RED STAR FALLING

ALSO BY **BRIAN FREEMANTLE**

BRIAN FREEMANTLE

RED STAR FALLING

A THRILLER

THOMAS DUNNE BOOKS
ST. MARTIN'S PRESS ⊠ NEW YORK

This is a work of fiction. All of the characters, organizations, and events portrayed in this novel are either products of the author's imagination or are used fictitiously.

THOMAS DUNNE BOOKS.
An imprint of St. Martin's Press.

www.thomasdunnebooks.com
www.stmartins.com

Library of Congress Cataloging-in-Publication Data

Freemantle, Brian.
   Red star falling / Brian Freemantle.
      pages cm
   ISBN 978-1-250-03224-9 (hardcover)
   ISBN 978-1-250-03225-6 (e-book)
   1. Muffin, Charlie (Fictitious character)—Fiction.   2. Intelligence service—Great Britain—Fiction.   3. Intelligence service—Russia (Federation)—Fiction.
4. Espionage—Fiction.   I. Title.
   PR6056.R43R33 2013
   823'.914—dc23

2013003987

St. Martin's Press books may be purchased for educational, business, or promotional use. For information on bulk purchases, please contact Macmillan Corporate and Premium Sales Department at 1-800-221-7945 extension 5442 or write specialmarkets@macmillan.com.

First Edition: June 2013

10 9 8 7 6 5 4 3 2 1

To Will and Harriet, with love

I need to look great for all patrons so please keep me away from food, drinks, pets, ink, pencils and other things that may harm me.

INSTINCT KICKED IN AT CHARLIE MUFFIN'S FIRST AWARENESS OF consciousness, not opening his eyes, not moving. Alive at least. But hurt: he had to be hurt, although there was no pain. Shots. He remembered several shots, and falling but no pain then; no pain now, either. Just numbness. He was numb, no feeling in his left side, and there was a strangely tight thickness on his right that he could feel. Bandaged. He was bandaged, his chest encased. Why? If he'd been shot, why didn't it hurt? A hospital, he supposed: he was definitely under bedcovering. What sort of hospital? Very cautiously, knowing the sheets and blankets would cover the movement, Charlie edged his right hand sideways, almost at once detecting unsecured restraining straps: two at least, each with heavy metal fixings against the bed frame. There would be more that he couldn't reach. At best an infirmary operated exclusively by Russia's international intelligence service, the Federalnaya Sluzhba Bezopasnosti, or FSB. At worst a psychiatric facility. Before the alleged end of communism in Russia in 1991, psychiatric institutions and their mind-destroying expertise were favourite KGB weapons against its prisoners and dissidents.

The FSB, the KGB's successor, wouldn't interfere with his mind, Charlie tried to reassure himself. Before they did that they'd drain its memory of every particle of every scrap of information embedded from twenty-five years of front-line espionage service in MI5, Britain's counter-espionage service. Or would they? They'd want to inflict the heaviest punishment possible for the incalculable damage he'd caused them.

Wherever he was, there'd be room-encompassing cameras, the fish-eye lenses fitted with infrared darkness penetration: maybe sound detectors or someone physically in the room. But he needed to assess his surroundings. He kept his eyes as narrowed as possible—the eyes of unconscious people were frequently half open—but didn't move his head. Charlie's impression was of near darkness, the room illuminated solely by two permanent low-emission night lights. There were two disinterested interior-ward guards at the half-opened, metal-backed door, in soft-voice conversation he couldn't hear with unseen people, possibly more guards, outside. The uniforms were more medical than military.

It had to be a psychiatric hospital, Charlie accepted, a different numbness moving through him. To do to him what they wanted, whenever they wanted. Before they took his sanity would he be able to answer the one and only question that mattered to him?

In the tree-bedecked LEGOLAND castle at London's Vauxhall Cross that is the headquarters of MI6, the UK's secret intelligence service, Director Gerald Monsford's imagery was of being in a room in which the ceiling and floor as well as the walls were contracting all around him, crushing from every direction his chances of survival.

He'd needed Charlie Muffin dead, not just wounded, for that survival: that was his hope, that Stephan Briddle, his designated assassin, would have succeeded and then fortunately been killed himself, neatly solving almost all his problems. Just as urgent—maybe more so, in the immediate short term—was locating the other two officers who'd been with Briddle. There was no reference to them in what Moscow had so far released and no response yet to his frantic embassy enquiries, which gave Monsford the straw-clutching hope that they'd escaped the shooting and would be returning to London. It was imperative he got to them first. So where were they? Why hadn't they made even the briefest of reassuring contact?

His threadbare professional existence depended upon Stephan Briddle's having withheld the assassination order from those other two, which regulations strictly decreed the man should have done. But regulations also dictated that the Director was never contacted at home, which Briddle had ignored, ironically giving Monsford the escape he was contemplating now. If Briddle had stayed silent and had managed to rehearse the other two, he might just be safe. Able, even, to overcome all the other things that had gone so disastrously wrong and endangered his intention to control not just MI6 but MI5 as well and establish himself as the country's intelligence supremo.

He needed help, Monsford conceded: people—a person—he could trust, as much as he trusted anyone. But he didn't have such a person. James Straughan would have been the one: known how to find out more before the impending confrontations. He could at least have sketched a ground plan with his operational director if the stupid bastard, who'd shown no sign of a breakdown, hadn't committed suicide and brought about the current internal headquarters-security investigation. That, by itself, would normally have dominated Monsford's priorities. Now it became one of several, all potentially professionally fatal.

There was, of course, Rebecca Street. But while he'd already established his newly appointed deputy as a satisfactorily inventive mistress, he wasn't any longer sure of her absolute loyalty, despite her inclusion, along with Straughan, in the assassination discussions. It was the very fact of her participation in those ambiguous, innuendo-cloaked exchanges that was belatedly causing Monsford's doubts. In the days immediately prior to Straughan's suicide, Monsford had isolated a closeness between the two which unsettled him.

Was his fragile escape plan possible? He had to make it so. Like a frightened child whistling in the dark—and totally without embarrassment in his empty office—Monsford, who feigned a classical education by quoting Shakespeare with monotonous frequency, recited his favourite aphorism—*Am I politic? Am I subtle? Am I a Machiavel?*

'Yes I am,' he answered, still aloud.

———

'It's been officially upgraded to crisis,' announced MI5 Director-General Aubrey Smith, a quiet-spoken man whose uncaring dishevelment betrayed the university professorship he'd held before his intelligence appointment. 'What's the practical update?'

'Charlie's alive,' declared John Passmore, a former SAS colonel seconded to MI5 after losing an arm in the first days of the Iraq invasion in 2003. 'The confirmation from the Russian Foreign Ministry is that he's wounded, shot, but there are no details of how badly. Four died in the airport shoot-out: two MI6 men, an uninvolved arab who was in front of Charlie and a militia security officer. We don't have a definitive number of wounded. The estimate is twelve, at least half of them seriously. We have to expect more deaths. I've forwarded to the emergency committee the very preliminary report from Ian Flood, who headed our extraction team.'

'You sure Flood's sound on everything he saw?' asked Jane Ambersom, the deputy director.

'One hundred percent sound,' insisted Passmore. 'Flood is definite he saw the gun in Briddle's hand.'

'Firing at whom?' broke in Jane Ambersom, tensed forward in her seat.

'Charlie,' declared the operations director, positively.

Silence settled in the suite, Aubrey Smith's concentration appearing to be upon a tandem-linked London barge making its arthritic way down the Thames. Eventually he said, 'We've got a credible, trained witness to a British MI6 officer shooting a British MI5 officer with the clear intent to kill.'

'Yes,' confirmed Passmore, reaching across to his empty left side, an unconscious habit familiar to the other two.

'Are we going to make the direct accusation against Monsford today?' asked Jane Ambersom, who'd initially seen her manipulated transfer from MI6 deputy to the parallel position in MI5 as an escape to the safer side of the internecine war between the two intelligence directors but wasn't totally sure now that she was on the winning side.

'No,' decided Smith, to the visible surprise of the other two. 'When we release what I wish was a real trapdoor I want to be sure that Gerald Monsford hangs by the neck until he's dead.'

'We realized you'd recovered consciousness an hour ago but I guess it was earlier than that,' declared a voice Charlie instantly recognized. 'Why don't you open your eyes so we can talk, Charlie? That's what you've got to learn now, how to talk about everything I want to hear.'

Mikhail Guzov, the FSB general whom Charlie had outwitted during his most recent assignment, smiled down at Charlie as he finally opened his eyes. Guzov was a tall man of pronounced ugliness, thin to the point of appearing skeletal. Charlie had months before determined that the man compensated for his physical appearance by dressing immaculately in suits hand tailored for him, which Charlie hadn't believed possible in Moscow. Today's was grey striped, Charlie saw, looking at Guzov at the side of his bed. 'You're certainly not who I expected to see.'

'There's going to be so much you didn't expect,' said Guzov, grimacing an intended smile of satisfaction. 'Who would have imagined things turning out like this?'

Charlie was able to look properly sideways to where his left side was virtually embalmed in bandages. 'It looks bad.'

The grimace this time came with a snorted laugh. 'The bullet missed every bone, anything important and stopped just short of your left shoulder: all you're suffering is extensive bruising and shock.'

'What about the bullet?'

'So close to the surface it popped out like a bean from its pod.'

'Sounds like I was lucky.'

'We've got all the time in the world for you to decide if you're lucky or not, Charlie. I really don't think you're going to feel lucky by the time it all ends.'

IT WAS A DEDICATED CONFERENCE ROOM, ENTERED FROM THE corridor overlooking the multi-tiered, floor-to-ceiling atrium of what is technically the Commonwealth section of the Foreign Office. Either end was dominated by large double doors which could be opened to extend the capacity. Today both sets were closed. There were, unusually, no oil portraits of bewigged former statesmen looking down in judgement from the walls upon entirely functional furniture, a long, central table against which were arranged chairs, twelve on either side. In front of each chair were individual leather-encased blotter settings, with notepad, pencil selection, water carafe, and tumbler. Not all places were name designated, although every unnamed section had a generic identification: MI5 and MI6 had both and confronted each other like courtroom lawyers. Behind the anonymous sectors were smaller tables and chairs, for support staff and aides. The secretarial provision of three stenographers, two women and a man, was directly in front of one set of double doors. The complementing recording facilities, one master set with the insurance of a secondary backup, were on an individual but almost-linked table, operated by two men, one of whom wore earphones to adjust his monitoring dials and sound levels. Suspended from the ceiling directly above the conference table and extending its entire length were four relay microphones.

Sir Archibald Bland, the Permanent Secretary to the Cabinet and, as such, head of the civil service, occupied the chairperson's position at the middle of the table, flanked on his left by his equally ranked counterpart,

Geoffrey Palmer, the Foreign Office liaison to the Joint Intelligence and Security Committee. Their normally shared responsibility was that of conduit between both intelligence agencies and the government, an arrangement providing Downing Street with plausible deniability of direct knowledge or involvement in any espionage activity, certainly any that became publicly embarrassing, as it had now. On Bland's right was Sir Peter Pickering, the attorney-general, who was recognizable to everyone but had no nameplate. Neither did the two men accompanying him. Behind them sat two aides, both women, just visible over a wall of legal books that had needed a trolley to bring them into the chamber.

'We'll start,' announced Bland, brusquely. The microphones were over-amplified, deepening his normally weak voice. 'And I'll do so with the reminder that all of us here are signatories to the Official Secrets Act. Today's situation has the highest security designation of that act. This meeting will, officially, remain in permanent session.'

Those on both sides of the table had properly arranged themselves during the preamble, making their spaces their own. The quickest to settle were the confrontationally positioned MI5 and MI6, director opposite director, deputy facing deputy. Inexplicably, there was a named place for James Straughan, leaving John Passmore facing an empty chair. Aubrey Smith was surprised, and therefore unsettled, at Gerald Monsford's composure, which Monsford was, in fact, only just managing to maintain, disconcerted by the provision for Straughan, convinced it had been manipulated by Smith with the support of Bland and Palmer to achieve the effect it was having. He'd been aware, too, of Rebecca Street almost imperceptibly easing away from him. From the brief smile he'd caught, Monsford was irritably sure Jane Ambersom had detected the minimal distancing, too.

'Which brings me to the next point,' continued the cherubic, pink-faced Bland. 'At all times this will be a totally open as well as a permanently convened committee. I expect full and immediate participation from everyone. We're confronting an unparalleled political emergency that has to be resolved as quickly and as completely as possible.' Bland stopped, drinking heavily from his water glass. 'It's essential the serious-ness is defined from the outset, for which I defer to my co-chairman.'

Geoffrey Palmer, a grey-haired, patrician-mannered man complet-ing a casting director's image of a professional civil servant with his black-jacketed, striped-trousered uniform, had his water glass already filled, sipping from it as he sorted through already prepared papers. 'The most effective way to achieve necessary clarity is to establish some chronology. Eight months ago the body of a one-armed Russian man was found in the grounds of the British embassy in Moscow. Before being brutally mur-dered he had been tortured. Shot as he was in the back of the head, his en-tire face and any teeth from which dental-record identification might have been possible were destroyed. The fingertips of his remaining hand, from which prints could have been obtained, had been burned away by acid.'

The majority around the table, with the exception of both intelli-gence groups, were making notes. The headphoned technician at the recording apparatus had adjusted his sound levels, reducing intrusive resonance.

'Under international diplomatic agreement, the embassy grounds, as well as the building itself, is British territory,' continued Palmer. 'A widely experienced MI5 officer, Charles Muffin, was sent to Moscow to investi-gate the crime. He did that with great success, very little of which was made public—'

'Is it to be made public to us?' interrupted a bespectacled, fair-haired man from GCHQ, the British government's Gloucestershire-based radio, electronic monitoring, and communications facility.

'Of course,' confirmed Palmer. 'Running in parallel with Muffin's in-vestigation was a Russian presidential election. The predicted victor was Stepan Lvov, a former KGB officer turned politician, as is Vladimir Putin . . .'

'Lvov was killed, weeks before the election,' came in a iron-corseted woman from the Foreign Office. 'It was a Russian mafia execution: Lvov was threatening to crack down on Russian organized-crime gangs, par-ticularly those operating in Moscow.'

'It was an execution, certainly,' agreed Palmer. 'But not by Russian mafia. Lvov hadn't quit the Russian intelligence organisation for politics. And he most definitely hadn't ceased being what America's CIA judged potentially to be the greatest intelligence coup in its history, having as a spy the president of the Russian Federation. It took over eighteen years for Russia to set up that coup, orchestrating Lvov's approach to the Americans, and over that period feeding through him to Washington genuine sacrificial material to convince the CIA of the spectacular asset they'd have when he became President of Russia, which he undoubtedly would have become because the FSB were ensuring the election result, ironically financed by payments to Lvov from a gullible CIA.'

There were shifts around the table, people momentarily looking up from their notes, taking in the growing realization of what they were being told.

Before the man could continue, Stanley Brown, the GCHQ director, said, 'The FSB would have been able to manipulate American foreign policy in whichever direction they chose with what Lvov supplied to the CIA. Why did the FSB kill him?'

'To silence him, as they silenced others involved, in the hope of keeping the operation secret, once it had been destroyed,' said Palmer. 'Muffin broke the plot by discovering the embassy-murder victim had been a KGB colleague of Lvov who tried to sell what he knew to the CIA! At the very last moment, to prevent Charlie making that discovery, the FSB colonel who'd supervised Lvov from the start, a woman named Irena Novikov, came forward claiming to have been the murdered man's lover: she even risked travelling to London with Muffin to destroy the proof of the Lvov operation she'd had to provide to convince Muffin she was genuine. Charlie unravelled it first. She's now in an American protection programme, undergoing interrogation likely to last for years. Muffin was put into a protection programme here in England. . . .'

'I hope Muffin got a medal,' said a woman from the GCHQ group.

'There's still a lot for you to hear,' cautioned the civil servant. 'Muffin abrogated the conditions of his programme, actually disappearing from his safe house to demonstrate he could guarantee his own safety. Within hours of his reappearance, the apartment in which he'd lived prior to going into protection was burgled by three FSB agents until then operating undetected from the Russian embassy here in London. Most if not all of you will be aware from the resulting publicity of their arrest: they remain in custody . . .' Palmer hesitated again, draining his glass and refilling it, needing the break. 'So far, I've sustained my chronology in a relatively logical sequence . . . now we come to the surreal. . . .'

There were further shifts around the table, note-taking suspended again.

'*Surreal* is the apposite word,' intervened Sir Archibald Bland, supportively.

'The Russians' arrests resulted from MI5 monitoring Muffin's apartment, as part of his protection. That included converting his apparently disconnected telephone into a detection device, in effect a burglar alarm. It also recorded, without any indication of it doing so, incoming calls,' recounted Palmer. 'During a period of little over a week there were five separate messages from a woman we subsequently learned to be Natalia Fedova. All the calls were from Moscow street kiosks. She holds the rank of lieutenant colonel in the FSB, in which she was then a senior analyst and interrogator. It has been confirmed that she is also the legal wife, under Russian law, of Charles Muffin, by whom she has a daughter. Those five calls were all pleas for Muffin's help to get her to England, which had apparently been arranged between them during his time in Moscow on the embassy-murder investigation—'

'I think this is the appropriate moment for a coffee break so that we properly digest what's been outlined,' interrupted Bland. 'This isn't by any means the end of the surrealism: it's little more than its beginning.'

There were coffee and tea urns on a long side table already set up in the overflow annexe beyond the unobstructed double doors, smaller tables and chairs arranged through the rest of the room. Neither Bland nor

Palmer followed the rest, all of whom remained within their individual groups, the majority standing. Gerald Monsford took Rebecca Street to the farthest end, leaving MI5 just inside the connecting doors.

From her position there Jane Ambersom said, 'For someone facing professional disgrace and potential imprisonment, Monsford looks remarkably sanguine.'

'Rebecca doesn't,' countered Aubrey Smith.

'The rumour is that their relationship extends intimately beyond the professional.'

'Probably why she's looking so uncomfortable, accommodating someone of his size can't be easy,' remarked Smith. who was a short-statured, thin man upon whom clothes carelessly hung rather than fitted. By contrast, the MI6 Director was tall, well over six feet, his size accentuated by a bull-shouldered, indulgence-bulged body that defeated the best of Savile Row's tailoring expertise to flatter.

'It's what they mean about making your own bed and lying in it,' said Jane, unsympathetically. Like the other deputy, Jane wore a business suit, but hers was an outdated Mao style that contributed to her androgyny, as did the shortly cropped hair and almost complete avoidance of makeup.

'A fate you avoided by crossing to my side of the river,' smiled Smith. He'd initially resisted Jane's appointment, misconstruing the transfer as a Monsford connivance to undermine his position as Director-General to install at MI5 his own chosen nominee through whom to control both intelligence agencies, which Smith suspected to have been the intention of a previous attempted overthrow.

'It wasn't difficult to resist: the only association I mourn from over there, now quite literally, is with Jamie Straughan,' said the woman, who'd retained the link with the MI6 operations director and knew from their last, pre-suicide meeting that Straughan had collated proof of Monsford's abuse of power. She still hoped Straughan had somehow bequeathed that evidence to her. So far there'd been no indication of its whereabouts.

They both turned at John Passmore's late arrival. At once the man said, 'Nothing new from Moscow. There's still no sighting of the other

MI6 guys who were with Briddle, either. And our own Moscow *rezidentura* confirm they haven't returned to the embassy.'

'They're coming back overland,' guessed Jane.

'That's the most obvious,' accepted Smith.

'What the hell are they talking about?' demanded Monsford, from the other end of the room. 'Where's Passmore been?'

'Probably in the toilet, like a lot of other people,' dismissed Rebecca.

'Why did you move away from me when we first sat down?' demanded Monsford.

'For Christ's sake, Gerald! I moved to give myself more room, that's all!'

'When Palmer finishes I want you to open the discussion: throw it onto MI5 to get their opening contribution first.'

'You're the Director. They'll expect any responses to be from you.' Having got up her skirt, the bastard was now trying to hide behind it. After today and whatever emerged from it she needed to think very seriously about when—and how—to explode the stratospheric bomb that Straughan had primed under Monsford's fat ass. Her dilemma, Rebecca feared, was that she was damned if she did and damned if she didn't.

'I'll choose my moment of responsibility.'

Or choose to avoid it, thought Rebecca, too accustomed to the man's manipulation to be surprised at what he was asking her to do. 'Won't it . . . ?' she began but was stopped by the reassembly summons.

'I will take over the background briefing,' resumed Sir Archibald Bland. 'Before I do, you should know that *Tass* has just announced from Moscow that another Russian and a Lebanese caught up in yesterday's shooting have died.'

Beside her, Rebecca was conscious of Monsford leaning forward, expecting more, seeing too that the Cabinet Secretary had turned towards them as if directly addressing them. Drawn by Bland's look, several other people were also staring, including the opposing MI5 hierarchy.

'But let's return to the chronology and the surreal,' hurried on Bland, turning back into the room. 'We were persuaded that extracting someone of such seniority and experience within Russian intelligence as Natalia Fedova was a professional advantage that had to be taken. We were also persuaded, after varying disagreements, that Muffin should lead the operation, supported by a six-man team made up equally from MI6 and MI5 officers. Muffin appeared publicly, although unidentified, during the embassy-murder enquiry. To avoid the Fedova extraction being compromised he was to work independent of the British embassy as well as from his support group, all of whom were housed within the embassy's residential compound. Muffin was to make the extraction arrangements with his wife and only call in help in the final stages of bringing her and their child out. A further identification precaution was for Muffin to travel separately to Moscow. . . .' There was a preparing pause. 'Muffin chose personally to avoid the risk of further identification by abandoning his Moscow flight at Amsterdam. He is known to have made his way back to England but then to have flown from Manchester to Moscow the following day using the cover of a tourist group. That entry was discovered by the FSB but Muffin had left the group by the time they were arrested by Russian militia. Since that arrest, one of the tourists, a man suffering a heart condition, has died. Most of you will remember the publicity that followed Muffin's disappearance and the seizure of the tourists, who remain in custody. . . .'

Bland hesitated again, for more water. Rebecca saw there was far less note-taking now but more head-together exchanges within the individual groups. It was particularly obvious among MI5. As well as whispered exchanges, Passmore was one of the few also writing, pushing slips of paper sideways to Aubrey Smith: twice, as Rebecca watched, the Director-General wrote a reply on the offered paper. She became aware of Gerald Monsford scribbling beside her, too, but was too far away to decipher the scrawl and Monsford didn't offer it to her.

'Muffin did not contact his support for over a week . . .' Bland was saying. 'When he did, it was to refuse any dealings or association with its

MI6 contingent. We do not know the reason for that refusal, nor anything of what Muffin was doing in Moscow during that period. There was disagreement between the agency directors here, as well as between MI6 and MI5 in Moscow. As a result, a second MI5 squad was sent to bring Natalia Fedova and the child out. That extraction was arranged for yesterday, Muffin joining it at the airport. . . .'

During Bland's second throat-easing break, Monsford finally passed Rebecca a single-line note that read, *The opening is weighted in our favour,* followed by three exclamation marks. Rebecca slid it back without comment. Her impression was that while appearing impartial, the civil-service-liaison duo were very adroitly sewing a self-incriminating minefield for both MI6 and MI5 to negotiate. And if she obeyed Monsford's instructions, she'd be taking the first exploratory step.

Bland coughed. 'On their way to the airport the new MI5 team leader suspected they were being followed. He warned Muffin, who decided upon a different flight to decoy the then unknown pursuers. . . .' He allowed another preparing pause. 'We have limited information of what followed. According to the MI5 team leader, the three MI6 support groups separated upon entering the airport terminal. One, Stephan Briddle, made directly for Muffin, who turned at a shout from David Halliday, an MI6 officer resident in Moscow. The MI5 witness heard shots before identifying the gunman, but he is definite he saw Briddle with a Russian-manufactured Makarov pistol in his hand. Briddle and Halliday were among the four initially killed, to which we now have to add the two who died subsequently. We know Muffin was injured, but not how badly. . . .'

Bland emptied his glass. 'We've kept this narrative consecutive as well as chronological. Throughout most of what we've outlined, however, there runs a further sequence. Simultaneously—but independently, with no foreknowledge of either MI5 or ourselves, the government liaison— MI6 was organizing an extraction of the deputy chairman of the Federalnaya Sluzhba Bezopasnosti. They succeeded in doing that but the man's wife, who'd gone to Paris to persuade their son to defect with them, was seized with the young man by French authorities as they were being brought here. So were MI6 officers and an aircrew. The wife was allowed to continue. The son refused. All our officers are still in French custody. We believe there is some relevance in linking these two events.'

The Cabinet Secretary looked invitingly to Palmer, who surveyed the room and said, 'That, in outline, is the emergency we confront and have to resolve. . . .' Palmer's survey stopped at Gerald Monsford. 'And I think, Director, that you should be the first contributor.'

Rebecca was aware of Monsford's attention but refused to meet the demanding look, saying nothing.

'Let's finish unpacking your things.'

'I don't want to unpack my things. I want to go home. I don't like it here.' Sasha was still wearing her pyjama suit, sitting on the side of her bed. Her curl-bubbled hair, naturally blond like her mother's, was dishevelled from her restless night following their arrival.

'You're going to meet your new teacher today,' promised Natalia, bent over the child's case.

'I'm going to school?'

'Just meeting her today, to say hello. You're going to learn a new language. We're in England.'

'I don't want to be in England! Go to a new school.'

'It won't be a new school exactly. It'll be just you and your new teacher.'

'What's happening, Mama? I don't understand what's happening.'

'We've come to live here for a while.'

'*Why?*' wailed the child.

'We came to be with someone but he's not here.'

'Can't we go home then?'

'Not yet. We have to wait.'

'It feels tight,' complained Irena Yakulova Novikov.

'It will,' accepted the cosmetic specialist, holding the mirror for the Russian to study the result of the corrective surgery. 'What do you think?'

Irena intently examined the left side of her face, for years burn-mottled not by a restaurant accident with Stepan Lvov, which she'd told Charlie, but in a Moscow car accident. She was attractive again, Irena decided: beautiful even. 'There's no discoloration at all.'

'We're very good at what we do.'

As she was good at what she did, Irena thought, facing the prospect of finally having to do what she'd so far managed to postpone since her transfer from Britain to Washington. 'Will it ever come back?'

'Not if you're careful. We'll prescribe some medication: creams, emollients, stuff like that. But your sunbathing days are over.'

'Thank you very much. I'm grateful.' It was going to be a long time before she said anything else even vaguely honest, reflected Irena. She'd expected to work in London—somewhere in England—not here. It made everything twice as difficult. She was frightened, Irena admitted to herself.

3

THE SECURITY FACILITIES FOR THE HERTFORDSHIRE SAFE HOUSE accommodating Maxim Mikhailovich Radtsic, the deputy chairman of the Federalnaya Sluzhba Bezopasnosti, and his wife were supervised from a building constructed to appear part of its garage block, more than half of which was further concealed by a stand of mature, heavy-leafed oaks. It had no outside windows or doors. Entry was through the garage itself to an inner, steel-lined door operated by a double-lock system. The largest wall area was completely filled by twenty closely placed but separately focused and operated TV screens monitoring every space within the house. It was possible to zoom each camera from within the security-control cabin. The volume of each could be adjusted. Both film and audio transmissions were recorded as well as being simultaneously relayed into the control centre. From there the simultaneous relay could be transmitted to London receiving facilities within MI6, MI5, and selected government sites. It did not, however, disclose the geographic location of the MI6 property.

A separate side section was similarly filled with TV and audio coverage of every outside access to the house. Always visible on these cameras were the permanent, twenty-four-hour foot patrols which were divided into squads of four, ensuring a permanent armed presence around the entire interior perimeter. Also monitored from this section was a mine-field of buried ground sensors, the sensitivity of which precluded any animals larger than rabbits in the extensively wooded grounds.

The control room worked on an overlapping round-the-clock shift system. Harry Jacobson, the MI6 Moscow station chief who'd brought Radtsic out, entered with the mid-morning changeover, standing aside as the interchanging groups, two men and two women, went through the required signing-on and -off formalities.

'Anything?' asked Jacobson, when it was finished.

The night-duty officer, a woman, shook her head. 'Elena's still got her bedroom door locked. Maxim tried to get in at about eleven. He was stumbling drunk by then. She told him to fuck off: her words, not mine. Hers again this morning when he asked her to come to breakfast. She's still locked in there. . . .' The officer gestured to the television picture showing a gently rising and falling bedclothed hump. 'Anything new from Moscow?'

'The body count's gone up to six,' said Jacobson. 'There's uproar everywhere. Our Lord and master and his Mary Magdalene are going to a crisis meeting sometime this morning.'

'What about Andrei?' asked one of the night men.

'I wish there were something about the kid.' As he wished a lot of other things, thought Jacobson. It was still too early to reach any sensible conclusion but he guessed the fallout from the Moscow shooting would in the short term bury the benefits he'd expected from organizing Radtsic's extraction, despite Andrei's refusal, for which he couldn't be blamed. As it was now, Jacobson wasn't sure how much there was to regret anyway: whether, in fact, it wasn't better to keep his head as far down as possible to avoid unfounded blame or recrimination. His worry was not knowing if Monsford's order to assassinate Charlie Muffin, a mission he'd escaped by personally supervising Radtsic's defection, had been officially registered in MI6's operational logs. It should have been, according to regulations. But Monsford made—and too frequently changed—his own regulations to suit the prevailing wind of the moment.

'What are you going to tell Maxim?' asked the day-shift supervisor, also a woman.

'There's nothing to tell him but I've got to generate some co-operation from the awkward bastard.'

'Best of luck. We'll try to film your best side,' said the woman and at once wished she hadn't. Jacobson was a trouser-creased, polished-shoes man whose short-haired neatness was marred by the unclipped walrus moustache cultivated to conceal a harelip, about which he was sensitive.

Radtsic was in the large, glassed conservatory he'd established as his favourite since arriving three days earlier. It was built to the rear of the house, overlooking expansively barbered lawns sloping to an open-air swimming pool and a faraway tributary of the Thames. The summer house was furnished predominantly in chintz fabric, loosely covered armchairs and couches, and scented by flowers cut daily from the garden. The patrolling guards were always intentionally out of sight.

Radtsic was dressed as he'd invariably been from the moment of his defection approach to Jacobson at a French embassy reception. The heavy serge three-piece suit was complete with a collar and tie. Today, for the first time since that initial Moscow encounter, Radtsic was smoking a pipe instead of the chain-lighted cigarettes he'd favoured during their Moscow meetings and which now, with the thick, greying hair and moustache almost as fulsome as Jacobson's, heightened the Russian's uncanny resemblance to Stalin. Radtsic was slumped in a solitary easy chair carefully positioned to prevent anyone sitting close to him. Within reach from his chair was a substantial side table upon which were full bottles of whisky and vodka, with ice, water, and tumblers. One glass was separated from the others, near enough for Radtsic to reach without stretching. It was empty, with no obvious residue from it already having been used.

'Good morning, Maxim Mikhailovich,' greeted Jacobson. 'Are you well?'

'As well as I was yesterday and the day before that,' awkwardly responded the Russian. The pipe's pungency was overwhelming the scent from the flowers.

Jacobson decided his association with the other man was sufficiently established for him not to suffer the shit the Russian was dumping on everyone else. It would also be satisfying to appear on sound-tracked film giving a better performance than Gerald Monsford. 'We can provide anything Elena wants to eat, you know.'

'What?' Radtsic frowned, confused by the opening.

'She hasn't eaten breakfast.'

'She doesn't want breakfast: she wants Andrei,' recovered the other man.

'We're making every diplomatic effort to get him here with you,' insisted Jacobson, who had no idea what efforts were being made. 'It's Andrei who's refusing to come: we can't do anything about that.'

'Arrange another two-way television conference so that I can persuade him.'

'Persuade him or rant at him as you did the first time, so uncontrolled that the French cut the link? Which they now won't restore.' Jacobson tensed for an outburst to his bullying.

'Why am I dealing with you, an underling? Where's Monsford? I was promised I'd be dealing personally with the Director.'

'No you weren't,' rejected Jacobson, surprised Radtsic had deferred to him. 'You were promised you'd be personally *welcomed* by the Director. Which you were. Now you're dealing with me, the underling who saved you from being purged by a country who'd decided you'd failed them. That failure wasn't a factor then; getting you out was. But we can talk about it now, now that you're safe. Why were you going to be purged as people were in the old days, Maxim Mikhailovich?'

'I'll co-operate, tell you all you want to know, when you get Andrei here. But not until then,' avoided Radtsic, no longer dismissive.

'You know what I'm really curious about, Maxim Mikhailovich?' continued Jacobson, conversationally, satisfied with how the encounter was going. 'I'm curious about that day on the Moskva River cruise when we were making your escape preparations: the time you told me you'd had nothing whatsoever to do with the FSB plan to get Stepan Lvov elected president and make a plaything of America, imagining he was the best spy they'd ever cultivated. How much did the Lvov affair have to do with your being purged?'

'It's exactly what I told you then,' refused Radtsic, loudly. 'I had no active part in the Lvov operation.'

'That's my point. All we'd ever talked about, up to that point, was getting you, Elena, and Andrei here. We hadn't spoken about anything operational. Why, after a lifetime at the very top of Russian intelligence, did you suddenly deny involvement in an operation that had never been discussed between us?'

'I didn't—don't—want to waste time upon things I don't know about when I start co-operating.'

'I want you to think very seriously indeed about co-operation. And I'd like us to start that co-operation as early as tomorrow,' said Jacobson, on his way to the door, wondering how it looked on the television monitor.

Rebecca sensed the tension in Gerald Monsford, turning when she knew he was no longer looking at her. His head was bowed over the table, both hands outstretched before him but flat, not clenched. He withdrew them as he came up to stare directly across the table at Aubrey Smith.

'It is going to be extremely difficult for me to respond to the situation we're confronting,' began the MI6 Director, inwardly fuming at the immediate smiling, head-bent exchange between Jane Ambersom and the MI5 Director-General. 'At best I can only offer my briefest suggestion of what might have contributed to the airport tragedy. What I am going to tell you now might substantially change. It might even prove entirely unfounded. . . .' He paused. 'And you'll understand, after what little I have to say, how much I'd welcome it being entirely unfounded: welcome being completely wrong.'

The room was completely silent, unmoving.

Monsford gestured farther along the table, to Bland and Palmer. 'Omitted from the eloquently presented background to the activities of the last few weeks was something I now want to introduce.'

Monsford cleared his throat, sipped some water. Rebecca no longer sensed the man's earlier tension.

'You've already been told of Muffin's Vauxhall flat being burgled by three FSB agents,' resumed Monsford. 'Neither my MI5 colleagues opposite, nor ourselves at MI6, could understand how that was possible. There is no publicly available documentation from which an identity can be discovered. . . .' The pause was longer this time. 'There is, in fact, only one way Muffin's correct name and address could have been obtained by the Russians: one that as Director of MI6 I am reluctant even now to confront but cannot ignore. . . .'

Aubrey Smith was engaged in a hurried, note-shuffling exchange between Jane on one side and John Passmore on the other.

Monsford's gesture this time was to the empty chair beside him. 'I imagine many of you are curious at this empty seat and of the identity of James Straughan, who should have been occupying it. . . .' Monsford raised the nameplate, displaying it more visibly. 'Until a week ago, James Straughan was the operations director of MI6, a man of outstanding ability and loyalty . . .' there was a pause, 'a man I believed, still want to believe, genuinely *was* someone of outstanding loyalty.'

Across the table, Jane Ambersom was no longer scribbling notes. She was rigid with emotion in her chair, her eyes fixed unblinkingly upon Monsford.

'A week ago James Straughan committed suicide,' declared Monsford. 'There was no note of explanation or excuse, no reason of which I am aware why he should have done such a thing. Because of the sensitivity of his function within MI6, coupled with an as-yet-unsubstantiated, anonymous allegation that MI6 contains a mole, a complete root and branch security sweep is currently under way within the service I head. Before coming here today I advised the head of that investigation of a conversation I had in the middle of last night with Stephan Briddle. He had no knowledge of the mole allegation or of the current investigation: he'd been in Moscow as part of Charles Muffin's support team for almost three weeks. . . .'

Monsford drank some water, gazing around the table, an actor's preparation for his denouement speech. 'In that conversation Briddle told me James Straughan was unsafe: that he had evidence of a disloyal cell to which David Halliday was also linked. Briddle believed Muffin, who'd spent long periods in Moscow and is, as you've been told, married to a high-ranking officer in the FSB, had some information pertinent to it. Briddle wanted to speak to Muffin before he left the country to find out what that information was. He said he'd call me within hours. We all know why he wasn't able to—'

'This is preposterous nonsense, all of it!' exploded Jane Ambersom.

'No-one would be happier, more relieved, than me for it all to be dismissed as exactly that, absolute and preposterous nonsense,' said Monsford, finally turning to look at Rebecca, who was thinking that nothing would make her happier, either, because she knew that what Monsford had told everyone in the room was precisely that, absolute and preposterous nonsense.

Monsford was sure he'd pushed back the immediate confrontation. Maybe not for long, maybe only for today, but the ceiling and walls were no longer crushing in on him, giving him more time to think. And to listen. That's what he had to do now, listen and sift everything possible from the settling dust for specks that might strengthen the story he was trying to build.

'Why are you rejecting the Director's account so vehemently?' Sir Archibald Bland demanded of Jane Ambersom.

The woman was flushed, a combination of anger at Monsford's accusation and embarrassment at losing control. 'Until a comparatively short time ago I was the deputy director of MI6. As such I came to know James Straughan extremely well. He *was* someone of extraordinary ability. He was also someone of outstanding integrity and above all else of total loyalty who had become extremely concerned with the management and manner of operations within MI6. *That* was James Straughan's burden: that and the strain of personally caring for a seriously ill mother. To suggest he was guilty of the slightest disloyalty, a spy, is not just nonsense, it is a total travesty.'

Monsford was the first to fill the following silence. 'It's gratifying to hear one colleague defend another in such a spirited manner. But I would remind all of us here that the defence used a moment ago is virtually an historical echo of that used to dismiss the initial accusations of treason against Kim Philby and his deeply embedded cell of KGB spies—also within MI6—responsible for the assassinations of dozens of MI6 and CIA officers.'

'Can we bring ourselves to the present and not dwell upon earlier MI6 failures, disastrous though they were,' hurried in Aubrey Smith, anxious to subdue his deputy. 'I do not believe at this stage, little more than hours after what's happened in Moscow, that we can do more than formally open this enquiry, urgent though it is to provide some response to government demands. . . .' Smith looked towards the secretariat. 'To that end I want listed that I will call an MI5 eyewitness to the events at Vnukovo Airport. And also produce all audio, filmed, and written communication between MI5 and its officers in Moscow during this entire operation. . . .' The pause now was more determined: concentrating totally upon Monsford, Smith said; 'I would welcome the positive commitment from the MI6 Director that a full and matching disclosure will be provided by them. . . .'

Monsford jerked up almost too theatrically, as if startled by the demand. 'Of course I give that assurance. But there's a difficulty. Regulations officially put materiel-release authority beyond me, resting during the internal security examination with those conducting it. That's why I've already consulted with them about Straughan, instead of beginning the enquiry myself. It's to the internal investigators that this committee has to make release requests.'

Jane Ambersom thrust herself exasperatedly back in her seat, holding herself against another outburst.

John Passmore said, 'Without a cross-referencing overview from within MI6, that could take months and even then not assemble it all!'

'I'm afraid so,' agreed Monsford, turning once more to Sir Archibald Bland. 'I am meeting the investigators later today, though. Another recourse could be to suspend the regulations for me to provide that overview.'

'Or me?'

There was a further familiar silence. Monsford's head snap was the first to bring the concentration upon Rebecca Street, who for the first time met the man's gaze, smiling up. Monsford remained expressionless, going back to the room, 'Or, of course, by my very able deputy.'

Which she'd guarantee included Straughan's protectively unedited digitally recorded version detailing the intended MI6 assassination of Charlie Muffin, Rebecca thought: the version Straughan had left for her to find. She'd be walking a fraying tightrope, revealing herself to have been present at that discussion. But hopefully she could pre-empt accusations of complicity by manoeuvring a personal appearance before the enquiry to produce it.

'The extraction of Maxim Radtsic was not a shared operation,' qualified Smith, quickly. 'But the MI5 dossier should provide a template from which a great deal of MI6 traffic can be traced.'

'It would greatly speed up this enquiry if a full schedule of possible witnesses and materiel were provided in advance by our two services, allowing us to have whatever's called upon to be instantly available,' attempted Monsford.

'Surely in an enquiry of this importance the requirement has to be for raw intelligence that Director Monsford and I are here to provide, not material prepared to be immediately comprehensible. Which, officially precluded as you are, neither you nor your deputy could provide anyway. It has to be produced as it is.'

I could still include my stratosphere bomb, thought Rebecca, desperately; *it wouldn't take longer than a second: a split second even.*

'I agree,' said Bland. 'My co-chairman and I want the full, raw intelligence dossier made available.'

'As we appear to be formulating an agenda, I'd like it registered that I intend consulting our legal attaché at the Moscow embassy, as well as getting advice from within my department here,' said Sir Peter Pickering. 'We have made repeated demands for diplomatic access to the detained Manchester tourists. I think that additionally we should strenuously press the Russians to establish if Muffin is being held on legal grounds or simply being treated for injuries sustained in the airport shooting. As far as I can see the only legal offence might be an entry irregularity, which is pretty low on the scale of things.' The man went to the Foreign Office group, 'I'm assuming we've already made the formal application for consular access to Muffin?'

'Delivered two hours ago,' confirmed a balding man, after a sideways glance to the woman next to him.

'I'd like—' started Smith, but Pickering talked over him.

'I'm well aware of the accustomed practice,' anticipated the attorney-general. 'And I can't imagine a situation more essential than this to include one of your people.'

'Two MI6 officers died and two more are missing,' reminded Monsford, anxiously. 'I think it's even more essential that I also have representation on the delegation.'

'Two would be too many,' objected Smith. 'The entire MI5 dossier will be made available. That complete disclosure will obviously include everything we get if our man gains access.'

'I'm satisfied with that undertaking. We'll restrict it to MI5,' decided Bland, collecting up his papers. 'I don't think there's anything further to be achieved today. . . .'

'We haven't decided who'll guide the collation of MI6 materiel,' reminded Rebecca.

Bland stopped his tidying. 'No decision is necessary upon that until after the Director's initial meeting today with the security officers.'

Shit, thought Rebecca, acknowledging a lost opportunity.

Monsford was thinking the same thing, although that wasn't his complete focus. That was upon Rome and the sudden realization how he could greatly add to the story he'd just fabricated.

So deep had the animosity between the FBI and the CIA become—and the petulant need to show who, currently, held the whip-cracking hand— that the Agency's deputy director had to travel into the city from Langley to the Bureau headquarters for the meeting he'd requested. The Bureau deputy, Mort Bering, rose at the entry of his CIA counterpart, Larry Stern, for the mandatory, forced-smile handshake.

'You got more problems?' demanded Bering at once, settling to face the other man across the small conference table. No record was being kept.

'You know damned well we have,' immediately admitted Stern, who affected a Louisiana country-boy persona, complete with pronounced accent, wide-buckle belts, and occasionally even hand-tooled boots; today he wore tasselled moccasins. 'The Lvov business double fucked us, information-wise, from ambassador downwards in both Moscow and London. Now we've got MI6 re-creating the gunfight at the OK Corral, with bodies all over the airport concourse in Moscow.'

'You think there's a connection?' asked Bering, intentionally awkward.

'For Christ's sake, Mort! One of the guys put down at the airport was Charlie Muffin, who broke the Lvov thing apart. Of course there's a connection.'

'What else?' pressed the FBI deputy, knowing there was more.

'Irena Novikov, whom we hoped to be some sort of compensation for all that we lost with Lvov. She's stringing us out. We had the plastic surgery done, which was the deal agreed by Charlie, and the surgeon says she's fit enough to be debriefed. But she's still stonewalling, insisting on more time to recuperate. We want something to undermine her: get the bitch to understand she's not on a free ride and to start talking.'

'My guy is pretty tight with his liaison, MI5's deputy,' disclosed Bering.

'Who's a gal,' identified Stern at once. 'How tight is tight?'

'We'll have to wait and see,' said Bering, unhelpfully.

'What do you think Pennsylvania Avenue would say if they knew this was happening?' said Jane.

'That I was properly fulfilling my liaison function between our services,' said Barry Elliott. It had been his idea that she cook dinner that night at his Chelsea Embankment apartment: they'd carried their wine with them into the bedroom and were drinking it now after the love-making. 'What do you think your people would say?'

'I don't know and don't care.'

'I'm glad you were able to make it,' gently embarked the American. She'd cancelled their previous date.

'You wouldn't believe what's happening.'

'I'd try, if you told me.'

Jane sipped her wine reflectively, sitting naked with her back against the headboard. 'It's a full-blown, official enquiry. A lot of it involves the MI6 penetration I told you about.'

'Don't you think I deserve to know more, after doing what I just did?'

Jane smiled at the innuendo. 'You'll know, before anyone else.'

Jane lapsed into silence again, accepting the refill Elliott poured. 'I know I asked you to leak the penetration to MI6, but it hasn't worked out as I'd hoped it would, not yet anyway.'

'You going to tell me when it does?'

'Of course. And a lot more.'

'Like what?'

'It's big: very big. And you'll be the first to know, outside.' She looked at her watch. 'I've got to get back. Aubrey Smith's arranged a late confer-ence and I'm not looking forward to it.'

'Why not?'

'I fucked up at the enquiry.'

'Badly?'

'I'll tell you tomorrow. Could we eat in again, here, like tonight?'

'Of course.'

Despite the conversation, Elliott was sure things were progressing beyond the professional for Jane, as it was for him.

4

'IT WAS A MISTAKE. I'M SORRY,'

'You let yourself get angry: lost perspective as well as control,' criticized Aubrey Smith. 'It cost us opportunities. We won't expose Monsford for what I'm sure he's done by losing our temper.'

'It won't happen again,' promised Jane Ambersom.

'We're the only people who know—or think we know—what he's done,' said the haphazardly dressed Director-General, from the window overlooking the night-lit river. 'We've got to prove it to everyone else.' He turned to Passmore. 'Our concentration has initially to be on Charlie and the big question—why did he so positively refuse to work with the MI6 officers in his support group? What did he learn in the lost week before making contact with our people?'

'Specifically made contact with Patrick Wilkinson, our team supervisor,' reminded Passmore. 'He wouldn't deal with anyone else.'

'Are our three on their way back?' queried Jane.

Passmore shook his head. 'I want them back, not picked up on some pretext. I'm waiting for some indication of Moscow's next move.'

'The greater need is to get Wilkinson back,' said Smith, moving from the window. 'He must have some indication of what MI6 were doing.'

'Briddle and his crew didn't find Charlie: Natalia led them to him,' Jane pointed out.

'Are you suggesting she intentionally led them?'

Now it was Jane who shook her head in denial. 'Just being pedantic.

Natalia Fedova remains our biggest professional mystery, but if she were leading him into a trap it would have been an FSB ambush, not one set up by MI6. We mustn't confuse ourselves by over-interpretation. Let's not forget Natalia's extraction began by us all believing it was she and the child we were getting out. During the joint planning Natalia and Sasha were identified. So was their flat at Pecatnikov Pereulok. All Briddle and the other two had to do was doorstep the place and follow Natalia when she made her move.'

'But we know they didn't sit outside Pecatnikov and wait,' Passmore pointed out. 'We know that until the day of Natalia's extraction they spent all their time running after our guys, hoping to be led to Charlie.'

'So why'd they switch: how did they know that Natalia was getting out on a specific day from a minor airport?' asked the Director-General.

'We can't answer with other hypothetical questions,' Jane warned again. 'The only thing we can establish is that Charlie was their target. Using Charlie as a diversion to get Radtsic out made professional sense. But Radtsic was *already* out. They didn't need a diversion. All they were trying to do was kill Charlie.'

'Killing Charlie makes sense if he found out something Monsford wanted kept secret,' argued Passmore.

'Which brings us back to where we began,' accepted Smith. 'We'll log the points. But at this moment it's more important we get Wilkinson here, to appear before the committee.'

'We decoy again,' declare Jane. 'We recall one of our other two. If one gets out okay, there's no watch alert. If he gets picked up, it doesn't matter—he's disposable to our needs and neither of them can be accused of anything: eventually they'd be repatriated. We provide Wilkinson with an entirely new identify, with all the Russian entry-and exit stamps our technical people can create here, and ship them to Wilkinson in the diplomatic pouch. All we risk then is CCTV identification. To lessen that danger he comes out of Moscow by train or boat on the same day our remaining decoy tries to get out direct from a Moscow airport.'

Neither man responded at once, examining the suggestion.

Passmore said, 'Overland train is quicker: all Wilkinson will have to do is get over a border; Poland is closest.'

'Give me a feasibility assessment,' ordered Aubrey Smith. 'I want Wilkinson on the move, the earlier the better.'

Passmore stretched his remaining arm across his body to its empty place. 'Ian Flood's our star witness, the man who watched almost everything at Vnukovo Airport. I've got time to go through it all in detail, create the chronology which appears to be Bland's preferred procedure.'

'No long-winded presentations,' cautioned Smith. 'Tell Flood I want it in bite-sized pieces, all easily digested.'

'We weren't given a procedural format,' Passmore pointed out.

'Warn Flood about that,' Smith continued to coach. 'Same guidance when it gets to questioning, which it obviously will. Tell all our witnesses that. Specific answers strictly kept to specific questions. No responses to inferences . . .' The man hesitated, glancing at Jane Ambersom. 'And no loss of temper. It's a ploy Monsford will use if he gets the opportunity.'

'Anyone got an opinion about Rebecca?' invited Passmore.

'In the absence of anything Jamie Straughan left me—and I'm still sure there's something, somewhere—Rebecca Street holds the golden key if she'd come across to us,' said Jane.

'There could be someone else with a lot to offer,' suggested Aubrey Smith, reflectively. 'The one thing we do know Charlie did during the lost week was make contact with Natalia Fedova. She could unlock a lot of doors, too.'

'Natalia is refusing to talk about anything,' reminded Jane.

'I'm thinking of our immediate problem, confronting Monsford as well as doing whatever we can to help Charlie,' said Smith. 'Natalia knows he's been seized but not that he's injured. Or how it happened. Go down again. Convince her she could show us a way to get Charlie back.'

'Do you truly believe we can get Charlie out?' challenged Jane, directly.

'Not totally,' replied the man, just as direct. 'But Charlie's the only one with anything to lose.'

The safe house assigned to Natalia and Sasha was in Hampshire, originally a lodge conveniently close to the police college at Bramshill. It formed the centrepiece of an annexe complex in which most of the protection squad was housed. The technical facilities were virtually the same as those at MI6's Hertfordshire house, including the geographic location restrictions on the London relays. The protection officers were predominantly female, adjusted for those they currently had to guard. The squad supervisor was a greying, comfortably rounded woman named Ethel Jackson, whose appearance belied a twenty-year MI5 career, fifteen of them as a front-line field officer, from which she'd had to be withdrawn after the accident-concealed disposal in Berlin of an FSB counter-intelligence operative on the point of exposing her. Ethel Jackson's legacy was a permanent limp from the fracture she'd sustained in the staged car crash: her leg ached in cold weather.

The woman was waiting at the door of the former lodge, forewarned by Jane's telephone call from London, and led the way into a side study. 'Natalia's with Sasha, in the kitchen, while the child eats supper. Natalia saw the BBC's lunchtime news; demanded to see someone. I've let her think that's why you're here.'

'It'll do,' said Jane. 'How is she?'

'All to hell since she saw the news. They showed footage from the airport CCTV.'

'I saw it.'

'Was Charlie killed?'

'Hurt. We don't know how badly.'

'I knew him. Worked with him in Athens and again in Vienna. Are we going to get him out?'

'If we can.'

'Do the Russians know who he really is?'

'Inevitably.' Personal relationships within the service, particularly between active field agents, were banned, but from his personnel file Jane knew that Charlie Muffin ignored virtually every regulation and every subclause and Jane suspected a personal concern in Ethel's interest.

'They'll sweat all sorts of shit out of him.'

'Yes,' agreed Jane.

'He'll give them a hell of a runaround, though.'

'You know him well enough to be sure of that?' asked Jane, confronting the professional uncertainty.

Ethel smiled, acknowledging the point of the question. 'Yes, I know him well enough to be able to tell you that.'

'How do you feel about Natalia?'

'Are we talking deputy director to senior officer or two women who don't know each other but understand what we're talking about?'

'Your choice,' avoided Jane.

Ethel hesitated. 'It was a wonderful affair, apart from not knowing what would happen literally from one minute to the next. I loved him: maybe still do although it could be that I'm sorry for what's happening to him. And I'm jealous of Natalia for being his wife, which he never asked me to be and which I'm glad he didn't because it probably wouldn't have lasted as long as it took to get to the registry door exit. Natalia and Sasha are going to be protected and cared for better and more thoroughly than anyone who's been in the programme before, because I've appointed myself their personal guardian . . .' She stopped, needing breath. 'So there's your choice. Replace me right now, this minute. Or go on letting me keep them safe until we get Charlie back to them.'

'I'd like to see Natalia right away,' said Jane, without hesitation.

'Thank you,' smiled the other woman.

'You'll watch it all, of course?' anticipated Jane, nodding to the single, momentarily dead-eyed screen on the study wall.

'That's my function, to watch to ensure no problems arise.'

'I want you to watch even more closely than normal,' urged Jane. 'If you detect anything, anything at all—an unguarded moment, a gesture or a remark to Sasha—that unsettles you, I want to know at once. Being in a protection programme is stressful enough. What's happened in Moscow is going to double that stress: treble it.'

Ethel glanced briefly at her watch. 'Sasha should be bathed and in bed by now. Natalia will be in the small drawing room, where the television is.'

It was tuned to BBC twenty-four-hour news when Jane entered, although at that moment it was showing a sports segment. Natalia was already half out of her chair, alerted by the door opening. Knowing already about the airport shooting—and having seen the blurred, imperfect Russian CCTV—Jane had expected Natalia to be distraught, hair-straggled, and disarrayed. She wasn't. She wore a skirt and sweater and her blond hair was neatly brushed. There was no makeup.

'Is Charlie dead?' Natalia demanded at once, her voice uneven.

'No,' assured Jane. 'He's hurt. We don't know how badly.'

'Why didn't you tell me before?'

'I didn't know before. We need to talk.'

Natalia hesitated before easing herself back into her chair. Jane sat opposite.

'What's he being held for—the charges, I mean.'

'Your people are drip feeding everything, forcing us too much upon assumptions,' said Jane. 'That's why I am here. If we're going to help Charlie, you've got to help us.'

'The Sluzhba won't let him go.'

'Natalia, listen to me! It wasn't a Sluzhba ambush; if it had been, you wouldn't have got away from Moscow either.'

The Russian shook her head, bewildered. 'Then who . . . I don't understand.'

'We don't properly understand ourselves. When we do—*if* we do—it could tell us how to help Charlie.'

'They'll never give him up,' repeated the woman, dully.

'So you're giving up?' challenged Jane, intentionally brusque.

Natalia smiled, sadly. 'You're forgetting what I did, how I'm trained. I won't be frightened or angered into a shell to be bullied into telling you all you want to know.'

'I'm not trying to compete,' said Jane.

'Why don't you tell me what I'm going to find so difficult to understand?' invited Natalia, settling farther into her chair.

The same BBC news service brought Radtsic and Elena properly together in the same room for the first time in twenty-four hours, Radtsic insisting his wife watch with him. Together, silently, they saw it twice more; on the last occasion, Radtsic stretched close to the screen better to see the CCTV background.

'I'm sure it was Vnukovo,' identified Radtsic.

'What was happening—*has* happened?' asked Elena, in her bewilderment forgetting her antipathy to her husband.

'It looked mafia: a turf war shoot-out.'

'You heard the Russian commentary, underneath the British translation,' corrected Elena, 'It was British intelligence: MI6.'

'A diversion from my crossing was talked about, at the very beginning,' remembered Radtsic. 'It was before things changed and you went to Paris to bring Andrei out. It was only mentioned once.'

Elena jerked her head towards the screen, the picture running without sound. 'Yesterday, they said. It can't have had anything to do with you—with us. Both of us were already here yesterday.'

Radtsic shook his head, equally bewildered. 'MI6 was identified. The two dead officers were named!'

'It's got to be a coincidence, whatever it was. We'll probably never know,' repeated Elena, recovering.

'I want to know,' said Radtsic, more to himself than to his wife.

Elena came forward towards the screen, turning up the volume to another repeat. The blurred CCTV footage was the same, as well as the MI6 identification, but the studio report was updated. The UK government continued to refuse to answer the demands made in a series of official diplomatic notes. London's refusal was understandable in view of that newly obtained information.

'It *has* to be something to do with me,' declared Radtsic. 'Whatever caused the shooting, all those deaths with more to follow, according to the statements. They're going to twist it: turn it into something to denigrate me.'

'You've betrayed Russia!' agreed Elena. 'What do you expect them to do?'

'I need you,' abruptly declared Radtsic, ignoring the television now, his entire concentration upon Elena. 'I *do* know what they'll do, what they'll make me out to be. I don't expect things to be the same between us now—know they can't be, just as I know all that you've sacrificed by coming with me. But you're not with me, are you? You're locking me out: I don't mean from the bedroom, from sex. I don't want sex. I just want you, with me. I need a friend, that's all. Just a friend.'

Elena didn't respond for a long time, looking neither at Radtsic nor at the repetitive television but seemingly unfocussed upon a checkmate-displayed chess set on a game table against a far wall.

Finally she said, 'I'd like to know that Andrei isn't suffering because of all this. He shouldn't be, should he? It really isn't like the old days, is it? He proved his loyalty by not defecting.'

'I want to know what's happened to Andrei, too.'

'If I knew he was all right, wasn't being punished, I wouldn't want him to come here to join us: for him to have to live as we're going to have to live. I'd want him to stay in Russia, with Russians.'

Now it was Radtsic who didn't quickly respond. At last, quiet-voiced, he said, 'That would be best. And it's not automatic that he'll be punished. Some things have changed.'

'I'll try to adjust: not lock you out.'

'Thank you.'

'I said I'll try. That's all I can promise, that I'll try.'

'That's all you can tell me?' anticipated Natalia, professionally.

'You know a lot more anyway,' confirmed Jane, who'd edited her account strictly to MI5's immediate needs.

'Internecine warfare between same-country intelligence agencies isn't unusual,' offered Natalia. 'It's happened between my service—both KGB and FSB—and the Glavnoye Razvedyatelnoye Upravlenlye, our military intelligence.'

'Extending as far as attempted sabotage of supposedly joint operations and murder, which is what this was—or attempted to be?'

'I don't know of a situation that's gone to that extreme,' conceded Natalia.

'We lost Charlie for a week—eight days to be precise—before he made contact with his support group at the embassy,' said Jane. 'The first thing he told our officer was that MI6 was to be totally cut out: that he was refusing any contact whatsoever.'

'You told me you were having doubts in London that MI6 weren't being straight with you,' reminded Natalia.

'Which we weren't able to pass on to Charlie during that lost week,' reminded Jane, in turn. 'And it was Charlie who told his embassy linkman first, not the other way round. We know, from the tourist flight, that he actually got to Moscow on the Monday. When did he first contact you?'

'Tuesday,' said Natalia, covering her caution with the quickness with which she replied. Charlie was injured but alive and she had to do everything conceivably possible to get him out of Russia. She didn't know in sufficient detail what Charlie had told them to justify the extraction of herself and Sasha.

'Tuesday morning or Tuesday evening?'

'Tuesday evening,' said Natalia, promptly again: there was no danger in that answer. 'When we were first together, before we lived together, we had a contact procedure, dead letter drops. Charlie used it and I picked up.'

'It was a very early arrival, on the Monday: four A.M. He must have filled the drop sometime during that first day,' calculated Jane. 'So he'd been able to move about in Moscow roughly thirty-six hours. That first time you met, did he tell you what he'd been doing?'

The safety of complete honesty seized Natalia. 'Nothing at all.'

'It's Charlie we're working to help,' prompted Jane, solemnly. 'Wasn't there the slightest indication?'

Natalia shook her head, maintaining the honesty. 'He was very careful about the actual meeting: wanted to guarantee I'd cleared my trail before he approached me. The drop was at Moscow's original Botanical Gardens. In those very first days of our originally getting together we'd used a hotel very close, the Mira. That's where Charlie was living at the beginning of what you're calling his lost week. It's virtually a rent-by-the-hour whorehouse now. We went there to hide, nothing more. And talk. But only about what was going to happen. There was all the publicity about the tourist arrests by then. I said we'd never get out: that I'd trapped him. He told me he'd make it work.'

'Charlie was ultra-cautious,' picked up Jane, searching for crumbs. 'Didn't you think there was some significance in that?'

Natalia shook her head again, still sure she was on safe ground. 'I have never known a more instinctive, more intuitive espionage professional than Charlie. He finishes other people's thoughts before they know how to finish them for themselves; knows what they're going to do or say before they do. . . .' She hesitated, weighing her words. 'The point I'm making is that I didn't see any significance in the precautions Charlie took. I saw Charlie Muffin being Charlie Muffin.'

Now it was Jane who hesitated, unsure how to continue. 'There's an interpretation that could be made from what you've just said.'

'What?' demanded Natalia, uneasy at not isolating the direction of the remark.

'Was that eulogy of Charlie Muffin the true character assessment? Or was he, in truth, the one you actually managed to turn into a double?' challenged Jane. 'There have been other assessments, assessments easily reached from your actually being married to him, that Charlie has for a long time been a double.'

Natalia remained blank faced, as she had throughout, constantly aware of the cameras and just as expertly now refusing the anger at the accusation, turning the irritation upon herself for allowing even the vaguest twitch of annoyance. For the benefit of the permanently attentive lenses she actually smiled. 'We began trying to find something that might help get Charlie out of whatever situation he's in, a situation in itself that makes ridiculous the accusation you've just made. I'm as much your captive here as Charlie is in Moscow, which compounds the ridiculousness. As difficult as it obviously is for you to believe, which I accept because our being married is even more difficult to believe, Charlie and I never, ever, exchanged a single operational detail until what you refer to as the lost week—'

'Which you haven't told me about,' instantly seized Jane.

'Because your questions haven't allowed me to.'

'Tell me now.'

'You have to tell me something first,' demanded Natalia. 'Did MI5 know Maxim Mikhailovich Radtsic was being extracted *before* he arrived in Britain?'

Jane hesitated. Throughout she'd felt comfortable with the other woman, not suspecting professional manipulation and believing that she was being told the truth: this was a reversal of roles she hadn't anticipated. But by being aware of it, she was forewarned, she reassured herself. 'No,' she said, intentionally short.

'Charlie knew,' Natalia announced.

'How?'

'I don't know,' conceded Natalia. 'But he definitely knew about Radtsic crossing over before I told him I had been appointed to the investigation into Radtsic's background. The only possible source can be MI6, who, according to what you've told me, staged the Vnukovo ambush in which they tried to kill Charlie. Nothing of which makes the slightest sense.'

'That's our problem,' agreed Jane. 'Nothing's made sense since the beginning of this mess.'

Gerald Monsford decided that he'd come out of it far better than he'd imagined possible, right up to the very moment he'd responded to the committee's demand. Unquestionably better, too, that it was he who'd provided the explanation in the way he had, instead of fielding Rebecca to provide his opening. But that hadn't been her ploy. The bitch had meant to leave him stranded, hanging back as she had. He regretted now stranding her in return, rejecting any conversation during their silent ride back to their Vauxhall Cross building. But she definitely had to believe she was safe, not coming forward as he'd instructed and before that physically pulling away from him in front of everyone. It was obvious that he had to get rid of her but he couldn't risk any move to achieve that until he discovered what she imagined to be her protection. So it remained a concern but not his most pressing one. That was building upon that morning's success by very precisely pointing the head of the security investigation to substantiate the doubts he'd already sown about James Straughan.

Matthew Timpson arrived with bank manager's punctuality befitting his black-suited, portly self-important demeanour. With him, unexpectedly, was the unnamed, crimp-haired, matronly woman, also in black, who'd been among the initial investigative hierarchy.

She wasn't introduced now, either. Instead Timpson said, 'Interviews are always formally witnessed.'

'I didn't see this as a formal interview.' Monsford frowned, having hoped for an unrecorded exchange.

'This is a formal investigation: every encounter is formally witnessed and recorded,' lectured Timpson. 'You'll be provided with a verbatim transcript in addition to a copied recording.'

While they'd talked, the woman had installed a slightly larger than pocket-size recorder on Monsford's desk, a bell-shaped receiver arm extended directly towards him.

Indicating his own system, Monsford said, 'I'll make my own copy, of course.'

'Of course.'

The sanctimonious bastard was patronizing him, Monsford decided. He'd take his time choosing the deflating moment.

'You've got something important to contribute to our enquiry?' invited Timpson. He'd chosen his own chair and was sitting with his hands comfortably joined across a plump, waistcoated stomach. His face, like his voice, was expressionless and oddly shone, as if he'd polished rather than washed it.

'Your investigation will encompass the apparent suicide of my former operations director, James Straughan?' embarked Monsford.

'It's of particular interest *because* it is inexplicable,' said Timpson, pedantically.

Timpson would have been a very difficult bank manager from whom to coax an overdraft, thought Monsford. 'Straughan was very closely involved, the architect in many ways, of much of what has become the very complicated and far-too-public difficulties in which both MI5 and my service currently find themselves.'

'Are you suggesting his suicide is directly connected?' asked the flat-voiced man.

Slightly better, judged Monsford. 'Your security classification enables you total access to all the operational details of both extractions?'

'All the appropriate documentation and authority has been provided to you,' insisted Timpson, pedantic again.

None of which gave this jumped-up clerk the right to sit as if in judgement, thought Monsford. Maybe it was deflation time. 'As you've been provided with all the case documentations and authorities of both extractions, what, in your opinion, is the outstanding indication that there is a security leak within MI6?'

'I'm here at your invitation, to hear what you have to tell me,' Timpson avoided, the self-satisfaction slipping slightly.

'From that reply it's obvious you haven't isolated it yet, which certainly makes this a necessary meeting,' said Monsford, aggressively. 'There is no conceivable way the FSB could have burgled Muffin's London flat unless its address came from one of our two agencies. I believe MI6 to be the source.'

'Straughan?' demanded the security head, at once.

Monsford had expected greater surprise. 'That's the indication.'

'What indication?' asked Timpson, a finger-snap question.

'One of my dead officers, Stephan Briddle, was the MI6 supervisor within Charlie Muffin's original support team,' set out Monsford, his concentration now entirely upon every word he uttered and the recordings being made of them. 'Just after midnight—I was asleep, didn't check the exact time—in the morning of the Vnukovo shooting I received a call at my apartment at Cheyne Walk. It was Briddle, in Moscow. He'd discovered a cell, he told me. It was a fragmented story. The gist was that David Halliday, my other dead officer, was part of that cell, together with Straughan, who was running it. Briddle believed Muffin knew more about it: had proof, even, which was why Muffin refused any MI6 association, fearing he'd be compromised—'

'You have a transcript of this conversation?' intruded Timpson, finally energized.

Monsford shook his head, carefully avoiding the denial being audibly recorded. 'Briddle broke operational security. My home telephone is technically an insecure line, not equipped for automatic recording. The conversation was too brief for me manually to switch my normal answering machine to record.'

'There'll be an automatic listing on your telephone record of the call being made, though?'

'Of course there will be. I've just told you mine is an ordinary public line.' Monsford's antipathy towards the other man vanished at the hoped-for question. Stephan Briddle *had* broken every operational security by making the panicked call on an open line just after midnight, but only to confirm by an ambiguous exchange the order to assassinate Charlie Muffin, whom David Halliday had chanced upon at the Savoy Hotel bar they'd used together during Charlie's embassy-murder assignment. But that all-important incoming-telephone record existed, to validate the story no-one could prove to be a lie.

Timpson hesitated, reflectively. 'I'm not clear of the connection with James Straughan. How does this have anything to do with the FSB learning of Muffin's London address?'

'I hadn't finished,' bullied Monsford. 'Briddle also told me that Halliday, maudlin drunk, had talked of arguing with Straughan about an FSB double agent in Rome. Briddle said it hadn't made sense because Halliday was so drunk but that it involved finding Charlie in London: that Charlie had been his friend and he didn't want Charlie physically harmed or betrayed, as Straughan had persuaded him to betray everything and everyone else.'

'Does Rome have any significance to you?' asked Timpson.

All the superciliousness had gone, Monsford recognized, satisfied: the sort of man Shakespeare called the resty sloth. Shaking his head once more, Monsford said, 'No. But that's why I'm pointing you towards Straughan's file: if there's anything, it should be there.' And would be, Monsford knew, because he'd proposed using the FSB's Rome double to leak Charlie Muffin's otherwise totally secure London address as part of his original assassination distraction to cover Maxim Radtsic's defection. Just as he also knew that in his log note Straughan, the consummate, rule-observing professional, would not have identified him as the source of the instruction.

'If Straughan was the mole he'd hardly leave proof behind, would he?'

Monsford shrugged. 'I'm offering all that I know in the hope of resolving this eroding uncertainty within my service. If it comes to nothing, if I'm wasting your time, then I'll apologize. And as I do so, be glad that an officer I always regarded with the highest respect did not, after all, betray his country.'

'We appreciate what you've told us,' said Timpson, rising. 'As of this moment it's the focus of our investigation.'

Monsford was surprised at the call from his deputy, smiling in expectation of a grovelling apology, deciding as he lifted the receiver of their internal line that he'd pressurize her further by rejecting whatever she said.

'There's been another Moscow announcement,' said Rebecca Street. 'Denning and Beckindale, our two other officers with Briddle, were arrested during the shooting. The statement says they are co-operating fully.'

'How was it last night?' asked Barry Elliott.

'Not as bad as I'd feared,' said Jane. They were in bed again, finishing off the dinner wine.

'What, exactly, did you do wrong?'

'Lost my temper: openly challenged Monsford, which was stupid of me.' She stretched, careless of the bedcovering falling away from her. 'This apartment really is more convenient than mine: it took me less than ten minutes to get here tonight. And your kitchen is better equipped than mine.'

'You going to stay over tonight?' asked Elliott, pleased at the way the conversation was going.

'The Watch Room would use my cell phone if there was no reply from my flat but it would mean my wearing tomorrow the same clothes as today.'

'Why not move some of your stuff in?'

'Do you think that's a good idea?' she asked, smiling sideways across the bed.

'I think it's a very good idea,' encouraged Elliott. 'Washington isn't pleased with me, either, so I might need a shoulder to cry on.'

'What's their problem?'

'Not knowing what the hell's going on in Moscow, of course.'

There was a familiar pause. 'We think Monsford set Charlie up for assassination.'

Elliott shifted directly to face the woman. 'You've got to be joking!'

'It started out as a considered diversion but we think that Monsford didn't call it off.'

He had to risk it, Elliott decided. 'Diversion from what?'

'MI6 had a walk-in.'

'Into the embassy?'

'At a government reception.'

'He still in Moscow?'

'Here.'

'How big?'

'The biggest.'

'We talking professional?'

'Personal: very personal. If it leaks, it can only have come from you.'

Fuck, thought Elliott. 'What are we proving here?'

'Each other. This is my commitment.'

5

CHARLIE EXPECTED THE WITHDRAWAL OF THE CATHETER TO BE roughly performed, intentionally to hurt, but it wasn't. It was extracted slowly, by a caressingly soft-handed, substantially busted blond nurse who frequently stopped to ask, smiling, if she was causing him discomfort. Each time Charlie assured her she wasn't, glad that the procedure was finished and the bedcovering restored before the assembled, expectantly smiling medical team witnessed his lie. There was no pain, either, when she was helped by others to extract the cannula from the back of his hand and disassemble the metal stands supporting the two drips. While he'd lain there Charlie was sure he'd isolated the listening attachment at the mouthpiece corner of the permanently available oxygen supply: he'd always manoeuvred himself in its direction when breaking wind.

'We're going to look at the wound, put on a lighter dressing,' announced the bearded, heavily moustached surgeon, coming out of the medical group. None had ever been identified.

'Everything still feels numb,' said Charlie. It was a pointless persistence, he accepted, but every gesture of resistance, no matter how minimal, was psychologically important. He guessed Mikhail Guzov was trying the same technique by ignoring him for an entire day to generate apprehension for what was to come.

'So you keep telling me,' said the physician. There was dutiful laughter among those assembled behind him.

Charlie stood unsteadily, momentarily dizzy from being upright on his usually uncomfortable feet for the first time in almost three days as well as from having only one free arm for natural balance. The team and the outside guards trailed behind when they emerged onto the corridor, giving Charlie an unobstructed view on his wheelchair journey, which he at once acknowledged to be another unsettling psychological trick. There were no obvious side corridors to general wards. Every door, its padded rubber exterior heavily studded by regimented, large-headed fixings, was closed. There were no sounds from inside any room he passed. Nor did they encounter another person in any of the half-lighted passages. The intention, Charlie knew, was for him to feel totally abandoned, which he did.

Charlie was stripped of his back-buttoned smock but retained the overly long trousers, which puddled around his ankles, making it difficult even to stumble the few steps to the examination table. He needed help to get onto it. This time the two assistants were men and far less careful, the purpose of which Charlie again recognized, staying rigid faced against the pain he was insisting he was still too numbed to feel. He tried to twist his head to his injured shoulder as the dressing was cut away but an unseen theatre nurse cupped his head and others turned him onto his uninjured side, giving the surgeon front and back access to his wounded shoulder. Charlie had to close his eyes against the blinding overhead light.

'Although you tell me there's no feeling we'll still have a little local anaesthetic, shall we?' mocked the surgeon.

Charlie counted three injections. Genuine numbness was very quick.

'This could heal with too much external scar tissue, which we don't need, do we?' continued the voice, from behind. 'Just a cosmetic snip, here and there.'

Charlie felt the pressure of an instrument, but no pain, then a different pressure, as if his shoulder was being prodded. A whispered conversation began, during which Charlie strained. He was sure he heard *heal* at least three times. Then what sounded like *flat* or maybe *flag*. *Week* was very clear. So was *infection*. The new dressing was far less mummifying, the bindings brought around his chest only to keep the bandages in place.

There was far more consideration getting him off the table. Once more, briefly upright, he needed support to regain the wheelchair.

'It's a perfect operation: with that little tidying there'll hardly be any scarring,' promised the surgeon.

'Was it really worth the effort?' asked Charlie. They'd expect the beginning of depression at his growing realization of helplessness.

The ever-ready smile clicked on. 'I take professional pride in everything I do. Whatever the circumstances.'

A smaller entourage took Charlie back to his room, only his ward guards and the two male nurses who'd manhandled him onto the examination table. They took another, seemingly longer route, although again through deserted, semi-lit corridors past silent, padded doors.

Mikhail Alexandrovich Guzov was already there.

'The doctor tells me you're making a remarkable recovery: that we can start today,' greeted the immaculate Russian, dismissing the room guards with a jerk of his head. The trouser of Guzov's crossed leg was arranged for the razor-sharp crease to run unbroken from knee to burnished boot.

The extended return had enabled a discussion with the surgeon, Charlie guessed, as his medical escorts helped him, more gently now, from the wheelchair to the bed, in which, in his absence, a back support had been fitted to put him into a virtually upright sitting position. Testing his assumption, Charlie said, 'I've just undergone surgery.'

'Surgical vanity,' said the FSB general, confirming Charlie's guess. 'There's no reason for further delay.'

'What's there to talk about?'

Guzov smiled, broadly. 'I'm not in any hurry, Charlie. I want what's going to happen between you and me to last as long as possible. My only impatience is for it to start.'

'You told me,' sighed Charlie, dismissively. His shoulder began to ache as the anaesthetic wore off.

'There's been the usual diplomatic request for consular access,' declared Guzov.

Don't hint eagerness, Charlie warned himself. 'It's nice to know somebody cares.'

'I don't imagine it's philanthropic concern, after all the problems you've caused.'

'I don't understand that.' When would the access be, for his chance to discover what had happened to Natalia and Sasha? Charlie agonized. Guzov would enjoy—would exacerbate—the torment if he knew its significance. Or *did* he know? Was this it, the beginning of the threatened torture? *Stop!* Charlie told himself, angrily: Guzov would be winning if he inculcated eroding uncertainty.

'They're not going to make any real effort to help you,' goaded Guzov. 'Not you or Denning or Beckindale. You know Denning and Beckindale, don't you, Charlie?'

He was achieving nothing from perpetual denial, Charlie recognized again. He had to convince Guzov and through him as many others as possible that they were achieving control and then mislead and misdirect them for as long as he could. The FSB would know from their embassy surveillance the precise arrival of all three MI6 men, just as they knew, from the same observation, that he hadn't been anywhere near the embassy during that period. So there was no provable link between him and the two back-up MI6 survivors. 'The names don't mean anything to me. Do they know me?'

'They've told us all there is to tell.'

A fatuous boast, discarded Charlie. 'That should minimize the time we need to be together, until I'm repatriated.'

'You imagine we're going to accept that you're not guilty of serious offences under Russian law?'

Charlie didn't imagine it for a moment but snatched at the indication of London's diplomatic response to his seizure. What else was there to deduce? All the identification was of MI6 personnel. Had Ian Flood—as

well as his original MI5 support—escaped? If they had, it logically followed that Natalia and Sasha had escaped as well. Too big an assumption
but Charlie was encouraged. He thought . . . The interrupting awareness
came in a rush, expanding into a physical stomach lurch at the realization of how close he'd come to missing the Russian's weakness. 'Finding
an offence to justify all the nonsense is going to be a problem.'

Guzov failed to stop the briefest facial twitch. 'How long are you going to persist in this stupid insistence of innocence?'

'Until you accept it to be the truth and put me into the care of the
British embassy,' recited Charlie.

'We have statements from Denning and Beckindale in which both
identify you as a senior MI5 field operative.'

Charlie at once saw the route—a positive shortcut, in fact—to follow,
although there was the one specific discovery he didn't want to make at
its end. 'What else have these two total strangers claimed to know about
me?'

On this occasion the anger was visible on Guzov's mood-mirroring
face. 'We have all we need. As well as sufficient, court-supporting evidence for a charge of active involvement in acts of espionage against the
Russian Federation.'

The Russian was bluffing, Charlie decided, surprised at the clumsiness: bluffing very badly and, even worse, inexpertly. That would have
been the moment to hit him with Natalia and Sasha: to gloat that they
had also been seized and watch, hopefully, for him to crumble. It was conceivable, even, that the Russians didn't have Denning or Beckindale, either.
Their association with the dead Briddle could easily have been established
through their arrival documentation, providing Guzov the names with
which to attempt the deception. And even if the two were detained, there
was nothing in Guzov's bluster to indicate confessional statements. Feeling a sudden sweep of tiredness, unsurprising after the minor surgery
and the concentration necessary for this encounter, Charlie settled himself more comfortably against his bed support and said, 'It all sounds
fascinating.'

'You're playing it as I'd hoped you would, Charlie. Imagining you're better than me: that you can beat me.'

'Something else I don't understand,' dismissed Charlie.

'How about something you will understand?' said the Russian, the smile broadening. 'We know about the woman.'

They convened at Thames House as they had the preceding day and again Aubrey Smith gave the opening to his deputy. Overnight, Jane Ambersom had organized a transcript of her conversation with Natalia, prefacing the verbatim account with what she considered the salient factors.

'Charlie knew about Radtsic's defection—and of Elena and Andrei's seizure in France—before Natalia told him?' queried the Director-General, coming up from the papers.

'I think there should be a qualification here,' warned Jane. 'In the full transcript she's adamant it was Maxim Radtsic whom Charlie knew about. I'm inclined to think he knew there was *something* else going on, but not that it was Radtsic's extraction as such.'

'You mean she's intentionally misleading us?' challenged Passmore, at once.

'Absolutely not,' denied Jane. 'I believe she fully understands she's got to do everything she can to help Charlie. I also believe she sincerely believes Charlie mentioned Radtsic by name, because of her own surprising involvement. There's also a lot of guilt. Knowing, too late, that she was cleared of suspicion—that her marriage to Charlie hadn't been discovered—she feels she trapped him into going back to get her and their daughter out.'

'She didn't talk about the Radtsic investigation?' asked Passmore.

'Before we started talking I specifically excluded anything other than what might help Charlie,' responded the woman. 'It was she who mentioned Radtsic but only to make her point of Charlie knowing or having discovered something during the lost week. And let's not overlook what else she said: that MI6 could have been the only source for Charlie's information, whether it was Radtsic by name or just a mysterious "something," which is my interpretation.'

'An MI6 source doesn't fit with what we know,' protested Smith, turning to the other man. 'I need our three back. What's happening to them?'

'Neil Preston's booked on this morning's direct Sheremetyevo flight to Heathrow. Peter Warren's at the airport, to see if he makes it. In last night's diplomatic bag to Moscow I sent a new passport, with all the necessary documentation for Wilkinson. It's in the name of Paul Mason. If Preston gets out, we could put Wilkinson on the lunchtime flight: we've already made a reservation. If Preston's intercepted, Wilkinson's on the eleven A.M. express to Poland. The flight from there will get him into London at 2300 tonight.'

'I wanted him here today,' reminded Smith, in his customarily flat voice.

'*Safely* here tonight,' qualified Passmore, heavily. 'This route is the quickest and gives us that safety.'

'Does it *ensure* it?' questioned the Director-General.

'No,' conceded the operations director. 'I judged it our best chance.'

'What about Warren, either way?' asked Jane.

'I'm keeping him there, whatever happens,' said Passmore. 'I'm briefing our man for Charlie's access delegation later today: the entire group is being assembled in readiness from here. The Foreign Office want as little connection as possible with the compromised Moscow embassy to avoid the Russians pulling another trick to exacerbate our embarrassment. Moscow's finally agreed to a delegation meeting with the Manchester tourists, too: they'll all go from here, distanced from the embassy for the same reason. I've got one of ours in that group. Warren will be the dedicated conduit for both our officers.'

'And despite all the distancing efforts, every single move of both delegations will get maximum media exposure to be relayed around the world to stoke the pressure upon us,' anticipated Smith, objectively.

'Has Moscow actually agreed to diplomatic access to Charlie, after delaying over the Manchester group for so long?' asked Jane.

'No,' admitted Passmore. 'It'll obviously depend upon how much humiliation they're determined to achieve. I'm guessing we'll get to Charlie more quickly to provide footage of a sorry trail of British diplomats getting on and off aircraft.'

'Are we thinking clearly enough?' asked Smith, rhetorically. 'We suspected Monsford was planning something but didn't know what it was; told Wilkinson to warn Charlie. But before Wilkinson opened his mouth, Charlie told him he wasn't working with his *assigned* MI6 group. Which makes Natalia's suggestion that MI6 was Charlie's source absurd: downright impossible. . . . Or does it?'

The others remained silent, waiting.

'Go back through Charlie's file,' Smith picked up. 'Jacobson and Halliday made up the MI6 *rezidentura* in Moscow. Did either of them overlap Charlie's Lvov assignment there?'

'The Lvov assignment that Gerald Monsford went practically insane trying to take over,' reminded Jane. 'Maybe it really is that, a genuinely insane preoccupation.'

'Jacobson brought Radtsic out,' said Passmore, in further recollection. 'Presumably he's still babysitting the man in a safe house somewhere.'

'We'd never get near him in an MI6 house, any more than we'd let them get within a million miles of Natalia,' said Jane.

'We'd be close enough if Jacobson were called as a witness before the committee,' said Aubrey Smith.

'There'd need to be a reason for calling him,' said Passmore. 'You think the arrest of Denning and Beckindale provides it?'

'We're certainly going to try,' decided the Director-General.

It was more than likely Monsford had been told independently, Rebecca accepted, but if he hadn't, the asshole had only himself to blame, refusing her calls and messages and leaving the curt instruction on her answering machine to make her own way to that morning's session. She'd more than covered her ass—which she'd determined to continue covering in every other way from now on—by spreading her alert not just to his voice mail at Cheyne Walk and at his headquarters office but to the operations room as well. She'd called minutes before leaving Vauxhall Cross and been told there'd been no contact from the Director.

Rebecca was intentionally early, conscious of the immediate attention from the secretariat supporting Sir Archibald Bland and Geoffrey Palmer, neither of whom had yet arrived. She was conscious, too, that yesterday's place setting for James Straughan had been removed. Surreptitiously, confident that she was unobserved, Rebecca eased her repositioned seat away from Monsford's. The general influx came about thirty minutes before the scheduled opening. Monsford came in just before MI5. Monsford wasn't openly smiling but appeared relaxed, surveying those already gathered around the table, which he joined differently from the preceding day, passing in front of the secretariat, at which he briefly paused before continuing on to his designated seat, nodding in satisfaction as he reached it at the absence of Straughan's place setting. He neither smiled nor greeted Rebecca.

'I've been calling you: leaving messages.'

'Something's come up. I've been busy.' He didn't look at her as he spoke.

Shit, she thought, disappointed. 'You've heard about Radtsic then?'

Monsford covered the lurch of surprise by noisily repositioning his chair, closing the gap Rebecca had created. 'I spoke to Jacobson half an hour ago. He didn't say anything!'

'The significance didn't register with our CCTV monitors in Hertfordshire: Christ knows why not!' criticized the woman. 'Radtsic made Elena watch yesterday's BBC coverage of the shooting, which included the Russian airport film. Radtsic talks about a diversion being discussed in the initial days of his extraction planning. The remark was isolated overnight by a committee monitor. I got the call at seven this morning, after they couldn't reach you. As I couldn't, until now.'

'Have you seen the clip!' demanded Monsford.

'The whole sequence,' confirmed Rebecca. She was curious at his comparatively calm reaction. But he'd never been the quickest off the mental starting block.

'Tell me: every word he said.'

Rebecca hesitated, conscious that everyone was gathered around the table. 'They're both bewildered by the film: can't understand it. Radtsic suggests it's mafia, a turf war shoot-out, which Elena ridicules. They're listening to the original Russian soundtrack, under the English voice-over. Which Elena reminds Radtsic specifically identifies MI6. That's when Radtsic talks of a diversion. . . .'

'Exactly!' insisted Monsford. 'Tell me Radtsic's exact words!'

The panic was settling, Rebecca thought, satisfied. '*"A diversion was talked about, at the very beginning,"*' she quoted, having anticipated the man's demand. '*"It was before things changed and you went to Paris to bring Andrei out with you. It was only mentioned once, as far as I recall. Nothing was ever said again, after that one time."*'

The room quieted at the entry of Bland and Palmer, which Monsford ignored. 'No actual mention of killing! Just a diversion? That's all he called it, a diversion?'

'Diversion was the word,' confirmed Rebecca. 'He never referred to assassination, although assassination was the context in which he said it.'

'Let's begin, shall we?' suggested Bland, from farther along the table.

The Cabinet Secretary's preamble was much briefer than the preceding day's, adding to the continuing official record with the Russian arrest of Robert Denning and Jeremy Beckindale and Moscow's agreement to a diplomatic visit to the Manchester tourists. Glancing briefly at a slip of paper passed up from the secretariat, Bland concluded, 'And there is a request from MI6 Director Gerald Monsford immediately to address this committee.'

So close had Monsford put himself to her with his earlier chair shifting that Rebecca was aware of his left leg sometimes touching hers. There was none of the nervous twitching of the day before. The man's briefcase remained unopened on the opposite side of his chair and there were no prompt notes in front of him.

'I have a number of matters that I believe takes forward the concerns I expressed yesterday at my service's penetration by foreign intelligence,' began Monsford, leaning comfortably back in his chair. Following yesterday's session, he continued, he had briefed the head of the security investigation within MI6. 'Within three hours, forensic technicians discovered illegal apparatus connected to the personal recording equipment in my office. The official installation of my equipment was personally supervised by James Straughan. The concealed illegal apparatus was operated from Straughan's private office. The only fingerprints upon it were those of James Straughan. . . .' Monsford paused, allowing the reaction to move throughout the room. 'Every conversation I have had over the last two months, either by telephone or with people in my office, has been illegally monitored and presumably passed on to whomever Straughan was working for. I have already ordered that all my audio records be scrutinized to learn the full extent of the potential damage. . . .'

Of course there would have been equipment! thought Rebecca. How else could Straughan have made the incriminating copies they'd hoped to be their insurance against being caught up in whatever Monsford was planning. Why hadn't she thought . . . ? Thought what: done what? Rebecca fought against the panic, trying to calm herself. She hadn't known where or how Straughan had rigged what he'd called his tie line. And even if she had, she wouldn't have been able to dismantle it. There was no connection to her, she reasoned, snatching for reassurances. So she was still safe. And had to stay that way. She had to hear it all through: do nothing, say nothing, but think harder and better than she'd ever thought before.

Directly across the table, Aubrey Smith had gradually, imperceptibly, reached out to grip Jane Ambersom's arm, conscious of the furious vibration coursing through the woman, tightening a warning against another outburst.

'. . . An even more recent indication,' Monsford was saying. 'Overnight a remark from Maxim Radtsic was isolated upon film. The reference is to a diversion presumably to be staged to facilitate his extraction. In the very early stages of the extraction of Natalia Fedova and her daughter, there was such discussion, which came to nothing. It was specifically in the context of Natalia and her daughter. I know nothing of a diversion in bringing Radtsic out. Radtsic is refusing to co-operate with us until his son is allowed to join them. After this meeting I am immediately going to pursue this distraction remark, not having the slightest idea to what it refers. About Radtsic—'

'You can surely do more than question Radtsic?' broke in Aubrey Smith, prepared from the earlier conference at Thames House. 'He was brought out of Russia by the head of your Moscow *rezidentura*, Harry Jacobson, who was Radtsic's control from the moment of Radtsic's defection approach. It would have been Jacobson who talked to Radtsic of a diversion, wouldn't it? We can bring Jacobson before this committee in person, as I intend producing some of my officers involved in Natalia's extraction.'

Rebecca at last detected the tightness spreading along Monsford's leg and felt a jump of satisfaction, her own concern lessened by calm reflection.

'It would certainly be an option, if Radtsic remains recalcitrant,' conceded Monsford, reluctantly.

'Why an option?' persisted the MI5 Director. 'Jacobson is an essential witness in his own right. He was at the embassy virtually throughout this entire series of events, would have known everything.'

'It's obvious we have to hear him,' declared Geoffrey Palmer, impatiently. 'Let's put him on the witness list.' Turning to Monsford, he said, 'What you've told us is potentially disastrous. The absolute essential now is our tracing the full extent of this cell and eradicating it.'

'To that end I propose we add to the witness list the head of the security probe into my service,' said Monsford.

'Agreed,' said Bland, quicker than his co-chairman.

Rebecca couldn't discern any tension from Monsford now and decided the man considered himself the finger-flicking master of ceremonies.

As if in confirmation, Monsford said, 'I also believe it's time to counter

Moscow's propaganda by disclosing Maxim Mikhailovich Radtsic's defection, as well as that of Natalia Fedova.'

'No!' objected Aubrey Smith, unusually loudly in his anxiety. 'We only yesterday got Moscow's agreement to a delegation to the Manchester group. We must not give them an excuse to delay or refuse contact with Charlie Muffin. Additionally, we now know Moscow has detained two MI6 officers. That inevitably means another delegation. There'll be a time—and an advantage to be gained—in announcing Radtsic's crossing. But this isn't it. To do it now would be entirely counter-productive.'

'We agree,' quickly came in the unidentified spokesman from the Foreign Office contingent. 'Confronting Moscow now would be a diplomatic mistake: we've got too many of our nationals exposed.'

'This is perhaps the moment for me to make a contribution that may have some relevance,' offered Stanley Brown, the GCHQ director. 'We intercept some material out of the Lubyanka but not enough. We get much more Russian Foreign Ministry chatter to their embassy here and occasionally their response to the Lubyanka. Translations of what we've picked up about this business will be available tomorrow but in essence there's an expectation of retaliation from us. But two days ago the traffic stopped—'

'Meaning?' broke in Palmer.

'They know we listen, just as we know they listen to us.' The man smiled. 'And knowing it we both seed a fair amount of disinformation in the hope of confusing each other. Stopping electronic communication altogether means they've gone to hard copy, hand delivery between ministries and the Lubyanka in Moscow and in the diplomatic pouch to the embassy here. They've got a contingency response about which they don't want us to get the slightest indication.'

'Which we defeat, delay at least to our advantage, by not providing a reason to initiate it,' pointed out Aubrey Smith.

'We'll hold back from public disclosure on either defector,' decided Bland. 'I would . . .'

The Cabinet Secretary stopped at the unexpected telephone intrusion from the secretariat's table and watched with everyone as a clerk hurried to the door to take a message slip from an outside attendant. The man went directly to Aubrey Smith. The Director-General pushed the envelope sideways to Passmore as he said, 'This morning we attempted to bring out one of Charlie Muffin's MI5 support team, Neil Preston. He was detained thirty minutes ago, going through passport control at Sheremetyevo Airport.'

'When in God's name is this fiasco going to end?' demanded Geoffrey Palmer, exasperated.

'My name's Birkitt, Edwin Birkitt,' introduced the CIA interrogator. 'We're going to spend a lot of time together.'

'You choose your own cover names or get them allocated?' came back Irena Yakulova Novikov. She'd fence for as long as she could, get what unsuspecting guidance she could.

'How's it done in the FSB?' came back Birkitt, just as quickly. He was a slight, nondescript man, apart from the thick-lensed spectacles. He was unencumbered by any note-taking paraphernalia, entirely dependent upon the automatic listening and filming installations. His Russian was excellent.

Irena smiled, in begrudging acknowledgement. 'They're allocated.'

'Same here. Guess I was lucky this time.'

'I'm not a defector. I went to England to save an operation.'

'And failed. At least you got a hell of a face job. You really get burned at a dinner party with Stepan Lvov?'

Irena smiled again. 'So the puppy dog British have given me to you in the expectation that you'll get more than I told that scruffy bastard who thought he'd fucked the Lvov operation?'

'You've got every reason to despise him, beating you as he did.'

'I went willingly, operationally, to England. I did not come willingly here, to the United States. Technically I have been kidnapped. I demand to see people from the Russian embassy.'

'We're kidnappers, remember? We don't do things legally.'

There was an almost imperceptible frown and Irena held back the words she had opened her mouth to utter. Instead she said, 'You can't do this!'

'We're doing it,' Birkitt pointed out, conversationally. 'According to what you told Charlie Muffin, you masterminded an operation over eighteen years that would have made the U.S. a client-state of the Russian Federation. That's got an awful lot of people as mad as hell and the last thing they're worried about is normal legality. Officially you're a disappeared, Irena Yakulova. You're here for as long as we choose to hold you, which is as long as it takes to learn every last scrap about your great plan.'

'You're out of your mind if you imagine I'm going to do that.'

'You're out of your mind if you imagine that we won't.'

6

'HELLO.'

Sasha squinted up against the cloud-broken sun. 'Hello.'

'Where are you off to?'

'Home.' Sasha was carrying a doll lopsidedly by its arm, with its clothes in a half-zipped bag in her other hand. She wore open sandals and a summer dress.

'You can't walk home from here. It's too far,' said Ethel Jackson.

'You're speaking Russian,' insisted the child.

'But we're not in Russia. Hasn't Mummy told you where you are?'

'I can't remember where she said.'

'We're in England.'

'I don't like it in England. I want to go home.'

'Have you told your mother where you're going?'

Sasha pulled her bottom lip uncertainly back and forth between her teeth. 'I'm going to.'

'It's always best to tell people where you're going,' said Ethel, aware of Natalia bursting through the open patio doors behind the child. Seeing Sasha with the protection supervisor, Natalia slowed but only slightly. 'Here she is now.'

Sasha turned and stood with her head bowed over the doll. Ethel put her hand lightly on the child's shoulder to pull her comfortingly closer. Sasha came without protest. Ethel felt the tremble in the child's shoulders. As Natalia came within hearing, Ethel said, 'Sasha and I are going to have cakes on the patio with . . . You haven't told me your baby's name, Sasha?'

'Ludmilla . . . Luda,' mumbled the girl.

'With Luda,' finished Ethel. 'Why don't we all have cakes together?'

Natalia looked at how Ethel was reassuring her daughter, then more directly up to the other woman. 'That would be nice.' She was short of breath from hurrying.

They were met at the patio by another protection officer, who nodded to the cake order: Natalia agreed to Sasha's having Coca-Cola as a treat. The child very studiously ignored the two women, fussily positioning the doll on the fourth chair, arranging and re-arranging its clothes. As she did so, Sasha said, 'We're going home, aren't we, Luda? Don't like it here, do we, Luda?' and more quietly mumbled on unintelligibly, a conversation entirely with her doll.

Natalia moved to speak but before she could, Ethel said, 'I told you it's too far to walk, Sasha. And look, you forgot the pram we got for Luda. Why don't you take her for a short walk in the garden until your Coke arrives?'

Looking properly to her mother for the first time, Sasha said, 'Can I take Luda into the garden?'

'Not too far. I want to be able to see you.'

Unspeaking for several moments, the two women watched Sasha, still heavily in conversation with her doll, trundle its pram out into the garden. Ethel said, 'You know she couldn't have gone anywhere.'

'I wasn't worried about her getting *out*. I was terrified about someone getting *in*.'

'That can't happen either. You're both safe.'

'Nothing's *supposed* to happen,' heavily qualified Natalia. 'You're in the business. You know the search is on: always will be. They don't give up. It won't matter that Sasha's a child.'

'Stop it, Natalia!' demanded Ethel, sharply. 'You're in a protection programme precisely to stop your ever being found, which you won't ever be.'

Natalia was silent for several minutes. 'Have you heard anything new?'

Ethel hesitated. 'There's been another arrest. An MI5 man.'

'Linked to Charlie?'

'One of his original back-up.'

'How?'

'At the airport, trying to get home.'

'They won't let anyone go,' insisted the Russian. 'They'll pick them all off, one after the other. The more they get, the more they have to match the loss of Maxim Mikhailovich.'

The tea, Coke, and cakes arrived. Looking out into the garden, Natalia said, 'We'll let Sasha come back when she's ready.'

Ethel said, 'Numbers can't balance their loss of Maxim Mikhailovich.'

'The more people they have, the more confusing they can make their retaliation.'

Ethel poured the tea. Neither bothered with cake. Ethel said, 'What retaliation would you expect?'

'The obvious, if they find him and Elena here: just as they'd eliminate Sasha and me. The KGB punishment rules haven't changed, even though the title has. The orders to hunt down and eliminate us will have been automatic. In the interim, they'll probably claim Maxim Mikhailovich and Elena were kidnapped, as they claimed with Elena in France; Andrei's refusal gives them a lot of ground in which to manoeuvre that sort of story.'

'What about you?'

Natalia shrugged. 'They won't bother about me, not publicly; the elimination order will have been promulgated, though. Why do you think I was terrified when I couldn't find Sasha? They'll ask for access to me, of course. I meant to talk to Jane about that. I don't want anyone getting to me from the embassy. I've got to agree to a meeting, haven't I?'

'Yes,' confirmed Ethel.

'I positively refuse to meet anyone from anywhere. Will you tell Jane that: tell her today?'

'I'll tell her,' promised Ethel. After a momentary pause, she said, 'Have you thought of anything else since you talked to Jane: something that could help Charlie?'

Natalia shook her head. 'You saw the film recording of me and Jane?'
'Yes.'

'Charlie's source must have been inside the embassy,' insisted Natalia. 'And if Charlie wasn't talking to his own people in the lost week, it must have been MI6, mustn't it?'

'Charlie didn't go anywhere near the embassy during the lost week,' reminded Ethel, disappointed at the repetition of Natalia's conversation with the deputy director. 'And after all the bugging discovered in the embassy, Charlie wouldn't have risked landlines.'

Natalia regarded the other woman curiously, as if she'd misunderstood. 'He didn't trust landlines, not at all. Nor the Russian cell phone you issued him here. He guessed you'd fit it with a tracker to know where he was all the time. He only used the phone issued here once, because it worked underground when he finally made contact and then more to confuse the MI6 hunting him. At all other times he used pay-as-you-go Russian cell phones, throwing them away after a single use: he gave me four and had even more himself. That's how he and I communicated after I was appointed to the committee investigating Maxim Mikhailovich's background to find the identity of whoever turned him.'

Ethel's wicker chair creaked when she moved, needing physical movement at the satisfaction that moved through her. 'Cell phones can be intercepted by scanners. The FSB would have ring-fenced the embassy with them.'

'Pay-as-you-go are one-off numbers, doubly more difficult to scan at random and that difficulty quadruples if they're discarded after a single use,' lectured Natalia, waving to Sasha, who waved back but didn't move towards them.

Ethel wasn't sure of the importance of what she'd learned but believed it was enough. She wasn't sure, either, whether openly to discuss it with Natalia: they were supposed to be working to a common aim and Ethel didn't want to destroy the bridge building by knocking away its fragile foundations. Say nothing until she got better guidance, Ethel decided. Following Natalia's waves to Sasha, Ethel said, 'It isn't unusual in ordinary circumstances for someone of Sasha's age to announce they're leaving home.'

'I know,' accepted the Russian. 'What's unusual—and makes it different—is what's happened to her in the last week. With which I haven't been helping, only thinking of Charlie.'

'But now it's happened you can help.'

'Can *we*?' asked Natalia, pointedly.

'If you'd like me to,' immediately responded Ethel. 'If you wouldn't consider it interfering.'

'I'd think of it as you helping me. You have children?'

'They're with their father. What I do—have done—isn't best suited to motherhood. It makes me pretty expert on how it goes wrong, though.'

'You worked in the field, before?'

'Yes.'

Natalia made as if to speak but didn't. After several moments she said, 'Thank you, for being kind. It's difficult for me, doing what I've done, not to despise myself as a traitor. That was always at the back of my mind when I was debriefing people who'd come across.'

'Maxim Mikhailovich fits the traitor profile,' disputed Ethel. 'I don't believe you do. There's a lot of difference.'

Once more Natalia appeared to be about to speak but again stopped herself.

'What?' encouraged Ethel.

'Nothing,' avoided Natalia, twisting in her equally creaking wicker seat at Sasha's return. 'We saved the cakes until you got back.'

No-one—maybe not even Gerald Monsford himself—knew how close he had been to collapse by the end of that day's regular session. Mentally he strained for the concentration to follow the concluding period but too many of the voices around him seemed disembodied and difficult to connect with their speakers, all of it distracted even more by his inner difficulty deciding which survival move to make next.

He was pulled towards the bombshell discovery of James Straughan's bugging, convinced that copies were what Rebecca considered her political strength. But did she actually *have* copies or only knowledge of their existence? According to Timpson, specialized versions were minuscule, measurable in millimetres: the type, Monsford knew, that Straughan, the ultimate specialist, would have used. But where the hell were they? Did Rebecca actually have them: some at least? Or had Straughan been the storekeeper as well as the recordist? And if he'd kept them, where had he stashed them? He had to be the first to find and destroy everything, Monsford acknowledged.

But the forensic team, the scientific experts, *hadn't* found anything yet. So wherever they were, his destruction wasn't guaranteed. It was more important, more immediately urgent, to get to Harry Jacobson before anyone else and he had to do that personally, not by telephone, technically secure from eavesdropping though they were supposed to be: under the current investigative scrutiny, Monsford wasn't sure if communications weren't now automatically being officially tapped.

He did, however, alert Jacobson by telephone that he was coming, relief surging through him that there'd been no official approach from the committee, concluding the call with the strict instruction that the man was to talk to no-one, not even Radtsic, until he got to the Hertfordshire safe house.

Rebecca responded at once to Monsford's summons. He let her settle in her customary chair, with his own audio apparatus visible to ensure she saw him activate it.

'What do you think about Straughan?' Monsford demanded, the question intentionally wide.

He knew, Rebecca accepted: hardly the deduction of the century, even for someone of Monsford's bovine speed of thought. But he didn't have any proof and until he did she couldn't be accused of anything. She had to fight back, find a way to get ahead again. 'Surprised, obviously. Shocked.'

'You had no idea what he was doing?'

The goading bastard was playing with her, like a sadistic child pulling the wings off butterflies. 'No. None.'

'I'm so glad,' said Monsford, unctuously. 'Irrespective of anything else that might be uncovered, what Straughan's done is a blatant breach of the Official Secrets Act, clear proof of hostile espionage. Anyone working with him, complicit in any way, would be equally guilty. That's a lock-the-cell-door-and-throw-away-the-key sort of punishment.'

'Nothing's been found?' questioned Rebecca, forcing a recovery. Monsford was staging the performance of his mentally uncertain life, she decided, reminding herself of her earlier committee-room conclusion. In whatever reality remained in that twisted mind, Monsford would be shitting himself at what the scientific investigators might find. But then, confronting her own reality, Rebecca accepted that she was, too, although unless a medical examination was forced upon her—which there couldn't be, because that would be criminal assault—no digitalized recordings would be found.

'No,' said Monsford, convinced he knew what she was thinking. 'And don't bother getting back to the local police investigating the suicide. Timpson's already taken that over, lock, stock and barrel. As Shakespeare put it, "with as little a web as this will I ensnare as great a fly as Cassio."'

More applicable to himself than to her, whoever Cassio was, thought Rebecca. But the bastard was closing every avenue against her. 'What do you want me to do?'

'Get all you can from the embassy about Denning and Beckindale. Their man, Preston, too, if you can. As far as the embassy is concerned it remains a joint operation. Get into official contact with whoever's organizing the diplomatic access to get one of our people aboard. . . .' He smiled what was supposed to be a just-between-ourselves smile. 'Wait for me to get back from Hertfordshire. We've both worked far too hard these last few days. Let's go out to dinner: enjoy ourselves.'

She'd have to endure it that night and for as long as it took afterwards until she found her way out. But when she did, Rebecca vowed, the final time she fucked Monsford wouldn't be physical and she'd enjoy it far more than he would. At least for tonight—and for those that necessarily had to follow—she could amuse herself at the thought that he'd never know what she had hidden in the tampon she'd have so carefully to withdraw and, even more carefully, and quickly, reinsert while he lay gasping and groaning.

'I didn't mean to get you out of a meeting,' apologized Ethel, the moment Jane came on the line. While she'd waited for the connection Ethel had watched Natalia and Sasha on the drawing-room monitor, curled foetal-like together in an encompassing easy chair.

'The message said it could be important,' said Jane.

'I hope it is,' said Ethel. 'I think I'm getting Natalia to trust me. It began with something small involving Sasha. Natalia's actually asked me to help her with the child.'

'Brilliant!' enthused the other woman.

'Did we know Natalia was part of an investigation into Radtsic's background: that the Russians believe he was part of a long-term spying operation they've got to uncover?'

'Not precisely. There was a message from Charlie about a committee-type scrutiny and that it had something to do with Radtsic: that it was important.' Jane paused. 'My understanding with her was that we wouldn't talk about it yet, only about whatever might affect Charlie.'

'It happened naturally, almost without my initially becoming aware of it,' said Ethel. 'I certainly didn't set out to move things forward and at this moment I haven't. I'm analyzing her reactions, without knowing their significance. I'm sure there's something about Radtsic. I thought, for a moment, that she was actually going to tell me. But at the last moment she drew back.'

'You think you could take her that close again?'

'I don't know,' Ethel answered, honestly. 'I could try.'

'Try,' urged Jane.

'The thing with Sasha: she'd packed her baby's things and told me she was going home. Natalia's agreed to my helping Sasha adjust.'

'You *have* become friends,' congratulated Jane.

'Too early to say yet but it could be,' cautioned Ethel. 'But before we go any further I want some guidance. Do I do things overtly or covertly?'

There was no instant response from the other end of the line. Ethel waited. On the monitor, Natalia and Sasha were still intricately entwined. Finally Jane said, 'It's a difficult call. If she thinks we're cheating, we'll have lost her.'

'That's why I asked the question,' said Ethel, faintly impatient.

'We'll go on as we are, at least for another few days,' decided Jane. 'The moment you become unsure, you back off: it's important you're the first to withdraw to prevent Natalia closing the door against us.'

Why was there a moment of disappointment at the professional practicality? wondered Ethel. Nothing could ever be personal, came the immediate answer. 'There's something more and it's my instinct, nothing more. Over the lost week, Natalia and Charlie communicated through pay-as-you-go Russian cell phones, discarding them after single use. She's suggesting he used the same channel with his embassy source, which she still insists has to be MI6. I'm just floating a former-field-operative thought here. Could it be that whoever that inside source was, he or she might *not* have discarded their phone: that somewhere lying about inside the MI6 *rezidentura* there might still be a throwaway phone with things on it that we could find very useful?'

'You've done well,' congratulated Jane. 'You've gotten a damned sight closer than I came within a million miles of achieving.'

'It's not difficult to be Natalia's friend. . . .'

'You're not thinking of . . . ?'

'No,' halted Ethel. 'I'm not thinking of late-night confessions over brandy snifters about my knowing Charlie. And I haven't finished. She's terrified, like they're all terrified in the early stages, of being found by the FSB. I'm to tell you, as positively as I'm able, that she will not see a diplomatic representation from the Russian embassy.'

'Moscow could use that refusal to block our access to any of our people,' recognized Jane, at once.

'That's what she's insisting: wants you to know,' said Ethel, glad to have moved the decision on.

Harry Jacobson was obediently waiting at Monsford's designated spot, virtually out of sight of the main Hertfordshire house, close to the garage complex. It would have been equally difficult for Monsford to be seen from the house getting from his car, which pulled in even closer to the buildings. Monsford led the way through the concealing stand of trees deeper into the wooded area, not speaking until he reached it.

'Just ground sensors here? No audio equipment?'

'Not until about another four metres,' assured Jacobson.

'You missed Radtsic's reference to a diversion,' accused the Director, at once.

'Yesterday was my rest day.' Where was the usual irrational anger at any mistake? wondered Jacobson.

'Who was monitoring?'

'Bullen?'

'You replaced him?'

'Of course,' said Jacobson, glad he'd anticipated the dismissal demand, even though it had created an atmosphere with the rest of the protection squad.

'What did you tell Radtsic in Moscow?'

'Exactly what he told Elena on film. At one of our meetings, before any plan had been formulated, I told him we might introduce a diversion into his extraction. . . .' Jacobson hesitated, believing he was beginning to understand, a swell of hopeful satisfaction moving through him. The assassination instructions would have been transferred to Stephan Briddle, he guessed. And Stephan Briddle was dead. '. . . Then the idea got dropped. I never discussed it in any way whatsoever with Radtsic . . . or with anyone else.' *Come on*, thought Jacobson, enjoying himself: *nibble at the bait for me to be sure.*

'The committee are attaching importance to the remark, after what happened at Vnukovo.'

Getting there, thought Jacobson. He had to be careful, though. He needed to gain every benefit while remaining as distanced as possible from this unnaturally subdued bully. 'I can understand that, after what happened.'

'You're to appear before them, to explain the remark.'

Savouring how perfect the analogy fitted the huge man, Jacobson recognized this to be the moment the subjugated bull was on its knees, the sword upraised for the killing thrust. 'There's surely nothing more for them to hear or understand beyond what they've already seen and heard on film.'

'They'll want to know what the intended diversion was to be.'

Jacobson hesitated, wanting the words to be right. Monsford even had his head lowered, as if in readiness for the kill. 'I actually find it difficult to remember the details of our conversation.'

Monsford's head came up, restoring his full bull-like stature, smiling briefly. 'I'm glad we've had this conversation.'

Oh no you don't, Jacobson thought at once. Could he take the chance: risk everything with just a few misplaced words? But it wasn't his risk, he reminded himself. 'We haven't talked of my next posting, now I quite obviously can't return to Moscow.'

'That has to be resolved,' allowed Monsford, tightly.

'I did put forward some preferences.'

'Washington, wasn't it?'

'And Paris.' The ballet wouldn't be as good as it had been in Moscow but on balance it would be better than America. And Covent Garden had been a total disappointment the night before.

'Yes, Paris,' accepted Monsford, reflectively.

'As head of station,' pressed Jacobson, knowing it all had to be finalized at this moment, with nothing left as a vague promise.

'Which do you want?'

'Paris.'

'It's yours.'

'As head of station.'

'As head of station,' echoed Monsford. His face was mask-like.

'And potentially deputy director after that.'

'That'll be yours, too, when the time comes.' Which it never would, determined Monsford, furious at the humiliation.

'When do you want me in London for the committee hearing?'

'Be on standby from tomorrow. Anything I need to know before seeing Radtsic?' That would be an easy encounter, Monsford knew, his survival-enhancing approach already determined.

'There's been a reconciliation of sorts with Elena: they're eating together, spending most of their day together, mostly watching television for anything more from Moscow. But she's still not sleeping with him.'

'What about the drinking.'

Jacobson looked unnecessarily at his watch. 'There'll be less than a quarter of a bottle left by now.'

It took almost four hours for Ian Flood to go minutely through the Vnukovo Airport shooting in preparation for MI5's enquiry presentation.

At the finish, Aubrey Smith said, 'I want to establish a movement pattern. The MI6 back-up split the moment they enter the terminal: Denning and Beckindale stay to one side, Briddle goes at once, on his own, towards Charlie, who's in the Cyprus flight check-in line, unaware of their arrival?'

'Yes,' confirmed Flood, an athletically bodied, controlled man.

'How long before Halliday entered?'

'A minute, no longer than two.'

'Was Halliday with the others?' came in Passmore. 'Did you get the impression all four arrived together, in the same car? Or might Halliday have followed separately?'

Flood nodded at the significance. 'I was only suspicious of one car following us from Natalia's apartment and assumed they were all in the same vehicle. Halliday could have travelled separately but it would have needed to be directly behind, in which case I think I would have isolated the second pursuit, too.'

'How long did it take Halliday to orientate himself?' picked up Smith.

'Again, minutes. He seemed immediately to see Briddle and simultaneously to locate Charlie from the direction in which Briddle was moving.'

'Or could he have expected Charlie to be in that particular check-in line?' asked Jane.

The question, again significant, briefly silenced the Director-General's Thames House suite. Flood said, 'Meeting there separately, by agreement, you mean? It would have been a hell of a coincidence for them to have been meeting by prior arrangement at the same time as a separate MI6 discovery of Charlie, wouldn't?'

'What did Denning and Beckindale do?' asked Jane.

'Nothing,' said Flood, shortly. 'I had them in my eyeline the entire time. They had Briddle, one of their own, as a marker. But they didn't appear to see Halliday. Or, if they did, they'd been ordered against intrusion.'

'If indeed it was an MI6 operation that had gone wrong,' qualified Smith.

'That's what you identified it to be, an operation?' followed up Jane.

Once more Flood paused, for thought. 'Charlie met me the previous night at the Savoy. That's when he gave me the very specific order against interfering if anything endangered Natalia and Sasha's extraction.'

'That previous night,' seized Jane. 'Tell us everything about that, in as much detail as you can!'

'He didn't give me any details of the Lvov assignment, but he said he'd appeared publicly on Russian television during it and that there'd been a security alert out for him: that he risked being picked up on official CCTV. . . .' Flood hesitated, shaking his head.

'What is it?' pressed Jane, curious at the man's gesture.

'Something I'd forgotten, until this moment. I don't know if it contributes anything—'

'Everything and anything contributes,' persisted the woman.

'That night, in the hotel bar, when he was talking of being identified, he said it would have been all right if he hadn't made the Amsterdam switch and got the Manchester people arrested. That none of it had been necessary.'

'What does that mean?' questioned Passmore.

'He didn't explain. The inference was that it would have been all right if he'd stayed on the original flight. That he'd created his own risk of identification.'

'He said that! That he staged that diversion because he thought he was going to be picked up the moment he arrived!' came in Smith.

Flood looked uncertainly at Jane before saying, 'His exact words were, "I fucked it up all by myself but it was fucked up before it ever started to get where we are now. Which has got to be done right."'

There was a digesting silence.

'Okay,' resumed Jane, cautiously. 'He'd created his own identification problem but the operation was fucked up before it started out from here. Did he explain that?'

'He said it had never been to extract Natalia, which everyone here thought. He'd suspected it wasn't right but couldn't work out why until he learned that Radtsic had defected. But that it was ongoing—'

'What was ongoing?' said Smith.

'MI6's determination to screw Natalia's extraction, even though they'd got Radtsic safely away. I said that didn't make sense. Charlie said he thought it went right back to the Lvov investigation but he didn't understand how or why.'

'We've gotten away from the movement pattern,' complained the Director-General. 'How were Halliday and Briddle moving towards Charlie—quietly, calmly, together or separately?'

Flood toyed with his long-empty coffee cup. 'Moving quickly, but they *weren't* together. Again, it's an impression but at first I didn't think Briddle was aware of Halliday behind him, trying to catch up.'

'That's what you believe Halliday was trying to do, catch up with Briddle?' asked Passmore.

'I'm not sure,' replied the man, awkwardly. 'That was my initial thought. I saw Halliday shout, although he was too far away for me to hear what he said. I thought it was to attract Briddle's attention but Charlie turned as well.'

'Distances,' demanded Jane. 'How far apart were they at this stage: Charlie's in the queue, then comes Briddle and after him Halliday. How far apart were they?'

Again Flood paused, considering. 'Charlie just stood there. At Halliday's shout, Briddle was about eighteen metres away. Halliday was about two metres behind him. It was then that Briddle turned and saw Halliday.'

'What did Briddle do, after looking around?' seized Passmore.

'Started to run towards Charlie,' replied Flood, again understanding the significance of the question. 'It was at this point that I heard the first shot. No-one else reacted. Both Briddle and Halliday were running by now—'

'Was it Briddle's shot?' demanded Smith.

There was no hesitation this time. 'I don't know. I didn't see a gun. Briddle was running peculiarly, arms around himself, hugging his jacket around his body. At last people became aware two men were running across the concourse . . . moved to let them through. Then I did see Briddle with a gun in his hand, a Makarov . . . saw him fire—'

'Stop!' insisted Smith. 'This is pivotal: at whom did Briddle shoot?'

'At Charlie,' replied Flood, again without hesitation. 'Charlie Muffin was unquestionably Briddle's target. Everything erupted then: it was pandemonium, gunfire, screaming, people running everywhere. I saw Charlie go down and decided it was time to get out.'

'And I think it's time for us to stop and analyze what we've got,' decided the Director-General.

Gerald Monsford strode determinedly through the safe house, more confident than he'd been for days, actually bemused at how perfectly the pieces were fitting together, knowing before he started how perfectly he could slot Maxim Radtsic into his survival frame. Both Radtsic and

Elena were in the favoured conservatory, the television turned to the permanent BBC news channel as Jacobson had predicted. The vodka bottle was still a quarter full.

'At last!' greeted the Russian, rising at Monsford's entry. 'What news of Andrei?'

Monsford pulled a seat closer to the two Russians and said, 'We've got other things to talk about today, Maxim Mikhailovich: important things.'

'There's only one thing of importance for us to discuss,' persisted Radtsic, frowning.

'Tell me about your penetration of MI6, my organization,' demanded Monsford. *The lie circumstantial... the lie direct*, came appropriately to Monsford's mind: he'd always liked Shakespeare's *Comedy of Errors*, although this confrontation was hardly likely to be a comedy.

Radtsic stared blankly across the intervening space, saying nothing.

'We know we've been penetrated: found the evidence,' bulldozed Monsford, shifting minimally towards the ever-running camera. 'I've also seen the film of you and Elena watching what happened at Vnukovo: heard you wondering at the connection with your defection. So let's stop all this posturing about refusing to cooperate until Andrei gets here. I've told you what we're doing to achieve that and now I want—I insist—on your telling me everything about the cell you created within MI6. It's over now, finished. Straughan's dead: you actually saw Halliday gunned down in the airport shooting.'

Radtsic remained blank faced, shaking his head. 'What are you talking about . . . ? I don't understand a word you're saying. . . .'

'I can't play games with you, Maxim Mikhailovich: *won't* play games,' hectored Monsford. 'Discovering your penetration of my organization changes things between us. I want it all: every name, precisely—to the actual date—how long you've run it, for us to calculate how much you've received, all the embassy Controls here in London, contact details, dead letter drops, codes you used. Everything! You understand that, Maxim Mikhailovich: everything!'

Radtsic partially reached out towards Elena, as if for physical support, then dropped his outstretched hand. 'This is a riddle: madness. I have not penetrated your organization. There is no cell. Stop it: you must stop this. It's nonsense.'

'I want an answer and I want it now!' persisted Monsford. 'If I don't get an answer, we're going to have completely to reconsider our situation. You're going to co-operate.'

Which was precisely what Charlie Muffin was being told, almost two thousand miles away in Moscow.

'We had a guy once, long time ago now, who was a legend within the CIA,' reminisced Edwin Birkitt. 'His name was James Jesus Angleton, head of CIA internal security. His legend, getting people to tell him things they wouldn't even tell their own mothers, was the problem: no-one realized he was going mad because he'd always been so eccentric no-one ever questioned him. . . .'

Irena sighed, slumped back in her chair, fingering the edge of her skirt, wondering how many cameras in total were focused upon her.

'We had this Russian defector, genuine guy with lots of stuff to tell us, but Angleton thought we were being jerked about. You wouldn't guess what Angleton did.'

'I know what he did.' Irena sighed again. 'He kept him in solitary confinement for six or seven years and no-one had the balls to challenge his authority for doing it. And if I'm supposed to be frightened by that as an analogy, I'm not. Langley put safeguards into the system after that, didn't they?'

'That's the point,' stressed Birkitt. 'You've been here a long time now, long enough to have that facial correction we promised, and you're not showing the gratitude Langley expects. There's still a lot of people in the Company who think Angleton got a rough deal in the end and wouldn't think it wrong to go back to the old days to find out what they want to know.'

'Am I supposed to be frightened?' repeated Irena.

'I think you should be.' Birkitt smiled.

CHARLIE WAS DISCOMFITED AT HIS SWAYING UNSTEADINESS, standing without a supporting hand for the first time in almost five days, and after such inactivity his normally awkward feet began to hurt, too.

'You need help?' asked Guzov, from the far side of the room. He didn't move to provide it. Neither did the two ward guards beside the man.

'I'm fine,' refused Charlie, wedging his thigh against the bed edge to keep himself upright.

'Hope you like your new clothes.' Guzov grimaced. 'Your old ones were only good enough to get your size. We managed to salvage your shoes, though.' The Russian held the Hush Puppies aloft like battlefield trophies: fittingly, they were blood spotted.

'I'm sure they'll be fine,' said Charlie. Laid out beside the bed were a rough work shirt, thick-cord trousers, and a traditional kulak-style smock rarely seen outside isolated farm communities on the Steppes. Charlie turned, grateful for the additional stability when he perched on the bed, but almost toppled forward struggling into his fortunately original although stiffly laundered underwear.

'You sure you're okay?' goaded the Russian, still not moving.

'Quite sure.' Charlie got into the trousers more easily, leaning backwards over the bed. The apparent clumsiness of putting on the shirt was intentional, scrubbing it back and forth in a back-drying motion to scratch the persistent irritation from his healing shoulder. The Hush Puppies were sufficiently stretched for Charlie to slip his feet into without bend-ing. The smock was too large, like the belt to go around it, and he saw the two guards were smiling along with Guzov.

'We got the size wrong after all,' said the Russian, in mock apology.

'I'm not going anywhere special.'

'You'd be surprised where you're going, Charlie,' promised Guzov.

Sure that he'd fall, stumble at least, Charlie refused the pace Guzov set along the deserted corridor, forcing Guzov to wait at the elevator. In the foyer they were totally ignored by three blue-uniformed receptionists at a central desk beyond which, through a glass screen, an open-plan office was visible. There were no ringing telephones or flickering computer screens: the silence was practically sepulchral.

Outside it was raining, that persistent, cloud-leaking drizzle that Charlie remembered sometimes fell day after day, painting Moscow a monochrome, suicide-tempting grey. There was as little evidence outside the building—no ambulances or canopied emergency bays or bustling, white-coated doctors or nurses—as there had been inside, of it being a medical facility. None of the entering or leaving staff wore hospital uniforms that would identify them outside the building. From the second storey upwards, all the windows were barred. From the elevator descent, Charlie knew he'd been on the fourth level.

There was a plainclothes guard beside the driver, also in a suit, of the waiting, dark-windowed BMW. Guzov left Charlie to get unaided into the car. The ward escorts stood back under the overhanging building to keep out of the rain. No-one spoke when Charlie finally, awkwardly, got into the vehicle or helped him secure his seat belt. There were no identifying hospital signs at the end of the drive and Charlie finally concluded it was the sort of psychiatric institution he'd initially suspected. As the car swept out into unfamiliar streets Charlie wondered if they actually were in Moscow: he'd been unconscious from the time he was shot until he'd awakened in the restraint-strapped bed, after the operation to remove the bullet. It was at least five minutes before Charlie recognized the ring-road approach and calculated he'd been held in the northwest, an area of Moscow with which he was unfamiliar. From the directional indicators on the slip road to the multi-lane highway, Charlie knew they were continuing north.

At last Guzov turned to him. 'You realize by now where we're going, of course?'

'I know the *direction* in which we're going,' qualified Charlie, not willing to volunteer his familiarity with the city.

'I promised you'd be surprised.'

He had to step back from positive confrontation, Charlie knew: the attitude he'd adopted since his seizure wasn't returning anything he could utilize. 'What puzzles me is our leaving Moscow before there's been consular access.'

'We're not leaving Moscow,' threw back Guzov, ignoring Charlie's response. 'We're going to the hills.'

That *did* surprise Charlie, although he didn't show it. Should he acknowledge his awareness of the cliché, showing his familiarity with the city after all, or fall back upon supposed ignorance? Every savvy Muscovite knew 'the hills' referred to a particular area of the high ground overlooking the city. In its exclusiveness, since the time of Stalin, lay the weekend and holiday retreats of the nation's ruling elite, up to and including the premier and the president. 'I've heard of the dachas but not of the prison facility. The gulags are surely a long way further east?'

Guzov smiled his gargoyle smile across the car. 'It'll be a very long time before you end up in a gulag.' The facial expression widened. 'If you're sensible, which I hope eventually you'll be, you could avoid going to one altogether.'

In his new mindset against confrontation, Charlie decided against the ritual challenge of legality and criminal charges. They were out of the city now, in the scrublands before the gentle upwards climb. The drizzle was heavier, scudding down in bursts: it had driven people and vehicles off the highway and everything looked as forbiddingly desolate as the psychiatric building he'd just left. The tree line was abrupt, almost barbered, empty no man's land one moment, straight-edged forest, mostly firs, the next. So densely cultivated and maintained was the forest for the

favoured few that it almost at once became half-light, occasionally interspersed by the sudden brightness of an opening into an unmarked road to
a hidden property.

The spur road was on a bend, which the driver would have known.
He braked hard instead of gradually, throwing Charlie forward against
his seat belt. The pain seared through Charlie's still-healing shoulder
but he managed to bite back the groan. Everyone else had expectantly
braced themselves, he saw. Just beyond what would have been visible
from the main road was a gatehouse-operated barrier that wasn't lifted
until the driver's documentation was cleared from within the check-
point.

Although narrower, the new road was properly metalled and maintained, built in Roman-style straightness as far as Charlie could see, but
the offshoot lanes were less frequently obvious, with few warning tree
breaks. Which meant Charlie was again totally unprepared when, after
the briefest of braking, the BMW slewed to the right. The abrupt jar
from hitting an uneven rough track again burst agonizingly through Charlie, the pain this time so bad he couldn't stop crying out.

'Slower,' Guzov ordered the driver. To Charlie he said, 'You all right?'

'That was fucking stupid,' complained Charlie. And intentional, he
knew. The turning off the public highway into the barrier-controlled
road was roughly two kilometres from the beginning of the tree line and
the third break to the left in those trees. The distance of this turn-off from
the Roman-straight road was far less, hardly a kilometre and the fourth
on its left, counting from the barrier.

'You're right: it was stupid,' agreed the Russian.

Charlie tensed his dressing-shielded shoulder to detect the first warm
sensation of the wound reopening. All he could feel was the heartbeat-
timed throb that replaced the initial excruciating pain.

Less than a kilometre, finally estimated Charlie, as the track bal-
looned into a clearing in the middle of which stood, as if on display, a
picture-postcard image of a Russian dacha. It was wood-built, even to its
steeped, snow-discarding shingle root, and completely encircled by an

open, balustraded veranda, the entire construction lifted high off the ground on stilts, again to defeat the winter snows.

Once more unaided, Charlie got from the car, relieved the unsteadiness was lessening although his shoulder still throbbed. The driver and guard remained by the car as he followed Guzov. Inside the cottage, most of the furniture was rough, country-carved wood. Guzov took one chair, waving Charlie to another fronting it.

'You can look around later,' Guzov decreed. 'What we're going to do now is understand how we're going to work. . . .' He gave an almost uncaring gesture around the dacha. 'Well?'

Go with the flow, Charlie reminded himself; he still had to find his rewarding level of response. 'I am surprised. Confused, in fact.' Which was, Charlie accepted, the entire purpose of this bizarre exercise.

'Did you expect a rat-nested Lubyanka cell, with water running down its walls?'

'It crossed my mind.'

'It still could be. Or a return to where you've just come from for a different type of specialized treatment . . .' There was another wave around the room. 'Or there's this, where you and I can talk. . . .' There was another pause, for the face-dividing smile. 'And before we start discussing that, let's really understand each other. I know you are going to lie: that's what we professionals are trained to do in the event of a seizure. I'm going to take a lot of time sifting through all your deceit to get to the eventual truth. You'll also try to escape. Which you can't possibly do, so don't try. You'll have a rotating staff, male and female, to cook and clean. . . .' The arm waving went beyond the cottage. 'This is a special complex—'

'In which live more specially trained men whose job it is to protect the even more special people who relax and holiday around here,' anticipated Charlie.

The grimace came and went. 'An elite *spetsnaz* company, a kind of imperial guard. Where we are now—where you're going to be—is where they're permanently barracked: those they protect aren't actually all around but they're not that far away.'

'An imperial guard for the rulers of a country that destroyed its imperial royal family,' remarked Charlie. He still wasn't getting his attitude right, he criticized himself.

'Imagine that!' persisted Guzov. 'You, a British intelligence agent, so close to the relaxation hideaways of Russia's hierarchy! You might as well be on the moon, trying to hurt them with a catapult for all the harm you can do. This is the most closely guarded, impregnable few square kilometres in the entire Russian Federation: in the world, maybe.'

He was being positively invited—challenged—to try, Charlie accepted. 'I'm surprised you feel able to take the chance.'

'What risk, Charlie? The only harm you can ever cause again is to yourself. Those special men you talk about have orders not to physically to harm you. But trained as the *spetsnaz* are, they might welcome a change from the norm to go bear hunting—with you as the bear.'

'I don't think I'd like that,' acknowledged Charlie. Better response, he decided.

'The choice is yours to make. And inevitably regret if it's the wrong one.'

Certainly not a challenge he felt like taking up at that moment. But he had to try something, he supposed. His jarred shoulder still ached, matched by that from his re-incarcerated feet. Neither of which distracted his thinking. Why was Guzov going through this performance? He didn't need a lecture like this, a performance like this, to convince him of the inevitable humiliation of an escape attempt, disguised as a kulak.

Time to re-introduce a little reality, Charlie decided. 'You surely don't intend the consular encounter to be here?'

There was a shrug of disinterest. 'You've been out of circulation for days: you're a long way behind developments.'

Apprehension moved through Charlie. 'What developments?'

'We've got so many of your people in custody now, although none with such accommodation as this. We scarcely know what to do with them all.'

Your people, picked out Charlie: but still no reference to Natalia, not even Guzov's earlier remark about their knowing of "the woman." Charlie said, 'In custody for what?'

'So many different offences,' dismissed the Russian.

'None of which affects my right to consular access that will be applied for.'

'As it has for all the others. That's the point I was making: the difficulty of finding time and space to fit everybody in. You're on the list.'

'I have the right of consular access,' insisted Charlie.

There was the familiar grimace. 'I'm the person who decides what rights you do or do not have, Charlie. No-one else. We'll eat, meet the first of your housekeepers. And after that we'll start work.'

'I was looking for you.'

'And you found me.'

'I learned five English words today,' boasted Sasha. 'There were pictures to help me.'

'What were they?' invited Ethel.

'Cow, dog, goat, horse . . .' The recital faltered. 'I've forgotten the last one.'

'Four out of five is very good,' praised Ethel.

'I can almost say the name of my teacher, too.'

'Mrs Elphick,' came Natalia's voice, from farther along the corridor. 'She wants you back in class. . . .' As she came into view, Natalia continued, 'And she's very pleased at how hard you're working now.'

'Can we have cake outside again today?'

'As a reward for working hard,' agreed Ethel.

'I wouldn't have believed the transformation if I hadn't seen it for myself,' said Natalia, watching her daughter go back along the corridor. Turning to the other woman, she said, 'Is there anything from Moscow?'

Ethel shook her head. 'Jane's staying in London to be on the spot. But we've spoken. She wants me to talk to you about some other developments.' Without waiting for a response, the protection supervisor started towards the lounge, where coffee was already set out.

As she handed Natalia her cup, Ethel said, 'The leader of your extraction team has given a detailed account of a meeting with Charlie the night before you came out.'

Natalia put her coffee untouched on a side table, waiting.

'There are things Charlie told him that you might be able to help us understand better: by themselves they're incomplete.'

'What things?'

'Did Charlie tell you about abandoning the plane bringing him to Moscow?'

Natalia finally sipped her coffee, considering her answer. 'It was really what I told him.'

Another chink of light through a gradually opening door? wondered Ethel, who wanted to justify Jane Ambersom's decision to let her continue the gentle questioning of Natalia. 'What was that?'

Natalia breathed in, preparing herself. 'I don't know anything of what happened with Stepan Lvov, just what I inferred from what followed. I knew Charlie was involved, of course: he appeared on Russian television.' She sipped more coffee. 'When Charlie and I got together, personally I mean, I cleansed the records to make it look as if Charlie's debriefing was passed on up the line to others. But my link with Charlie, sanitized though it was, had to remain in the records. I was called in for interrogation the day Lvov was assassinated. I told the questioning officer the story that Charlie and I had rehearsed and from the initial reaction I believed it had been accepted. But I was called back the following day. The first interrogation had been one-to-one. This time there was a panel of three and the questioning was far more aggressive, although more general. I kept rigidly to my initial account, without the slightest deviation. I was, after all, on my own ground: knew all the interrogation ploys and traps. The more general stuff wasn't a problem. The interrogation, which I considered hostile, continued the following day and when it ended I was warned I might be recalled.'

Natalia drained her cup and accepted a refill from the other woman. 'Charlie and I were very careful about our relationship, particularly after we got married. One insistence, when he came back to England, hoping I would join him, was that I always called him from public telephones, never from my home line, which could be tapped. After the third interrogation and the warning of possibly more, I guessed I hadn't cleansed the records as thoroughly as I'd imagined: that there was something that could trap me. I called Charlie from the public phones as he insisted. He never picked up but I left messages, pleading with him to help Sasha and me. That was always my fear, having Sasha taken away from me. But then it all changed. . . .' Natalia straggled to a halt, breathing heavily.

'What changed?' prompted Ethel, cautiously, when Natalia didn't continue.

'I made a terrible mistake . . . it's all my fault. . . .'

'Natalia, I need to understand what you're telling me.'

'They didn't suspect me, not after the first interview. Those that followed, the aggressive ones, were to satisfy them I was sufficiently loyal for the job I was being transferred to do. After I started I learned that everyone else had been tested as I had.'

'What job were you being tested for?' coaxed Ethel.

Natalia remained silent for several moments.

'Natalia?' pressed Ethel, keeping the impatience from her voice.

'I said, when I got here, that I wouldn't co-operate until you got Charlie back, but I've got to, haven't I: tell you everything that might make that possible?'

'Yes, you have,' said Ethel, forceful for the first time.

'The loss of Radtsic was cataclysmic within the FSB. They started the investigation within hours of getting the confirmation from airport CCTV of his boarding the plane. By the second day they began creating the committees. That's where I was transferred, to one of the first-level groups tooth-combing Radtsic's complete professional background from the day he joining the KGB. They're convinced there's been a long-term cell operating throughout Radtsic's entire professional career.'

'How many committees?' asked Ethel, sure she was concealing her excitement.

'I don't know, not precisely. I gave Charlie an estimate of ten at my level, the lowest. Each group was separate from the others: that's why I can only estimate the total. Each member of each committee worked on a batch of material at a time. If we believed we'd found something deserving further examination, we had to alert the rest of the group, in case others came across the same name or discrepancy. After being annotated, to avoid whatever it was being permanently misplaced, it was forwarded up to the next examination level, where the search is, apparently, being speeded up by computer analysis.'

Now it was Ethel who lapsed into a brief silence, mentally assembling what Natalia was telling her. 'So your mistake was telephoning Charlie?'

'The mistake was telephoning him in the panic that I did,' elaborated Natalia. 'I told him at the end of his Lvov investigation that I'd finally decided to leave Russia for good, bringing Sasha here. If I'd simply told him I was coming he wouldn't have needed to come to get us. All that business of changing planes and joining a tourist party wrecked everything.'

'What did Charlie say?'

'That it wasn't wrecked: that he'd get us out. Which he did, didn't he, by sacrificing himself?'

'Did he say anything about your extraction being endangered by anything other than his detection by the Russian authorities?'

'Not specifically. He made several references to there being things, situations, that he didn't understand. It was my impression that he felt threatened but that he didn't want to make me more nervous than I already was.'

'What about the extraction itself? How did he prepare you for that?'

Once more there was a moment of consideration. 'He simply told me to take Sasha to the airport and go through the formalities with the tickets and passports he'd given me the previous day. There would be escorts who'd be with me throughout the flight, first to Helsinki and then on to here. I wouldn't know them but they'd know Sasha and me.'

'Where did Charlie say he'd be?'

'The FSB knew he was in Moscow, so it was obvious there'd be an airport alert for him. The arrangement was to show himself to me outside the terminal, which he did. He told me that after that I wouldn't see him again until we were all safely on the plane. . . .' There was a gulped pause. 'He also told me that if I became aware of any commotion I wasn't to stop but keep going. But I wasn't aware of anything. I expected him to get on the plane but he never did.'

'How long did you work with your committee, going through Radtsic's personal archive?' asked Ethel, tensed against the question off-balancing the other woman.

'Five days.' Natalia straightened in her chair, recognizing the changed direction.

'How much did you read?' Ethel pressed.

'I'm not sure.'

She was looking for an escape, Ethel knew. 'You said you worked in batches: how many batches did you clear in a day?'

'Maybe ten.'

'A day?' repeated Ethel, determined upon as much accuracy as possible.

'Yes.'

'How big was each batch?'

Natalia created a measurement between her outstretched hands, saying nothing.

'Multiply that estimated size by fifty, ten batches over five days, you must have gone through roughly six kilos of material?'

Natalia hesitated. 'I suppose so.'

'We'll need to talk about it, Natalia. We'll want it all,' reminded Ethel.

'When we know what's happened to Charlie.'

The door burst open, interrupting them. 'I got a star!' announced Sasha, proudly.

Aubrey Smith led the reaction, but not in the way expected by the others who'd watched the simultaneous transmission from the police-college safe house in Hampshire. Looking to Jane Ambersom, he said, 'Not many people—certainly not anyone I've encountered since becoming Director-General—would have officially acknowledged, as you did, that Ethel would achieve more than you could in the time available. That's not just a verbal commendation: it'll be on your personnel file by the end of the day.'

Jane hesitated, seeking more than a platitude but couldn't. 'Thank you very much.'

'From her success so far, maybe Ethel should get a commendation, too,' suggested Passmore.

'She's well on her way,' promised the Director-General. 'It's essential we learn everything Natalia got from Radtsic's file.'

'We're having one success with the woman-to-woman situation,' Passmore pointed out. 'Why don't we try another?'

'Agreed.' Smith smiled, understanding. He turned to Jane. 'From the chair shifting and body language, despite rumours to the contrary, I don't think rapacious Rebecca is enjoying the sidelines,' said the Director-General. 'I believe the dissatisfaction I'm seeing in Rebecca could be encouraged by comparison with the authority and responsibility accorded to Jane.'

'You surely don't imagine she'd ally herself with us!' questioned Jane.

'Depends how overlooked or even threatened Rebecca feels herself to be,' shrugged Smith. 'All you've got to do is present the Natalia disclosure.'

Passmore's pager beeped, directly followed by a call on the internal link to the communications room. The operations director smiled, turning to the two others. 'Patrick Wilkinson's made coded contact, on an open line. His message is that it was an exciting trip but that it's good to be home.'

'At least that's one officer spared from the diplomatic-access machinery,' remarked Jane.

'I've got people on standby for all the others when the Russians eventually agree: Charlie's at the top of the list,' said Passmore.

'Let's hope Charlie's man gets the chance to perform the function if the Russians ever offer it,' said Smith, doubtfully.

It was virtually automatic for Charlie to identify the dacha as a brilliantly positioned safe house, as impossible to get *into* as it was to escape *from*, the myriad nooks and crannies of its rough timber construction tailored for the inner observation equipment in addition to the specialized guarding army outside. The easily smiling middle-aged woman who served the excellent stroganoff was attractive enough to have been a swallow in the Cold War days of diplomat-targeting sexual entrapment, the male minder sufficiently handsome to have been a raven offering the same temptations to lonely female embassy staff. Charlie noted that the offered wine was his Georgian favourite and that the rack was fully stocked. Mikhail Guzov maintained the exchanges throughout the meal with stories of two undetected years as a KGB officer in the London embassy, which Charlie dismissed as complete invention from the word-perfect tourist-guide recitation of the places and sights Guzov claimed to have visited. Charlie's disbelief was confirmed by Guzov's account of a weekend at a Shakespeare festival at Stratford-on-Avon when the movements of Russian diplomats were officially restricted to a twenty-mile radius of London.

'And now we talk,' announced Guzov, as their plates were cleared.

'About what?' asked Charlie, pleased at the gravy spot besmirching the Russian's lapel.

'Irena Yakulova,' announced the Russian.

Charlie was relieved there was no longer any unsteadiness when he stood: he wasn't surprised in the circumstances that his feet hurt.

'It's huge,' declared Mort Bering. As a concession—and because the essential point had been made—the FBI deputy director had travelled out to the CIA headquarters in Virginia.

'What!' demanded Larry Stern. At Bering's request, today's encounter was in the FBI man's car, driving without direction through Rock Creek Park.

'Everything's tied up with the Lvov thing but the steer Elliott's getting is that it's moved on a long way from how you guys got screwed.'

'What about our getting involved: try to salvage something from the fucking disaster?' suggested Stern. 'We need something to impress the Intelligence Committee on the Hill to prevent their discovering what a total fuck-up we made and how many top-echelon guys it's cost us.'

'We're a long way from there yet,' cautioned Bering. 'What about the Novikov woman?'

'We finally got her in the chair: got our best guy on it but she's still stonewalling. Claims she was kidnapped, demanding access to her embassy.'

'What's she being told?'

'That as far as anyone knows she doesn't exist anymore; that unless she gives us every last detail of the Lvov emplacement, she'll stay here until she's old and grey.'

'You think she'll buckle?'

'There are a lot of mirrors in the safe house, so she can watch that pretty new face of hers wither along with the grey hair if she doesn't.'

8

CHARLIE WAS MOMENTARILY BEWILDERED AT GUZOV'S DECLARA-
tion that the architect of the Stepan Lvov emplacement was to be the focus of their opening session, from which the obvious conclusion had to be
that the FSB believed Irena Yakulova Novikov was under British, not
American, protection. But then why shouldn't they believe that?

How could he use it? As much and in as many misleading directions
as he could invent, came the answer. But not randomly: not sowing the
disinformation seeds like a gardener in a March wind. He could plant
offshoots where it was fertile but there had to be a central theme if he
was to convince Guzov and those who'd analyze more closely his every
inference and innuendo that a thread of truth held together the lies
they'd expect him to tell.

What they'd anticipated would be the key, Charlie knew: so the way to
convince them was to tell them what they'd prepared themselves to hear,
spiced with just the misted shadow of a deception they'd almost sublimi-
nally accepted. Had he been with Irena Novikov long enough to fabricate
enough to trick those who professionally knew her intimately and who
would, inevitably, be called upon to examine microscopically the account
he concocted? A step—into the dark—at a time he determined.

'How is she?' abruptly began Guzov.

A hesitation would be natural and he had to guard against facial ex-
pressions; body language, too. 'Well enough: she's hardly going to be ill
treated.'

'So you expect her to come over to you?'

Not the response of a trained interrogator, judged Charlie; conceivably, though, intentionally gauche, to lure him into overconfidence. 'That's what she did, came over *with* me, didn't she?'

Guzov's mouth tightened. 'Under what duress?'

Irena would have been subjected to a lot of FSB rehearsal and planning, right up to the moment she'd left Moscow with him. But she wouldn't have disclosed any of that during a debriefing. What then? What she might *not* have mentioned, he decided. 'Duress of her own making, not mine.'

'I don't understand that answer.'

'How could you? You don't know the mistakes she made: the mistakes others made. All that she did and said in an effort to save the Lvov operation.' His first unchallengeable opportunity to sow seeds, Charlie recognized, hoping his slight relaxation in the enveloping chair would have been picked up on film.

'There hasn't been any official diplomatic response to our request for consular access,' said Guzov. 'Your Foreign Office isn't even acknowledging her presence in England.'

Creakingly thin ice, Charlie realized at once: how long before London disclosed where Irena really was? 'Maybe it's Irena Yakulova who doesn't want to acknowledge it.'

'*Is* she refusing?' demanded Guzov, directly.

Where was the safe ground? groped Charlie. Spurred by a sudden thought, he said, 'I'm not going to be allowed consular access until you are granted the same to Irena, am I?'

'What do you think?'

What Charlie thought was that he was in a box within a box, denied any possibility of confirming Natalia and Sasha's escape. 'I wouldn't know anything about consular access. That's a diplomatic negotiation.'

'We believe Irena Yakulova is being held against her will.'

Charlie had days earlier acknowledged that Mikhail Guzov wasn't a trained interrogator but this was scarcely competent: he had to be careful that his leading the encounter wasn't obvious to the unknown monitoring professionals who'd analyze everything. 'Irena Yakulova was not nor is under duress. Neither is she being held against her will. Her cooperation is entirely voluntary.' That would surely prompt a more useful exchange!

'Neither do we believe that she's co-operating voluntarily.'

Was that a clumsy encouragement to prove the contrary? At least it gave him an opening. 'Lvov was a brilliant concept, wasn't it?'

An obvious wariness settled about the other man. 'Britain and America, led by the nose! It's more than brilliant.'

Shit, thought Charlie, disappointed, but caught by the tense in which Guzov had replied. '*Was* brilliant,' Charlie corrected. 'And all ruined by those mistakes of the amateurs.' Which Irena had virtually accused Guzov of being, Charlie remembered, warily.

'What amateurs?' the Russian demanded, on cue.

'It would have all gone to plan if Ivan Nikolaevich Oskin's body hadn't been dumped in the grounds of the British embassy, wouldn't it?' lured Charlie.

'Did Irena Yakulova tell you that?'

Blocked, Charlie conceded, at the same time as recognizing his chance to add to what the FSB would know to be true. 'As well as a lot of other things. Her greatest anger was with the CIA for dumping it as they did. It didn't make any sense. Any more than the other stupidities.'

'What other stupidities?' demanded Guzov, on cue again.

It was verbal tennis, Charlie accepted. He had to play carefully not to infer Irena's criticism of the man confronting him. 'I know there was a lot she didn't tell me. But you yourself were furious at the militia's unauthorized arrest of Svetlana Modin, the TV anchorwoman. You were using her, weren't you, Mikhail Alexandrovich?' He was coming close to suggesting too much, Charlie cautioned himself, and they were a long way now from Irena Yakulova. Was Guzov really inept? Or had the man undergone a crash training course in the hope of his seizure from the moment the FSB learned of his return to Moscow?

'As you used her.'

He had to redirect the encounter, Charlie determined, switch Guzov back into the lead. 'But I didn't have anything to do with her assassination. Or with Lvov's. More mistakes.'

'Irena Yakulov called the assassinations a mistake?'

Better! thought Charlie, encouraged. 'She said there was no purpose: no benefit.'

'There wasn't any, not for us.'

Charlie let in the pause, knowing it would be expected both by Guzov and those later studying the film footage, as well as needing the reflection himself. Subjectively, the humiliatingly manipulated CIA had more cover-up reasons to assassinate the president-elect and the sensation-seeking TV presenter than the instinctively suspected FSB. Which prompted another, inevitable speculation. Had it been an American finger that fired the bullet that put him down in Vnukovo Airport and not the pistol-wielding MI6 man who was his last conscious recollection? 'No, there wasn't, was there?'

'I'm surprised you needed Irena Yakulova's guidance; it was a mistake for her to have offered it.'

His had been a careless remark, Charlie criticized himself at once. 'It depends upon whose opinion you're judging it.'

'It wasn't her first, either, was it?'

'Wasn't it?' hedged Charlie.

'What threat did you use to get her on the plane with you to London, Charlie?'

'You've recovered the airport CCTV by now. Nothing, no-one, *made* her get on the plane to London. She came of her own free will.'

'But hasn't come back.'

'Again, a choice made of her own free will. As Maxim Mikhailovich Radtsic came of his own free will. As did his wife, who was actually *given* the choice. That's quite an exodus, don't you think, Mikhail Alexandrovich?' Surely that would prompt a reference to Natalia if they knew of her importance to him?

Guzov's face flushed as well as tightened. 'We're not discussing Maxim Mikhailovich or his wife.'

The FSB didn't know! Or of his awareness of Natalia's brief secondment to one of the groups vetting Radtsic's background. 'A lot of people are discussing it, though, aren't they? I'd guess it's going to take years for you to uncover all the contacts Radtsic had, all the information he's leaked. I'd go as far as to say that you never will uncover it all. There'll always be the fear that you've missed someone: that there's one leaking source you haven't been able to plug. Nothing's ever been as bad, not in your entire history, has it? That's what Irena Yakulova thinks.'

The grimaced smile was weak, overly forced. 'We'll survive: recover.'

'Not for a very long time: all those years I suggested.'

'We'll see. Before which we've got a great deal more to talk about, haven't we? We've not really made any progress whatsoever this afternoon: not achieved anything worthwhile.'

Charlie hoped he had, although he couldn't at that moment isolate exactly what. He was being distracted quite a lot by the jungle-drum throbbing in both feet, which was never a good sign.

'Where are we going?' excitedly demanded Sasha before they reached the end of the drive.

'It's a surprise,' said Ethel, from the driving seat.

'I want to know now!' It was childish frustration, not precociousness.

'It wouldn't be a surprise then, would it?' said Natalia. Reverting to English as they turned out onto the main road, she said, 'I'm not happy doing this.'

'This car is fitted with a tracker—and a back-up if the first one malfunctions, which it won't—permanently monitored by the control room back at Bramshill: they know to the yard where we are at all times,' soothed Ethel, speaking English, too. 'There's a permanent tri-connection between us, Bramshill, and the protection car behind us, with a four-man— actually women—crew. That car's also got independent electronic back-up. And there's absolutely no way your whereabouts could have become known anyway. It's right, necessary, that you get out like this: more so, perhaps, for Sasha than for you at this time. You're not going to spend the rest of your life under self-imposed house arrest, are you?'

'I don't know how I'm going to spend the rest of my life,' said Natalia. 'Our talking like this is being monitored too, isn't it?'

'Simultaneously relayed,' confirmed Ethel, shifting in her seat, regretting Natalia's lapse into self-pity. 'Moscow hasn't responded to three requests from our Foreign Office for consular access to Charlie.'

'Why!' demanded Natalia, abruptly twisting in her seat to look directly across the car. 'Is he dead?'

'No,' denied Ethel, just as urgently. 'There's no indication that he's even seriously injured. Your people are just being as obstructive as possible; we need something to overcome that obstruction.'

'What's wrong, Mama?' said Sasha, her voice uneven, from the rear of the vehicle. 'Why are you angry?'

'I'm not angry . . . I . . . I didn't properly understand something.'

'I don't know what you're saying . . . talking about. Why don't you speak so that I can hear what you're saying?'

'We have to talk this way,' said Natalia, too sharply.

'It's not far now,' quickly came in Ethel, seeing the child's face begin to crumple in the rearview mirror. 'We'll play a game. The first one to see . . . to see a red car gets a prize.'

'Thank you,' said Natalia, recovering.

'Do you know Irena Yakulova Novikov?'

There was no outburst this time, although Natalia remained sideways in her seat. 'No. Why do you imagine I would?'

'Charlie brought her out of Moscow with him. She devised the Lvov operation from its inception.'

When Natalia didn't respond, instead staying silent but frowning across the car, Ethel chanced a quick sideways look. 'What?'

'Who said she devised the whole thing?'

'She did, when Charlie trapped her.'

'She's FSB?' Natalia was still frowning.

'Of course she is and before that KGB,' said Ethel, disconcerted by the other woman's reaction. 'She made contact with Charlie after a press-conference appeal: tried to close down his investigation by admitting to being the architect as well as Lvov's lover. She tried to keep everything intact by insisting that Lvov was a genuine CIA source, not a plant.' Ethel hesitated. 'What's wrong?'

'She shouldn't have done that.'

'Of course she shouldn't have done it!' agreed Ethel, impatiently. 'Charlie caught her out, threatened to send her back to Moscow to FSB punishment.'

'But . . .' started Natalia, but stopped. 'Where is she now?'

'Washington.'

'There's one!' shouted Sasha from the back, as Ethel joined the motorway.

'First prize to you,' said Ethel.

'What's the prize!'

'You've got to wait until we get to where we're going.'

'Is she co-operating there?' asked Natalia.

'I don't know,' admitted Ethel.

'Did she co-operate here?'

'I believe Charlie recorded her collapse, after he caught her out. I don't think there was a positive debriefing.'

'There must have been something more . . . something that proved she was the Control of the Lvov scheme.'

'Why's this important, Natalia?'

'I'd like to see it: what she said to Charlie. And know what else she provided: how it was provided.'

'There's another one!' came Sasha's voice from the rear seat.

'And another prize,' promised Ethel. To Natalia she said, 'Why?'

'It might tell me something.'

'Like what?'

'I need to see a pattern: that's what interrogations have, a pattern, a direction, that this woman. . . . ?'

'Irena Yakulova,' supplied Ethel.

'That should be obvious if I can see what Irena Yakulova said.'

'I told you I wasn't sure that she underwent a proper debriefing.'

'There'll still be indicators,' insisted the Russian. 'Will you tell London—Jane—what I've said?'

'I also told you our conversation is being relayed to London.' Leaning her head back towards the child, Ethel said, 'We're here.'

'A zoo!' exclaimed the child.

'And your prizes are models of the animals you like the most,' declared Ethel.

'I want a tiger,' immediately determined Sasha. 'I coloured a picture of a tiger for your friend who's going to meet us, didn't I, Mama? When's he going to get here?'

'I'm not sure,' said Natalia, her voice thick.

'That went in a direction I didn't expect,' said Aubrey Smith, turning away from the voice relay.

'We didn't get anything about what she did—and might have found—going into Radtsic's background,' complained Passmore. The review sessions had become completely informal: Smith and Jane Ambersom were sitting in easy chairs in the office annexe, coffee cups and percolator on the table separating them. The operations director was perched on a radiator cover by the window, the Thames behind him.

'Ethel did the obvious, the only thing, going with the flow instead of trying to direct the conversation,' rejected Jane, defensively.

'And where did that flow take us?' questioned Passmore.

'I don't know but I want to find out,' said the Director-General.

'We've taken, accepted, a lot about Natalia Fedova on unproven trust, haven't we?' said Passmore. 'We've only got Charlie's word for everything about her. And he's not here to give us anything more.'

'What are you suggesting?' demanded Jane, her face creased.

'I'm not *suggesting* anything,' said the operations director. 'I know

I'm a comparative newcomer to this business, without the experience that either of you have, and I also know we're seeking her help, in our current circumstances. But would it be wise to give her everything that Charlie got from Irena Yakulova?'

Jane looked to Aubrey Smith to respond. The Director-General said, 'Normally it wouldn't be contemplated and I totally accept your reservations. But nothing about our current circumstances are normal: there's no criteria to draw upon and I hope this won't provide one for the future. As experienced as we all might consider ourselves to be, we've only got our own perspective from which to look in from the outside. Natalia's been on the *inside* for more than twenty years. She's our asset—an invaluable asset able to see and interpret in a way we never could.'

'So we show Natalia everything we've got?' pressed Passmore, seeking a positive decision.

'I haven't definitely decided,' avoided Smith. 'Let's consider what's more immediate. I've had an advisory call from the enquiry secretariat. Monsford's producing Jacobson, his Moscow station chief who brought Radtsic out. Do we match their man with Flood and Wilkinson?'

'Wilkinson's getting cleaned up but I've had an hour with him,' reported the operations chief. 'He doesn't know anything about the shooting: all the MI6 men, including Halliday, slipped out of the embassy in the middle of the night—'

'Together?' interrupted Jane.

'That's the indication from the embassy log. Wilkinson had three meetings with Charlie, literally chased on all of them by the three MI6 sent in as part of Charlie's original back-up. Wilkinson doesn't know what Charlie was doing when he was operating alone, but thinks from Charlie's refusal to have any MI6 contact even before their first meeting—and before we warned from here that he should watch his back—that Charlie was suspicious of some physical move against him. Charlie didn't give the slightest lead but Wilkinson got the impression that he might even have had a source—'

'Who?' broke in Jane. 'The three supposed to be supporting him were hunting him!'

'Halliday was on station when Charlie was there on the original investigation into the embassy murder,' remembered Smith. 'Did Halliday work with the three shipped in from here? And what about Jacobson?'

'Neither of them,' said Passmore, at once. 'Wilkinson says the back-up group scarcely saw Jacobson: that he positively ignored them. And the three MI6, in turn, practically ignored Halliday: kept him on the periphery, never properly including him. Halliday certainly wasn't involved in the runaround to locate Charlie.'

'Could Halliday have been Charlie's inside source?' wondered Jane.

Passmore shrugged. 'We're not going to get the answer to that until we speak to Charlie again: *if* we speak to Charlie ever again.'

'We don't compete with Monsford and his witness,' decided the Director-General. 'We'll leave the entire concentration on Jacobson and do our best to undermine whatever he produces. And I want you,' Smith turned to Jane, 'to do even more to undermine Rebecca Street in the way we've discussed.'

'I'll try,' promised Jane.

'And we will let Natalia see how Charlie broke Irena Yakulova Novikov,' the man finally decided.

Before his suicide James Straughan had described to Rebecca the miniaturized digital bugging device he'd installed in Gerald Monsford's office as a thumb drive. The preceding night the Director hadn't been able to manage a thumb-size proportion, making it unnecessary for her to have briefly removed her tampon concealment, but Rebecca knew Monsford's inability wasn't the blame-shifting cause of her being ostracized that morning, but the locked-door closeting with Harry Jacobson.

Which Rebecca actually welcomed, deciding there was safety in as much professionally visible separation as possible between them while she devised her escape from any responsibility for the Vnukovo shooting. Her most obvious evasion would be to dispose of the chip: literally to flush it down the toilet in the tampon in which it remained hidden.

Which was too obvious and too dangerous. Self-incriminating though it was, its contents could conceivably provide—although she didn't know how—a shield against whatever Monsford was inevitably planning if the internal-security investigation exposed the supposed mole penetration as the survival straw to which the desperate man was clinging.

What then? Finding Straughan's copy—or rather, the location—of the digitally recorded assassination discussion would be a near-guaranteed way out. There'd be the reassurance of actually having both in her possession, enabling her to destroy one and have the other discovered during the ongoing security search. The correction came at once. She provably, vocally, featured on it, knowing that Monsford was lying about there being no intended assassination, leaving her complicit with the man on the one hand and equally responsible on the other by not speaking out at the opening of the committee enquiry.

Sticking to her intention publicly to be seen distancing herself from Monsford, Rebecca arrived early at the committee chamber, glad no preparation appeared yet to have been made for Jacobson. Picking up the man's printed nameplate, Rebecca led a chair-carrying attendant to the designated MI6 location and made much of rearranging the seating to put Jacobson between herself and Monsford.

She was in the process of doing that when Jane Ambersom, also alone, arrived at MI5's opposite position, pleased at the other woman's obvious, quizzical attention. Smiling across the conference table, Rebecca said, 'It's difficult to fit in any more people.'

'It's fortunate we didn't call our witnesses today.' Jane smiled back, leaving both women satisfied.

He'd done well, Charlie congratulated himself. If just one of his disinformation seeds germinated, the encounter would have been a success. And he'd planted enough for the crop to be far greater. What else had he got? The most important had to be his belief that Natalia and Sasha had safely got away. Which made the tit-for-tat delay in consular access less important, although he still needed positive confirmation of their safety.

Had he—as well as a lot of other people—wrongly believed the FSB to be the assassins of Svetlana Modin, the TV anchorwoman through whom he'd publicly exposed the Stepan Lvov plot? There was far more logic—and reason—for her and Lvov to have been killed by the damage-limiting CIA, who would equally have been his far more logical pursuers through a willing MI6 surrogate and would provide every explanation for the airport attack.

All of which, until proved otherwise, were reasonable conclusions, Charlie decided. But why the totally inexplicable concentration upon Irena Yakulova Novikov and Guzov's equally inexplicable assertion that the woman had been forced from Moscow and was now held against her will?

Try as he could—and he'd tried every possible conjecture since Guzov's departure—Charlie couldn't find anything vaguely close to answers to those conundrums. Which left him worrying that the afternoon had indeed been very carefully and cleverly programmed, too cleverly yet for him to work out how or why.

They hadn't foreseen this—couldn't have foreseen this, Irena accepted. Now she didn't know what to do, denied access to anyone from the embassy. They hadn't foreseen that refusal, either: everything too rushed, too panicked. But she wouldn't panic. She had to make some concessions and she had enough to begin with. But for how long? Could she hope for any indication from Birkitt, who'd shown his apparent inexperience by naming the scruffy man who'd caught her out in Moscow as Charlie Muffin? Unlikely, she accepted, realistically. She'd thought there might have been, at first, but she'd changed that initial impression. Believing she could recognize like for like, Irena had now decided that Birkitt's seemingly unfocused demeanour, the apparently rambling approach, wasn't unfocused or rambling at all: that there was a rat-trap mind hearing everything, analyzing everything. That the man who had to be at least twenty years her junior was better at his job than she might be at hers. Most worrying of all was that she believed that he, and the CIA he represented, were quite prepared to carry out every threat he'd made: that she really could simply disappear.

9

BOTH INTELLIGENCE-AGENCY DEPUTIES WERE, IN FACT, MORE than satisfied with the enquiry-chamber encounter. To Jane Ambersom—and to Aubrey Smith, whom she told the moment he entered the room—Rebecca's remark, innocuous though it appeared, eased Jane's intended approach. To Rebecca Street, Jane's response was a pinprick to deflate the balloon-thin confidence with which Gerald Monsford arrived, his entry with Harry Jacobson timed to gain the maximum attention from the almost-assembled tribunal.

'Witness*es*!' stressed the MI6 Director, drawing Rebecca beyond the hearing of anyone else. 'You mean there are several?'

'Certainly more than one.' This was definitely closer to orgasmic than the farce she'd frustratingly endured the previous night.

'But not today?'

'I don't think so, not from the way she spoke.'

'We need to know who they are, get an idea of what they're going to say, before they're called.'

'Something might emerge today.' It was so easy to nudge the man off his self-constructed pinnacle, Rebecca thought. She even knew enough Shakespeare to find the mockery—*I have a faint cold fear thrills through my veins.* The only inconsistency after the last night's farce was that it came from *Romeo and Juliet.*

'What I . . .' began Monsford but was halted, needing to return to the table, by the arrival of Geoffrey Palmer and Sir Archibald Bland.

Monsford did not immediately respond to MI6 becoming the focus of attention at Bland's announcement of Harry Jacobson's appearance, hunched instead over his pad. It was in the momentary hiatus of Bland's invitation for Monsford to take his witness through his evidence that the MI6 Director slipped his palm-concealed note to Rebecca, who left the folded paper unopened, preferring instead to watch the unintended difficulty she'd created by putting Monsford and Jacobson beside each other.

Monsford had to twist awkwardly sideways to lead Jacobson, who had matching difficulty needing to face across the table, not at his director, for his responses. Rebecca's imagery was of a ventriloquist operating his mouth-shuttered dummy, which was totally appropriate in view of the rehearsal she knew Jacobson had undergone.

He had, deposed Jacobson, become Radtsic's Control from the moment of the Russian's approach at a French-embassy reception. He had not, at that stage, known the man was Maxim Mikhailovich Radtsic, the executive deputy of the Federalnaya Sluzhba Bezopasnosti. Over the course of several clandestine meetings at various Moscow locations, Radtsic had made clear his determination to defect, with his family, believing he was about to be purged. He had not given any positive reason for that belief but allowed the inference that he was being held personally responsible for the Lvov debacle. Throughout the planning of Radtsic's extraction, Jacobson had dealt primarily and directly with the Director but also logistically with the operations director, James Straughan. He was also aware, from both men, that the deputy MI6 director, Rebecca Street, was an active participant at every stage of the planning. A difficulty arose in that planning from Radtsic's son being a student at the Sorbonne, in Paris. To persuade the son to defect, Radtsic's wife travelled to Paris. Because of Radtsic's intelligence expertise, it was decided by James Straughan that a large extraction-support team was unnecessary— that Jacobson alone was sufficient Control and escort for the man— particularly acknowledging the possibility of the FSB becoming aware from airport and embassy surveillance of the arrival in Moscow of a

British intelligence contingent for a separate, MI5 extraction of Natalia Fedova. The defection of Maxim Radtsic went flawlessly but that of the man's wife and son was intercepted by French security. He knew nothing of the circumstances of that interception. Nor did he have any detailed knowledge of the Natalia Fedova extraction.

'Was there, during the planning with either myself or the operations director, any discussion of a staged diversion to draw attention from Maxim Radtsic's crossing?' asked Monsford.

'Not with you, sir.'

Jane's exasperated move was halted by Aubrey Smith's leg jamming into hers.

'Which is not a complete answer,' prompted Monsford.

'There was one reference from operational director Straughan. He said he was thinking of introducing a diversion.'

'What was that diversion to be?'

'I don't know. It was never referred to again by operations director Straughan.'

'Was there any discussion of a diversion with anyone else: deputy director Rebecca Street, for instance?'

'I do not recall any such discussion. I cannot categorically say that one never took place. If it did, I can't remember it.'

Aubrey Smith's leg was painfully into Jane's: he felt the anger throbbing through her.

'Did you ever, either in discussion or as a rumour within either the MI6 or MI5 *rezidentura* of the Moscow embassy, hear of an intended distracting assassination?'

'No, sir. My instructions from operations director Straughan were to keep myself completely separate from the second extraction.'

Properly turning his chair back into the room, Monsford said, 'I do not think I can help this enquiry any further.'

'There'll be a refreshment break,' decreed Bland.

Rebecca at last opened Monsford's note. It read, 'FIND OUT ABOUT MI5 WITNESSES.'

It was Jane's idea to go alone into the adjoining annexe, leaving Smith and Passmore in the enquiry room analyzing Harry Jacobson's anodyne puppetry. Jane got there first, putting the onus of approach upon the other woman, quickly getting tea she didn't want and an empty table, away from which she moved one chair and put her sagged briefcase on the third, leaving only one place vacant. It was physically a mechanical, unthinking process, Jane's mind blocked by a single mantra: *beat him, beat him, beat him.*

'I guess this vacant chair is for me?' said Rebecca, standing behind it.

'Why not?' invited Jane.

'Thank you for saving it.' Straughan had disdained the MI6 headquarters ribaldry at the other woman's androgyny and Rebecca trusted the sadly dead man's judgement.

'With whatever questioning there might be for Jacobson, it made every sense to keep your witnesses back, didn't it?' began Rebecca, covering the silence by opening and pouring her mineral water.

'We haven't decided a specific day: there's a lot to be discussed.' It was her lead, with Rebecca having to follow, Jane decided.

It would be naïve for her to expect any other attitude from the woman whom she'd replaced, Rebecca acknowledged. Objectively considering the circumstances, Jane Ambersom was being remarkably receptive, even though she was sure the attitude was motivated by the same reasons as her own. Knowing the concessions had to come from her, Rebecca said, 'We've both got far too many of our people in Russian custody.'

'And too many innocents totally unaware what the fuck's happening to them, largely because of Charlie Muffin.' It would appear too much, as the all-girls-together obscenity was too much, but Jane hoped it would cloak the direction in which she wanted to lead the other woman.

More than receptive, judged Rebecca. Cautiously, she said, 'Some people other than the innocents don't know what's going on, either.'

'That was a pretty shitty trick Monsford pulled, getting you into the records.'

There was almost a physical wince of withdrawal from Rebecca. She sipped her water, needing the pause, discomfited by the reminder of how Jacobson's remark had been manipulated. 'I didn't have anything to do with what happened to you at Vauxhall Cross. I want you to know that.'

A clever evasion, conceded Jane. 'If for a moment I believed you had, I'd thank you as sincerely as I knew how. Where I am now, among the people I am with now, is the luckiest escape I'm ever likely to have.'

'We're straying into generalities,' complained Rebecca, further unsettled by the other woman's response.

'What, specifically, should we talk about?' pounced Jane.

'This, all of it, has gone beyond any sensible rivalry: beyond any sense at all.'

'I think so, too.' Jane hadn't expected such a commitment.

The summons bell signalled the resumption of the hearing.

'Are your witnesses going to cause us difficulty?'

Jane was briefly off-balanced by the directness. Deciding to match it, she said, 'The one who was actually at the airport and saw it all, could . . .' The pause now was for emphasis. 'But not to you, personally: you personally haven't made any claims, have you? We're judging your inclusion by Jacobson to be yet another of Monsford's responsibility insurances, having someone else at whom to point the finger if he thinks it necessary.'

Rebecca rose, to prevent their being the last to return. 'I think we should talk again.'

'I think so too,' agreed Jane.

Natalia looked up expectantly at Ethel's entry. 'You've heard something!'

'Not about Charlie,' quickly calmed the security supervisor.

'What then?' It was close to a disinterested question, Natalia even turning to where Sasha was playing with her zoo-animal models. She'd chosen a giraffe to go with the tiger.

'They've agreed to your seeing Irena Yakulova's admission to Charlie.'

Natalia came back, frowning, to the other woman. 'We only spoke about it this morning?'

'I told you the conversation was being relayed from the car. Are you surprised?'

Natalia gauged the question. Finally she said, 'Yes, I am.'

'Why?'

'Are you debriefing me?' demanded the Russian. It wasn't resentment.

'I don't think I'm professionally competent enough, do you?'

'Not if there was something I wanted to keep from you.'

'Something like why you're surprised to be seeing Charlie's confrontation with Irena Yakulova?'

Natalia smiled at last. 'Normally it wouldn't be contemplated with someone who hadn't proved themselves during a full interrogation: it definitely wouldn't be conceivable in Russia.'

'The judgement is that these are anything but normal circumstances.'

'That's certainly true.'

'What Irena said isn't being electronically transmitted, for obvious security reasons, so it won't be here today. It's being couriered from London.'

'A courier could be followed!' objected Natalia, the concern immediate.

'Not by helicopter, making an intermediate transfer stop to prevent the initial flight plan being hacked into,' assured Ethel.

'You were testing me for right answers, though, weren't you?' challenged Natalia.

'Weren't you expecting me to test you, being included as closely and as quickly as you are?'

'I was waiting, hoping not to be disappointed.'

Knowing before he even set out on his experiment that the warning ache in both feet would make it difficult—and determined against worsening the discomfort by encountering any unpredictable *spetsnaz*—Charlie limited the expedition to the dacha's immediate surroundings, not expecting to confirm the extent of the cottage's outside electronic surveillance, despite believing he'd isolated the most likely internal observation in the main rooms. He tested that belief by slipping out a side door onto the encircling veranda but sat at once on one of its rough-hewn seats to assess the quickness of the male housekeeper's pursuit. He spent the fifteen minutes he allowed for the man's appearance intently studying as much of the exterior of the building as he was able to see, confident he also identified two devices beyond his eyeline from their internal supply cables.

Charlie was careful to avoid both when he finally moved, sticking to the inside of the raised walkway, along which he detected two more telltale supply leads, and by visually estimating the distances between them left the dacha beyond their scope. The usual provision in such safe houses was that every potentially detectable camera or CCTV was duplicated by at least one so well hidden as to be invisible, no matter how well trained or experienced the searcher. And here that invisibility was doubly compounded by the tightly encircling firs among the branches of which a profusion of unseen cameras could be mounted.

None of which was the point or purpose of Charlie's so-far-uninterrupted excursion, which he was surprised—as well as increasingly concerned—he was being allowed to continue.

The unevenness of the track to the paved road was even more pronounced than it had been during the agonizing car approach, slowing him to a groping foot-at-a-time progress, and he was relieved at the tree break he'd memorized, smiling at the instantly more comfortable pine-needle path through trees so closely packed together that almost at once he was shrouded in near-total darkness. Charlie stopped after about fifteen metres, conscious of the undergrowth scurrying and tree-branch scraping, waving his arms about him in a pointless battle against the miasma of flying, stinging things protesting his intrusion. The movement made his shoulder itch.

The pine-needle carpet was so thick—and the approach so professional—that his housekeeper guard was practically upon him before Charlie realized the man's presence, despite the intensity with which Charlie was both listening and expectantly looking.

'It's easy to become disorientated, lost, in woods this dense,' said his house guard, conversationally.

'I was just turning back,' responded Charlie, still waving his arms around his head. 'And I'm being badly stung.'

'They're a particularly vicious type of mosquito,' said the man, turning. 'It's easier if we go back this way: shorter, too.'

It was, conceded Charlie, shuffling gratefully behind. He'd probably get away with the same experiment once more but after that he'd have to find something different. But this had been an encouraging confirmation.

It was not until she re-entered the enquiry that Jane Ambersom fully realized that she could, if sufficiently adept, at least humiliate and at best expose as a lying megalomaniac the man who'd tried to destroy her professionally. And if that near-hypnotic intensity with which Monsford was staring at her was attempted intimidation, it wasn't going to be any more successful than his thick-fingered seduction efforts when she'd been his deputy.

'Let's get on,' formally reconvened Sir Archibald Bland, mirroring the open surprise of almost everyone else at Aubrey Smith's announcement that Jane would open the MI5 questioning.

Bullet points were set out for her on a single sheet and John Passmore, close beside her, had a second sheet of corollary targets dependent upon Harry Jacobson's initial responses. Following the first written prompt, Jane said, 'We have been left to assume a great deal, perhaps too much, from what you've told this enquiry. I'd like you to be far more specific because what little you've offered so far is very directly contradicted by MI5's understanding of events. . . .'

A stir went around the chamber, the concentration settling upon Monsford and Jacobson who remained like statues in their seats.

'So let's start from the absolute beginning,' Jane continued. 'Maxim Mikhailovich Radtsic approached you at a French-embassy reception?'

'That's what I've already deposed,' said Jacobson, the words measured.

'How?' Jane demanded, sharply.

Jacobson shifted, uncertainly. 'I don't understand that question.'

Jane exaggerated the sigh. 'How, exactly, did Radtsic approach you?'

'He came up to me; I was standing alone.'

'And said? I'm sure you can recall his words exactly.'

' "I want to talk to you of something of great importance," ' quoted the man.

'Just that: just those eleven words?'

'Yes.'

'What was your reaction?'

'I asked him who he was. He said he was someone who could be of great interest and value to my country.'

'Did he identify himself?'

'No.'

'Did he address you by name?'

It was another sharp question and almost imperceptibly Jacobson moved to look to Monsford for guidance, the gesture stopped as quickly as it began. 'He called me Mr Jacobson.'

'In English?'

There was another hesitation. 'Yes.'

'And you acknowledged the identification by continuing the conversation?'

'I believed it was an approach that could prove useful.'

'Why?'

'He'd arrived as part of a Russian-government group.'

'In front of which he openly approached you, addressing you, in English, by name and in such a way that showed he knew you were an intelligence officer attached to the British embassy? Didn't it occur to you that you were being targeted by Russian intelligence?'

'Of course it did!' insisted Jacobson, indignantly. 'It was my immediate thought then and remained my concern throughout the entire extraction.'

'What's the purpose of all this!' abruptly intruded Monsford. 'This officer successfully brought to England Maxim Mikhailovich Radtsic, the executive deputy director of Russian intelligence. What is there to be questioned, beyond that?'

Satisfaction surged through Jane at the opportunity, openly and in front of his peers, to confront the man she loathed. 'So very, very much. We believe it's important to discover how many inviolable precautions against entrapment your officer ignored, and which could have led to subsequent events at Vnukovo Airport. We also want to learn, which I imagine also to be of primary importance to you, if there were any indications of Radtsic's alleged treason from exchanges James Straughan might have had with your officer. And then there's—'

'I don't think there's any need for you to expand any further or for this intervention to have been made.' broke in Geoffrey Palmer, from his joint chairman's position beside Bland. 'Let's continue with the examination.'

Jane only just held back the smile of triumph at the public rebuke to the MI6 Director, conscious that Rebecca Street hadn't tried so hard to conceal the quick facial twitch. 'You were telling us of your fear of entrapment?' Jane picked up. 'Did you follow the prescribed MI6 procedure for defections: particularly a defection of this importance? There were, after all, sufficient MI6 officers on Moscow station for protective surveillance during your encounter with Radtsic.'

There was a further hesitation from Jacobson. 'My orders were to keep Radtsic's extraction quite separate from those MI6 officers involved in Muffin's operation.'

The man's reply opened several pathways, and Jane chose the most personally important. 'Orders from whom?'

This time Jacobson completed the look towards Monsford, answering the question without needing to speak, which he did anyway. 'The Director.'

Jane hoped there hadn't been sufficient rehearsal. 'You had a resident officer, David Halliday, permanently on station with you.'

'He was also precluded.' The answer was less assured.

'Upon whose orders?' She scarcely needed the bullet-point prompts, Jane decided.

'The Director.'

'Was Radtsic's extraction controlled entirely by the Director?'

'Not entirely.'

The man was apprehensive of an unanticipated question, Jane knew, that thought at once replaced by another at Rebecca's shift on the opposite side of the table. 'With whom else did you deal directly?'

'The operations director, James Straughan.'

There was another stir around the room. 'With whom did you deal the most, the Director or James Straughan?'

Jacobson appeared to consider the question and again Jane decided the rehearsal had been inadequate. 'I would estimate more with Straughan than with the Director.'

'Were some of the exchanges shared or were they always one-to-one?'

'As far as I am aware, they were always one-to-one.'

'Again, as far as you are aware, were the conversations between yourself, the Director, and James Straughan always recorded?'

'It's standard practice for them to be recorded.'

'Were you aware of any exchange, with either man, being unrecorded?'

'No.'

'Would you have been aware?'

'Not unless I was told: it's always done from London.'

'So there's a full voice record of everything that passed between yourself, the Director, and the operations director, James Straughan?'

'I told you the recording systems are operated from London. I was in Moscow. I cannot say whether everything was recorded or not.'

On his secondary sheet Passmore marked a series of exclamation marks. Time for another question she didn't imagine had been rehearsed, decided Jane. 'How many one-to-one, presumably recorded, discussions did you have with your deputy director, Rebecca Street?'

Jacobson moved to speak but seemingly changed his mind, briefly looking down at the table before saying, 'I don't recall any *direct* discussion between us.'

'Not thirty minutes ago you suggested there had been!' challenged Jane.

'I didn't mean to convey that impression.'

'So any exchanges that might have involved the deputy director, Rebecca Street, were shared either with the Director or James Straughan?'

'They would have been, yes.'

'And as it is standard practice, they would have been recorded, providing a positive log of every occasion in which Rebecca Street was involved, along with the subjects of whatever those conversations were?'

'Yes.' The admission strained from the man.

'From your exchanges with either the Director or James Straughan, did you get the impression that Rebecca Street was being excluded, as people in Moscow were excluded?'

'No, I did not get any such impression.'

'But let's stay with impressions,' encouraged Jane, disregarding her prompt list entirely, totally confident of where she was going and how to get there. 'What were your impressions of the operations director throughout all your dealings with him?'

Jacobson stared across the table, appearing nonplussed. 'I'm not sure I got any particular impression!'

'Let me help you,' intentionally patronized Jane. 'Was it your impression that he was competent?'

'Yes,' said Jacobson, uncertainly.

'Was there ever an instruction or a remark from which you got the impression that James Straughan was trying to obstruct or misdirect you?'

'No.' The man frowned, still uncertain.

'Did the operations director ever appear stressed, out of control?'

The frown deepened. 'No, never.'

'To whom did you first speak about Maxim Mikhailovich's approach to defect?'

'The Director,' replied Jacobson, at once.

'How soon afterwards did Straughan become involved?'

'Virtually immediately: the same day, I think. The official recordings will be dated and timed.'

'And how soon was that after Radtsic's approach at the French embassy?'

'The following day. I'm sure it was the following day.'

'You have told us Radtsic did not identify himself at the French embassy that evening. How were you able the following day to name him, both to your Director and James Straughan?'

'At the French embassy I gave him one of the reserved contact numbers at our *rezidentura*. He called the following day, to arrange a meeting. At that meeting he told me his name.'

The moment, decided Jane. 'Was that when you talked of a diversion?'

'It was . . .' started Jacobson, then stopped. 'I don't recall mentioning a diversion to Maxim Mikhailovich.'

'He appears to recall it very easily.'

'I don't.'

'Nor what the diversion was going to be?' tried Jane.

'It was never mentioned.'

'Did the word *assassination* come into it?'

'This has already been exhaustively covered and denied!' intervened Monsford, flushed.

'Do you have any evidence to support this line of questioning?' Bland asked Jane.

'Not at this stage, but I would like to register the request to recall this witness after evidence still to be produced by this side,' conceded Jane.

'The request is registered but for now move on to other points,' ordered the chairman.

'Did you recognize the name Maxim Mikhailovich Radtsic?' resumed Jane.

'Of course. He's named as the FSB's executive deputy on our watch list.'

'The additional function of protective surveillance by a fellow officer at this first open meeting would have been to photograph the man,' said Jane, baiting her trap.

'There is a photograph on our watch list.'

Jane was aware of Monsford's discomforted fidgeting. She said, 'I know the watch list, from my time at Vauxhall Cross. And I know the photograph. It was snatched, from a distance, at a Presidium meeting sixteen years ago.'

'It was sufficient for initial confirmation of his identity.'

Turning directly to the joint chairmen, Jane said, 'I would ask that this photograph is subsequently produced to give this committee the opportunity to decide upon its clarity for positive identification.'

'Let's have it, shall we?' Palmer said to Monsford.

'What reason did Radtsic give for wanting to flee Russia with his family?' demanded Jane.

'Radtsic is still being debriefed,' intruded Monsford, hurriedly.

A second opportunity she hadn't imagined, seized Jane. 'It's our understanding that Radtsic is refusing any co-operation until he is reunited with his son, who in turn has refused to follow his father here. Which surely creates an impasse for you. But that's another entirely separate matter. I am not asking about any debriefing. I'm asking what reason Maxim Radtsic gave for defecting, which is quite different.'

'Radtsic's been given an ultimatum in the light of the hostile penetration of my service,' persisted Monsford, flushed again by a confrontation he knew he was losing.

'Which again does not affect my question,' insisted Jane, in turn,

'I'd like to hear the reason,' once more supported Geoffrey Palmer.

Monsford, defeated, jerked his head as if in permission to Jacobson, who said, 'He told me he was about to be purged, although he had no personal involvement in the Stepan Lvov affair.'

'Learning much more about that could be key in getting a lot of our people—certainly those innocently caught up—out of Russia,' unexpectedly declared Sir Archibald Bland.

'Which I assure you we will learn, very quickly,' said Monsford, anxious to recover.

Next to Jane, Passmore hurriedly wrote *disclose*, followed by more exclamation marks, on his secondary prompt sheet.

Jane said, 'An assurance I can also give. In the days immediately prior to her extraction, Natalia Fedova, who was successfully brought to this country despite the events at Vnukovo Airport, had open access to the personnel files of Maxim Mikhailovich Radtsic.'

'You sure this Fedova woman isn't the witness Ambersom thinks will cause us the most difficulty?' demanded Monsford.

Us, picked out Rebecca, recognizing the familiar responsibility shuffle as quickly as she'd earlier established that the man hadn't activated his recording system. 'Of course I'm not sure. I understood it was one of their people who witnessed the shooting but she could have been trying to put us off track.' Rebecca didn't think the MI5 deputy had been attempting anything of the sort but she was enjoying unsettling Monsford.

'It was a personal attack upon me: a positive decision by Aubrey Smith to nominate her as Jacobson's questioner. Bastards, both of them! And Palmer, too. He was definitely against me.'

She had to make contact with the woman to thank her for the particular questioning that took her out of the direct firing line, acknowledged Rebecca. 'It didn't go well, did it?'

'Jacobson fucked up. He definitely isn't getting Paris after today's performance.'

So that was the promised reward, accepted Rebecca: the original assassination order had to have been given to Jacobson. 'Do you want me to tell Timpson that all the voice recordings between Jacobson and here have to be handed over to the enquiry?'

'No!' said Monsford, at once. 'I want you to concentrate on Radtsic. I'm appointing you his interrogator. I want everything he knows about

Lvov and the penetration here. I'll notify Timpson: I've given notice that I'm calling him tomorrow. I'm expecting him to be good.'

At that moment Monsford had no way of knowing just how good.

'Sounds like you won,' congratulated Barry Elliott.

'Aubrey Smith seemed to think so: told me afterwards there was no need for either him or Passmore to have taken over the questioning.' She was in the kitchen, preparing the spaghetti sauce.

'Congratulations.'

'I didn't mean to tell you in so much detail.'

'I'm glad you trust me enough to do so.'

'You know why I did?'

'Why?'

Everything at a snail's pace, she warned herself. 'You kept your word, about Radtsic's defection. Neither your people nor the CIA could have held back if there'd been the slightest hint.'

'I've got a dilemma about the way things are going between us. If they knew, Washington would accuse me of losing professional objectivity.' That night he'd made closet space for some clothes with which Jane arrived.

'I don't think there's going to be a conflict,' said Jane, coming into the room to accept the offered wine.

'I hope you're right.'

'Trust me,' said Jane. She hoped she didn't have to make the choice between professional and personal, either. Despite the perfection of it all—being in a personal relationship that until now she'd only ever dreamt of, never imagining it ever happening—she was unsure what that choice would be. She had to be very careful not to appear too eager and spoil everything, certainly not until she was positive that Barry's professional dependence had become personal.

10

GERALD MONSFORD STAGE-MANAGED HIS ENTRANCE INTO THE enquiry chamber to the maximum effect, arriving last and remaining standing to direct attendants where to place additional chairs and a minuscule table for the two support staff—one the matronly, grey-haired woman—whom Matthew Timpson insisted upon accompanying him: it would have been physically difficult to accommodate all three if Rebecca Street had that day been part of the MI6 group.

'Looks like another virtuoso performance,' remarked John Passmore, dryly.

'Where's Rebecca?' wondered Jane Ambersom, rhetorically, at the double-act entry of Sir Archibald Bland and Geoffrey Palmer.

Monsford didn't hurry recounting Timpson's official function or the unit's highest security clearance, pleased at the obvious, heads-together MI5 curiosity from across the table. Beside Monsford, as he spoke, Timpson prepared himself with bank-manager efficiency, meticulously placing a jotting ledger in the very centre of his blotter, two capped fountain pens alongside, and poured water in readiness. Rehearsed, the woman aide, unasked, handed forward two loose-leaf folders when Timpson half turned.

'The discoveries to date of the internal investigation into MI6 will be presented in the preferred chronological order, upon which my witness has already been briefed,' assured Monsford.

The note Aubrey Smith passed to Passmore read, *too confident*.

The discovery of the eavesdropping bug on the Director's recording system had been remarkably quick, on their second day at Vauxhall Cross, commenced Timpson. Technically, the illegal device was known as a tie-line and ran parallel to the legitimate system supervised by James Straughan. The assumption had to be that the bugging had been in place from the time of the official system's installation, which covered a period of three and a half months and involved the detailed examination of forty-three hundred registered calls to be assessed for potential security damage. Some had been with Downing Street, at least six directly with the prime minister.

The tie-line had been operated from James Straughan's private office, adjacent to the permanent Watch Room. The office was always locked in Straughan's absence by a combination code, randomly chosen and changed daily, which would not function without secondary eye-retina recognition: it had taken an entire afternoon to override the security and gain access to the man's office. All inward and outward traffic on the tie-line would have been digitally preserved.

The receiving chip in the apparatus at the time of its discovery had been blank. The assumption had therefore to be that Straughan transferred each recording at the end of each day onto an electronic thumb or memory stick. Despite the most extensive, technically assisted search of Straughan's office, safe, personal locker and closet, and the man's Berkhamsted home, no digital thumbs had been located. The man had no safe deposit facilities at his bank. Nothing had been stored in the vaults of either the man's solicitor or his accountant. No documentation or indication had been found in any search so far to lead the investigators to a hiding place for what Straughan had copied. Searches were, of course, continuing. The Berkhamsted house was in the process of demolition, literally brick by brick, and all pipe work opened. The garden and the basement were being excavated to a depth of two feet.

'Were there fingerprints upon the listening apparatus and wiring?' asked Monsford.

'A substantial amount,' confirmed Timpson. 'All were those of James

Straughan. From the most recent it was possible forensically to lift perspiration residue and in a total of six places in the office human hair was recovered. From the hair and perspiration, DNA was established. The DNA and the fingerprints were those of James Straughan.'

'Were there fingerprints or DNA traces of anyone other than James Straughan?' pressed Monsford.

'None whatsoever,' replied Timpson.

'So the reasonable, circumstantial evidence is that no-one other than James Straughan had any access to, or use of, the illegal listening apparatus.'

'Not to the apparatus itself. It would have been a simple computer process to replicate any recording made.'

'Were such computers available to Straughan?'

Timpson frowned at the question. 'Every computer in the Watch Room, as well as that in Straughan's office, has the capability.'

'Is there any technical way to establish if copies were made on any of the computers?'

'Not if it were a simple duplicating process. We are examining the hard drive of every computer conveniently available to Straughan,' assured Timpson. 'So far we have found nothing.'

Monsford stopped, shuffling for affect through his own, so-far-unused briefcase papers, coming up empty-handed. After a further pause, he said, 'You have made an additional, extremely important discovery?'

Timpson turned to the attentive woman already waiting to pass him a further loose-leaf file. Turning back into the room, Timpson said, 'Following upon the finding of the eavesdropping installation, our investigation has quite obviously been concentrated upon James Straughan. A particular focus has been upon the records of his own known electronic and verbal communications traffic. On November twelfth last year a telephone call was logged from MI6's Vauxhall headquarters to Rome. By "logged" I mean a written record, not a verbatim transcript of a conversation. The automatic telephone register timed the call as lasting fourteen minutes—'

'A written log would have recorded the recipient's identity and the subject discussion,' abruptly interrupted Jane, at once regretting the interjection from the smirk of satisfaction that instantly registered on Monsford's face.

'We're coming to that in good time,' he patronized, nodding to Timpson to continue.

'The recipient of Straughan's call is listed on the log as Vasili Okulov, although that is obviously an operational name,' disclosed the investigator, opening the new folder. 'The call was to a private, unlisted number, which we have on our files. Publicly, Okulov is regarded as a vehement opponent of the current Russian regime, particularly critical of Vladimir Putin. Okulov was involved in a hit-and-run accident last year he claimed to have been a Russian assassination attempt. All of which, according to an MI6 investigation, was a cover for his true function, which is to locate through his anti-Russian reputation genuine Russian opponents to be identified to the FSB. He's considered an active double through whom MI6 have dealt in the past to leak misinformation to the FSB. Our contact with him is always by phone, through a Berlin cut-out connection: Okulov believes the MI6 approaches are through an anti-Russian organization—'

'I am aware of this history,' Jane risked again. 'What's its relevance here?'

'The relevance is the subject matter to which you've already referred and which, as you've so correctly told us, would have been recorded,' said Timpson, taking a single piece of paper from his file. 'It reads: *CM location*. The entry has been subjected to graphology analysis: the handwriting is unquestionably that of James Straughan.'

Monsford said, 'The off-duty residence of an agent is one of the most sacrosanct of all security precautions. On November twentieth, three Russians, later identified as FSB officers, were arrested breaking into Charlie Muffin's London flat: it had been fitted with intrusion detectors after the man's entry into a witness protection programme following his destruction of the Lvov penetration.'

The victory is twice itself when the achiever brings home full numbers, mentally recited Monsford, looking across the separating table at the MI5 group: Shakespeare had an appropriate expression for every situation.

———

'It wasn't a debriefing—it wasn't intended as a debriefing,' declared Natalia Fedova. The television upon which, over and over, stopping and starting the Freeze button, she'd studied Charlie's confrontation with Irena Novikov, was blank now, although the DVD was still in its slot. Her separately provided transcript of the encounter, now heavily annotated and symbol marked, lay on the table separating her from Ethel Jackson.

'Is that significant?' asked Ethel, cautiously

Natalia smiled, apologetic in advance. 'To a certain degree, yes. To another degree, not at all. From the background you've given me, Charlie needed confirmation, a confession, from Irena that her shrine to the man found in the British-embassy grounds was a fake, even though he'd scientifically proved that the photographs of her and Ivan Oskin were superimposed. . . .'

'Based solely on that evidence, he'd had a Moscow TV anchorwoman, later assassinated, claim on air that Lvov was a CIA spy,' agreed Ethel. 'The Agency actually had a plane on standby at an RAF base here to take Charlie on a rendition-interrogation flight to God knows where! He was in the biggest hurry you can imagine!'

'Charlie was frightened he wasn't going to get that admission.' assessed Natalia, bluntly. 'From her demeanour, her responses, I don't believe Irena picked it up, which was fortunate for Charlie. . . .' She paused. 'But I'm not totally convinced about that.'

'You're still losing me,' complained Ethel.

'I don't believe Irena was frightened,' declared Natalia. 'Not as frightened as she should have been, threatened with return to Russia after failing to salvage the biggest operation in Russian-intelligence history.'

Ethel jerked her head towards the dead TV. 'I sat through all your replays! Irena was terrified of being returned!'

'My job's fear: recognizing it, using it. Irena Novikov was nervous, maybe frightened to a point but just that, only up to a point, no further. . . .' One by one, in front of the security supervisor, Natalia laid out copies of the still photographs from Irena's shrine. 'What's odd, strikes you as unusual, about any of these phoney, superimposed prints?'

Ethel studied the display with the concentration with which Natalia had earlier watched the video, twice rearranging the pictures in different sequences before finally looking up, shrugging. 'Nothing. I know they're superimposed but I can't see anything odd or unusual apart from that in any of them.'

'According to what Irena originally told Charlie, she was on station in Cairo with both Oskin *and* Lvov, although it was Lvov who was her lover and with whom she was totally involved, setting up her White House infiltration. Why aren't there photographs—okay, superimposed photographs—of her and Oskin in those days: the obligatory camel pose with a pyramid in the background; on the Nile in a felucca? Certainly one of her before her face was marked? That's not a pictorial record stretching over more than eighteen years. I don't think any of those pictures span more than a four-year period.'

'You've answered your own doubts,' argued Ethel, forcefully. 'She wasn't ever *with* Oskin: couldn't have given a damn about him until he tried to sell what he believed he knew and she didn't know that until he was found dead in the embassy grounds. They had what, a month, five weeks, to put all the phoney stuff together from what was available from Oskin's belongings to match as best they could with what Irena could produce to create a half-credible story. And don't forget that's all they wanted, a passable match: it was never intended the shrine should be brought to England, risking exposure. It was theatre, for a one-shot performance when Charlie was taken to a flat he believed to be the one she'd shared with Oskin. It was your soft-hearted, romantic husband who scooped it all up and shipped it here in the diplomatic bag for her to have the memorabilia. That's the only reason Irena *came* here, to destroy the one thing that could expose her as a phoney and with that exposure wreck the whole Lvov concept.'

'That's an impressive rebuttal,' conceded Natalia.

'Which you're not buying?' anticipated Ethel.

'I need to watch the video again, in addition to a lot more analysis,' insisted Natalia. 'I've got a vested and very special reason not to get anything wrong, remember? I'm trying to get my husband back.'

'You think we failed—that I failed—because it didn't work at the end?'

Edward Birkitt smiled at the scorn, refusing any other reaction to the apparent reversal of the woman's previous resistance: he'd very early discerned her underlying irritation at his remaining unresponsive to every effort Irena Novikov made to surprise or shock him. Persisting that way, he said, 'Hasn't it?'

'I'm disappointed, Ed. I'd had you down as being more intelligent than that.'

'Than what?'

'Than what your response indicates.' Irena Yakulova Navikov was nervous although sure it wasn't showing: rather that the disparagement was now the right way for her to go.

'What does it indicate?' asked Birkitt, determined to surrender the questioning role only on his terms, not hers.

'A total misunderstanding, misconception, of the incredible success we've achieved.'

'I'm looking forward to your telling me all about that.'

'You want to know something?'

'I want to know everything.'

'Twenty years, longer even, nearer thirty, that's how long we had your CIA sitting up on their hindquarters, begging for every little scrap we chose to toss their way. Who was in the White House then? Carter, wasn't it? Maybe it was Reagan: you work it out, he was your president. Remember what a mess you guys made trying to get your hostages from the Tehran embassy?'

'You claiming credit for screwing that up?'

'That's my problem—your problem—my remembering with any accuracy everything we did do. There was so much, so very much and in so many different ways in which we sent you guys running every which way. But the Tehran debacle has a familiarity about it and it was a disaster, wasn't it?'

'You want me to admit a CIA failing?' invited Birkitt, following apparent interrogator openness when nothing was compromised. 'Okay, the CIA screwed up the advice we offered the outgoing president.'

Irena spread her hands in a gesture of helplessness. 'And who do you think spread the information that led to the Company screwing up, Ed? And did the same to screw George Bush in the first Gulf War?'

'You telling me you introduced Stepan Lvov to the CIA with something about that?'

'I told you, it's hard to remember.'

'Do that, try real hard,' urged Birkitt. He had to shift his approach, to match hers.

'Why don't you work it out?' suggested Irena, knowing now she could make it all sound credible. 'America's leading the cavalry charge, as always. So why did the invasion stop short of Baghdad with the chance then of unseating Saddam Hussein and getting the oil-crazed Bush family's eager little fingers on all that black gold? You think it was because the United Nations mandate didn't technically authorize it? There wasn't a UN mandate in 2003 but that didn't stop jackass Bush Junior going in, did it? Look at it another way. How about the first invasion being stopped because intelligence guidance at that time was that Saddam really *did* have weapons of mass destruction and would have used them? That was the intelligence we made sure George Senior was getting, that Saddam had biological weapons and would use them. That was the story we changed—telling the truth, would you believe!—that sent George W scuttling in. And that didn't have anything to do with 9/11 and Saddam's supposed support for Al Qaeda but everything to do with that precious oil and which politically connected construction company was going to get the exclusive rights physically to rebuild a country that was going to be flattened.'

'For someone with a memory problem, that was pretty comprehensive, if contrary to a lot of the known facts?' coaxed Birkitt, relieved that at last the dam had been breached.

Irena shrugged. 'I was talking in broad outline but you can check it out, can't you? Your State Department will have all the records from 1990, 1991. And your CIA archives will provide the cross-reference, showing the intelligence that was coming in.'

'I'm following your scenario and I've got my own idea of why Moscow would want to get involved like this, but why don't you give me your take, to avoid my disappointing you a second time about my intelligence?' invited Birkitt.

'It's surely a long way short of Einstein's Theory of Relativity,' sneered Irena, confident enough to risk sarcasm. 'Saddam was only ever a danger to his own people but we didn't want America in general and the Bush family in particular getting their hands on Iraqi oil: we've got a lot of our own to sell at a premium to the West. And we didn't want America and the West gaining influence by overthrowing a man universally despised by every other Arab nation. So look what we achieved, by manipulating the intelligence as we did. By stopping the first invasion at the gates of Baghdad, we made the United States look weak and ineffectual in the eyes of every other Arab country and sold billions of dollars more of our own oil to the West at the same time as increasing our own influence throughout the region. As well as getting a lot more assets in place when we wanted to use them. Which we did, after 9/11. All we had to do then was tell the truth, let the CIA know that Saddam had dismantled his weapons programme and wait for little George Junior to go in like a Wild West robber baron and get that oil so long denied the family.'

'You claiming you achieved all that?'

'I'm suggesting you establish your own proof. It's there for you to find and check how close what I've told you tallies with what you've already got on record.'

'Why the change, Irena Yakulova?' demanded Birkitt, sharply. 'A few days ago all you did was tell me to go to hell. Today you're giving me an overview I'd never imagined ever getting.'

'A few days ago you threatened me with a lifetime in solitary confine-ment. Maybe I believed you,' said Irena, the answer prepared.

'I like the change.' said Birkitt.

She'd done it, decided Irena. No, she at once corrected herself. She hadn't got away with anything. She'd prepared herself with a game plan and from the American's reaction she hadn't simply hooked him, she'd pulled him in, gaffed him, and hung him out to dry. By insisting that over twenty years there had been too many such Russian intelligence coups for her ever to recall in specific detail, she avoided the risk of be-ing trapped by any factual challenge. A near masterstroke had been the 1990s fear of Iraqi weapons of mass destruction, which had been widely known and about which there would inevitably be references in the CIA's Middle East traffic of the time, supported in State Department papers.

All of which would convince them from the outset she was finally co-operating as they expected. Which just might, she calculated, get her the so-far-refused diplomatic access and the guidance she so desperately needed when she couldn't carry on the charade any longer.

'Where's Monsford?' belligerently demanded Maxim Radtsic, before Re-becca even seated herself.

'There are things keeping him in London.' She'd have to be very cau-tious insinuating doubts about Gerald Monsford without it being obvious on the recording apparatus.

'Things like an enquiry into the insanity of our last meeting!'

Maybe she wouldn't need to insinuate after all, thought Rebecca; but she'd still try, when she considered it safe. 'You've got television. You know there's a lot going on.'

'Does that mean getting Andrei here with us is being put to one side?' demanded Elena. As always, the couple sat some distance apart on sepa-rate conservatory seats.

'Not at all. Director Monsford hopes to have something to tell you very soon,' assured Rebecca. It wasn't much but it was something the irascible Russian might remember to throw at Monsford later.

'I'd like to believe that,' said Elena. 'We both would.'

'You know you have Director Monsford's personal promise on this,' said Rebecca, seizing the better opportunity. Glad of the care with which she'd planned the encounter, she heaved her briefcase onto her lap, pulling out the two thick books that had given it its weight, and offering them one by one to the woman. 'They're in English, I'm afraid. But I know you weren't able to bring anything out with you and I thought you might like something of our research discipline. . . .' She smiled. 'And I apologize if I've chosen badly.'

Elena smiled back. 'English isn't a problem, and I haven't read them: it's very thoughtful.'

'And I know Jacobson offered you the chance to meet some other professionals you might find interesting.' She was disappointed that it was Jacobson's rest day: she'd been curious at his attitude towards her after the committee-room session.

'No!' refused Radtsic, at once. 'I've told Monsford we're not co-operating with anyone until we get Andrei here.'

'Haven't you thought how that refusal might actually be preventing— obstructing—your getting Andrei back?'

Radtsic hesitated at the point of adding more vodka to his glass. 'What do you mean?'

'You've seen the television: got an idea at least of how bad things are between us,' said Rebecca, tentatively, setting out the idea that had occurred to her on the journey to Hertfordshire. 'We scarcely have any proper functioning communication with Moscow: we've made three separate approaches for just such a channel to pass messages between yourselves and Andrei. There hasn't yet been any response. If you began to co-operate, gave us something genuine with which we might indicate you were talking openly to us, at the same time as telling Andrei in a letter—a letter your FSB would logically open and read—that you were going to tell us everything we want to know because you were being denied access to him, you could very easily open the closed door.'

'Do it, Maxim Mikhailovich!' implored Elena. 'You must do it! You know you can't go on refusing forever. And now you know a possible way of getting through to Andrei!'

'Why didn't that bullying idiot Monsford tell me all this from the beginning?' demanded Radtsic, reluctant to capitulate.

Why had she agonized over insinuation! 'We've already talked about how much is going on: he expected to get here today.'

'But decided it wasn't important enough,' picked up Radtsic, exactly as Rebecca had hoped.

'I've told you why he couldn't.'

'I'll think about it,' begrudged Radtsic. 'But if I change my mind I don't want to talk to Monsford.'

It couldn't have gone better if she'd scripted the entire exchange, thought Rebecca as she entered her car. Now she had to hope that however she worked out her approach to Jane Ambersom on the return journey, it would be half as successful.

Without the white coat and the sniggering entourage, there was a second's delay in Charlie's recognition of the doctor from the psychiatric institution who followed Mikhail Guzov into the dacha. In a three-piece business suit the man appeared fatter than he had at the hospital. He was carrying a bellows-expanding medical case.

'See how concerned we are about your well-being!' greeted Guzov.

'It's comforting,' said Charlie, matching the mockery.

The surgeon was ignoring both of them, busying himself with the case, which expanded open to create a flat ledge for the compartmented instruments. The layout completed, the man said, 'Let's look at the shoulder, shall we?'

Charlie shrugged the peasant's smock over his head, the difficulty its awkwardness, not actual pain from his shoulder. There was no pain, either, at the removal of the dressing but an irritation persisted.

'Enjoy your walk in the woods?' asked Guzov, from a corner chair.

'The mosquitoes were a problem.' He felt the surgeon behind him prodding with various pressures around what he assumed to be the bullet exit point. There was still yellow-and-black bruising around what had to have been the bullet's entry.

'You should have stuck to the road,' said Guzov.

'I didn't want to risk going that far.'

'It's healed very cleanly,' intruded the unseen surgeon, from behind him. 'And there's obviously no pain?'

'No.'

'What about the numbness you were always complaining about?'

'Gone now, fortunately.'

'Any other problems with it?'

'None,' lied Charlie.

'There's no need for a further dressing,' announced the physician, coming into view but talking to Guzov. 'Or for me to see him again.'

'There!' said Guzov. 'A complete recovery. They were as bad at shooting as they were at being intelligence officers.'

'I'm glad about that,' said Charlie, struggling back into his smock and sitting back expectantly, not bothering with the outer belt, which was also too big.

'A day off today,' announced Guzov, standing. 'Today was making sure you've fully recovered.'

Maybe it wasn't so essential to make too many more outside expeditions, thought Charlie; no more than one or two at the most. He didn't think Guzov had been exaggerating how *spetsnaz* troops might relieve their boredom.

In the J. Edgar Hoover Building on Washington's Pennsylvania Avenue, the CIA's Larry Stern waited impatiently until his FBI counterpart finished reading that morning's transcript of Irena Novikov's interrogation before declaring, 'Bingo!'

'We haven't got the Full House yet,' warned the more guarded Mort Bering.

'We'll get it!' said Stern.

'If this is the beginning, we just haven't got a can of worms, we've got a whole fucking truck load,' persisted the cautious FBI deputy.

'But I'm squeaky clean, Mort: untouched by any of the fallout from the fuck-up all those other guys allowed themselves to be suckered into. Just like you, safely untouched and protected. All we've got to ensure is that we stay that way.'

'That's all we've got to do,' agreed Bering.

11

'HOW DID IT GO?' THEY DIDN'T EAT OUT AS MUCH SINCE JANE HAD virtually moved in, and Barry Elliott was particularly glad they weren't that night, after the Washington exchanges throughout the afternoon.

Jane sipped her wine reflectively. 'Not good. We could only challenge the total illogicality of Straughan leaving provable records of his dealing with an FSB double, and Monsford threw that right back at us, demanding a reasonable alternative for what his evidence showed, which we didn't have. Straughan did provably make a call to a known FSB operative—it doesn't matter that he's a double—and within days Charlie's flat was burgled by the FSB.'

Elliott spread his hands out towards her. 'You must have *some* argument against Straughan going bad!'

'We can't find one,' admitted Jane, reluctantly. 'You in a hurry to eat? Your T-bones are too big for one person: I thought we'd split one between us.'

'No hurry,' dismissed Elliott, quickly. Which there wasn't: he wanted to get around to things gradually, as part of the normal end-of-the-day conversation, hoping she'd fully recognize what—but more important, why—he'd done. 'What's tomorrow's schedule?'

'Wilkinson, the only one of the original support group to meet Charlie face-to-face. And Flood, who was briefly with him and actually witnessed the shooting.'

'Neither is going to be able to knock Monsford's story of an MI6 penetration, are they?' That was important to implant in her mind for later.

Jane nodded in agreement. 'But we can show up all the inconsistencies of the attack on Charlie. But from our near-total failure today, tomorrow might not be worth a row of beans either. Monsford can just shrug his great fat shoulders again and say he can't explain anything with Briddle and Halliday dead.'

'Have you thought yet that Monsford could be right about the penetration: that Straughan wasn't ever your friend, just trying to con you about Monsford working to wreck everything?' asked Elliott, hopefully starting to move the conversation in the direction he wanted.

'He wasn't conning me!' refused Jane, the defensive belligerence immediate.

'Just setting out the chessboard,' quickly retreated the American. 'It seems from where I'm sitting that Monsford is a long way ahead and that you're an even longer way behind.'

Jane poured more wine, saying nothing.

This wasn't going the way he wanted, Elliott recognized. 'What about Rebecca being your way in?'

'Got an inconsistency there, too,' offered Jane. 'She wasn't at today's hearing.'

His second chance, hoped Elliott. 'Any reason given?'

Jane hunched her shoulders, lapsing into silence again. Then she said, 'I'll start dinner.'

'You haven't asked about my day,' stopped Elliott.

Jane smiled up, apologetically. 'Sorry. How was your day?'

'Irena's dynamited the logjam, quite literally.'

Jane came anxiously forward in her chair. 'With something to help us with Charlie?'

'Not yet,' said the American, to Jane's visible disappointment. 'But I'm setting up a deal that keeps you right inside the loop. . . .' He hesitated. 'And I've put myself on the line doing it.'

'How?'

'It's a CIA bag, so logically the co-operation should be with Monsford and MI6. But I've argued Irena was your case first: that Charlie broke her and that the Bureau, me, maintained the liaison with you because the CIA wanted to distance itself from more fallout.'

'And?' pressed Jane, hoping she was correctly following what he was saying.

'The Agency wants everything, and I mean everything, that happened between Charlie and Irena. Their psychological profilers, those guys, want a comparison from which to judge her now. She's started off claiming that through Lvov in the very beginning the FSB manipulated America in both Iraq wars.'

Jane snorted a laugh. 'You've got to be joking!'

'That's what I said when Washington first told me. Irena challenged her interrogator to check CIA and State Department intelligence in 1990 against 2003. There's a fit, a good enough fit to make it believable. The CIA certainly believe it.'

'Jesus!'

'I said that, too. Here's the deal I want to set up: you give me everything and I'll get you back as much as I can persuade them to give me in return. The better—the fuller—your stuff, the more I can negotiate to get back.'

'Cutting out Monsford?'

'I've warned my guys about the MI6 penetration: said involving MI6 could blow it all away. After what happened with Lvov in the beginning, nobody's going to risk another CIA earthquake. The aftershocks haven't subsided yet.'

'It's not going to help us with Charlie, is it?' said Jane, reflective again.

'No,' admitted Elliott, at once. 'But it'll sure as hell help you and me. Which is what I'm trying to do, help us.'

She wasn't as excited, as grateful, as he'd expected, decided Elliott, disappointed.

————

He'd destroy her, Gerald Monsford determined: destroy her far more effectively, more completely, than he'd destroyed Jane Ambersom, because that bitch hadn't directly challenged him like this one with yesterday's filmed performance from Hertfordshire, which most of the people in the enquiry would have seen by now or at least heard about from those who had. The retribution had to be what Shakespeare had Othello call a 'capable and wide revenge.' And he was sure as hell going to achieve that. He was going to ensure that Rebecca Street was helplessly entwined in the tangling labyrinth he was creating, eventually to be exposed as James Straughan would be exposed, the joint architects of all that had gone wrong. Which Monsford knew he could do, as painstakingly as he was enmeshing everyone else, layered strand of culpability after layered strand of culpability. But this wasn't the time: not even the moment to think any further about it. This was the day MI5 was introducing its initial witnesses, people who'd actually been there, seen what happened, and he couldn't risk the slightest distraction.

It was enough, then, that Rebecca be alongside him, after Jacobson's overnight advice that Radtsic was refusing to see anyone, talk to anyone, until he and Elena had sufficiently considered Rebecca's proposal. Having her with him—supported as well by some of the comments she'd made in Hertfordshire—was enough to imply that Radtsic's suggestion might even have come from him and that her function had been merely to relay it.

The entry of the co-chairmen and the opening formality had by now become so ritualized that those participating came close to ignoring it, rearranging themselves and their belongings and whispering asides. There were no huddled exchanges between the MI5 group, though. Unlike the preceding day, provision had been made in advance for Patrick Wilkinson and Ian Flood. The five entered together and took their seats without any conversation. Jane Ambersom stared intently but blank faced across at Rebecca, who returned the look just as expressionlessly. Rebecca's impression was that the opposing group looked confidently well rehearsed.

Beside her, Monsford came forward over his prepared notepad, his concentration absolute.

Patrick Wilkinson, a vaguely distracted, clearly nervous man, identified himself as the field supervisor of the MI5 support team for an extraction of which Charlie Muffin was overall Control. Initially there had been some confusion among the group at Charlie's apparent disappearance in Amsterdam. Wilkinson had expected the central, co-ordinated supervision to be from MI5's Thames House headquarters after Charlie's disappearance but realized by the second day that the three MI6 officers were communicating independently with London. The two groups were physically thrown together within the embassy but the socializing was limited, even awkward. The three MI6 officers spent most of their day within their closed-off *rezidentura:* with nothing to do but await orders, Wilkinson and his two colleagues had spent a lot of time in the embassy gymnasium and indoor swimming pool. The MI6 men had never joined them. Wilkinson said that on the third day he'd openly challenged Stephan Briddle about the separate contact with London, concerned that two command structures could lead to confusion and endanger the extraction.

'Briddle replied that his orders to deal direct with London came personally from the Director,' declared Wilkinson; and Aubrey Smith, who was leading the testimony, paused, looking expectantly across the table for an intervention, but Monsford made no attempt to speak.

'What was your reaction to that?' resumed Smith.

'I said I'd talk to London about it. My thought, to prevent confusion, was that control might be concentrated through MI6. Briddle told me not to bother. Which is what I was told when I spoke to my own operational director. I was told that there were concerns about the joint operation and that I was appointed field supervisor of my two MI5 colleagues and we, too, were to work separately. That order was reiterated after the Russian arrest of the tourist group Charlie had used.'

'What was the response of the MI6 officers to that arrest and the awareness that Charlie Muffin was in Moscow?'

'They virtually put us under observation, which was initially ridiculous, restricted as we all were to the embassy. Neil Preston, one of my colleagues now under Russian arrest, lost his temper and asked what the hell was going on. Robert Denning, one of the MI6 officers also now under arrest, replied that they didn't know: that they were getting orders, without explanation, from day to day. Stephan Briddle overheard and there was an argument between them.'

'What about the two resident MI6 officers?' switched Smith.

They scarcely ever saw Harry Jacobson, the head of station, insisted Wilkinson. The man actually appeared to have distanced himself from his own people. There was not a single occasion during their time in Moscow when Jacobson had mixed socially. In contrast, David Halliday, the other resident, had tried very hard to mix but was ostracized by his MI6 colleagues, which Wilkinson and the other two MI5 men didn't understand. Halliday had eaten with them twice in the embassy canteen, wanting to know about Charlie, whom he'd known from Charlie's earlier posting. Halliday had called Charlie the most unpredictable but best intelligence officer he'd ever known.

'What did Halliday say about his relationship with his own people?' asked Aubrey Smith.

'That his face didn't fit and that he feared he was on his way out. And that it wasn't fair,' replied Wilkinson, at once.

The stiffening expectation across the table was almost too fleeting for Rebecca to isolate before Smith added, 'Was that all Halliday said?'

'No,' replied Wilkinson. 'He told us he thought he was being set up to be a fall guy, like Charlie.'

'He thought he was being set up, just like Charlie?' echoed Aubrey Smith.

'Those were his exact words.'

Monsford scribbled furiously.

———

The ladies' toilets were the most obvious contact place apart from the refreshment annexe but Rebecca hesitated for Jane's confirmation from the direction she took leaving the enquiry room. By the time Rebecca entered, it seemed most of the other attending women were ahead of her in the Victorian-era mausoleum of floor-to-ceiling white tiles and echoing, constantly throbbing pipe work. Both Jane and Rebecca initially ignored each other. Both let others beat them to cubicles to clear the sprawling room. Between them they reduced the remaining occupancy to three, in addition to themselves, when they finally emerged from stalls neither had needed anyway, managing adjoining washbasins and mirrors. Their original interest gone, the three remaining women ignored them, engrossed in their own conversation.

Talking directly into her own reflection, Rebecca said, 'I tried to reach you last night, to thank you for what you tried to do questioning Jacobson.'

'I was staying with friends,' comfortably avoided Jane, rearranging already arranged hair. 'I wondered where you were yesterday until I caught up with the safe-house transmission.'

The three other women trailed out. Still using her reflection, Rebecca smiled at them. Only one smiled back.

Jane said, 'You thought any more about our coffee-break chat?'

'A lot.'

'And?'

'I'm still thinking.'

'What Monsford's trying is bullshit: it'll be exposed as such.'

Rebecca didn't respond.

Deciding the risk was justified, Jane said, 'I met Jamie the week before it happened,' and admired the other woman's tight-faced control.

Rebecca finally said, 'He was very frightened at the end.'

'Aren't you?' When Rebecca again didn't respond, Jane said, 'With Jamie gone, you need support from the sort of people you most certainly haven't got where you are now.'

Rebecca finally turned directly to the other woman. 'What is it for you, personal or professional?'

Jane considered the question. 'Mostly personal at the beginning, I suppose, when the opportunity was suddenly there. I don't think it is anymore. It's gone way beyond that now: now it's very much professional. Monsford's the danger to himself—and to you—but not any longer to me. You sure you can win all by yourself?'

'I didn't have the slightest doubt before Jamie died.'

'You don't have Jamie anymore. You're by yourself.'

Rebecca shook her head, a gesture of uncertainty.

Time for further risk, Jane determined. 'Do you have it, Rebecca? Have what Jamie made.'

'I didn't know—don't know—about Rome,' unexpectedly declared Rebecca.

Jane was too surprised immediately to respond. 'You surely don't believe . . . can't believe . . . !'

'How do you explain it?'

'I don't explain it. But don't forget Vasili Okulov is a known double MI6 used a lot in the past.'

'The log entry unquestionably referring to Charlie Muffin was in Straughan's handwriting,' persisted Rebecca.

'However incontestable the supposed proof, it's just not possible for Jamie to have gone over: to have betrayed anyone or anything,' rejected Jane, loudly.

'I need to be surer,' protested Rebecca, her uncertainties seeping through.

'Maybe it's in what Jamie set up before he died,' chanced Jane.

'It's . . .' started Rebecca, the denial half formed, but stopped.

'What, Rebecca?' demanded Jane, guessing the nearness of finally learning just what Straughan had achieved.

'I need to be sure,' repeated Rebecca, lamely.

'Whenever are we one-hundred-percent, no-doubt-whatsoever-sure about what we do?' pressed Jane, maintaining the pressure. 'You've got a simple choice. The way it's turned out for me, I actually beat the bastard.

That's all you've got to be sure about: where it's safer—survivable—for you to be.'

The reassembly summons sounded distantly through the heavy Victorian door.

'My mobile's there,' said Jane, offering her card. 'I don't want any more missed calls. But I *do* want calls: the quicker and the sooner the better.'

The resonance of Wilkinson's session-closing remark still hung sufficiently in the enquiry room for Aubrey Smith to refocus it simply by a third repetition. 'David Halliday, one of the two MI6 resident officers in Moscow, told you he believed he was being set up to be a fall guy?'

'Yes, sir.'

'For what?'

'He didn't know. His answer, when I very directly asked him, was a fall guy for everything that was going on but from which he was being kept out. Charlie said practically the same when we finally met.'

Aubrey Smith allowed the second echo to reverberate throughout the room. 'When, precisely again, was that?'

'When he made his first call to the embassy Charlie told me at once that nothing he said, no arrangements we made, were to be shared with MI6,' recounted Wilkinson. 'On the second call, he said he believed MI6 were working on something different from what we thought to be the operation we were there for, something that was being kept from us: that his involvement with any of us was going to be limited to an absolute minimum.'

'Did you have, or get, any indication of MI6 working upon something quite separate from what you understood to be the MI5 extraction?'

'London lifted the restriction upon our leaving the embassy after Charlie surfaced, which very clearly activated MI6. Whenever we left, they attempted to follow. On the day I finally met Charlie there was a near-farcical situation, but for its unknown, underlying seriousness. I realized later that Charlie was setting his own safety test. He had us move around the Moscow

Metro, to his direction, before he and I met. And he monitored it all. From the moment of our going underground, we were followed by MI6. Charlie was communicating on one of the cell phones issued from here. From wherever it was he concealed himself, Charlie had my two officers lead MI6 in the wrong direction all over the underground system.'

There was a shift of irritation from Gerald Monsford and another scribbled note. Caught by the movement, Smith paused again, looking to the other director. Unmoving again, Monsford gazed back, saying nothing.

'Your two colleagues led MI6 all over Moscow,' picked up Smith. 'What were you doing?'

'What they were doing was for my benefit: for me to meet Charlie undetected as he demanded. It was to exchange passports, to enable Natalia Fedova and her daughter to fly out.'

'Which you succeeded in doing?'

'Which I *thought* I'd succeeded in doing,' qualified Wilkinson. 'Charlie didn't trust anyone, even his own colleagues. I didn't know where he was living, what he was doing. He knew I'd try to follow him when we finished: my instructions from London were to bring him back into the extraction as it had been planned. To prevent my following he personally escorted me back into the underground—we'd actually gone up to street level, to a park, to talk—and remained on the platform to ensure I left. The following day he told me he'd seen Stephan Briddle two carriages behind the one in which I was sitting. Charlie believed Briddle had been with us all the time, apart from in the park, and had boarded the train ahead of us, expecting Charlie to be with me.'

'To do what?'

'Charlie believed he was in physical danger that might even go as far as an attempt upon his life.'

He'd missed something, Charlie acknowledged. Probably missed several things, because nothing was ever totally understood in the wilderness of intelligence, but there'd been one all-important, pivotal mistake and because of it he'd been thinking wrongly, assessing and judging wrongly, ever since.

What was it? How far back had it occurred? Could he recover: do anything to reverse or correct it? Most important of all, did it endanger Natalia and Sasha, whose escape from Moscow still wasn't positively confirmed? And could he really be so confident that there was no risk of his being shuttled off to oblivion in a Siberian gulag?

His first demand, inextricably linked to the second, was the core to everything, and the answers to that weren't going to come, if they came at all, like divine guidance on the road to Damascus. He had to go back, to the very beginning, to the moment he'd stood at the side of an autopsy slab in a Moscow mortuary looking down at the faceless, tortured body of a man who'd imagined himself capable of walking away from the CIA and the FSB with a bagful of money for keeping the secret of the Lvov penetration.

What about recovery, reversing any potential damage? He was hardly in a physical position to recover or reverse anything. But he didn't need to be, came another, quick contradiction. His physical situation wasn't relevant. What he needed was to *know*. Knowing, or believing he knew, where he'd gone wrong could provide the guide he so desperately needed to so much else.

Which brought him to Natalia and Sasha. He *had* to be right about their getting to England! It was inconceivable that Mikhail Guzov, who believed bullying to be an interrogation technique, would not have used their interception as a weapon, a mentally crushing club with which to beat him, if they'd been seized at Vnukovo airport. It remained unconfirmed but with so much else to resolve it had to stay an outstanding uncertainty, not a forefront concern.

As did, Charlie objectively conceded, his growing conviction that whatever transpired in the coming weeks, maybe even months, it was no longer an automatic outcome that he'd be transferred to some distant gulag.

He'd have to continue with his own experiments, Charlie reluctantly concluded, even if they did threaten an encounter with the *spetsnaz*, which he very much wanted to avoid.

'I don't understand why there had to be a suspension,' complained John Passmore, as they settled back into the Director-General's Thames House suite. 'No statement the Russians issue this afternoon can affect what we were producing. . . .' He extended a cupped right hand. 'We had the room like that! Monsford was squirming.'

Aubrey Smith smiled at the ex-soldier's military exasperation. 'For all their esoteric titles and pretensions to understand intelligence workings, we're dealing with very senior Whitehall civil servants, the ruling mandarins, dealing in turn with Westminster politicians each and both of whom prefer their lives to run in straight lines, unhindered or derailed by the unexpected. To them, Moscow's advance announcement is a worrying uncertainty, a diversion from the straight line. Until they've heard what Moscow's going to say or do, Bland and Palmer—and all their little backroom dwarfs—are disconnected, slowed if not actually paralyzed by the uncertainty of the unknown.' The man smiled again. 'Which, I agree—and hope—could be close to how Gerald Monsford feels despite our losing our momentum. But we really have done well with Wilkinson and I believe this adjournment is to our advantage: it gives time for what Wilkinson said to be properly absorbed. There's less chance now of it being confused by whatever challenges Monsford makes or by Flood's account of the actual shooting.'

'I couldn't be happier at the interruption,' declared Jane, impatiently. 'I've got a lot to tell you about Irena Novikov in America and of the conversation I had with Rebecca Street during this morning's break.'

She recounted both in sequence, taking a full half hour to ensure she omitted nothing, conscious of the growing reaction from both men towards the end.

'America will cheat: keep a lot back for themselves,' assessed Passmore, at once.

'Of course they will: so will we,' accepted Smith, pragmatically. 'But again I think whatever we get will be to our benefit. It sounds as if Irena is opening up far more than she did to Charlie—'

'And let's not forget Natalia's feeling about that,' reminded Jane.

'You think we should pick up Washington's offer?' questioned Passmore.

'Absolutely,' enthused the Director-General. 'We've got everything to gain and at this moment I can't see what we've got to lose.' Looking to Jane, he said, 'What's Elliott think they're going to get through us?'

'Everything there was between Charlie and Irena: not just the confrontation but everything that happened between them in Moscow, before he brought her here,' set out the woman. 'And what Radtsic gives us.'

'So you've told him about Radtsic?' seized Smith, sharply.

'I wanted to reciprocate the offer of getting everything from Irena Novikov,' replied Jane, twisting the truth against the criticism. 'As you said, we stand to get more from them than they can get from us.'

'Particularly as Radtsic isn't telling us anything,' Passmore pointed out.

'He won't be telling *us* anything anyway, will he?' said Smith. 'Monsford's got Radtsic, when he eventually starts to talk. It's the enquiry decision we have to assess at the moment, but that doesn't extend to our sharing with America.'

'And the CIA have Irena,' added Passmore. 'The logic's surely that they'll go direct to Monsford.'

She shouldn't have expected they'd accept the American offer without considering the potential difficulties, acknowledged Jane. 'The liaison was established through the FBI because so many in the CIA hierarchy got burned in the aftermath of the Lvov exposure,' reminded Jane. 'I've worked hard maintaining that conduit, which has come good with Elliott's offer. As far as he's concerned, the co-operation with both FBI and CIA continues through us.'

'So what are you proposing?' pressed Smith.

'What I thought you'd already decided,' hurried Jane, anxious to avoid further difficult questioning. 'We take the offer, reciprocate the exchange as much and as best we can. . . .' She hesitated, momentarily undecided. 'In the circumstances in which we're currently embroiled with MI6—and already having told you about this morning, with Rebecca Street—I didn't think we were considering the finer niceties of inter-agency behaviour?'

Aubrey Smith looked up quickly at the remark, went as if to speak but by not doing so created an awkward silence that Passmore hurried to fill. 'You really believe Rebecca's got what Straughan bugged?'

'Without the slightest doubt, after this morning,' said Jane, relieved to move on. 'It's Straughan's provable contact with Vasili Okulov that's spooked her.'

'You think Wilkinson's evidence, with Flood's to follow, might persuade her?' asked Smith.

Jane shook her head, uncertainly. 'I don't think it's Monsford's manoeuvring she's worried about. And I don't think she seriously doubts Jamie's loyalty for a moment, either. I think she's using Rome as an excuse, an escape, from making the final commitment.'

'Where does that leave us?' asked Passmore.

'Where we've always been with Rebecca, knowing—knowing without doubt now—that she's got what we need to bring Monsford down but having to wait until she comes to us,' said Jane. 'Which she will, eventually.'

John Passmore responded at once to his pager, looking up as he read it. 'Moscow is milking every last drop from this. Their statement's being released in an hour, our time, according to TASS.'

'Time enough for me to have a moment, alone, with Jane,' said Aubrey Smith.

'I'm sorry,' Jane apologized at once. 'I shouldn't have spoken as I did.'

'That's not what I want to talk to you about, although it fits in with what you had to tell us,' said Aubrey Smith. 'I've had a lengthy internal security report, telling me about you and Barry Elliott.' He raised a hand against an interruption. 'It was nothing targeted: just routine.'

'It's a private, personal situation.'

'It can't be, from what you told John and me minutes ago.'

'There's a separation between what I told you minutes ago and what's happening between Barry and me,' insisted Jane.

'Did he tell you that's how it is for him?'

'He's not using me: wouldn't use me.' She couldn't be more positive of anything, thought Jane.

'Aren't you using him?'

'I don't think I am.'

'I think it's indivisible, for both of you. And I think it's a hell of a weapon for Monsford to use against you, both personally and professionally, if he ever learned what's going on.'

'I do not want to stop it personally. And I don't believe I can stop it professionally, either,' said Jane.

'Which, very succinctly, encompasses the problem.'

'I'm not conceding that at the moment there is a problem, although I admit Monsford could turn it into one.'

'Be very careful, far more careful than you've been so far,' urged Smith.

'Do I have your support?' Jane asked directly.

Smith hesitated. 'I will professionally support you for as long as I can if things go wrong.'

'Thank you,' said Jane. It was, she accepted, the most she could expect: maybe more than she could have expected. Having freed herself of him, it was unsettling to confront the thought that she was providing a weapon that Monsford would use, given the slightest chance.

12

JUDGED AS A THEATRICAL PERFORMANCE, WHICH WAS HOW Russia staged the repatriation of the Manchester tourists, the production was of Oscar–winning proportions.

The announcement of their release, by a smiling, strikingly attractive Interior Ministry spokeswoman, began from a brightly backdropped studio but in less than a minute the picture dissolved into live, outside coverage of the event itself, with the voice-over commentary switched to English. The group was filmed emerging, mostly smiling, from an unnamed Moscow hotel, their clothes very obviously freshly cleaned and pressed, all the women professionally coiffured; two of the men and one woman were in wheelchairs pushed by uniformed nurses. They were greeted in the hotel forecourt by a waiting delegation of six, two men and four women, from the Moscow tourist board. As ferried-forward bouquets were presented to each of the English women—with vodka for the men— the delegation leader referred to the tourists as totally innocent, manipulated victims dismissively used as pawns by uncaring British intelligence agencies engaged in hostile activities against the Russian Federation.

The perpetrator of their deception was in Russian custody, as were others involved in associated espionage acts for which they would all face appropriate Russian justice. The tourists were being returned to their homes and to their families with every good wish from the Russian authorities, with a warm invitation to return to Moscow as guests of the city, the authorities of which sympathized with their initial ordeal, as they sympathized with the family of the one member of the group whose premature death, from a heart attack, was the obvious result of the incident. A heavy-busted girl wearing a T-shirt emblazoned with the logo of the Manchester tour company and identified in a caption as the group leader, Muriel Simpson, thanked the Russian authorities for their care, kindness, and help after it was established none of her group was in any way involved in activities against the country. They had been disgracefully deceived and used by intelligence organizations of the British government, which she hoped, upon her return to Britain, to find the subject of legal action by her company.

It was past six in the evening before the committee reassembled and there was no preamble from the co-chairmen. Sir Archibald Bland announced at once, 'The plane's arriving at Heathrow, not Manchester, in an hour. The company have arranged an immediate press conference. The *Mail* and the *Express* are offering contracts for exclusive personal stories.' As he spoke he looked accusingly between the two intelligence chairmen.

Aubrey Smith said, 'It's a good thing they're free. It can't have been pleasant for them. At least now all the others detained are professionals, with some idea of what to expect.'

There were isolated stirrings around the table. Geoffrey Palmer said, 'Is that really all you've got to say!'

Smith frowned, curiously. 'What else would you have me say? They were wrongly used, by one of my officers, which was unfortunate. I regret whatever treatment and hardship to which they were subjected. It'll have been a bad experience, upon which the Russians—and now they—are capitalizing. But there's nothing practicable we can do to defuse what's happened.'

'Except endure yet another publicity circus!' said Bland. 'Downing Street is furious.'

Smith went to continue but before he could Gerald Monsford said, 'We should announce the defection of Maxim Radtsic, which I've argued for days now. The sensation of that would overwhelm whatever fuss these tourists are going to make.'

'No, it wouldn't: it would hugely escalate the whole thing, making the tourists appear far more important than they are,' rejected the MI5 Director-General. 'Do nothing and the media interest will fade. Associate them with the defection of the second-most-important man in Russian intelligence and it'll be a sensation that'll go on for weeks.'

'That reflects the initial feeling elsewhere,' disclosed the Cabinet Secretary. 'We'll return to the remit with which we were convened and only officially consider this if we're called upon to do so.' Turning to Monsford, he said, 'We adjourned at the moment of your examining of Mr Wilkinson.'

'Which created the opportunity for me very thoroughly to consider everything that Mr Wilkinson told this enquiry,' responded Monsford, his voice thick with disdain. 'Every word of which was totally unsubstantiated by any factual evidence or documentation from someone who—which *is* substantiated by him and his colleagues being replaced—was considered to be incapable of fulfilling the purpose for which they were sent to Moscow. I don't believe this enquiry would be usefully served by anything further from Mr Wilkinson.'

Monsford's move seriously disconcerted Aubrey Smith, who'd so confidently expected that day's hearing to conclude with Wilkinson's cross-examination that he'd considered not including Ian Flood in their return that evening. Their pre-hearing preparation—along with their professionalism—prevented its being obvious.

In what appeared an instant rebuttal to Monsford's dismissal, Flood at once isolated Charlie Muffin's fear—'more a positive expectation'—of physical intervention within minutes of their meeting at the Savoy Hotel the night before Natalia and Sasha's extraction. Because of that conversation, recounted Flood, he was particularly alert for surveillance the following morning and became aware of a following car just before clearing the city on their way to Vnukovo Airport. He warned Charlie when they met, as arranged, outside the departure terminal. Charlie refused an offered gun, for protection, and abandoned his original intention to leave on the same plane as Natalia and the child. Instead he switched to a

Cyprus-bound flight to draw attention from the extraction route. Charlie was third in the Cyprus check-in queue when three MI6 officers—Stephan Briddle, Jeremy Beckindale, and Robert Denning—entered the terminal. Briddle separated from the two others and headed directly towards Charlie Muffin, who was initially unaware of what was happening. Beckindale and Denning remained by a perimeter wall, giving no reaction to David Halliday's arrival several moments after the first three MI6 men. Halliday appeared to see Charlie and Briddle, breaking into a run in their directions. Flood believed, from the man's facial expression, that Halliday shouted, although he was unable to hear what the man yelled. Briddle heard, though, at the same time as Charlie, and both turned in Halliday's direction. Briddle began to run too but awkwardly, holding his jacket around him. Charlie did not move, just watched. Flood saw a pistol in Briddle's hand when the man was about eighteen metres from Charlie. There was the sound of a shot—Flood did not see who fired it—and a militia officer fell. Flood then very clearly saw the gun in Briddle's hand, thrust out from beneath his jacket.

'And I saw him fire. The gun, a Russian Makarov, was aimed at Charlie. From the recoil movement of Briddle's hand I believe he fired twice. Charlie jerked, obviously hit, and twisted to his left and fell. My orders—Charlie's specific orders to me—were not to intervene but to get Natalia and the child safely away. Which I did.'

'How far away were you from the shooting?' questioned Smith.

'Approximately fifty metres.'

'Was the terminal building crowded, putting people between you and the other three, Charlie, Briddle, and Halliday?'

'It was busy, but not crowded. At no time was my view seriously impaired by people.'

'Was Stephan Briddle shooting at Charlie Muffin?'

'Yes.'

'You have no doubt about that?'

'No doubt whatsoever.'

'With intent to kill?'

'There is absolutely no doubt in my mind that it was Briddle's intention to kill Charlie.'

'Fifty metres is a substantial distance,' declared Gerald Monsford. He appeared quite confident, picking up the questioning at once at Aubrey Smith's invitation. The scribbled notepad was in front of him but he didn't consult it as he began.

'I do not regard it as substantial,' refused Flood. The wariness was obvious.

'You were able quite easily to see Briddle, Halliday, and Muffin over such a distance without your view being obscured by the crowds milling about the departure terminal?'

'My view was never obscured.'

'What colour was Charlie's suit?'

'Grey,' replied Flood, at once. 'Over it he wore a beige raincoat: it was very crumpled. And what appeared to be very old suede shoes.'

Monsford hesitated, off-balanced by the detail of Flood's reply. 'Describe the view you had, from where you were standing.'

'The entry into the terminal was to my left. The various check-in desks were directly in front of me. The way into the passport checks and the embarkation lounge was to my right.'

'Where was the MEA desk for the Cyprus flight positioned in the bank of check-in desks directly in front of you?'

'To my right.'

'Explain the episode from your viewpoint in Vnukovo Airport.'

Now it was Flood who briefly hesitated. 'Charlie was in the check-in. The two who came in with Briddle were to my left, about thirty metres from me, against the wall. Briddle first walked and then ran directly in front of my line of vision, with Halliday running behind, both towards Charlie.'

'A tableau, directly in front of you?' pressed Monsford.

'It happened directly in front of me, my being separated by a distance of about fifty metres,' replied Flood, pedantically.

'Which didn't give you the perspective from which to judge, did it?' pounced Monsford.

Flood remained silent for several moments, staring across the intervening table. Eventually he said, 'Perspective? To judge what? I don't follow the question.'

'It's all happening in front of you, from left to right: literally a stage setting,' established Monsford. 'But from where you were you can't tell this enquiry with any accuracy that Charlie Muffin was Briddle's target, can you?'

'Briddle fired at least twice at Charlie Muffin,' insisted Flood.

'According to the airport CCTV, which the Russians have shown— the camera in an entirely different position from your view—a militia officer fell before Charlie?'

'Yes, I saw a militia officer go down.'

'How far was the officer from Charlie?'

'Close. About two metres, between two check-in lines.'

'Who shot him?'

'I don't know.'

'You don't know! It was all happening before your very eyes: eyes that were in no way obscured by other passengers, allowing you a perfect view of everything.'

'My concentration was upon Briddle, Halliday, and Charlie.'

'You've just told us you saw the officer fall.'

'Of course I saw the officer fall: his was the direction in which I was looking, although not specifically *at* him.'

'What about Halliday? Did he have a gun?'

'I did not see him carrying a weapon, nor did I see him with one on the CCTV the Russians made available.'

'I'm not asking you what was on the CCTV. I'm asking you what you saw David Halliday carrying.'

'I did not see Halliday with a gun.'

'You did not *see* David Halliday carrying a gun. But you can't be sure that he didn't have one.'

Flood hesitated. 'No, I can't be sure.'

'How many people did you see with guns, in addition to Briddle?'

'I believe the militia officer who fell had his pistol in his hand. And I saw another militia officer behind Charlie take his weapon out when the shooting began.'

'Just two men! You are surely aware of the number of people seriously injured by gunshots, in addition to those who actually died!'

'I have already given evidence that I followed my orders when the shooting started and left the outer terminal area to ensure the extraction of the woman and child.'

'What do you say to my suggestion that Stephan Briddle was not shooting *at* Charlie Muffin with intent to kill but at others who were closing in to arrest him after his identification on CCTV?'

'That just isn't the way it happened?'

'But you don't know and therefore can't tell us how it happened, can you, Mr Flood? By the time it all happened you'd already left the main concourse to get on the plane to Helsinki, hadn't you? Your account, like that of Mr. Wilkinson before you, does nothing to help this enquiry.'

From the opposite side of the table Jane Ambersom tried to gauge a reaction from Rebecca, but the woman turned away, refusing to answer the look.

'Thanks for delaying the meeting: for telling me there was to be a televised statement,' said Irena Novikov, determined to control the exchange as she believed she'd conducted their previous session.

'I guessed you'd want to watch it,' said Edwin Birkitt, who hoped Irena would regard his alerting her to Moscow's release of the English tourists as an indication of their growing and improving relationship.

If only you knew how vital my seeing it really is! thought Irena, further tightening any outward satisfaction. 'It'll increase the public pressure on the British, won't it?'

'It's not a mess I'd like to be part of,' said Birkitt.

'You heard how badly hurt Charlie Muffin was?'

'We don't believe it was serious.'

'He was very good,' reflected Irena. 'He'll be a loss to the British.' It was important that they believed everything she'd told Charlie in Moscow.

'What do you imagine will happen to him?' pressed Birkitt, anxious to bring the interrogation on track.

Irena made a doleful expression. '*Guessing* he's having a bad time won't get you anywhere close to what it'll be like. He's the guy that ruined twenty years of espionage planning, remember?'

'Which you were telling me about last time,' encouraged Birkitt, seizing the opportunity.

Irena smiled across at the man, inwardly amused at the eagerness. 'I was right, wasn't I? You found what I told you you'd find in CIA and State Department files, about the first Gulf War? Why the U.S. backed off?'

'Yes,' allowed Birkitt. It was his interrogation technique always to flatter the subject whenever possible.

'That established us, those of us formulating the Lvov penetration,' embarked Irena, everything prepared. 'And we needed it. Don't forget what was happening in 1991, Gorbachev surrendering it all and talking shit like perestroika and glasnost. We were frightened that our particular operation was going to be tossed away before it properly began and that Gorbachev might actually take the KGB apart, which was one of his earliest promises coming into power. But with just that one success, which was a *hell* of a success, actually first stopping America in its tracks and then letting you sink into what later became a quagmire, changed a lot of the thinking about what to do about the KGB.'

'What did—?' broke in Birkitt, at once halted by an over-eager coughing fit. 'What were the changes to the KGB?' he managed to finish.

Irena sniggered a laugh. 'Precious little, compared to what some of the early suggestions were. There was the change of name but that was cosmetic, as it's always been when it's politically suited. The clearing out of dead wood, which needed clearing out anyway. Amalgamation of Records and Archives. And then we had another success.'

'What was that?' Birkitt frowned, struggling to keep up.

'Showing us how completely, because of the Gulf success, your people trusted Lvov,' said Irena, close to patronizing. 'Through Lvov we drip-fed all sorts of changes and watched them being fed to the media: picked a lot up intercepting your station-to-station chatter, too. We couldn't believe how easily it was all turning out.'

'I'd like to make a comparison test,' said Birkitt. 'Could you make a list?'

'I'll try to remember as much as I can.'

'That would be great,' encouraged Birkitt, pushing a yellow legal pad across the table towards her.

Irena carefully began her list, frequently pausing for apparent recollection. During one hesitation, she said, 'I don't suppose Charlie knows his unhappy band of tricked travellers have been freed.'

'I don't know,' admitted Birkitt.

Charlie did.

'A prime example of Russian compassion,' declared Mikhail Guzov, turning off the portable DVD player with which he'd arrived at the dacha an hour earlier.

'And a far more important example of a very effective use of propaganda,' conceded Charlie. 'What about my consular access?'

'I've already told you about that but it was you who made that propaganda possible; we should really make some gesture to thank you, shouldn't we?' goaded Guzov. 'I'm having the London press conference recorded for you to watch later. From what I heard in the car on my way here, you really aren't their favourite person.'

'I'm rarely anyone's favourite person.'

'Make yourself mine,' urged Guzov. 'Tell me from the very beginning everything that passed between you and Irena Yakulova, right from the moment of her anonymous telephone call to the contact number you set up at the embassy after the murder.'

Was that a guess? wondered Charlie. Or a test? The truth as much as possible, the intentional disinformation in the finest threads, Charlie reminded himself. 'She staged it brilliantly,' he began, settling in the rough wood chair.

13

WAS THIS HER CHANCE? WONDERED REBECCA STREET, AS SHE approached the Hertfordshire house: maybe, even, her last chance? Or was she misjudging this as she'd probably misjudged other ways out, too frightened of the absolute commitment. Maxim Mikhailovich Radtsic's refusal to deal with anyone but her sealed in stone the now-unconcealed enmity of Gerald Monsford. And she'd virtually disclosed to Jane Ambersom the existence of James Straughan's precious record. But none of the inferred promises of protection from Jane overcame the insurmountable fact that she identifiably featured on that snugly nestling chip that would destroy her as effectively as it destroyed Monsford if it became public. As well as further destroying the reputation of James Straughan, whose incontrovertible link to a known active FSB agent had strengthened Monsford's claim of MI6 penetration. And which she could not dismiss even though she found it difficult to conceive the man was a traitor. The overwhelming—practically automatic—likelihood was that Monsford had connived that incriminating contact, as he was conniving everything else. But . . . ? But what? Was she showing acceptable, reasonable professional caution? Or was she using Rome as an excuse to do nothing, say nothing, as she suspected Jane Ambersom believed? Twenty percent acceptable, reasonable caution against an eighty-percent excuse for remaining silent, Rebecca calculated.

The protracted, alerting security precautions at the Hertfordshire safe house gave ample time for Harry Jacobson to be waiting in his supervisor's office by the time Rebecca reached the protection compound. He remained behind his desk, not bothering to rise at her entry, the greeting restricted to a curt nod.

'London said you're moving in?' opened Jacobson.

'For a couple of days, seeing how things go,' generalized Rebecca. She noticed Jacobson's lip-concealing moustache needed trimming, like the rest of his normally more tightly clipped hair. All the wall-mounted CCTV was functioning but Rebecca couldn't see Radtsic or Elena on any of the monitors.

'I thought we were anticipating his debriefing in terms of years?'

'We are, if he tells us all we want to hear. I'm here to decide how genuine this promised co-operation is going to be.' This conversation was being televised, too, Rebecca realized, consciously stopping herself looking around for the operating camera.

'Best of luck. You're going to need all—and more—that you can get.'

Was it being recorded? Rebecca abruptly wondered, caught by Jacobson's attitude. She understood the takeover animosity but didn't imagine that later analysts would. Gesturing to the wall displays, Rebecca said, 'I can't see Radtsic or Elena?'

'It's scarcely surprising. They're walking in the grounds.'

Irritation swept through Rebecca at the man's studied disrespect. 'Being filmed, of course?'

'It's standard regulations.'

'Do they often walk in the grounds?'

'Proper exercise is also a standard regulation.'

Rebecca only just held back from the anger-flared pomposity of insubordination. Instead she said, 'Has every exercise walk been filmed, according to standard regulations, for lip-read translation and interpretation?'

Jacobson stirred at the demand, straightening slightly from how he was slumped behind the desk. 'A complete, comprehensible translation has not been possible.'

'Not from *any* of them?'

'Not according to the lip-reading specialists here.'

Rebecca let the silence build. 'Where are the films?'

Jacobson vaguely gestured to a bank of filing cabinets to his left. 'Here.'

A decisive opportunity, remembered Rebecca. 'Is the Director aware of their existence and their retention here?'

'Exercise periods are always logged in daily reports,' recited Jacobson, anxiously. 'It's—'

'Standard regulations,' cut off Rebecca, impatiently. 'I want every film you've retained here, together with their attempted deciphering, no matter how incomprehensible or incomplete, packed up today and couriered, again today, to London for forensic audio enhancement and segmented analysis by additional Russian-language lip-readers. I also want a personal memorandum, from you, with a copy to the Director, explaining why this hasn't automatically been done, according to standard regulations, since Radtsic and his wife have been here.'

'They've refused co-operation until now,' defended Jacobson, awkward in his belated concern.

'All the more reason for us to know whatever might have passed between them when they believed themselves beyond our internal cameras, which I know from watching that internally recorded footage they are very much aware of,' crushed Rebecca.

'They haven't committed a crime: you're treating them like suspects.'

'I'm treating them as they properly should be treated, people who still need to prove themselves.'

'Are you replacing me as head of this protection operation?' Jacobson's challenge was spoiled by the falter in his voice.

'Of course I'm not!' irritably rejected Rebecca, at once. 'I'm here specifically—and *only*—to begin the debriefing of Maxim Radtsic: again, hopefully, to elicit something from which we can judge the man. The day-to-day supervision and security remains your responsibility or that of anyone chosen to replace you. . . .' There was scarcely a pause as the disquieting possibility occurred. 'You must be looking forward to the change, although you weren't in Moscow that long, were you?' she tried again.

'Long enough. The Bolshoi was Moscow's only saving grace and I had

to enjoy that in its temporary premises because of all the delays rebuild-
ing their proper theatre.'

'At least you'll be spared that now.'

'Even the best of what's available in Paris won't match the Bolshoi,
even in temporary accommodation.'

The poor fool actually imagined he could trust Monsford, Rebecca
recognized. 'I suppose there isn't any reason for your hanging around
here. Why don't you raise your reassignment with the Director?'

'I will,' said Jacobson, positively.

'*After* you've done what I've asked about the exercise films,' Rebecca
qualified, heavily.

'I can do both before the day's out,' insisted the man.

'Best of luck: you'll need it,' said Rebecca, throwing the man's earlier
arrogance back at him.

They were, predictably, in the conservatory but the french windows were
fully opened onto the veranda upon which Elena had arranged her re-
clining chair. Radtsic was in his accustomed place, his liquor tray within
reach, but Rebecca couldn't see a glass in use. Elena rose to go back into
the room at Rebecca's entry but Radtsic didn't move.

Rebecca said, 'We were very glad to get your reply.'

'You gave us an undertaking we're expecting you to honour, unlike
other assurances we've been given,' said Radtsic.

'I will honour every undertaking I gave, which I expect you to match
with the co-operation we discussed,' persisted Rebecca, putting herself
opposite the man. 'Each is dependent upon the other, which is not my is-
suing an ultimatum. Moscow has to be convinced of the agreement we've
reached if they're to agree some communication between you and Andrei.'

Radtsic hesitated, as if he were about to reply, but instead he reached
into the side of his chair and brought out two folded sheets of paper, rising at last to offer both. 'You have sufficient Russian?'

'Yes,' assured Rebecca, scanning both sheets before actually reading the script. Radtsic's Cyrillic was in an open, almost childish hand, Elena's postscript by comparison in the hurried, academic scrawl, more difficult to read. Conscious of the concentration from both Russians as she read the letter, Rebecca held herself rigidly against its surprise that she was sure Radtsic expected. Rebecca said, 'We never understood that episode in Moscow when you told Jacobson, without being asked, that you knew nothing about the Lvov scheme.'

'At that time I hadn't fully decided who to go to, you or the Americans,' replied Radtsic. 'I was very uncertain who would be best: the safest. America would have had the most to offer but the CIA had exposed themselves too much to us, which they hadn't realized but would have done if I told them everything: I felt there was danger, physical danger, in approaching them. But that day with Jacobson I wasn't satisfied with how things were going. Jacobson was frightened—too frightened. I thought he was a weakness. I was actually thinking of how to approach America when I said what I did, spoke aloud what was going on in my head, which was stupid.'

Rebecca fluttered the paper. 'But here's your admission.'

Radtsic allowed a smile. 'That's what I want the Lubyanka to know I'm prepared to talk about unless they let me have my son.'

Rebecca held up a warning hand. 'Let's take this a step at a time, Maxim Mikhailovich. What do you know about Lvov?'

Radtsic's disbelieving frown came with a snort of derision. 'How can you ask me that!'

'I can ask you because so far I don't understand this conversation or what you've written in this letter. So, a step at a time. What do you know about Stepan Lvov and the long-established plan to install him as president of the Russian Federation, from which he was to manipulate a CIA who believed him to be their committed spy?'

'I was the executive director, the overseer and ultimate controller of operations of the Federalnaya Sluzhba Bezopasnosti. I was the man who approved the Lvov infiltration at its inception! What other reason is there for my being purged, as I was about to be purged? Within the FSB, I *was* the Lvov operation. Your blundering Gerald Monsford was surely able to work that out without being told!'

'There has to be a proper, sensible understanding between us, Maxim Mikhailovich,' stressed Rebecca, forward in her seat, her concentration and her intention entirely professional, nothing any longer personal. 'You've crossed to us: sought our protection, which we've provided and will continue to provide. But the arrangement isn't going to work on assumptions or surmises or working things out. You have to *tell* us, very clearly and in the closest possible detail. Are you following what I'm saying?'

'Of course I understand what you're saying!' said Radtsic, angrily. 'Don't patronize me!'

'Let you and me reach a personal agreement, here today, Maxim Mikhailovich. Let you and me undertake not to patronize or in any other way talk down or be discourteous to each other,' demanded Rebecca. 'Let's be—and behave—as we're trained to be, professionals.'

Radtsic stared steadily across at her for several moments. 'You are accusing me of being arrogant!'

'I am proposing that we behave towards each other in a way and in a manner that achieves, properly and amicably, what we're both working towards.'

For the first time Radtsic looked towards his wife, who'd come farther into the room. He said, 'I've been rebuked! Told to mend my manners and behave myself!'

Elena said nothing.

Turning back to Rebecca, Radtsic said, 'I think it would be a good working relationship to establish between the two of us.'

'I think so, too.' Rebecca smiled. Allowing the shortest of pauses, she demanded, 'You were in charge of the Lvov operation from its inception?'

'I chaired the internal operational planning committee. Irena Yakulova was a member: I brought her down with me from St Petersburg. She'd established herself as equally capable at forward planning and active field work. The actual concept, of convincing the CIA they had the eventual Russian president as an asset, was that of Irena Yakulova: I ensured she received the highest commendation, even for the idea. There was a lot of opposition. There were arguments against the amount of time it would take, the very impracticality of the whole idea, and then at the time, with the ascent of Gorbachev to power, the KGB itself—which we then still were—came under scrutiny. There were even preliminary discussions of greatly reducing its size, particularly with the dissolution of the Soviet Union into its republics.'

'You had the overview control, from the Lubyanka,' set out Rebecca, determined upon absolute detail from the outset. 'And Irena Yakulova—'

'Was the field Control,' completed Radtsic. 'I hope she knows I've come across to you, too.' There was a smile. 'I expect she's settled in more quickly than I have.'

'Jesus!' exclaimed Jane Ambersom, turning away from the concluding relay from Hertfordshire. 'How's all that going to fit in to the scheme of things! There are times, and this is one of them, when I'm not sure that I any longer know what the scheme of things is!'

'In our favour,' assessed Aubrey Smith, who'd been chairing the MI5 assessment of the committee session before the Hertfordshire interruption. 'Radtsic's Monsford's prize, certainly. But Radtsic's taken against him and says so, at each and every opportunity. And of which there's going to be a reminder at every debriefing session.'

'And at every session further alienate Monsford from Rebecca,' reflected Jane.

'Hopefully to push Rebecca more and more towards us,' agreed Smith.

'Monsford won't let it go on,' predicted Passmore. 'He'll try to get these simultaneous relays stopped: I would, if I were he. He only accepted the committee ruling in the first place to showcase his coup to as big an internal audience as possible. Now that it's soured, he'll try to block it.'

'We'd accepted, before this, that he'd done well confronting our witnesses,' reminded Smith. 'This will have wiped out any gain he might have achieved.'

'I *am* seeing a scheme of things,' Jane contradicted herself, still reflective. 'Radtsic and Irena together provide the very pinnacle of the Lvov hierarchy. We've got access—once removed, I agree, with Irena being in America, but still access—to both. We can overlay one account with the other and sift out all the half-truths and exaggerations. These are dream defections: double-dream defections.'

'Dreams from which there's going to be rude awakenings,' Passmore continued to caution. 'Monsford will try everything in the book to close off the CCTV link. And go ape-shit if he knows he's being sidelined from Irena Novikov's American debriefings, from which we've at least got some access. And Rebecca was right about the danger of assumptions. Let's not assume Radtsic's going to lay everything out on a silver salver.' The man smiled at Jane. 'Radtsic's working to his scheme of things, not ours—futile though it is for him to imagine it's going to get his son here.'

'You're right: let's not assume,' accepted Smith, realistically. 'Let's itemize and evaluate what we got today.'

'The most and very obvious has to be Radtsic identifying himself as the operational director at the Lubyanka and as such direct head of the Lvov plan of which Irena Novikov was the field Control,' set out Passmore. 'That's the one operation we believe ourselves familiar with but it would be a big mistake to let ourselves be blinded.' The ex-soldier paused for emphasis, looking between the two others. 'Operational director at the Lubyanka! Over twenty years! That's twenty years of total control and ultimate supervision of every major activity mounted against the West by the KGB and after them by the FSB. If that's true, if that's what we've potentially got access to, it's impossible even to conceive the value. It really, genuinely, is invaluable. He'll die of old age before he's able to tell us half there is to tell.'

For several minutes all three remained silent, considering the evaluation. Eventually Jane said, very quietly, 'Yes, that is the enormity of it, isn't it?'

'Which others, as well as us, will have already realized by now,' warned Passmore. 'And Gerald Monsford will have been one of them: probably the first.'

'We can't, under any circumstance, be cut out of this,' insisted Aubrey Smith. 'Nothing else really matters, not this internal war with Monsford or whatever happens with the CIA or to our people in Moscow, as well as the diplomatic fallout—all of it is inconsequential, irrelevant even. This has to be handled, judged, properly, above all professionally: everything else we've been doing properly until now becomes peripheral, needing our attention when it's appropriate, relegated for later consideration when it's not.'

'That's the philosophical argument,' acknowledged Passmore, pragmatic as always. 'What's the practical one?'

'My being the first to confront Palmer and Bland honestly to set out the incredible potential, if this is handled as it has to be,' said Smith, soberly. 'And the total, disastrous loss it will be if it isn't.'

'What happens if you fail?' asked Passmore.

'I can't fail.'

On the drive through the New Forest it had seemed a calm day but Ethel needed three windbreaks to create a protective camp against the wind-blown sand when they reached the beach at Mudeford. The sea was also too cold for Sasha, but she was contented now, proclaiming her doll had become Princess Luda for the castle she was building. Sasha was in a bathing costume but the only concession Ethel and Natalia made was to be barefooted. Two of the protection group, also dressed apart from their shoes, were slightly behind, sheltering under their own windbreaks. The rest were using the elevation of the concrete promenade to maintain their wider protective surveillance.

'Not such a good idea after all,' apologized Ethel.

'You couldn't anticipate how strong the wind would be,' said Natalia.

'I wanted to bring my daughter, for Sasha to have someone to play with: Beatrice is twelve,' said Ethel. 'They wouldn't approve it, which I didn't expect they would, but I thought it was worth a try. It would be good for Sasha to have another child to be with, occasionally.'

'She does need other children,' agreed Natalia. 'But she's settling down much better.'

'I'm pleased the bedwetting's stopped.'

'So am I. It worried me.'

'It was Jane I spoke to, about Beatrice.'

Natalia looked across at the other woman, knowing there was more.

'Irena Yakulova is co-operating with the Americans. Making some pretty extraordinary disclosures, apparently.'

'I haven't changed my mind about what passed between Charlie and her: none of it.'

'I've told Jane.'

'What did she say?'

'That she appreciated the analysis. The Americans want to compare what Irena told Charlie with what she's telling them: not just the ultimate confession, about Lvov, but everything he reported about their earlier meetings in Moscow. Their profilers think it might help assess her reliability.'

'I doubt it.' Natalia frowned. 'What's Jane want?'

Ethel smiled at the professional anticipation. 'Washington is offering to exchange something of what Irena's telling them. Jane wants your analysis of that, too.'

'How's my doing that going to help Charlie?' demanded Natalia, a reminder of her narrow, personal concentration.

'How will we know that until you do it?' Ethel shrugged.

'*Something of what Irena's telling them?*' echoed Natalia, questioningly.

'Those are the words as I heard them,' said Ethel.

'No,' accepted Natalia, as if in conversation with herself. 'The CIA will only release the minimum, to give the impression of an exchange. It'll make accuracy very difficult.'

'But you will look at what they do let us see?'

'Of course I will.'

'And we're obviously going to balance what we release against what they let us have.'

'Obviously,' acknowledged Natalia. 'What about Charlie, officially I mean?'

'We're still waiting for a response to the access request. The latest thinking is that the release of the Manchester group is a good sign.'

Natalia shook her head. 'They're not going to grant access to Charlie. They want him too much for what he did to them: what he wrecked.'

'What you're doing could change that,' encouraged Ethel. 'You're the one who'll see things from a Russian-intelligence perspective that none of our other analysts will.'

'I've already told you something about Irena Yakulova's admission to Charlie. Don't let it be forgotten.'

'I won't,' assured Ethel, looking across to the child. 'Sasha's getting cold.'

'Charlie promised to show us the English seaside,' remembered Natalia.

'Let's hope it'll be a better day when he does.'

'*If* he ever does,' qualified Natalia.

Charlie dismissed the first sound as an animal call but not the quick answering response. Charlie's fear was immediate and very real. He remained quite still, straining for more sounds, for some idea what it was, staring into the permanently dark twilight of the enclosed forest, seeing nothing, hearing nothing now. Mosquitoes gorged off his neck and face and hands, anywhere that was exposed. Were they in front or behind? He needed another noise to be sure—several more sudden noises, different from the first, to be really sure. They couldn't be behind, Charlie reasoned. Behind was more deeply into the forest, with no obvious path but the narrow, single person track that began at the dacha and which he'd found after sneaking from the rear of the building, where he'd calculated the CCTV to be the most ineffectively placed. No squad—and he was sure it would be a squad—could move unheard along what was less than a footpath, scarcely a passage at all.

The next supposed animal call was definitely human, at once confused by what very clearly was a genuine animal, a deep, guttural growl: something large, maybe a bear unexpectedly disturbed. Very positively from behind. It couldn't be a bear: something as wild and as dangerous as a bear wouldn't be allowed anywhere near the special people who had their special country houses comparatively close. Almost at once came the low-throated answer, but just as positively this time from the front.

He'd made a mistake, Charlie acknowledged, the fear spreading through him: a very stupid mistake for which he was already being mocked by the intentionally recognizable human animal sounds. Shouldn't move, he told himself. Or should he? The forest was so thick, the undergrowth and floor-covering tree brush and branches so dense that he'd be invisible just a metre off the track. But that would be hiding, attempting to escape, not simply exercising, which was his excuse: his justification. If he was right about the initial animal calls, pleading exercise against escaping would be irrelevant. Still better to stay where he was. Try to explain: to plead. What real animals made noises like those interspersing the mockery? What sort of men handled them?

Sweat was leaking from Charlie, the rivulets that coursed down his face irritating as much as the feeding insects, his shirt and the kulak smock glued to his body but he was cold: it wasn't the coldness, though, that was making him shake as he was shaking, tremors vibrating through him.

He heard the growl seconds before he identified its source, and despite the numbing shock Charlie was amazed that the animal and its handlers, and those that followed, could have got so close without his being aware of them. From the opposite direction there was a matching grunt and Charlie saw the pincering squad was in front and behind him. On an unheard cue and even more frightening, those who'd obviously been moving parallel with him on either side of the path abruptly rose into view, visibly hardly human, aliens emerging from a dark sea, from what Charlie had imagined impenetrably closed—and audibly betraying—undergrowth and tree brush.

Lights burst on, further startling Charlie, angled not to blind but perfectly to illuminate the ambush. Initially there was total silence, even from the shaggy-coated, tightly muzzled hunting dogs, a breed Charlie had never before seen or known to exist. They were huge, scarcely recognizable as dogs at all, each needing two handlers, one on either side with individual leashes. Each of the handlers was well over six feet tall but the animals stood higher than the men's waists.

Charlie guessed there were twenty in the squad, all in tightly patterned camouflage assault suits and aerial-fitted, head-enclosing helmets. The camouflage continued to their faces, streaked by black-and-green tiger stripes. Those in front and behind him on the path had strapped across their front short-barrelled, silencer-mounted automatic weapons of a type Charlie couldn't identify, holstered pistols and short-sword knives at their waists. Each had separate grenade webbing. Those still partially submerged in the forest undergrowth would be similarity armed, Charlie guessed.

Charlie cleared his throat, twice, to avoid the uncertainty sounding. 'I am permitted exercise.' His voice cracked before he got to the end.

There was laughter all around him. Both dogs lurched forward, their snarling triggered by the words, needing all their handlers to hold them in place. Charlie didn't see from whom the order came but in unison the handlers to the left of the animals snapped off their muzzles. Both dogs emitted mournful howls before lurching again towards Charlie, slavering mouths open. There was jeering laughter at Charlie's instinctive recoil and there were isolated shouts of 'let them go' and 'one at a time' and 'make him run.' Both sets of handlers staggered closer, fighting to restrain their animals.

'This is wrong. I am allowed here,' Charlie tried again, more loudly the second time, but the jeering overwhelmed his effort. 'Make him run, make him run' became a chant, picked up all around him: the dog to Charlie's left reared onto its hind legs in its snarling frenzy to get to him, its thrown-back head far above those of either of its handlers.

The shrill of a whistle startled everyone, bringing instant silence again. Charlie's house guard came from his left, easing past the intervening soldiers and showing no fear of the dog pulled marginally to one side by its handlers. Strong-voiced, the guard said, 'You're out of control!'

There were several shouts of 'fuck off' and one of 'make them both run' and an attempt to turn it into another chant but it straggled away, dying.

Putting himself directly beside Charlie, the guard looked around the encircling *spetsnaz* and said, 'The general is here, with your colonel. They know where I am: where both of us are. You are going to stay exactly as you are: re-muzzle those dogs and hold them. We are going to walk away. You are going to do nothing: not try to obstruct us.'

Charlie felt the pressure against his arm and began to move, not initially aware of his usually protesting feet actually shuffling forward, glad the guard led their way past the re-muzzled but still slavering animals. The man didn't speak until they got close to where the path widened at its approach to the dacha, where they could walk side by side. The man said, 'Those dogs kill. They're a strain of Siberian wolfhound.'

The retreat from the *spetsnaz* ambush had allowed Charlie outwardly to recover. 'How could you intervene like that?'

'It was an exercise, approved by their colonel. We weren't told until it was under way. They've done it before and it's gone wrong: people have been killed. There's little difference between them and their animals. That's how I know they're trained to kill.'

'You still took a hell of a chance.'

'Don't expect me to do it again,' said the man, nodding up to an obvious CCTV mounting. 'You're lucky I'd seen which way you'd gone.'

'I won't expect you to do it again,' assured Charlie. Because he didn't need any further confirmation, confident he'd completely evaded the camera the Russian indicated.

There was no-one at the dacha. The house guard said, 'The *spetsnaz* colonel's on his way, but I decided it wasn't a good idea to wait.'

'I'm glad you didn't,' said Charlie, sincerely. 'What about Guzov?'

'Delayed in Moscow until tomorrow.'

By what? wondered Charlie.

14

AUBREY SMITH WASN'T THE FIRST TO REACH THE EMERGENCY-committee co-chairmen. Rebecca Street was, going directly from the conservatory to Jacobson's fortunately empty office to confirm Sir Archibald Bland had seen the transmission. The Cabinet Secretary ordered her personally to bring Maxim Radtsic's letter to an immediately convened subcommittee session of MI5 and MI6, allowing her two hours for the journey from Hertfordshire. Jacobson arrived as Rebecca replaced the telephone, clearly surprised to find her there. Rebecca didn't get up from the man's chair.

'I've been on the phone from the control room, telling the Director about your debriefing.'

'He wasn't watching!'

'He's studying the replay now. I told him about Radtsic's letter.' Jacobson extended his hand. 'He wants me to take it to London tonight.'

'I've been ordered by the Cabinet Secretary to deliver it to him at a special meeting of both directors in two hours' time,' said Rebecca, not fully realizing the unintended mocking echo until she was halfway through. 'Didn't Gerald tell you one had been convened as a result of the debriefing?'

Jacobson gave up waiting for Rebecca to vacate his chair, taking the smaller one to which she'd earlier been relegated. 'No, he didn't. He wants the letter. I saw you take it with you from the conservatory.'

'Who'd you say's got more clout in the pecking order, the Director of

MI6 or the Downing Street–appointed Cabinet Secretary co-chairing an investigation into the current intelligence fiasco?'

'I'll tell the Director that Bland wants it.'

Another moment of commitment, Rebecca reminded herself. 'No. I'll ensure a copy is taken for Gerald tonight. The original has a diplomatic purpose, forlorn though we all expect that to be.'

'We can take a copy before you go,' desperately tried Jacobson.

'Diplomacy has the priority, which includes the extent of the letter's internal circulation,' refused Rebecca.

'The Director is not going to like this,' finally threatened Jacobson.

'I'll make everything very clear to him when we meet tonight,' promised Rebecca, more conscious of the permanent monitoring than Jacobson appeared to be. 'But I expect you'll have spoken to him again by then, won't you?'

Jacobson had, of course.

Gerald Monsford was moving between the annexe to the main committee chamber and its approach from the outside corridor and the ground floor below, determined to intercept Rebecca, which he did at the top of the expansive Victorian staircase, putting them in full view of Foreign Office night staff, as well as those still to respond to Bland's summons.

'What game do you think you're playing?' Monsford demanded.

'We're not involved in any game, Gerald. If I can persuade Maxim Radtsic to tell us all there is to be told, we've got the biggest intelligence coup of our lives, far bigger and more sensational than we ever imagined,' said Rebecca, calmly.

'I want his letter!'

'So does Sir Archibald Bland, to whom I'm going to give it.'

'Have you forgotten who I am!'

From any other man in any other circumstance, the arrogance would have been risible: here it seemed entirely fitting. 'Of course I haven't. Nor have I forgotten who Sir Archibald Bland is, either.' Rebecca heard footsteps mounting the stairs behind her, knowing from Monsford's fleeting expression that the newcomers were for their meeting and that Monsford hadn't wanted to be caught as he had been.

'You're through! You know that, don't you? Through!'

'We should go in,' smiled Rebecca, looking sideways at last as Jane Ambersom drew level. Aubrey Smith and John Passmore were still only halfway up the stairs.

'I'm hardly surprised it's a special meeting,' greeted Jane, although she was looking after the retreating Monsford. Sure the man was beyond hearing, she added, 'I've been waiting for your call.'

'This has intervened.' She'd done it, Rebecca thought: declared herself and made the break! She'd expected some sensation, a feeling, but at that moment there was nothing. It would come, she supposed?

'There's no reason why it should have done.'

'Radtsic's talking to me! *Only* to me. I don't want to lose that: none of us can lose that.'

Aubrey Smith and Passmore reached the first floor but didn't stop. As he passed Smith said, 'Well done.'

Jane said, 'We could still talk, you and me.'

'I've been recalled just for tonight. I'm staying—' Rebecca stopped abruptly. 'It's not convenient for us to meet at the moment.'

'Don't run away from it, Rebecca. We're going to have to talk....' Jane looked beyond, farther along the corridor. 'We're being called.'

The secretariat and support staff outnumbered those officially assembled. In addition to the two intelligence groups, the unidentified Foreign Office contingent had been reduced to four, positioned behind Bland and Palmer halfway along a much smaller oval table than that in the main room.

'We've all of us seen today's recording of Maxim Radtsic's encounter with MI6 deputy director Street. In the opinion of my co-chairman and myself, it's extremely encouraging, with a potential none of us can yet predict....' He smiled directly at Rebecca. 'And before we get into general discussion I want to place on record my congratulations for the manner in which Deputy Director Street has handled Maxim Radtsic, whom we all recognize to be an extremely difficult man. Those congratulations will be expressed as a listed commendation—'

'I would like to endorse those congratulations on behalf of MI5,' unexpectedly broke in Smith, to the visible surprise of everyone around the table.

The most obviously amazed was Gerald Monsford, whose mouth briefly worked without words before he managed, 'It was my intention to recommend such an official recognition. I obviously want to add my congratulations to those that have been expressed.'

Rebecca dipped her head in modest acceptance but continued briskly, 'This might be the moment for me to deposit with the committee the letter given to me by Radtsic, in the expectation of it being forwarded through diplomatic channels to his son, Andrei. It's an undertaking I gave him and which I think we should honour, in view of his reaction.' She acted upon the thought as it occurred to her, not handing the envelope to one of the waiting attendants but sideways to Monsford to deliver, conscious as she did so of the anger shaking through the man as he was forced to accept it.

Monsford managed to keep the emotion from his voice, though. 'You obviously have to be the official recipient, Sir Archibald, but I would welcome a copy as I'm sure my MI5 colleague also would.'

'Don't touch it!' stopped Aubrey Smith, as Bland reached out for the envelope from the now ferrying attendant. To Rebecca, Smith said, 'Have you handled the letter or just the envelope?'

Professionally recognizing the interjection, Rebecca said, 'The very outer edges of the letter, as little as possible: Radtsic handed it to me outside the envelope. I put it in. The only other prints will be Radtsic's. Elena's too, I guess: she wrote the postscript.'

'Four in total,' numbered the MI5 Director-General. 'The envelope and the letter must be forensically cleansed of every fingerprint but those of Radtsic and his wife—apart from an attendant handling—to be untraceable to FSB forensic examination, to which it will be subjected. We don't want to give the Russians the prints of the Director and deputy director of MI6, do we? Or those of the Cabinet Secretary?'

Bland nodded for the envelope to be dropped onto the blotter in front of him, continuing the gesture across the table to Smith. 'Thank you for the timely intervention.' Turning to Monsford, he said, 'Of course copies will be made, after the forensic cleaning. And the Director-General is right: we certainly don't want your fingerprints on your Lubyanka file, along with whatever else they've probably already got.'

From where she sat Rebecca saw Monsford's hands were white from the fury with which he was gripping them beneath the table.

And they stayed tightly bunched during the general discussion that followed. Geoffrey Palmer warned that to stop Radtsic carrying out his revelation threat, Moscow might make quick concessions, even producing Andrei for another televised linkup, making it essential that the maximum be extracted as quickly as possible from the Russian intelligence chief ahead of a Moscow reaction. To delay that, the letter would not be delivered for at least a week. Rebecca was to be permanently seconded to the MI6 safe house, apart from any necessary consultation recalls, and to take back to Radtsic the assurance that his letter would be personally handed to the Russian Foreign Ministry by a senior British-embassy diplomat. Radtsic's apparent change of heart both elevated and divided the remit of the emergency committee, endorsed Bland. It would continue in the manner in which it was currently functioning, with the interrogation of Radtsic proceeding in parallel, but with liaison constantly maintained beyond the simultaneous relay of the sessions between Rebecca and MI5 deputy Jane Ambersom.

Although comfortably distanced from the man, Rebecca saw Monsford now had one white-knuckled hand clamped over the other as if to restrain some physical outburst. The man's frustration was becoming facially obvious, too, a mottled redness moving up from his neck.

Taking Palmer's pause as an invitation, Aubrey Smith said, 'I think all that perfectly fits the situation. Irena Novikov's begun to talk. And we've been approached by the CIA, through their FBI conduit, for the fullest comparison exchange of what she told Charlie, in Moscow as well as here. I've agreed, on condition we get access to what she tells the Americans. It will make an even more invaluable comparison with what Radtsic might tell us.'

'Absolutely!' enthused Bland. 'This is tonight's second big step forward.'

'Do the Americans know that I've got Radtsic?' demanded Monsford, anxious to establish a footing.

'We've let it be known we've got someone valuable. Obviously there's been no names,' avoided Smith, smoothly.

'What about Natalia Fedova?' questioned Palmer, seeking further disclosure.

'Her only interest, matching ours, is doing everything she can to help Charlie Muffin,' said Smith, continuing the sanitized avoidance. 'She's studying everything that might contribute towards that. Our concentration has to be upon Radtsic and to a slightly lesser extent upon Irena Novikov. It's an unprecedented situation for us to find ourselves in.'

'I should have been more personally involved in this,' protested Monsford. 'MI6 is the communication conduit with the CIA. It was my organization that brought Radtsic out!'

'Which I totally recognize, even though it was *my* organization that brought Irena Novikov out,' responded Smith, prepared. 'The point was put to the FBI head of station here in London, who reminded us that in the immediate aftermath of the Lvov disaster it was your personal decision that MI6–CIA communications be maintained through MI5 and the FBI, to safeguard against any still-embedded Russian infiltration of the CIA compromising MI6. . . .' Smith hesitated, wanting to extend the confrontation as long as possible. 'Now, of course, with just such an infiltration investigation under way within MI6, it's unthinkable that there should be any sensitive traffic between you here in London and Washington—'

'And it's Radtsic's personal decision not to co-operate with you,' completed Bland, for the first time sharing his co-chairman's irritation.

Monsford once more had the sensation of the floor and ceiling crushing together as the walls closed in upon him. 'I have a right to be kept fully informed upon every development!'

'Every member of this committee is being kept fully informed of every development,' insisted Aubrey Smith, patiently.

Eager for some public demonstration to increase the obvious discomfort of the man who'd tried so hard to destroy her professionally, Jane slid another of her already provided cards across the table to Rebecca. 'You're going to need these numbers for us to stay in touch: always try the mobile first. It's never off.'

'You were very stupid.'

'Their colonel lectured me: called them animals when he arrived to herd them up,' said Charlie. He was anxious to resume the debriefing, wishing there hadn't been a day's interruption.

'Which I told you they were before he did,' reminded Mikhail Guzov. 'You should have believed me.'

'I do now.' Charlie still wasn't totally convinced the ambush hadn't been orchestrated but he'd sufficiently satisfied another suspicion and hadn't any intention of further woodland experiments.

'You've been very honest.'

'It wasn't an easily forgotten experience,' Charlie looked instinctively towards the footpath leading to the scene of the *spetsnaz* episode, his skin itching at the memory.

'We're finished with the *spetsnaz*,' impatiently dismissed Guzov. 'I spent yesterday reviewing everything you've so far told me. And couldn't find a single lie.'

Because there hadn't been one to find, reflected Charlie, finally coming to his recurring concern, to which he at once added the smaller question: what comparison did Guzov possess to assess his honesty? Not something to let intrude upon his far greater, all-important search for the self-made mistake that had led him for too long in the wrong direction. Which was, ironically, why he'd been so totally truthful with Mikhail Guzov: the tooth-comb examination of everything he'd said and done was not for the Russian's benefit but for his own essential hunt to find that one wrongly taken step. Charlie said, 'I'm not going to achieve much by lying, am I?'

Guzov gave his gargoyle grimace. 'Charlie Muffin, admitting defeat! That's not the profile we've compiled on you.'

The profile that Natalia had sanitized? Or a new one compiled after the first murder and all that had resulted from the uncovering of the attempted Lvov emplacement? 'It can provide the epitaph.'

'Not yet, Charlie. Not for a very long time. We stopped, the day before yesterday, with your getting to the militia investigator's offer to work behind my back.'

'Sergei Pavel was a good detective: an honest one, which should impress you, *honesty* being the new watchword.'

'He was stupid,' dismissed Guzov. 'What reason did he give for wanting to work like that?'

This might lead somewhere after all, thought Charlie. Cautiously he said, 'He told me you were determined to screw up the investigation, leaving him and me the scapegoats. He didn't want to be made a public scapegoat.'

'So he preferred to die instead.' The Russian sighed, still dismissive.

'I don't think he really imagined you'd go as far as murder.' It always had to be at Guzov's pace, the man imagining he was leading.

'We didn't,' denied Guzov, the impatience growing. 'We didn't need to kill Pavel: we could have transferred him off the case or fed you information through him he didn't know to be wrong. That was *why* he was assigned in the first place—to prove to you the sort of man he was and for us to use that honesty. What we didn't anticipate was that he'd be as straight as he turned out to be. Killing Pavel created entirely the opposite from what we wanted.'

Where could this lead? wondered Charlie, increasingly curious. 'You already told me it was the Americans.'

'Ordered—approved at least—by Ed Bundy. He told Lvov it was his idea, after it happened. If he'd told us in advance we could have stopped the idiot.'

'Why are you telling me this?' Charlie openly demanded, trying to pick his way through the contradictions, which he suspected were intentional.

'Why not? It's not as if I'm giving you anything you can use in the future: you haven't got a future, have you?'

That would have been a clever reminder of his helplessness if he hadn't taken his walks in the woods, reflected Charlie. 'I never had Bundy down as someone who couldn't make up his mind.'

'I don't understand that,' frowned the Russian.

'Something else you've told me is that Bundy was furious at the first murder: that the Lvov infiltration would have worked if Oskin's body had been dumped anywhere else but in the embassy grounds. Why attract more attention by killing Pavel?'

Guzov's frown remained. 'You're missing the entire point, Charlie: all of it! You're thinking from our point of view, the ultimate Russian intention. Bundy thought Lvov was *his* creation, *his* masterstroke: his entire CIA career was built around it. He was already landed with a sensation he didn't want, with the dumping of Oskin's body. He was thinking of *his* damage limitation by having Pavel killed. His stupidly ill-thought-out reasoning was that by killing Pavel he'd warn you off. That's what he told Lvov: that London would withdraw you and turn the whole affair over to us when we invented the story of Oskin's murder being a mafia crime. How about a trade?'

The Russian had taken long enough getting round to it, Charlie thought, caught by the abruptness: he hoped his wait was worthwhile. 'What's to trade?'

'Pavel was talking to you from a public phone when he was shot,' Guzov reminded. 'You never told me what he was telling you and there was nothing on the embassy tapes you made available to me when I officially took over.'

An uncertainty solved! Charlie at once recognized. Guzov knew he'd so far told the truth because the FSB would have recorded his every exchange with everyone over whom they had control and most definitely those with Irena Novikov when the FSB imagined they were setting him up with the false story to save Lvov. But Guzov didn't have that comparison with Pavel. Here was his first, absolutely unchallengeable opportunity to lie. But properly: professionally. Guzov had to convince himself that he was still being told the truth. 'I already told you, he didn't want to be made the scapegoat.'

'That doesn't sound like a good beginning, Charlie.'

That reaction sounded very good to Charlie. 'I don't understand.'

'I asked a very specific question.'

Keep stumbling forward towards me, thought Charlie. 'About the night he was killed?'

'You know that's what I was asking.'

Not good enough that time. 'It was the first of the intended covert calls. Bundy would have told Lvov that: there would have needed to be a lot of American surveillance.'

Guzov failed by the merest fraction to hold back the agreeing head movement. Charlie's hopes ratcheted up. 'He'd heard something, something he wasn't supposed to hear. I don't know what. I'm guessing at a conversation or part of a conversation. It wasn't clear whether it was between people in the headquarters building or on the telephone. . . .' Charlie was inventing as he talked and, as the thought came, went on, 'I don't know why, I might be completely wrong because it was never actually said, but my impression was that Pavel had overheard a conversation into which he had been wrongly plugged: an ongoing exchange he wasn't supposed to be part of. Would that have been possible with all that extra telephone equipment brought into the building for the communications centre after we appealed for public response to help identify Ivan Oskin?'

'I don't know.'

The uncertainty in the Russian's voice told Charlie that the man very definitely believed it was possible, as well as there having been calls that Pavel hadn't been intended to hear. 'And with Pavel dead, we never will.'

'There must have been something more positive—actual words—that gave an indication!' Guzov's voice was tightly controlled, each word spaced.

'Pavel wanted to meet, to work it out between us: he talked about a recovery—of the Lvov operation, maybe—but there was something wrong with dates. There was a mistake that shouldn't have been made. . . .' *Why did he invent that out of nowhere?* Charlie asked himself and for the second time resolved his own uncertainty. It hadn't come from nowhere. He was sure Natalia had talked about a mistake being made: of something being wrong. But what?

'You're sure you're clear?'

'Yes,' said Harry Jacobson.

'We're not anywhere near any voice sensors?' persisted Monsford.

'I'm on the far side of the coppice covering the command centre. It's clear of sensors.' Jacobson shivered, discomfited by the cold as well as this sudden summons.

'She's on her way back. Made me look ridiculous in front of everyone and now has the other bitch, Jane Ambersom, as a direct liaison to the committee. We've been sidelined!'

We've, picked out Jacobson, nervously. 'There's surely no way they can do anything without your being aware?'

'Of course there is,' rejected Monsford, irritably. 'They've got to be monitored.'

'We can't additionally monitor our own safe house!' exclaimed Jacobson, incredulously. 'Any unofficial electronic equipment will immediately sound an alarm. It's technically impossible.'

'I want to know how many times they meet. How friendly they appear. Try to get close, to hear something, maybe an aside they don't imagine will be picked up on a recording. Do whatever it takes to ensure we stay ahead of this.'

Gerald Monsford was becoming increasingly irrational, Jacobson decided: more serious, maybe, than irrational. Maybe, even, he'd tied himself to someone who was genuinely mentally ill.

'Monsford made an absolute mess of it,' judged John Passmore. 'He even forgot to try to close down the safe-house relay!'

'And knows he screwed up,' agreed Smith. 'We just stand back, let him go on deepening that grave we set out to help him dig.'

'Where's that leave me with Rebecca?' questioned Jane, anxious to get away from the Thames House analysis. She'd already warned Barry Elliott of a development, without telling him what it was on an open line.

'The big question,' accepted Smith. 'On the face of it, it's to our advantage, but I want us to move carefully. It goes beyond the unpredictability of Gerald Monsford. He is coming out badly at the moment, making Rebecca a potential successor. Which is how she might calculate it. I want to use her, not have her use us.'

'I wonder how frightened she is at the opportunity,' reflected Jane. 'I think I'd be scared to death.'

'She'd be stupid not to be,' agreed Passmore.

All of which, as she drove carefully back to Hertfordshire, was exactly what Rebecca Street was thinking as all the delayed doubts and hopes closed around her. She had a lot to think about, Rebecca accepted: a lot to work out.

15

THE DRINKS TRAY WAS AT HAND BUT UNTOUCHED, AND MAXIM Radtsic greeted Rebecca smiling broadly, an expression she couldn't recall from any previous film relay involving Monsford or Jacobson. Elena had moved her chair closer to her husband's accustomed place in the conservatory. She was smiling, too, and as always immaculate: today's dress was a Paris-purchased blue cashmere.

'The letter's on its way?' demanded the man.

'I personally took it to London last night,' assured Rebecca. 'By now it should be on its way to Moscow, if indeed it's not already there. It will be delivered to your Foreign Ministry by a senior diplomat from our embassy.'

'Why not by the ambassador himself?' Radtsic frowned. The aggression had gone but the arrogance was still there.

'He's on standby for whatever negotiation might arise from your letter,' replied Rebecca, smoothly. 'It's all being very carefully, properly, handled.'

'That's good,' accepted Radtsic, nodding an invitation for Elena to agree. He looked towards the drinks but didn't reach out towards then.

'Very good,' echoed the woman, dutifully.

'I'm pleased you're satisfied we've kept our side of our agreement,' prompted Rebecca.

'So today we properly begin,' accepted the Russian. 'It's going to take a very long time.'

Conscious of the preceding night's insistence upon maximizing Radtsic's disclosures in anticipation of Moscow obstruction, Rebecca risked the directness: 'You were telling me how you evolved the Lvov scheme: let's go on talking about that.'

In what Rebecca inferred to be the man's final awareness of his professional betrayal, Radtsic looked very obviously towards where he'd located a camera, holding the gaze for several moments. Elena broke her husband's concentration, tentatively half reaching out towards him: Radtsic shifted the look towards the hand still too far away for him to touch, physically shaking himself like a water-soaked animal discarding its burden.

'It was so good, so brilliant in every way. Oriental in its concept and execution: none of the do-this-day hurry of you or the CIA. It was cultivated, allowed to grow at its own pace.'

This wasn't boastfulness, an exaggerated beginning to enhance his value, Rebecca determined. Radtsic was stating a fact beyond challenge or qualification. But more to himself than to her or to unknowns beyond the watchful camera lens. Radtsic had lapsed into a reverie, in retreat maybe from his betrayal: she shouldn't try to bring him out from it, not unless the reminiscence stalled altogether. She feared it had when he didn't resume but instead remained, slumped now, seeming oblivious to his surroundings, and this time there was no outstretched hand from Elena, who stayed motionless. Rebecca did, too, deciding it was too soon to intervene. Moments stretched to positive, countable minutes. Way beyond the conservatory, at the edge of one of the far-away coppices, she got the impression of the movement of outside guards, although not a definite sighting. Rebecca hoped, anxiously, that Harry Jacobson, with whom there had been no contact since the day before, wouldn't be tempted by the frozen scene relayed on the monitor to intrude, ruining the mood. She'd give it a little longer: a minute or two.

'It was to have made me a legend.' Radtsic's oddly cracked voice suddenly came into the conservatory, close to startling the two women despite their expectation. 'There would have been medals: a commemorative plaque in the Lubyanka close to Feliks Djerzhinsky, our founder.'

She'd done the right thing remaining silent, Rebecca congratulated herself. That had to be her strategy, letting the man talk: the omissions could be memorized or picked up from the transcript to be queried later.

The coming to power of Gorbachev and Yeltsin had been a genuine revolution that no-one within the KGB had anticipated, Radtsic disclosed, head sunk in memory. The entrenched politburo waged its internecine wars and musical-chair coups, which occasionally brought about one of the familiar cosmetic name changes to the intelligence structures but in reality the government within a government apparatus had *been* the Soviet Union, the fabric holding it together: it was unimaginable that a political change could result in anything more unsettling than another renaming, which within the Lubyanka scarcely amounted to more than reprinting official stationery.

Ironically, it was the shattering reality of the Gorbachov upheaval that saved the Lvov scheme: that and its already having been sanctioned, protecting it from review because of its low-profile planning as a long-term, slow-maturing operation. And the carefully selected participants required the training that had brought them so close to such outstanding success.

Stepan Lvov had been Radtsic's personal choice, as he'd personally selected Irena Yakulova Novikov to be Lvov's permanent Control and case officer. He'd identified the potential of both from the moment of their KGB induction: he'd been the regional KGB chairman in St Petersburg, able to groom them from the beginning and bring both with him to Moscow within a month of his own executive-directorship promotion.

Rebecca was relaxed now, intent on every word but able at the same time to study Radtsic: Elena, too. Radtsic wasn't any longer worrying about the camera, seemingly still unaware of anyone else in the room. He needed frequent pauses, sometimes groping for a word and other times correcting his choice. Elena was actually leaning forward in her seat, listening so intently that Rebecca guessed that this was probably the first time in their married life that the woman had heard any details of her husband's work.

He'd considered the Lvov proposal constantly endangered throughout Gorbachev's era, continued Radtsic, particularly when the dismantling of the Soviet Union began. From the beginning, he'd shielded his operation and his protégés from postings to republics in which the KGB and later the FSB were disbanded and their officers reassigned or dismissed altogether. He'd further protected them by assigning them away from Moscow's immediate political focus or interest.

Abruptly, unexpectedly, Radtsic openly laughed but still to himself and remained smiling when he talked again of the irony that his idea had never required Lvov to emerge a star within the KGB or the FSB. It was America's CIA that Lvov had to convince that he was the most valuable intelligence asset they had ever turned into a double agent.

'It really was the greatest irony of all,' insisted the still-smiling Radtsic. 'Imagine it if you can. The Russian intelligence service, literally trawling the world through all its *rezidentura* for the suitable CIA victim gradually to be convinced that in Stepan Lvov he had the career opportunity of a lifetime. And you wouldn't believe how long it took us finally to settle upon Ed Bundy.'

Their first potential candidate was Steve Brogan, who was the CIA bureau chief in Santiago but who became more useful as a sacrifice when Brogan began trading in Chilean cocaine. His exposure seriously destabilized the Chilean government of the time through Brogan's trafficking links with two ministers as well as deeply embarrassing Washington when it became public. There were encouraging meetings and the bait of at least two genuine intelligence leaks to Luke Morpeth, the CIA deputy at Canberra, before he was medevaced back to Washington after a heart attack. A permanent assignment at Langley after his recovery ruled him out of Lvov involvement, although obviously contact had been maintained. It had been ridiculously easy sexually entrapping Josh Atkins soon after his secondment to the U.S. embassy in Helsinki and just as easy to tempt the man, again with genuine although low-level intelligence, but he was too eager to boast of CIA as well as FSB connections to his Russian seductress: his premature detection would have been inevitable. Atkins, too, had been kept on an FSB leash. There'd been more money and effort—and hope—expended on Harvey Flaxman than on any of his predecessors after the Harvard graduate's appointment as CIA station

head at the London embassy and what was judged to be his perfect suit-
ability for the role the FSB sought: Lvov was on the point of being transferred from his wait-until-called post at Russia's Rome embassy to
coincide with Flaxman's arrival in London.

'And then I made a mistake,' admitted Radtsic, the smile apologetic
now. 'Finding our CIA dupe was taking too long and I was frustrated by
the failures. I allowed the leaking of an FSB-manipulated political
change in the French government, the repercussions of which hadn't
fully been analyzed. The government fell as the result of Russian intelligence infiltration and Flaxman was moved to Brussels specifically to
head the CIA's intelligence apparatus within the European Union, with
no other function or purpose.'

Radtsic coughed, clearing his throat with difficulty, and Elena crossed
to the drinks tray to pour mineral water, which the man took with smiled
thanks.

'And at last we found Ed Bundy,' resumed Radtsic, out of his reverie
now, occasionally glancing towards the identified camera. 'He had been
suggested as a possibility when he was serving at the Ankara embassy
but left to one side because the profile was that of a man of almost robot-
like, unmotivated predictability. But after so many false starts—and a lot
of fresh profile analysis—it came to me that an automaton was *precisely*
the sort of man we were looking for. Bundy doesn't drink. He doesn't smoke.
In all the years he's been virtually under our control and manipulation—
which he's never once suspected—he's never so much as once looked at a
woman: to test him we even put the temptation in front of him and he
didn't appear to recognize what he was being offered. He's a notebook
keeper, a clock watcher and timekeeper. One of the freely available jokes
on the intelligence circuit in Ankara was that he consulted the CIA
manual before taking a shit, to ensure he wiped his ass the correct way.
The search that finally ended with Bundy took exactly eleven months,
from the time it began. At one time, after we moved in on him, I thought it
was going to take twice as long to make him ours, so regulations-constipated
was the man.'

Radtsic cleared his throat again and for several moments remained frowning as if he'd forgotten the point he'd reached. Abruptly, with another animal-like shake, Radtsic went on that by the time it was decided to target Bundy, the American had been moved to Cairo. Stepan Lvov was posted there within three months of Bundy's arrival. Irena Novikov followed a month after that.

'It really was a slow process. And I was too slow recognizing another mistake,' confessed Radtsic.

'What?' questioned Rebecca, after several silent minutes.

'Lvov and Irena,' picked up Radtsic, simply. 'It was obvious, upon reflection, so closely together were they always going to be, but an affair was a complication I didn't foresee. . . .' The Russian held up a forefinger narrowed against his thumb. 'It came that close to wrecking everything I'd worked so long to achieve. I actually . . .'

An opening door to Rebecca's left halted whatever Radtsic had intended to say. Harry Jacobson said, 'It's almost one forty-five. I thought you'd like to break for lunch?'

'A break would be good,' accepted Radtsic, at once. 'In fact I think I've talked enough for today. I'm tired. I need to think to make sure I'm not forgetting anything.'

'Of course,' accepted Rebecca, tight with anger at the interruption. 'That's quite enough for today.'

Radtsic poured his first vodka. 'It's been nostalgic, talking of the past. How is she?'

Rebecca came within a hair's breadth of a stumbled response. 'Irena's good. Settling in well.'

'She had nothing to keep her in Moscow, the operation destroyed as Stepan was destroyed by the moronic CIA.'

'I have no personal contact with her,' said Rebecca, cautiously. The CIA remark needed later analysis.

'Of course you wouldn't,' accepted the Russian. 'Would she know that I was here, in England?'

Rebecca hesitated. 'There's been no official announcement.'

'I'd like her to know that she wasn't alone: that we both got away from our own people as well as the Americans.'

Rebecca said nothing.

'But I don't suppose that's possible, is it? Letting her know, I mean.'

'No, it's not.'

'Pity.'

All the intrusion traps that Rebecca had set in her room remained in place and the white-noise transmitter to defeat telephone monitoring appeared untouched. Rebecca became the immediate focus of the five—three women and two men—still remaining in the security-quarters canteen. She responded to the tentative smiles and nods but chose a separate table at which to eat the Caesar salad she didn't really want, although she was surprised at how good it was. The burgundy was better than she'd expected, too. She was pouring her second glass when Jacobson entered. He chose a salad, too, but no wine and came directly to her table. 'Do you mind if I join you?'

Rebecca shook her head, anticipating the intended exchange more than she imagined Jacobson would by the time it finished.

The man said, 'There's no executive dining room. I expected you'd eat with the Radtsics. We could probably set something up.'

'This is okay.' Rebecca was determined not to let her anger show too early.

'Are the lights in your room okay? There were some odd readings on the control circuits last night.'

'The lights are fine. I did a security sweep when I got back from London.'

Jacobson stopped with his knife and fork suspended over his plate, and Rebecca wished he'd wipe away a spot of salad dressing on his overflowing moustache. 'You did *what*?'

'Electronically swept my room.' She decided against disclosing the white-noise protection. She intended to repeat the sweeps and intrusion traps every day to guard against his believing she'd imagine herself to be safe after just one security check. It would be a relief to take Straughan's protective recording from its present concealment for another safe hiding place, she thought in passing.

'You checked for unofficial bugs in an official MI6 safe house!' Jacobson ignored the waved farewell from one of the five diners as they left.

The man's disbelief was genuine, Rebecca judged. 'Isn't MI6 under a security investigation?'

Jacobson pushed his plate aside. 'This place is tighter than a drum. You don't need to worry.'

'Don't I, Harry?' pressed Rebecca, wanting to direct the conversation. 'There's too much uncertainty within MI6 at the moment, wouldn't you say?'

Jacobson hesitated. 'There's a lot I don't understand.'

'What *do* you understand, Harry?' seized Rebecca.

'Not enough,' avoided the man, awkwardly.

'You got written confirmation of your Paris posting yet?'

Jacobson faced her with apparent difficulty. 'I don't imagine the director's got time for that, with everything else that's going on.'

'It would have come from the personnel director, after Monsford's authorization. It's an automatic process.'

'I only had the conversation with him a day or two ago.'

'You spent some time together before you appeared before the committee.'

'Nothing was said,' admitted the man.

'You tried calling him?'

'No.'

'What about the lip-reading footage you sent for forensic examination?' Rebecca was intent on keeping him on edge.

There was another hesitation. 'I haven't heard back yet.'

'And you haven't called to check that, either?'

'They've only had it a little over twenty-four hours!'

Rebecca poured herself more wine, ignoring an empty spare glass on the table close to the man. 'I'm resuming Radtsic's debriefing at ten to-morrow. Before then, giving me time to read and assess it all, I want a complete written fact sheet setting out everything that's been transcribed, even if it's just isolated, apparently meaningless words. Because it might not be a meaningless word. It might be something absolutely essential to put to Radtsic.'

Jacobson was avoiding looking directly at her once more. 'I thought today was very good: a lot more productive than I imagined it would be.'

It was the best opening she was likely to get, Rebecca supposed. And she'd grown impatient with the man. 'I think it was going very well and could have got a great deal better if you hadn't blundered in as you did. Which is the only mistake, if mistake it genuinely was, that I'm going to allow you. Don't you dare do anything like that again as long as I am here, doing the job I'm trying to do. You step out of line just once more and you're out of here, which I'm sure the Director would be most unhappy about, but which I have the authority and certainly the official backing to make happen. And that official backing is something for you to keep very much in mind from now on. Do you hear and understand what I'm telling you, Harry?'

'I think I do.'

'I very much *hope* you do.'

By now both men fully realized—and had actually agreed—that the pro-fessional advantages to them both far outweighed the traditional antipa-thy between their two agencies, and Larry Stern didn't resent the short drive into Georgetown from the socially impractical woodland surround-ings of Langley. Mort Bering was already in the French restaurant on M Street, their table carefully isolated from others. As he lowered himself into his seat the CIA deputy director nodded his acceptance of a martini to match that already before his FBI counterpart and said, 'From what you told me on the phone, we've got reason enough to celebrate.'

'Elliott can't help much yet with a positive time frame but Radtsic's debriefing is definitely under way.' Bering smiled. 'The big unknown is how much the Brits will keep back for themselves.'

'But there's definitely going to be an exchange?' demanded Stern.

'Nothing written down, of course. But Elliott says it's one hundred percent guaranteed.'

Stern smiled back at last, touching his arriving martini against the other man's glass. 'You know what we've got! We're got a check and cross-reference on what Radtsic says against what Irena tells us. And vice versa.'

Bering shook his head, in correction. 'Far more, far better, than that. We're going to get the account of a defecting FSB deputy chairman to put against the story of the case officer of probably the FSB's *almost* perfect penetration of our country. This is better than we ever imagined.'

Stern ordered more drinks and to avoid further interruption they disinterestedly both chose steak and a side salad while the waiter was at their table.

'What about Irena's claim that the Lvov project was all her idea?' queried Bering.

Stern shrugged. 'We're going to drain her dry before we start asking who had the key to the executive washroom. You know what it's like, everyone claiming the credit for initiating the big one. We get enough from the Brits, we'll be able to judge for ourselves who thought it up in the first place.'

Bering gestured beneath the table to where he knew the unseen briefcase was tightly held between the other man's legs. 'How much have you taken out from what I'm sending to London?'

'Not a lot,' said Stern. 'Just the actual names she's given us. The less we keep back, the less, hopefully, the Brits will hold from us. But this gal is giving us a lot of worries.'

'How?'

'She fingered a guy in Yemen, a member of the Arab League we've been using and trusting for years, as an FSB plant.'

'Bad?'

'It's going to take us a long time to be sure but we've already isolated one wrong steer the son of a bitch gave us.'

Their steaks arrived and Bering hesitated for the waiter to leave before he said, 'You're right about the potential of what we've got, in total. It's important we keep it that way, tight to ourselves.'

'That's what I thought we were doing: it's certainly what I'm doing. I'm not sharing a piece of this pie with anyone.'

'I had breakfast with the Director yesterday. He started talking about a minimal task force.'

'Fuck!'

'I told him it wasn't necessary. That we had it all boxed and wrapped between us.'

'What can you do to block it if it comes up again?' queried Stern.

'Convince him we're getting everything possible, as we are, but I've warned Elliott against an approach from anyone but me.'

'I'll monitor it from my side. Nothing's going to happen without my knowing about it.'

'Something else,' said Bering, as the thought came to him. 'If Irena comes up with anything internal, here in the U.S., you won't forget jurisdiction, will you? We can't risk giving either director an excuse to move in.'

Briefly, almost imperceptibly, Stern's face clouded. 'We're doing this straight, okay? Mutual co-operation, mutual benefit, both of us happy.'

'That's the deal, both of us happy,' agreed Bering, belatedly aware he'd come close to impugning the other man's integrity. 'I'm not likely to forget it.'

'That's good to hear,' said Stern, limiting the rebuke. 'Let's neither of us forget it.'

'I've attached a specific note to the internal case files that the decision to exchange debriefings with America is entirely mine, reached without any consultation with either of you,' announced Aubrey Smith. 'If there is any subsequent enquiry—if anything backfires—you're totally uninvolved.'

'That wasn't necessary. I agree with what we're doing,' said Passmore.

'I agree, too,' said Jane Ambersom, disconcerted at the man's self-doubt at this late stage. There'd been suggestions when she'd still been at MI6 that Smith wasn't ruthless enough totally to destroy Monsford.

'It's technically a decision I've the authority to take: I'm ultimately responsible for the American liaison,' Smith pointed out. 'I'm exceeding that authority by not telling Bland or Palmer: keeping it from the enquiry committee. There's no reason for either of you to be part of it.'

'I've already alerted Natalia, through Ethel,' said Jane. 'The first of Irena's transcripts is due from Washington in tonight's diplomatic bag.'

'What about Radtsic's debriefing?' queried Passmore. Today's had been the shortest committee gathering yet, limited to an assessment of Rebecca's morning encounter with the Russian.

'Let's establish—have Natalia establish if she can—how much the Americans have edited from Irena's text,' said Smith. 'We've got more to offer than they have. I don't want to give away too much: not give away anything without getting something in return.' He turned to his deputy. 'What about Rebecca?'

'Too soon to hear,' said Jane. 'Realistically we've got to give her a couple of days.'

She stopped, waiting like Aubrey Smith while Passmore responded to his pager. 'You've got a reason for making it quicker,' said the operations direction, looking up. 'Moscow's just officially requested diplomatic access to Maxim Radtsic—'

'We can bargain for access to Charlie and all the others,' seized Jane, at once.

'I haven't finished,' warned Passmore. 'They've also asked for access to Natalia Fedova and Irena Yakulova Novikov. We know Natalia's answer already. But what are we going to do about Irena? How the hell are we going to handle that?'

16

'IS THIS A LOYALTY TEST?' UNEXPECTEDLY DEMANDED NATALIA, looking down at the helicopter-delivered dossier Ethel Jackson had put on the breakfast-room table between them. Natalia didn't attempt to pick it up.

Ethel half smiled, quizzically. 'A what?'

'All that you're asking me to do, to assess. Is it all genuine, something on which you need a judgement? Or am I being set a defector test?'

Ethel's smile broadened. 'You arrived here with pretty positive credentials as the wife of Charlie Muffin.'

'That's not an answer to my question.'

'No, Natalia,' agreed Ethel, patiently. 'Nor is this a loyalty test. What I'm asking you to look at is the transcript of an early CIA debriefing of Irena Yakulova Novikov, which we're asking you to give your professional opinion upon the extent of her co-operation. In what we're asking you to examine she's made some claims. We want you to judge those claims, if you can: tell us whether you believe they're genuine or whether she's trying to inflate her importance to negotiate a better resettlement deal—'

'With the Americans?' interrupted Natalia.

'We're liaising with the CIA.'

'How's that going to help free Charlie? That's our understanding: what I'm trying to do is find anything that'll help get Charlie out of Russia. I'm not here as a defector, needing to prove my worth. I'm here as Charlie's wife, with his child.'

'Which I already told you is how you're being treated. But there is something you should know: something I was going to tell you if we hadn't got into a loyalty discussion. Moscow has officially asked for diplomatic access to Maxim and Elena Radtsic. And to Irena Novikov, whom they believe still to be in this country.' The woman paused. 'And access to you.'

Natalia lapsed into silence, her forgotten coffee mug cupped in both hands. Finally looking up, she said, 'You know my answer.'

Ethel shook her head. 'I have to advise you of the approach.'

'You know my answer,' Natalia repeated.

'Then Moscow will be told you absolutely refuse,' said Ethel.

Gesturing to the blank-eyed television in the corner of the room, Natalia said, 'I haven't seen any official Moscow announcement of any defections.'

'There hasn't been any,' confirmed Ethel.

'That's not normal.'

'Neither is the defection of the executive deputy of the FSB. The guess is that they intend using his son to pressure Radtsic to go back.'

Natalia shook her head. 'There should have been an official announcement.'

'What's the decision going to be on the others?'

'The requests were only lodged last night, our time. I doubt they've been told: certainly not Irena, with the American time difference.'

Natalia once more looked to the American package on the separating table. 'Is Radtsic co-operating as she is?'

'I believe he is.'

'Believe?' queried Natalia. 'Don't you know?'

'No, I don't know,' replied Ethel sharply, letting her irritation finally show at the other woman's attitude. 'And I'm not seeking your help about Maxim Radtsic, not yet at least. I'm looking for your professional guidance to use to Charlie's benefit, particularly now there's likely to be diplomatic contact to learn what's physically happened to him. Which I thought you were as anxious to learn as a lot of other people who know, respect, and want to do everything they can to help him.'

Natalia became silent again, staring this time at the diplomatic package. At last, all belligerency gone, she said, 'I'm sorry. That wasn't right . . . how I've been behaving wasn't right.'

Now Ethel remained silent, not giving Natalia an easy escape, needing the pause anyway to recover from her near mistake of talking not of people who knew Charlie but of those who loved him, which Natalia might have misconstrued. Finally she said, 'Sylvia Elphick, Sasha's teacher, talked to me last night: wanted to clear something before mentioning it to you.'

'Clear what?' said Natalia, instantly attentive. Sasha had left with the woman fifteen minutes earlier. Ethel had waited until they'd left before producing the American material.

'She's seconded here because of her obvious clearance: normally she teaches children of our diplomats about to be posted overseas,' explained Ethel. 'None of the children are there for long: everything's transitory, no binding friendships, no exchange of family details. She's thought, as we both have, about Sasha being here by herself and wondered if she wouldn't benefit from going there. She thinks—'

'No!' rejected Natalia, positively. 'It's an obvious place for the Sluzhba to look: find her and trace her back here. Or just take Sasha, by herself, knowing that would be worse than killing me outright.'

'My people wouldn't consider it without carrying out every check.'

'No,' refused Natalia again, just as positively. 'It's too dangerous, whatever checks were carried out. It's not a decision that needs to be made this soon. I need Charlie here, to talk it through with him.'

'I won't mention it to London, take it forward at all,' soothed Ethel.

'What about Sylvia Elphick?' demanded Natalia. 'Has she mentioned it to anyone at the school?'

'She's got the highest security clearance. She knows better than that. And she's not at the school, is she? She's here, tutoring Sasha.'

'I want it independently screened: Sylvia Elphick screened,' insisted Natalia. 'It's the sort of simple mistake that could lead them here to Sasha and me.'

'I'll see it's done,' promised Ethel. 'And I'll talk to Sylvia myself.'

'I should do it.'

'I should,' contradicted Ethel. 'I'm the officer with the authority here.'

Natalia finally picked up the package, hefting it in her hand. 'I'm not being paranoid. This is how careful I'm always going to have to be.'

She *was* verging on paranoia, thought Ethel. She'd seen it before but this was the first time that a child had been involved. She'd have very carefully to monitor it: Natalia and the Sasha were her responsibility in every definition of that word. Had she loved Charlie? Ethel asked herself, giving way to the nagging reflection. Very much, she answered herself. Was it, in everyone's wildest dreams, conceivably possible to get him out of whatever he was going through now? No, she accepted, in another immediate answer. Which wasn't any reason at all to stop trying.

After a largely sleepless night of brief hope, quickly dashed by unusually objective examination, Gerald Monsford reluctantly acknowledged that the Russian approach wasn't his desperately sought chance to reestablish some lost presence before a tribunal he gauged clearly to be siding against him. And with it, even more hopefully, the chance to puncture Rebecca Street's over-inflated conviction that she had the authority to handle the Russian approach to Maxim Radtsic without him, which had been the dismissive message relayed through Harry Jacobson when he'd telephoned Hertfordshire. Jacobson hadn't shown the proper respect, either, trying to talk about his Paris posting instead of admitting he'd failed to establish the demanded monitoring of the woman. As always, Monsford timed his close-to-last entry into the committee room to avoid any impression of uncertain nervousness and didn't try, either, to be the first to speak after Sir Archibald Bland's formal repetition of the Russian's overnight diplomatic note. Neither, to Monsford's irritation, did Aubrey Smith. Which resulted in Bland's invitation, which Monsford momentarily didn't understand, for Jane Ambersom to respond.

'I agreed with Ms Street last night that she should immediately tell Radtsic and his wife: we know how closely Radtsic watches television news and we both decided it would have been a mistake for them to have heard of Moscow's request through an official announcement from any-one but us,' took up Jane, at once. 'She told me during our second conver-sation, less than an hour later, that Radtsic was subdued by the news, which didn't particularly surprise either of us although he would obvi-ously have expected the request. Radtsic said he wanted to think about it overnight. Ms Street's delayed her meeting with them today until after our session here. She expects Radtsic to agree. It'll be his opportunity to raise the situation of Andrei with Russian officials.'

The anger boiled through Monsford at the arrogant impudence of the two women, cutting him out of it all, as if he didn't exist! He was sure, too, they would have spoken to Bland or Palmer or maybe both, further isolating him.

'Telling Radtsic at once was the right thing for her to have done,' Palmer was saying, the praise increasing Monsford's fury. 'Diplomatically we can't oppose or obstruct any meeting. It's entirely a decision for Radtsic and his wife.'

'What about Irena Novikov?' asked Monsford, hoping to generate some criticism with which to get into the discussion. 'Aren't we diplo-matically in a difficult position, my MI5 colleagues having handed her over to the Americans without informing Moscow?'

'No,' deflated Palmer, at once. 'She officially sought sanctuary in the West and having been given the choice, chose America. The decision to tell Moscow is Washington's and only then if she requested it; whether she did or not I don't know.'

'We've obviously told Washington about Moscow's request, through their FBI liaison here,' came in Aubrey Smith. 'We don't expect to hear back until tomorrow.'

'I was thinking more of how Moscow might react at learning where she is,' struggled Monsford.

'Whatever they might do or say, it would be an empty gesture,' dismissed Smith. 'And they'd be risking our disclosing their failed CIA penetration, wouldn't they?'

He was losing again, Monsford recognized, the impression of being in a contracting box returning. 'I believe this is the opportunity and the time for us again to consider the public disclosure of Radtsic's defection. It might have been sensible to tell Radtsic ahead of a Russian announcement but at the moment of my coming here today there still hadn't been any disclosure from Moscow. But inevitably there will be: it could even be that they're planning to cause us some fresh embarrassment. I believe we should pre-empt whatever they do with our own media release that we've got the executive deputy of the Russian FSB here in Britain. . . .' He looked directly at Aubrey Smith. 'It's not now going to affect the outcome of what happens to our people they're holding. And for the first time we'd be ahead, not behind this situation. We could link it to the French episode and gain a lot of publicity advantages there, too.'

'I think there's more reason than ever for us to hold back,' disputed Smith. 'God knows what it is, but I agree Moscow's probably saying nothing at the moment for a reason. I think we should wait to discover what that reason is.'

'Leaving us again to follow, not lead.' Monsford sneered, judging himself on safe ground at last.

'I think there's an argument in favour of our getting ahead of the Russians,' said Attorney-General Sir Peter Pickering, making a rare non-legal contribution. 'After five days we've not come up with anything to counter Moscow's accusations or in any way deflect or minimize the media attacks, which is, let's not forget, the reason we've been brought together like this.'

'I know something proactive would be welcome within my section of the government,' said the unnamed head of the anonymous Foreign Office group.

'That's certainly more generally true,' supported the Cabinet Secretary. 'So much so that it's a decision that could be reached here and now, without the need for Sir Archibald and myself to consult elsewhere.'

At last! thought Monsford: he was carrying the meeting with him, overwhelming the no-longer-smirking bastards opposite. With that thought came another, how he might further restore his image, but he needed to think it fully through, ensure he'd considered all the potential pitfalls. He had only himself to depend upon now: had to think of everything, do everything, without anyone else's input. He said, 'The decision appears practically unanimous.'

'I'd like my dissent recorded,' said Smith, looking in the direction of the secretariat. 'I also want, to the point of insisting, to ensure that no reference whatsoever is made of Natalia Fedova or of her refusal to meet anyone from the Russian embassy.'

'Agreed, of course,' accepted Bland, at once.

Perfect, thought Monsford. Should he press for the Russian declaration to be announced through MI6? Leave it while he was ahead, he decided. His next move had to be with the CIA, in what Shakespeare so aptly called in terms of friendship with thine enemies.

Maxim Radtsic exchanged looks with his wife at Rebecca's announcement. Neither spoke. Recalling her earlier strategy, Rebecca remained silent, too.

Finally Radtsic said, 'Announcing my defection at this moment makes it a challenge to their demand for access.'

'There hasn't yet been a public demand,' qualified Rebecca, ready for the reaction. 'London felt when it comes there might be something derogatory towards you: something that might affect what you're hoping to achieve with Andrei.'

There was another unspoken exchange between husband and wife. Radtsic said, 'So now the people of Russia will know I am a traitor: the world will know.'

'It's your decision whether to tell the world why you chose our protection against what was going to happen to you if you remained in Russia,' countered Rebecca.

'That's what they'll call me, if I meet the diplomats: a traitor, betraying his country!' declared Radtsic, familiarly talking more to himself than to the two women.

'It's also your decision whether or not to meet them,' reminded Rebecca.

'It would have to be safe,' insisted the Russian. '*We* would have to be safe, Elena and I.'

'You will be, I can guarantee that,' assured Rebecca. She was annoyed at the Russian request coming now. It was a distraction, an entire day's interruption into what was going so well.

'Where will it be?' asked Elena.

'London. A government building,' said Rebecca, glad of Jane's briefing thirty minutes earlier.

'When could it be?' asked Radtsic.

'As soon as possible.'

'Will you be there?' pressed Radtsic.

'No. There will be two Russian-speaking lawyers.'

'That's no guarantee of safety!' dismissed Radtsic.

'Every member of the Russian contingent has to be diplomat accredited to the Russian embassy, someone known and approved by the British government.'

'There will be FSB officers among them.'

'There is a routine: an understanding,' set out Rebecca. 'Their contingent is limited to six diplomats. Is it conceivable that Moscow would risk the automatic arrest of six accredited diplomats by making any physical move against you in a room fitted with an alarm that would bring protection into the room within seconds?'

'To kill me, prevent my telling you all that I've learned and know from twenty-two years as executive director of both the KGB and the FSB, it's entirely conceivable that Moscow would sacrifice six diplomats, a dozen diplomats, whatever the repercussions.'

'Then I take it you're refusing a diplomatic meeting?' said Rebecca, hopefully. There was still time to resume yesterday's debriefing.

'No!' denied Radtsic, hurriedly. 'This can't be as the result of my letter, can it?'

'No,' agreed Rebecca, well aware the letter was still in London.

'This will be my opportunity to talk about Andrei: arrange his coming here.'

Rebecca decided there was nothing to be achieved by arguing against the man's deluded conviction that getting his son to England would be as simple as that. Elena looked quickly sideways at her husband, as if she were about to make the point, but looked away just as quickly. Rebecca spread her hands in a gesture of helplessness and said, 'Then how can a meeting be held?'

'Your prison facilities? Are the visits conducted through protective glass screens?'

'I'm not sure,' admitted Rebecca, wishing she knew the answer.

'Find out,' ordered Radtsic, peremptorily. 'I'll meet them but only inside a prison where Elena and I are on one side of a bulletproofed screen, with them on the other. There must be no way they can get to us.'

'What if your embassy won't agree to their diplomats conducting the meeting under those conditions?' anticipated Rebecca.

'I'm the executive deputy of the FSB they want to get back to Moscow,' recited Radtsic, like a mantra. 'To achieve that they'll meet me anywhere I dictate. Tell them it's a prison or no meeting. It's not negotiable.'

Maxim Radtsic must have been a bigger bastard to work for than Gerald Monsford, although for entirely different reasons, thought Rebecca. 'I'll make it very clear.'

'Soon,' insisted Radtsic. 'I want it as soon as possible: tomorrow, the day after at the latest.'

'We'll try to arrange it as soon as we can,' promised Rebecca.

'Until I've had the meeting we won't talk as we have been talking. Understood?' said Monsford.

Fuck! thought Rebecca. 'Understood,' she said.

'You watched?' anticipated Rebecca. The Hertfordshire facilities were designed for an outwardly impenetrable, inwardly electronically monitored safe house which did not require a totally isolating telephone pod within the control room. Rebecca still decided it was preferable to talk from there than from her room, where she would have had to disassemble the white-noise protection to make an audible call.

'All of it,' confirmed Jane. 'A prison's easy enough, Belmarsh is obvious, but you're right about Russian objection. The most obvious is that the visitor facilities have CCTV, to which they're sure to object.'

'Is the volume okay at your end? I'm in the control room as I was for our earlier call,' warned Rebecca. The conversations would be recorded, she knew.

'I can hear fine,' acknowledged Jane.

'His refusal to continue talking to me is a setback.'

'The Foreign Office is going to push for the day after tomorrow.'

'I don't believe in quick Russian decisions like I don't believe magic wands bringing rabbits out of a top hat, particularly after what you told me earlier about our going public with Radtsic's defection.'

'We lost our argument against doing so.'

'He isn't happy about it.'

'You think he might use that as a reason for stopping the debrief?'

'Maxim Radtsic's not someone you can second-guess about anything.'

'Until we get a decision from Moscow you're going to have some time on your hands, aren't you?' pressed Jane.

'I've got a lot of lip-reading transcription to go through.' From what she'd briefly scanned so far, Harry Jacobson had been right: what little there had been to transcribe contributed nothing.

'Won't you be coming back to London at all?'

It would be another commitment, acknowledged Rebecca: one that could totally jeopardize her succeeding Monsford if the overstuffed pig was successfully driven out of office. Or would it? Couldn't it, conducted with the finesse of the Machiavelli that Monsford boasted of being—recorded for later disclosure even, which would be truly Machiavellian—

represent completely the opposite, not the action of a betrayer but that of a loyal, guidance-seeking executive concerned at the behaviour and mental fitness of a superior? Rebecca said, 'I would certainly expect to, if only briefly. I need to be here the moment there's a positive response from Moscow.'

'Of course you have,' agreed Jane, following the other woman's lead. 'And it's my function, as your officially appointed liaison, to make sure you are. I have all your numbers.'

'I look forward to hearing from you,' said Rebecca.

'There's a recording of it all?' demanded Monsford, glad now that he'd broken away from preparing his approach to the CIA to take Harry Jacobson's call, which he'd initially refused.

'It's automatic and instant, like the film: it will already be with you,' reminded Jacobson, cautiously. He put himself at that part of the control-room tree shield where he knew there were no sound sensors to pick up his cell phone conversation.

'I meant one for me, for the proof that she's conspiring against us with the bastards across the river!' said Monsford, in an irritable mood swing.

'Jane Ambersom's her officially appointed liaison with the committee,' said Jacobson, carefully.

'For Christ's sake, stop reciting like a parrot and tell me what I want to know! Was there any indication in anything they said that they're working together against me?'

'Nothing that I can remember but I wasn't listening for anything like that!' said Jacobson, pushing the anxiety into his voice. 'Is that what you suspect?'

'It's what I damned well know to be happening. I'll listen to it here but I want you to get me my own copy. There might be something I can use.'

'Shouldn't you report what you suspect to the security investigation: it's surely relevant?'

'Leave me to decide what's relevant. I just want you to get me a copy,'

said Monsford, slamming down the telephone and turning back to the
Eyes Only e-mail with which he intended to open his personal communication with the CIA director in Langley, Virginia.

What I've copied isn't what you want to hear, mused Harry Jacobson
back in Hertfordshire, disconnecting the digital system from his cell
phone. His uncertainty now was what to do with it to guarantee his best
personal advantage.

'Enough!' declared Mikhail Guzov, slapping his hands against his knees.
'We've talked sufficiently for today.'

Charlie was glad to end the final session supposedly detailing his unrecorded conversations with the assassinated militia detective Sergei
Pavel, knowing he'd unsettled Guzov with the misinformation he'd introduced. 'I'll be able to exercise earlier than I expected.'

'It is a wonderful day,' unexpectedly enthused the Russian. 'Let's
walk together.'

'Aren't you frightened of being ambushed by special forces with mon-
ster dogs?'

'Today you're known to be with me, so we'll be quite safe from over-
sensitive dogs,' assured Guzov, giving his impression of a smile.

'If it's safe, I'd like very much to get beyond the immediate surroundings of the house,' hurried Charlie, rising to bring the Russian up with
him, not wanting the man to realize the revelation. Charlie's *spetsnaz*
remark had been a throwaway line, with no intended substance, certainly
not to get an unnecessary confirmation of the deception the Russians had
never imagined his isolating.

Having hurried the man outside, Charlie held back for Guzov to pick
the route, falling into uncomfortable parallel step to a path through the
trees.

'You appear to have had far longer conversations with Pavel than I'd
imagined,' said Guzov.

The interrogation hadn't ended, Charlie acknowledged: Guzov was obviously equipped for the conversation to be recorded as they walked. Charlie was unconcerned at the al fresco resumption, confident his carefully limited lies and misinformation were beyond challenge, despite the constant distraction of believing he was fingertip close finally to realizing his own personal misdirection. 'A lot can be said in a short time if the conversations were detailed, as ours were.'

Guzov swatted ineffectually at the inevitable mosquito attack. 'It all fits, makes sense, but at the same time I feel something is wrong.'

That had been Natalia's remark, about the Radtsic dossiers she'd been given to analyze, remembered Charlie, in his split-minded concentration: wrong but easily explained then by the dossier material being freshly copied, not duplicated from old files. 'Wrong in what way?'

'I can't pinpoint it,' admitted Guzov. 'The dates, maybe. How could that much conversation have been fitted into so little time. That's what has to be wrong, how much it's possible to fit in the time you had available.'

'You must believe me it was more than sufficient,' insisted Charlie, only just managing to finish the easy answer as the long-sought awareness engulfed him. No, Charlie refused. It had to be a mistake, another ridiculous misdirection.

'We've reached the road,' announced Guzov, beside him. 'Have you come far enough?

'More than far enough,' said Charlie, for the first time in his life regretting his elephantine mental recall.

17

THE LATE-NIGHT DISCLOSURE OF THE DEFECTION OF MAXIM Mikhailovich Radtsic, the deputy chairman of Russia's Federalnaya Sluzhba Bezopasnosti, exploded worldwide. In the time-differentiated space of twenty-four hours it not only dominated print, radio, and television media in the West but even more sensationally throughout every former communist-dominated eastern-bloc country and the Soviet republic. In America and England a number of previous Russian intelligence defectors, the majority of whose apostasy had been described as unrivalled coups for the West, emerged unanimously to declare Radtsic's loss so great that Moscow would have to rebuild totally its intelligence organizations and hugely curtail if not completely abandon its global ongoing operations for fear of exposure. Practically without exception those opinions were confirmed, again unanimously, by a matching number of former American, British, French, and Polish intelligence chiefs encouraged out of retirement for their judgement. Pages of newsprint were occupied by known or suspected intelligence operations during Radtsic's twenty-plus years of KGB and FSB power and described as a fraction of the inner secrets the man would eventually divulge. Which in turn would require complete intelligence re-evaluation and assessment by intelligence and security organizations worldwide.

The paucity of biographical information about Radtsic produced exaggeration beyond the imagination of spy writers, the most famous of whom were variously commissioned openly to fictionalize for print media the sort of man Maxim Radtsic might be. That idea was instantly copied by a variety of television organizations which scrambled into instant production fictionalized biopics which they abandoned scheduled programmes to show.

The title of master spy was universally bestowed. Radtsic's guessed age ranged between fifty and sixty-five and there was a diversity of invention between his espionage career beginning in the West—accompanied by association with believed Russian espionage successes—to his always having been a shadowy, chess-master genius evolving superlative internationally disruptive espionage plots. No authentic photograph appeared anywhere, and the rare but vague publicly recorded descriptions of Radtsic's remarkable resemblance to Stalin, some additionally suggesting a facial injury sustained on an espionage assignment, greatly hampered artists' attempts to re-create an image of the mysterious man. The most fanciful put Stalin's face on a tuxedoed James Bond body, some further enhanced by scantily clad girls in the background. There was a crop that followed the chess-master-genius fantasy and put a drawing of a scarred Stalin look-alike on a shade-wreathed Buddha-like figure. A lot just drew Stalin from various facial angles.

The connection between Radtsic and the French seizure of Elena and Andrei was logically made during that first full day, published initially in *Le Monde* and picked up or syndicated worldwide within hours. It provided sidebars to the main story and filled in a little of the biographical vacuum, although the French did not officially confirm the link or name Elena or Andrei. Nor were any photographs produced in advance of which, however, Elena was correctly described as beautiful and Andrei as darkly handsome.

There was cross-party parliamentary agreement not to pursue or question the prime minister's late-afternoon confirmation of Radtsic's presence in the United Kingdom, along with that of his wife. The emergency committee session had been postponed, pending that statement, until that night to allow practically twenty-four hours to gauge the global reaction to the defection, upon which, predictably, there was no comment from Moscow.

'Well?' questioned Aubrey Smith, as they crossed Parliament Square on their short walk to the Foreign Office building.

'A complete recovery from all the bad publicity of the past week,' judged John Passmore, objectively.

'Which also means recovery for Gerald Monsford,' Jane Ambersom pointed out, bitterly.

The requirement to stand to address the group had been abandoned at the convening session, along with the oath, but Attorney-General Sir Peter Pickering rose to adopt a courtroom lawyer's stance for his legal presentation. He had personally prepared the response to the Russian request for access to Maxim Radtsic, which had been hand delivered to the embassy that midday, along with the outright refusal of Natalia Fedova. Radtsic's acceptance demands had been very specifically set out and an extra copy kept if the committee decided it should be given to Radtsic, to prove to the man that his insistences had been fully established. In covering correspondence the requests for diplomatic meetings with all the Britons in Russian custody had been repeated, in the strongest diplomatic language considered possible, for early responses to each with the implication that any encounter with Radtsic depended upon reciprocal return agreements from Moscow: the request for physical contact with Charlie Muffin, with more immediately supplied medical details of his injuries and current condition, had headed the repeated access demands. In the hope of encouraging a Russian reaction, Radtsic's fingerprint-cleansed letter to his son had been included in the correspondence. Prior to preparing his official reply, Pickering had consulted diplomats and legal staff on the Foreign Office's Russian desk, whose general consensus was that meeting Radtsic in a British prison would be unacceptable to Moscow. The Home Office had confirmed there would be no difficulty conducting an encounter at Belmarsh prison, which had the facilities for which Radtsic had asked. Pickering had delayed acknowledging the separate Russian request to Irena Novikov, pending the decision of that night's meeting upon whether it should be raised with Washington through the MI5 conduit or officially by him to the American Justice Department. An unanticipated outcome from the public announcement of Radtsic's defection had been tentative indications from the French foreign minister that the Britons currently detained in France after Elena's interception would be freed without any official action against them.

Monsford was ready for the hiatus at Pickering's conclusion. 'I'm glad the long-overdue agreement to disclose Radtsic's presence here has been so productive. I'm further advising tonight's meeting that the secretariat have bound copies not only of every telephone conversation possibly intercepted by Straughan's illegal wiretap but also of conversations within my office over the entire recording-machine period. There are twenty-five copies, assembled by the internal investigation group. Each is security numbered for the identities of their recipients to be registered....' There was a staged hesitation, cueing the denouement: 'The potential security damage is incalculable....' He looked to the joint chairmen. 'There are sufficient copies for at least three to be made personally available to the prime minister: there are five conversations in which he identifiably features....' More directly addressing the Cabinet Secretary, Monsford smiled apologetically. 'There are sixteen recordings of conversations between you and me, Sir Archibald, all of which would require Eyes Only security classification.'

The second hiatus lasted longer than the first, finally filled by Bland's instruction for the transcripts to be distributed around the table, with five held back for Downing Street or the Cabinet Office. Caught by the pronounced sound of each slapping down upon the table, Bland lifted and let drop his copy and said, 'With the signatory registration assuring its security, I think for this to be properly assimilated it might be necessary to suspend the earlier rule against taking material from the room.'

John Passmore came up from the MI5 copy and said, 'Is an audio transcript to be made available as well?'

'Our request to the MI6 internal investigators was for a verbatim transcript, which this surely is,' frowned Geoffrey Palmer.

Aubrey Smith and Jane Ambersom were among others around the table looking curiously at the MI5 operational director.

'It certainly appears to be, with no attempt to turn the hesitations and pauses into a consecutive, coherent narrative,' acknowledged Passmore. 'But there's no indication of the lengths of the breaks, which could easily—and technically—not be those of every normal conversational interchange but an actual on-and-off interruption.'

'You've obviously overlooked the frontispiece note from the investigation team that there is no evidence of electronic tampering or unexplained intrusions on any of the recovered disks,' said Monsford, feeling the first flicker of apprehension: he'd very carefully explored the explanatory wording with Matthew Timpson specifically to avoid such a query.

'I've read that note very thoroughly, twice,' contradicted Passmore. 'It's very precise but doesn't cover what I'm talking about.'

'What, *exactly*, are you referring to?' persisted Monsford, encouraged by the curiosity still directed at the MI5 operational director.

'What I thought I'd made perfectly clear: how, transcribed like this, there is no indication whether, during a conversation either within your office or on the telephone, that conversation was interrupted by the recording facility briefly being turned off,' said Passmore, looking steadily across the intervening table at the MI6 Director.

He had directly to confront the accusation, Monsford knew, aware of the curiosity switching from the other man to him. Allowing the loud-voiced indignation, Monsford said, 'Turned off by whom?'

Passmore shrugged, as if nonplussed by the tone of the question. 'That's surely a matter for your current internal investigators.'

The bastard! thought Monsford, too late realizing the trap. 'With whom I'll raise it as soon as possible.'

'And audio copies?' pressed Aubrey Smith, understanding at last.

'We think that would be too much as well as being unnecessary,' intervened Bland, to his co-chairman's nodded agreement. 'We believe this uncertainty can be more conveniently resolved by the investigators carrying out this specific additional test.'

He'd escaped for the moment, Monsford accepted. But it was supposed to have been his triumphal recovery, not another reversal.

'*Is* there such an audio test?' asked Smith, as they walked back towards Thames House.

'I've no idea if it's scientifically possible,' admitted Passmore, smiling between the other two. 'There's usually some background sounds, however faint, if there's a pause or a hesitation in a recorded conversation: breathing at least. If a machine's turned off, it goes dead. I just punted the question to see if I could tilt Monsford off centre.'

'Which you did,' judged Jane.

'And which brings us back yet again to Rebecca,' said Smith. 'When the hell are you going to talk sense into that woman?'

'Hopefully tomorrow,' said Jane.

It was not established that they always ate together after Sasha was settled for the night and normally, when it happened, it was at Ethel's invitation, but that night the suggestion came from Natalia. Ethel always offered wine, and Natalia always refused, as she did now. She'd let Natalia lead, Ethel decided.

'I told Sylvia Elphick it was a bad idea for Sasha to go to the diplomatic school,' Natalia abruptly announced.

'I know,' said Ethel, sipping her wine. 'She told me.'

'I didn't want you to think I was disregarding your authority, going behind your back.'

'I didn't think that,' assured Ethel.

'It was important to me that you knew.'

Ethel swapped the used plates for clean and returned with the cheese, knowing they hadn't got to the reason for Natalia's dinner request. Ethel offered wine again as she refilled her own glass but Natalia once more shook her head, paring from its block slivers of cheese too small properly to eat and at once seemed embarrassed at doing it.

Abruptly again Natalia said, 'It isn't going to work, is it? Charlie, I mean. I knew, from the beginning, but I went along with it but there doesn't seem any point anymore. You're using me because I know the Russian espionage system, which I professionally understand and accept, but it's because I know it so very well that I also know they'll never let Charlie go.'

It had taken longer than Ethel had expected but because she'd anticipated that it would eventually happen she was ready, knowing it was important she deal with it honestly. 'No, I don't think they're going to let him go either: he's damaged them too badly.'

'Thank you for telling me the truth.'

'You'd have known—it would have destroyed our trust—if I hadn't.'

'Thank you, just the same.'

'What else do you want me to be honest about?' pressed Ethel, guessing there was still more.

Natalia made an uncertain gesture, pushing her uneaten cheese parings aside. 'If it weren't for Sasha I'd go back. She's always been the priority for both of us, having done what we did by getting married. The selfishness of it never came to me, not until now.'

'But you can't go back,' said Ethel, positively, wanting to halt a descent into self-pity. 'You're in a protection programme that's going to keep you safe. Nothing can ever happen, to Sasha or to you. You'll eventually be settled, wherever you want to be. You won't have Charlie, maybe. But you'll have his daughter, your daughter. That's how it's worked out.'

Natalia reached forward, pouring her own wine. 'You going to tell me it could have been far worse?'

'No,' said Ethel. 'You've got to work that out, decide that, for yourself.'

'I have to *know*!' Natalia declared, more angry than vehement. 'It'll take a lot of me away, hurt me more than I'm hurting now, but I must know what happens to him!'

Ethel hesitated, undecided whether at last to lie. Then she said, 'We'll never know that, Natalia. Whatever we're officially told, criminal charges, court hearings, things like that, won't even be the truth.'

'I love him so much!'

'Yes,' accepted Ethel, glad Natalia was too enclosed in her own emotion to be aware of hers.

'But he won't know that, will he?'

'He does. I'm sure he does. He came back to get you and Sasha out, knowing full well how badly it could go wrong, didn't he?'

'Yes, he came back,' agreed Natalia, distantly. 'Charlie never ever thought he could lose.'

Which was a belief mixed in among Charlie's far more muddled reflections, hunched in his log-cabin prison in the Moscow hills, eighteen hundred miles away. It wasn't, though, in the forefront of his mind, more a lingering self-accusation constantly pinpricking all his other more-relevant considerations, chief among them—consuming them—that he'd again, stupidly, come close to going in another wrong direction, this one more unimaginably worse than any other. Circumstantially the stomach-hollowing possibility could be made to fit all that had happened, but against every indicator that he could, circumstantially again, produce an unarguably innocent explanation.

So he still hadn't found his all-important mistake.

What then had he positively discovered? That it wasn't all over but rather that he was part of something, without the slightest idea what that something was, which came down familiarly to his accustomed role as the ass end of the pantomime horse, unable to see what was happening in front of him. Which had to be his focus, the unknown that was in front, not the unfathomable that was behind.

The one thing of which he believed he could be reasonably sure was that he wasn't eventually destined for a Siberian gulag. Which was a relief. His feet were always at their worst in the cold.

18

REBECCA STREET AMUSED HERSELF CHOOSING THE WATERSIDE Inn at Bray for their meeting. It was there that Gerald Monsford, determined to impress, had taken her the night they became lovers and she wondered if this encounter would be better: it could scarcely be worse. She even selected the same river-bordering table and was waiting when Jane Ambersom arrived, at once—and unexpectedly—smiling broadly as she crossed the Michelin-bestowed restaurant. The smile stayed as she sat.

'What?' demanded Rebecca, knowing there was a significance.

'Same place, same table. I said no.'

Rebecca laughed outright, glad of the atmosphere breaker. 'I wish I had.'

'And now?' It was far earlier, more direct, than Jane had intended but the opening was unavoidable.

'Let's order,' avoided Rebecca, the initial smile disappearing.

They both accepted that day's lobster specialty. At once trying to overcome the reservation she'd created, Jane continued their shared reminiscence, asking for Montrachet without consulting the wine list, and Rebecca's uncertain smile returned. 'Predictable bastard, isn't he?'

Taking her time now, Jane tapped the briefcase at her side and said, 'You'll have to sign an acceptance-register slip for the Moscow stuff.'

'Whose idea was it to let Radtsic see it?'

'Pickering's. What was Radtsic's reaction when you told him it was coming?'

'Snatched at the offer.'

'You think it'll change his mind about resuming the debriefing?'

Rebecca shrugged, waiting while their lobster was served. 'It depends, I suppose, if he likes all the covering material: I'm obviously going to press as hard as I can.'

'It's the best argument that could have been made on his behalf.'

'It'll be *his* opinion, not ours,' reminded Rebecca.

Rebecca was more relaxed now, Jane decided, but she'd still have to be cautious. 'There's been an incredible response, worldwide, to the defection disclosure.'

'I've watched a lot of it on television,' said Rebecca. 'So have Radtsic and Elena.'

'It was Monsford's idea to announce it publicly. He's treating it as a personal triumph.'

Rebecca was only toying with her food, seemingly more interested in her wine. 'Like I said, predictable.'

'But we might have caught him out with the disk transcripts.'

Rebecca's head came up, warily. 'How?'

She had to indicate that they knew more than they did, Jane knew, but avoid later being accused of lying. Which brought it down to presentation. 'I know now what you've got: how it was made.'

Rebecca remained slightly forward over the table but said nothing to help Jane better understand.

'He simply stopped and started the recording, editing out anything incriminating as he went along, didn't he?' pressed Jane, primed by Passmore's exchange with Monsford. 'But Jamie kept everything in full from his wiretap. That's what you've got, isn't it, Rebecca: the complete discussion and decision to assassinate Charlie?'

Rebecca still didn't respond, her face immobile.

Say something, for Christ's sake! thought Jane. 'But why, Rebecca? Radtsic was out! You didn't *need* a diversion. Why did Charlie have to be killed?'

Rebecca's head was bent reflectively again, too low for Jane properly to see her face, and Jane imagined the other woman might be crying until she looked up, dry eyed. And finally spoke. 'He never gave a proper reason, not one that made any sense. He just said it was necessary, as if he had a reason he wasn't disclosing.'

At last! thought Jane, the satisfaction moving through her; she had to keep the admission going, not give the other woman a reason suddenly to stop. 'But that's insane! Jamie—and you—must have argued against it? Asked why? Didn't Jamie ask why?'

'It didn't start out like that, not a positive discussion that led to the decision. I don't honestly remember Jamie asking why. Or asking myself. It was some time before we realized how Gerald was manipulating the recording. That was when Jamie said we had to protect ourselves: that we didn't know what Gerald was doing but that he was dangerous. Jamie was very worried, very frightened, about doing what he did. Jamie was actually permanently frightened of Gerald.'

Jane shook her head against the waiter's intrusion to remove their abandoned plates. 'Why didn't you do something when Jamie died! Why did you hold back?'

'Do what? Approach whom?' demanded the woman, defensively. 'I thought of what Jamie had done as protection but it incriminated me, as well: made me complicit. . . . It was better that I waited, to see what happened if they found Jamie's copy. And then there was the business with Vasili Okulov in Rome, which didn't make sense. There was no discussion about that and I didn't understand—thought there actually might be a mole—and by then it was too late.'

It was all nonsense, Jane thought: nothing in sequence, everything jumbled into excuses for doing nothing. Jane hadn't formed any personal opinion or feeling about the other woman but now, instantly, she did. Rebecca Street was as vainglorious a self-serving opportunist as Gerald Monsford, differing from the man only in possible mental instability. Each, Jane decided, deserved the other. Which wasn't a judgement with any bearing upon what she still had to achieve. 'But now it's not too late.'

'How can I produce it this late without being doubly incriminated?' protested Rebecca.

'You don't produce it,' argued Jane. 'I do, when you give it to me. Jamie was known to be my friend. I expected from the beginning that he'd leave something for me. The delay's easily explained away.'

'I was involved in the discussion: didn't do anything to oppose or stop it!' repeated Rebecca. 'I wouldn't be allowed to remain where I am. I could face prosecution. Certainly dismissal.'

'We'll erase your being on the disk,' improvised Jane. 'Monsford will probably claim you were present but there'll be no proof. It'll be your word against his and the proof will be against him.'

'What's the proof that Gerald stop-started his machine?' demanded Rebecca, alertly.

Shit! thought Jane. 'The blanks when the machine was turned off are detectable when it's played: there's complete silence. What you're going to give me will fill in those blanks.'

'Erasing me would also be detectable. It won't work!'

'Of course it will work!' Jane continued to improvise. 'Monsford did it himself, manually, didn't he? What you've got won't be stopped to create moments of silence. The wiping will be forensic, done by our technical people, as it's running.'

'Is that technically possible?'

She was almost there, thought Jane. 'I wouldn't have told you how it would be done if I hadn't already gone into it.'

'I'm putting my total trust in you.'

'It's your way out, home free.'

Rebecca remained motionless for a long time, head bent again. Jane had difficulty hearing when Rebecca finally mumbled, 'I want to do it.'

It would be a mistake to say anything, Jane knew: Rebecca had to think herself into doing it.

'I'm never going to put myself in a position like this again,' declared Rebecca, bringing her head up.

'I wouldn't agonize over it if I were in your position.'

'I need to go to the lavatory.'

She'd lost her: lost the chance, thought Jane, allowing the table to be cleared, automatically agreeing to coffee. She shouldn't have accused Rebecca of agonizing, even though she clearly had been: virtually crumbling into a collapse. It had been a challenging comparison, stirring a recovery. Definitely a recovery, Jane decided, watching the other woman return across the room, makeup repaired, hair freshly combed.

Rebecca sat and, unspeaking, stretched a closed hand across the table, which Jane reached out to meet and accept the tightly wrapped tissue.

Rebecca said, 'I should have washed it but I thought water might damage it.'

'I'm glad you didn't,' said Jane, guessing its concealment.

'I'd like a brandy.'

'We'll both have brandy,' determined Jane, gesturing to the waiter. Hers would probably be better used to sterilize what she had wrapped in tissue than to drink, she decided. Raising the glass, she said, 'You've made the right decision: the only decision.'

Rebecca didn't respond.

'I wouldn't touch it if I were you,' warned Jane, as John Passmore reached out towards the minuscule, unwrapped memory stick. 'She hid it internally, the centre of her universe.'

'And Monsford's, which he'll regret,' predicted Aubrey Smith. 'You did bloody well, getting her to part with it at last.'

'I've promised all evidence of her being on it will be untraceably wiped.'

'I need to check with the technical guys that it's possible to do that,' cautioned Passmore.

'Too bad if it isn't,' dismissed Jane, uncaring. 'It's ours now. And have them keep a totally complete copy before any erasing is done. I want evidence of her taking part in whatever discussions there were.'

'I'd do that anyway,' assured Passmore. 'But why do you want an additional copy?'

'She's the favourite to become the next MI6 Director, isn't she?'

'Make several copies,' ordered Aubrey Smith.

'It's far worse than I expected,' declared Natalia. 'It's worldwide ridicule, in Moscow's eyes. It could be disastrous for Charlie.'

'We've virtually made it a condition of access to Radtsic that we're allowed to see everyone held in Moscow and Charlie heads the list,' hopefully reminded Ethel. She'd officially registered Natalia's reservation to the Radtsic announcement, after warning Natalia in advance, and was glad she'd followed safe-house regulations by doing so.

'They invariably confront direct public humiliation, which is how they'll see it,' insisted Natalia, who'd sat with Ethel for a long time watching the global television round-up of the media coverage. 'Charlie's their obvious retaliation.'

Which he's always been, thought Ethel, surprised after Natalia's earlier self-flagellation that she appeared genuinely to retain any hope of Charlie's freedom. 'They had to know it was coming: expect it. And we can't use normal judgements here. We're talking of Maxim Mikhailovich Radtsic! We've got the overwhelming bargaining advantage.'

'You might get your other people back, those who don't matter, but not Charlie,' insisted Natalia.

They were on a conversational roundabout, Ethel recognized. And were anyway supposed to be discussing Natalia's assessment of Irena Novikov's American debriefing. 'Moscow haven't come up with a response yet.'

Natalia's laugh was condescending. 'How could you have forgotten what you've just said—that Moscow was expecting it. They've been ready for it—although probably not the sensationalism—within an hour of discovering Radtsic had gone and been prepared ever since, both with a public reaction and what they'd do in retaliation, although I'd guess they adjusted that after Charlie's shooting and all the deaths. Vnukovo made everything so very much easier for them. It gave them a choice.'

She had to get rid of this barrier, Ethel knew. It was technically a breach of regulations but the circumstances of Natalia's presence were as abnormal as those of Radtsic: probably even more so. 'There was something else that went to Moscow, in our reply to their access request. Radtsic wrote a personal letter to Andrei, begging him to join him and Elena, knowing the FSB would read and analyze every word and implication. One of those implications, more an open threat, was that he'd start telling us everything he knows about the organization he was at the very centre of for more than two decades.'

'Where's the threat in that?' demanded Natalia, unimpressed. 'That's what Radtsic's got to do to remain in a protection programme, isn't it?'

'He has to tell us *enough* to remain in a protection programme,' qualified Ethel, professionally. 'No-one's expecting him to disclose everything. And to stop him doing that, our reasoning is that they'll *make* Andrei come here, even though he refused in France.'

'How's that benefit Charlie?' persisted Natalia, still unimpressed.

'The same heavy implication included Charlie, heading the list of those whose release we expect in exchange,' risked Ethel.

'Is that the truth?' asked Natalia, even-voiced, looking directly at the safe-house supervisor.

'I thought we'd established honesty as the basis of our relationship,' said Ethel. Which wasn't exactly a dishonest answer upon which she could ever be challenged anyway; and she was anxious once again to get to the real purpose of today's encounter.

'I thought so, too,' said Natalia, doubtfully.

'Is Irena Novikov being honest?' seized Ethel, hurriedly.

There was a hesitation, a reluctance, to surrender the existing conversation but after several moments Natalia said, 'I need some background. How long has she been in America?'

'Five months, getting on for six.'

'And refused to co-operate in any way until just over a week ago?'

'She insisted upon a cosmetic operation to repair some burn damage to her face.'

'Which doesn't take five months.'

'There was some bargaining, apparently, at the beginning: the CIA demanding she start giving them stuff first, Irena arguing to get her face fixed first.'

'And she won?'

Ethel nodded. 'After the operation she stayed difficult until there was some pressure. I don't know precisely what that pressure was.'

'Whatever it was, it burst the dam, providing this?' queried Natalia, gesturing to the transcript on the coffee table between them. 'Have you read it?'

'Skimmed through it.'

'What's your professional assessment?'

Ethel hesitated, uncomfortable at the onus being put upon her. 'She's co-operating very fully.'

'After months of positive refusal.'

'What's your point?' pressed Ethel.

'My career's been questioning and assessing people, intelligence professionals, a number of whom we'd trapped and from whom we wanted every last thing they could tell us about every operation in which they'd ever been involved. All were trained in interrogation resistance, as Irena Novikov would have been trained. I broke every one—except Charlie—none by physical violence or threats of violence. But none collapsed, as Irena Novikov appears from these transcripts to have collapsed.'

'Are you suggesting she's lying, working a disinformation operation?'

'No!' refused Natalia, at once. 'She's giving names, events, and episodes that can be sufficiently checked from CIA sources. She'd have been caught out by now if she'd been lying.'

'What then?' demanded Ethel, curbing the exasperation at the thought of another verbal carousel.

Natalia gave an apologetic half smile. 'I don't know. Which is me being totally honest with you, instead of keeping the uncertainty to myself. What she's disclosing is the verifiable truth and the CIA must think, with every justification, that they've got an overflowing source. Which they have.'

Ethel sat unspeaking for several moments. 'I'm glad this conversation's been recorded: I wouldn't like to have paraphrased it.'

'It might help if I could compare what Radtsic's saying.'

'Which is also on the disk.'

'I'll go on trying to think it through.'

But think more, forlornly more, about Charlie, Ethel knew.

They'd sat side by side intently to read the London submission, Elena tracing the words with her forefinger, the first occasion Rebecca could remember from all the relayed films of the couple being that close since their arrival. Both eventually came up together, both smiling.

'Good,' judged Radtsic. 'Very good. This, as well as all the publicity, will get the result I want.'

'We hope so,' said Rebecca, guardedly, still trying to push from her mind her earlier decision to surrender the full recording of the assassination discussion with Monsford. 'But we don't expect it to be immediate.'

'Just days,' predicted Radtsic, with customary arrogance.

'Days during which there's no reason why we shouldn't go on talking,' urged Rebecca. 'We've been totally honest and open with you, Maxim Mikhailovich. I believe the co-operation should be reciprocated from your side, don't you?'

Radtsic's smile dimmed, but only slightly, hinting at the apologetic. 'I over-reacted to that fool, didn't I?'

What—who—the hell was he talking about? struggled Rebecca. 'I'll go along with your judgement to hear why,' she dodged, tensed for an indication.

'I never thought he'd get me out of Russia: actually told the twitching idiot that I was thinking of changing my mind to go to the Americans instead.'

Jacobson! identified Rebecca, relieved, although still not properly understanding. 'I'm glad you didn't. What about now?'

'I still think Jacobson's an idiot, but it would make me the greater idiot if we didn't go on talking, wouldn't it?'

Jacobson's ridiculous intervention, finally concluded Rebecca, relaxing. 'Yes, it would.'

'You're the first person I consider a proper intelligence professional since I've come over. We've known every MI6 officer you've put into Moscow during the past ten years practically before they've unpacked their luggage. And maintained that trace everywhere they've subsequently been posted, which has led us to even more. It's been so easy for us.'

Could they claim a similar success rate identifying FSB agents? Rebecca wondered. It was a relayed encounter and would drive Monsford into paroxysms of fury, which was a satisfying thought, one of the few she was now having. 'Thank you for the compliment.'

'Have you uncovered your hostile penetration?'

The question startled Rebecca out of any relaxation. There were too many conflicting, compounding facets to encourage a continuation without Radtsic realizing her ignorance, the most obvious of which was the potential escape it would provide Gerald Monsford. Ignorance, Rebecca determined, the word echoing in her mind: her only way forward, only way in any direction, was to let Radtsic play the puppet master. 'Are you going to help me do that?'

'So you haven't found it!'

Shit! thought Rebecca: hers had been a badly phrased question and would be all too obvious on film. 'You told us you didn't know anything about a hostile penetration.'

'Monsford's another fool, the biggest. How was he ever appointed?'

She was being outmanoeuvred—perhaps as she'd been outmanoeuvred by Jane Ambersom—too clearly reduced to the puppet role she'd assigned herself. 'We're talking co-operation, Maxim Mikhailovich. This isn't co-operation. This is playing games. Have you penetrated us?'

'Isn't that a question from a previous era, an automatic assumption that every hostile act has to emanate from Russia, the West's only adversary. You want me to make you a complete list of alternatives?'

'I want you to answer my direct question with a direct answer,' persisted Rebecca. 'Has MI6 been penetrated, either by the KGB, their FSB successors, or any other intelligence organization that would feature on the list you've just offered me?'

'I told your ineffectual director that I knew nothing whatsoever about any penetration.' Radtsic smiled.

'What are you telling me?'

'That I, personally, know nothing about a penetration of your service. Which I would have done, had there been a KGB or FSB success,' replied Radtsic, pedantically. 'But that is not to say there hasn't been one by another intelligence service. And if there has, I wouldn't expect your current director to have a chance in hell of uncovering it.'

Edwin Birkitt was the best at what he did because he had a regimented, train-line-straight mind and what he'd been ordered to do now was a derailment he didn't like. It should have been someone else's job, a more senior responsibility, which meant it was shit-dodging time and he didn't know from which direction to duck. Birkitt politely stood, as he always did, at Irena Novikov's entry, waiting until she was settled before he resumed his seat and said, again part of their ritual, 'How are you today?'

'It's more important you tell me how you and your English brothers are today,' Irena threw back. 'You all must be feeling pretty damned pleased with yourselves at the entire world knowing who you've bagged. Who ever would have thought the executive chairman of the FSB would cross the great divide? And to such worldwide acclaim!'

He'd been overruled, ordered to allow Irena Novikov unfettered access to television, just as his protests against that day's instructions had been dismissed, and Birkitt hoped that the later analysis would show both to be bad decisions without associating him with the mistakes. 'Some of the assessments are that it will wreck your entire organization: that it'll have to be restructured from top to bottom.'

'Never underestimate the Russian resilience.'

'I never have. Nor ever will,' assured Birkitt.

'Makes what I've offered irrelevant against what he's likely to disclose.'

'It doesn't make you—or what you can tell me—irrelevant at all,' contradicted Birkitt, immediately alert to the tense in which she'd phrased her remark. 'And I know that you know it, too.'

Irena shrugged, stretched back in her chair. 'You're going to have to beg and plead with the Brits to give you the crumbs, aren't you? And that's all they will give you, the stalest of crumbs.'

There was no point in any longer postponing what he had to do, giving her more opportunity for the filmed mockery. 'There's been a request from Moscow, for diplomatic access.'

Irena straightened, actually coming forward. 'Request to whom?'

Bitch! thought Birkitt, disconcerted by her prescience. 'Passed on to us from England. It's part of the diplomatic procedure that you have to be advised, which is what I'm now doing. And for you to tell us if you wish that access to be granted.' He sounded like a message-delivering clerk, he thought, miserably.

'Whoa!' smirked the woman. 'It's not part of any diplomatic process that I tell you anything. I wasn't asked whether I wanted to come here to America. I was thrown on a CIA plane by a bunch of assholes that I'd made look stupid and who are probably now stacking shelves in a 7/11. And after that, threatened by you with a lifetime of solitary confinement if I didn't co-operate. You know what I think? I think when I tell that to people from my embassy here—who I very definitely want to meet, as soon as possible—that they'll say I was kidnapped and questioned under duress, with which I'll agree and testify to. And the great U.S. of A. will be looking at a diplomatic incident that'll risk making public how very, very easy it was for me to make the CIA look a total bunch of amateurs over a very, very long period. How do you think that'll play in Des Moines, Ed?'

Birkitt hoped the diatribe had given him the time to devise a response. 'You're a self-admitted espionage agent and architect of an operation to infiltrate the very heart of the American administration. Under American law we've got every right to hold you and subject you to whatever interrogation we consider necessary.'

Irena shrugged again, the smirk still in place. 'I didn't admit to you being the architect of anything, Ed. What positive legal justification do you have for holding me as you're doing? That's something I'll need to talk about in very close detail to the embassy lawyers, too. But I don't think there's anything more for you and me to talk about, do you? I think we're through, Ed. All done.'

He'd known it wasn't going to be easy but he hadn't imagined it was going to be as bad as this, reflected Birkitt.

Charlie hadn't been aware of the changeover, which he thought he should have been—there would have been at least one vehicle, coming and going—and was unsettled at not being prepared. His new guard was a squat, swarthy man, Georgian maybe. The housekeeper was equally short and Charlie guessed she was heavier than the man by at least fourteen pounds.

'Good to see new faces,' lied Charlie, at the surprise breakfast encounter.

The man looked at him, unsmiling, not bothering to reply as he turned back towards the kitchen.

'You going to take as good care of me as my last guardian angel?' persisted Charlie.

The man halted at the door. 'I wouldn't have stopped the dogs getting to you. And won't if you try any more shit like that with me. So don't.'

The FSB variation on good cop, bad cop, gauged Charlie. 'What time's General Guzov getting here today?'

The guard continued on, again not replying. Charlie knew that Guzov's unexplained absence the day before, like the silent guard changeover, was all part of an intended disorientation process and because he recognized it he shouldn't have been as affected as he was, which was irritating. Because he'd had time to assess it, he further recognized that being incarcerated in the silent dacha deep in the middle of the silent forest—isolated from any certainty, almost from reality—was another part of the process. The technique was to make him psychologically dependent upon Guzov, anxious for the man's visits, even more anxious to ingratiate himself by telling the man whatever he wanted to know. They'd believe it was working, from his question a few minutes earlier. He'd have to be careful that it wasn't.

19

TO PREVENT HIS PRESENCE IN DOWNING STREET BEING PHOTO-
graphed by the permanent media posse, Aubrey Smith reached Sir
Archibald Bland's Cabinet Office in its rear annexe along the smallest of
subterranean corridors from the Foreign Office. There was an instant
impression of déjà vu as he entered the suite at the unexpected disorder
of Bland's desk, overflowed bookshelves all around it and an aged and
scuffed leather desk chair in which the shirtsleeved, collar-loosened man
sat. Geoffrey Palmer, also in shirtsleeves, was in a matching ancient
armchair that threatened to engulf him, completing Smith's nostalgic
recollection of the rarefied gentility of his former university existence
abandoned for the opposite extreme of government-sanctioned criminal-
ity up to and including assassination.

'I'm still concerned this contravenes the remit under which the committee was convened,' at once protested Bland. 'We hope whatever it is
you're going to tell us is as sensitive as you indicated on the telephone.'

Deniable responsibility for any mistaken decision, Smith recognized:
it was a credo with which he had to replace appreciation of after-dinner
port at High Table and esoteric disagreements about the wisdom of Plato
and Pliny. 'If you're unsatisfied that it is, I'll repeat it all before the full
committee later,' replied Smith. There'd be no recording devices here, he
was sure.

'Which we've postponed, as you requested,' said Palmer, struggling
forward from the depths in which he was submerged.

Smith took his time extracting the disk player from his overfilled briefcase, glad he'd anticipated Palmer's presence and brought sufficiently marked copies of the Monsford transcripts. He didn't hurry, either, handing them to both civil-servant mandarins or, after that, locating a power source, remaining by it as he turned back to the two men.

'What you've got in front of you are specifically marked extracts from what Gerald Monsford claims to be accurate and complete copies from the recording apparatus installed in his office by James Straughan. Those facilities automatically register the time and date of every conversation. At today's full-committee session will be produced the audio examination of those office disks. That examination will identify gaps where the manually operated system was stopped and restarted exactly where I've indicated on what you're now looking at. . . .'

Both men were bent forward now, their concentration divided between what Smith was saying and the documentation in front of them.

Gesturing to the disk player, Smith went on, 'What I'm going to play to you fills in those gaps. They irrefutably show that Gerald Monsford ordered the assassination of Charlie Muffin *after* the successful Moscow extraction of Maxim Radtsic. That murder, fortunately, failed. But the attempt brought about the carnage at Vnukovo Airport and the international catastrophe we're now trying to minimize. It also indicates the supposed hostile infiltration of MI6 to be a fabrication made easy by the deaths of their two officers in Moscow and that of James Straughan here in England to conceal Gerald Monsford's culpability in attempted murder. Gerald Monsford is dangerously, mentally unstable, someone who should be restrained as a risk to national security. Legal but closed court provisions for such restraint exist under the provisions of the Official Secrets Act.'

Both mandarins sat momentarily speechless, Palmer actually with his mouth slightly open, at the equivalent of a megaton charge imploding in the middle of their bombproof lives. Before either recovered sufficiently for words, Smith activated the machine beside him and said, 'We start with the marked blank on the first of your pages. It's timed and dated three days before Radtsic's successful extraction. Monsford is

responding to Straughan's warning from Harry Jacobson in Moscow that
Radtsic is arrogant and talking of telephoning Elena, in Paris, about his
intended defection.'

MONSFORD: *Tell him he's got to spell out to Radtsic the risk to which he's
putting himself: putting everyone, his wife and son most of all.*

STRAUGHAN: *There's something else. I've made it very clear to Jacobson
that Charlie Muffin's assassination, as a diversion, is aborted: that everything's cancelled.*

MONSFORD: *We intended using Charlie Muffin's killing as a diversion
for Radtsic's extraction. Muffin was never going to leave Moscow and neither were his wife and child.*

Smith paused the disk. 'The next marked section, on your second selected page, comes at the point when Monsford is insisting that there had
to have been a leak to enable the French to intercept Elena and Andrei on
their way here from Paris. You'll note it's timed and dated the day Radtsic
arrived in London.'

MONSFORD: *What about Charlie Muffin?*

STRAUGHAN: *He was always the unknown decoy, the diversion. He didn't
know anything.*

MONSFORD: *He's a double: tricked us all. He's gone over to the Russians!*

STRAUGHAN: *Charlie Muffin didn't know anything about Radtsic: if he
had—and has gone over—the first thing he'd surely have done was stop
Radtsic defecting.*

MONSFORD: *Charlie Muffin has to have had something to do with this!'*

'Your third marked section follows Charlie Muffin's contact with the
British embassy in Moscow with the refusal to deal with the three MI6
officers—the dead Stephan Briddle, and Robert Denning and Jeremy
Beckindale, both currently in custody,' guided Smith, pressing the Re-
start button.

STRAUGHAN: *What do we do about our three in Moscow?*

MONSFORD: *They stay. Now Muffin's crawled out from beneath the stone
he's been under, I want to be his shadow: every time he farts, I want to hear it.
I'm not having the Radtsic coup taken away from me by Charlie Muffin....*

'I'm pausing the disk intentionally here, although it's a continuing narrative,' said Smith. 'I want you to take particular note of it because of remarks I'm going to make later.'

STRAUGHAN: *I've nominally appointed Briddle our field supervisor of our three. Do you have any specific instructions?*

MONSFORD: *Tell him to call me at ten promptly tomorrow, his time. I'll take the call personally.*

'These are the relevant sections I consider most important today,' concluded the Director-General. 'There is a much wider selection of conversations and discussion between both men on these and other disks. We've subjected all these deleted extracts to extensive voice-print tests. The two speakers are unquestionably James Straughan and Gerald Monsford.'

He'd crossed the Rubicon from which he had for too long held back, accepted Smith, until now acknowledging the lies and deceits of others but wrongly, stupidly, clinging to what he'd considered some personal integrity by not lying and deceiving and cheating himself. And by so doing come so very close to being destroyed first by his overly ambitious deputy Jeffrey Smale and this time by a mentally deranged Gerald Monsford. Disappointingly, still hoping some integrity remained, Smith didn't feel any guilt: there was no satisfaction, either.

Geoffrey Palmer finally recovered, pulling himself fully out of the armchair for a more upright seat closer to Bland's desk, seemingly discomfited at finding himself without a jacket. Prompting a response from his partner, Palmer said, 'We need Sir Peter Pickering's legal advice.'

'And further, independent proof, damning though this is,' obliged Bland.

'We'll have to suspend the committee until it's resolved,' proposed Palmer.

'Unquestionably, but we won't make it official, not yet,' agreed the Cabinet Secretary.

Tweedledum and Tweedledee, undecided what to do about the Mad Hatter, thought Smith, bemused by the two men who appeared to have forgotten his presence in their back-protecting double act. 'I'd like to pick up my earlier remark about believing there's some importance in the last section I played to you, which might, in fact, go some way towards finding further, independent evidence of what I believe to be Monsford's guilt. Throughout the whole selection, Harry Jacobson features heavily. He certainly knew about the planned assassination of Charlie Muffin, which he denied before the committee. I believe the final extract to which I drew attention indicates that Stephan Briddle, with whom Monsford insisted upon dealing personally, had been ordered to take over the killing of Charlie Muffin from Harry Jacobson, which would explain Briddle's inexplicable Vnukovo attack.'

'He should certainly be re-examined,' said Bland, blinking as he brought his attention back to the MI5 Director-General.

'Without warning,' cautioned Smith. 'He'd inevitably query a recall with Monsford.'

'There's surely no grounds yet for arresting him?' questioned Palmer.

'Timpson's investigators have the authority to bring him back to London,' said Smith, glad of the midnight preparations after the copy of James Straughan's bugging had been analyzed and all trace of Rebecca Street erased. 'It doesn't officially constitute arrest but Jacobson won't know that: it might encourage the man into telling the truth. And there's something else he could help us with. He was MI6 station chief in Moscow. According to my deputy, who as you know was recently transferred from there, MI6 do not hold Russian weapons in their Moscow *rezidentura*. Which begs the question of where Stephan Briddle got the Makarov pistol clearly visible in his hand in the Russian CCTV footage. Again according to my deputy, any weapon shipped in a diplomatic bag needs the counter-signed authority of the director. It's not accepted for shipment without it. There isn't, apparently, a back-up register upon which proof of authority would be listed.'

'But a shipment log is maintained at the Foreign Office,' insisted Palmer, making the first positive contribution.

'Which would constitute further independent evidence if there was such an authorization in Monsford's name, wouldn't it,' suggested Smith.

'There's something you haven't told us,' suddenly challenged Bland, quizzically. 'How did you come to be in possession of this material?'

His most vulnerable point, Smith conceded. 'Straughan became a friend as well as a colleague of my deputy, Jane Ambersom, during her tenure at MI6. She lives in a mansion block which has in its lobby individual letter boxes for each occupant. She found the memory thumb, holding everything you've heard—obviously copied from the original disk recording—in her box yesterday. It had been hand delivered, not posted. We've forensically examined the packaging, of course. There are no fingerprints or evidence of source. The address was composed of letters cut from the previous day's copy of *The Times*.'

Both men stared steadily at him for several moments. Aubrey Smith stared steadily back, believing neither would question further for fear of an answer making them complicit, unable to deny their knowledge of the unknowable, the function for which they'd been appointed by their contentedly innocent political superiors.

Finally, Bland said, 'We'll expect you on standby throughout today. And your deputy, as well.'

'Of course.'

'And we thank you for bringing this to our attention,' said Palmer.

Officially, that other essential mantra—the meeting had never happened—Smith accepted, making his way back along the underground corridor. He didn't believe the feeling he was finally experiencing to be either guilt or satisfaction: it had, he supposed, at last to be apprehension, which was better than nothing.

'Does it mean I'll confront the bastard in court?' demanded Jane Ambersom immediately after Aubrey Smith finished his account of the Downing Street encounter.

'I don't know,' admitted Smith, discomfited at the prospect of questioning from a qualified lawyer even in a closed court. 'There should be some indication sometime today.'

'I'd like a court hearing,' savoured Jane.

'I'd imagine it would require evidence being given under oath, whatever the security restrictions,' said Passmore.

'I'll have no problem with that,' said the woman at once, looking towards the Director-General.

'We'll hear more later today,' avoided Smith.

'We've got another potential difficulty,' declared Passmore. 'There's been an overnight decision from the American Justice Department about diplomatic access to Irena Novikov.'

'Legally, under their asylum and witnesses'-protection legislation, Irena can justifiably claim kidnap,' came in Jane. 'She wasn't offered and therefore didn't sign a formal protection application.'

'That's bullshit,' dismissed Smith. 'After what she admitted—boasted—of doing, they can surely hold her on criminal charges.'

'Admitted and boasted to us—to Charlie—which is inadmissible in an American court because it wasn't made under their protective self-incriminating Miranda legislation,' rejected Passmore.

'What about us?' queried Smith, head to one side. 'Didn't she formally, properly, ask us for defector protection?'

'Which is Washington's argument,' confirmed Passmore. 'They're terrified they'll get burned again as they were by the Lvov business, only this time publicly. They want to ship her back here, to where the kidnap accusation won't stick and to which the access application was officially made.'

'Abandoning her completely?' questioned Smith, doubtfully.

'With their people discreetly in the background of the access meeting as well as during any further interrogations.'

'What's our guaranteed return going to be?' demanded Smith, pragmatically.

'Ours to demand,' said Passmore.

'We should certainly insist on getting all the film and audio of Irena's U.S. interrogation up to now,' said Jane. 'Natalia's unsure about the transcripts, without being able to pinpoint the reason, and thinks seeing and hearing might help.'

'I want a CIA commitment beyond that,' insisted Aubrey Smith.

'So we take Irena back?' pressed Passmore.

'And use her,' agreed Smith. 'We'll play her and Radtsic off against each other, see what that produces.'

Hopefully no more uncertainty and confusion, thought Jane, curious at the decisiveness she detected in Aubrey Smith.

Charlie tried to subdue the feeling, recognizing it as unneeded confirmation of his reliance upon the other man, but couldn't fully prevent the relief at Mikhail Guzov's reappearance.

'Missed me?' greeted the Russian, carefully straightening the trouser crease of his grey flannel suit as he seated himself.

'Desperately,' Charlie mocked back. 'No letters, no flowers, no chocolates.'

'But you had the peace and tranquillity of your surroundings,' Guzov came back.

The man was operating with some psychological guidance, Charlie accepted. 'Just the sort of convalescence I needed.'

'With the guarantee of so much more to come.'

That wasn't true, Charlie knew. So why had he let himself mentally sink as low as he had? The refused conclusion about the mistakes he'd made? No reason to give up, to allow the self-erosion as he had. The quickness and comparative ease with which he'd been manipulated was worrying. No it wasn't, refused Charlie at once, with his usual self-honesty. It would be worrying if it were his professionalism at fault, which it had been but only minimally. What he was really suffering was hurt pride at allowing it to happen at all, so confident—perhaps *arrogant* was a better word—had he always been that he could resist capture and incarceration for months, years even.

'There's a lot happening in the world of which you're no longer a part,' continued Guzov.

The man was hurrying whatever psychological guidance he'd been getting, judged Charlie. 'Which I'm sure you want to tell me.'

'Your people are making fools of themselves again, publicly boasting about defections, which we don't believe are legal.'

'That's what Irena Yakulova did,' insisted Charlie, curious where the lead would take them. 'I actually witnessed her request for protection: watched as she signed it.'

'To what sort of duress was she subjected?'

'There was no duress. I've told you that already, several times.'

'And expected us to believe it!'

Us, isolated Charlie: this was a conversation for a much wider audience. But for what purpose? 'You'd be making a mistake not to believe it. It's you who'd look foolish if London produced Irena Yakulova's signed application, together with the film of her making it. My recollection is of her laughing and joking, which certainly isn't the behaviour of someone under pressure or threat.'

'We'll see what she's got to say about that,' said Guzov.

Diplomatic access, Charlie realized: and he was helping them prepare for it! Or was he? A more logical interpretation was that Guzov had been trying out the duress accusation, which he'd denied them by disclosing that Irena Yakulova had been filmed smiling and relaxed as she signed the officially required documentation. And if he had succeeded in doing that, the Russians would have to evolve a new strategy. Testing in return, Charlie said, 'Ask whoever gets to see Irena to give her my love, will you?' and knew from the quick stiffening of Guzov's face that he'd scored.

'You're never again going to be in a position to send your love to anyone,' said Guzov, petulantly, and Charlie decided he'd won the entire exchange, as well. It was a better feeling than the others that had been eroding his reasoning over the past few days.

20

THERE WERE, OF COURSE, THE INEVITABLE AND INCREASINGLY hysterical diatribes of denial, but apart from that Gerald Monsford's professional as well as final mental demise seemed to those most directly responsible for it to be a disappointing anticlimax. Aubrey Smith and Jane Ambersom were summoned, with unintended symbolism, to the Whitehall building from which King Charles I had been publicly beheaded in 1649. The verdict upon Monsford was returned much less publicly in an anonymously furnished but uncomfortably large, ground-floor room that Smith thought similar to Sir Archibald Bland's office earlier that day, with the marked exception that all the books were neatly ordered behind their glassed, floor-to-ceiling cases, none of the furniture, although genuinely old, scuffed, and with a dividing, although not raised, judicial-style bench at one end. Behind it sat Sir Archibald Bland and Geoffrey Palmer, both now jacketed, Attorney-General Sir Peter Pickering, and two unnamed although identifiable Supreme Court judges. The persistently objecting Monsford was flanked by two Supreme Court lawyers. Two stenographers were supported by two sound technicians supervising a back-up recording system and there were four separate electronic and sound technicians to operate the complete record of Monsford's audio systems produced earlier by Smith from James Straughan's copies. Smith unhesitatingly testified under oath to their anonymous discovery. Harry Jacobson predictably crumbled at the moment of his detention by Matthew Timpson's officers and babbled in unprompted detail Monsford's specific orders to assassinate Charlie Muffin and remained unshakable under questioning from Monsford's counsel, both of whom were constantly hampered and interrupted by Monsford. One of the electronic experts produced technical proof of Monsford's voice on Jacobson's mobile-phone recording of his Hertfordshire safe-house instructions to spy upon Rebecca Street. The television image of Stephan Briddle clearly carrying a Russian Makarov pistol as he ran towards Charlie Muffin at Vnukovo Airport was shown prior to the production of the Foreign Office copy, with Monsford's signature authorizing the diplomatic shipment of the weapon.

Monsford's hysteria mounted with the tangible evidence against him. He repeatedly denounced the judicial hearing as a Star Chamber, which Aubrey Smith considered justified, and with increasing, rambling desperation rejected the undeniable evidence of his lying, murderous manipulation as, instead, further proof of James Straughan's double-agent spying.

Monsford's degeneration into complete breakdown came when he was invited to address the tribunal, which he did for the first time no longer hysterically but in a mannered, calm voice. He reiterated the Star Chamber denunciation with the additional insistence that Bland and Palmer were part of the MI6 infiltrating conspiracy attempting to conceal Straughan's espionage, in which all his other accusers were involved.

'Controlled not by Straughan—that was always the cover only I saw through from the beginning—but by *him*,' Monsford insisted, pointing a wavering finger at Aubrey Smith. 'I tried to prevent it, replace him with Jeffrey Smale, through whom I could have ensured both services remained safe, but it was too late: they were too well entrenched. But Smith hasn't won. I'll still bring all you traitors down, when this nonsense is over, and all the rest of you will go down with him. Straughan knew that: knew I'd discovered what was happening and was going to smash your entire cell. That's why he killed himself, knowing I was onto him, like I was onto Charlie Muffin and stopped him, too—'

'I think it is all over,' interrupted Sir Archibald Bland, completing his gesture to the already moving Matthew Timpson. 'This examination is over. . . .' To Timpson, he said, 'Help him to where he has to go.'

'A car,' said Monsford, unresistingly accepting Timpson's hand cupping his arm. 'I need a car right away. It's very important.' He stopped abruptly at the door, turning back into the room. 'Shakespeare talked of people like you—"O villains, vipers, damn'd without redemption." And I'll see that you are. You're finished, all of you."

'You know what frightens me?' asked Jane Ambersom, rhetorically. 'Apart from the ranting, to anyone who didn't know, he would have looked and sounded totally sane.' As had become their custom, they were walking back to Thames House.

'I hadn't realized how bad he really was,' said Aubrey Smith, somberly. 'I didn't expect him to be led away as docilely as he was, either.'

'He actually did want to run both services, didn't he? And probably would have managed it if he'd manoeuvred Smale into your job.' Which was prevented only by Charlie Muffin's entrapment of Irena Novikov, Jane remembered.

'It wouldn't have been the first time a man got into power without a lot of supposedly sane people recognizing he was mad.'

'What are we left with now?' wondered Jane.

'God knows,' said Smith, with an uncertainty that wasn't to last long that day.

It actually took ninety minutes.

Moscow's response to the public announcement of Maxim Radtsic's defection was timed precisely for that evening's main television and radio news bulletins to dwarf the worldwide sensation of London's disclosure, which it did over the following twenty-four hours. The officially issued news-agency statement was preceded by simultaneous declarations of its importance on all Moscow's main TV and radio channels. Interspersed with carefully selected and edited segments from the television link-up between Radtsic in England and Elena and Andrei in France, every anchorperson announced that General Maxim Mikhailovich Radtsic, a senior member of Russian state security, had not defected, as the United Kingdom claimed, but been criminally kidnapped by its intelligence agencies. Moscow had until now refrained from public disclosure while unsuccessful attempts were made for an explanation and to achieve a resolution. Radtsic's wife had involved herself in those efforts, continuing on to England to plead for her husband's freedom despite her attempted seizure by British agents being prevented by French authorities. She was now being held with her husband.

In perfect unison, the Moscow television screens switched to a picture of a haggard and dishevelled Andrei Radtsic, with identical voice-over introductions of a personal plea to the British government. His father's seizure and his mother's detention were illegal, insisted Andrei, his nervously shaking hands washing one over the other as he spoke. Their release was being argued politically: his appeal was personal. At this point, the wavering voice cracked and Andrei visibly began to cry, his voice still clear behind the handkerchief he hurriedly scrubbed across his face. His father was a sick man, suffering hypertension and high cholesterol. His inexplicable seizure was potentially life threatening; if he died, the British government would be responsible. The picture faded to the studios and anchor presenters who concluded that urgent demands had been made for diplomatic access to Radtsic and his wife.

Within an hour of the duplicated news-agency release, the Russian ambassador to London delivered to the Foreign Office a formal acceptance of all the conditions insisted upon by Radtsic for such an encounter.

'Bastards!' exploded the Russian the moment Rebecca Street entered the conservatory. 'Did you see what they did? Parading Andrei. Total fucking bastards!'

'They've got him in custody: not treating him well,' said Elena, more controlled. 'I knew that's what they'd do, make him suffer because of what we've done.'

'They've agreed to every access demand,' disclosed Rebecca. 'I've just had the call from London.' Where she should have been, witnessing Monsford's destruction. She had to get to London as soon as possible to see Bland or Palmer: certainly not try to arrange a meeting through Jane Ambersom.

'When?'

'That's what we've got to discuss.'

'I already told you,' said the Russian, his voice over-loud, 'As soon as possible. Tomorrow. I can't wait to get to the bastards!'

'Don't let everything collapse, as it did during the television linkup,' warned Rebecca.

'They're never going to let Andrei go, are they?' said Elena, more to herself than to the two others. 'We've lost him.'

'I'll not give way to temper, not this time,' insisted Radtsic, calming. 'And I will get Andrei back. I've got too much, know too much. And I'll let them know what I'm going to do with it if they don't give me back Andrei.'

'It's too late now to arrange anything for tomorrow,' said Rebecca. 'But I'll have it set up as soon as possible: certainly this week.'

'It *must* be this week!'

'It will be,' assured Rebecca, wondering how someone with the obvious intellectual composure of Elena came to be married to such a boorish bully. Which led her mind obviously back to Gerald Monsford. God, how much she would like to have been there, watching him fall apart! 'There's something else from the broadcast. You didn't tell us about hypertension or cholesterol.'

Radtsic waved a dismissive hand. 'It's nothing.'

'What about medication?'

'I told you it's nothing.'

'We'd like to bring forward the scheduled medical examination.'

'After the meeting with the embassy people,' insisted Radtsic.

'The medical examination can be tomorrow. The diplomatic meeting can't. Everything will be brought here for eleven tomorrow. And after that we could resume our talks.'

Radtsic's face hardened but just as quickly softened into a surprising smile. 'I would have enjoyed having you work for me.'

Which she wouldn't have enjoyed for a moment, Rebecca knew, remembering at once Radtsic's ambiguous reaction the last time the question had been put and deciding to risk it again. 'Did any of my colleagues ever work for you?'

The smile faded. 'Your past traitors are well documented, aren't they?'

'I'm asking about those who aren't yet documented.'

'That's an indication I'm holding back for the bastards treating Andrei as they are.'

'Moscow's beaten us again, sucked us up and blown us out in bubbles,' admitted Jane Ambersom. 'Everyone's running around in circles accusing everyone else of wrong decisions and judgements without the slightest idea how to make one that doesn't blow up in our faces.'

'I'm sorry it's got to be rushed like this,' apologized Barry Elliott. They were eating early, in their Mount Street favourite: he needed to be back in the embassy in conveniently close Grovesnor Square by eight to co-ordinate the arrival of Irena Novikov. 'And for all the shit you guys appear to be getting, too.'

'At the moment we're missing most of it, but it's overwhelmed our success in nailing Monsford and his infiltration nonsense. But it's made us the focus for all answers now that the emergency committee has been disbanded and Monsford isn't involved any longer.'

'Radtsic's access meeting is surely your opportunity?'

'That's diplomatically sacrosanct. We touch that, we set a precedent for Christ knows what in the future.'

'Moscow's statement talks of seeking access,' reminded Elliott. 'You sure it isn't going to be their next shit-dumping trick?'

'No,' conceded Jane, resigned. 'I don't have any idea what the hell their next trick is going to be, just that there's going to be one.'

'I wish I could contribute,' said Elliott, sincerely.

Jane shrugged. 'I'll go back to the flat while you're at the embassy, shall I?'

'Tonight, yes, but we might need to be a little more circumspect for a while.'

Jane's chill was immediate, like ice water thrown into her face. 'Why's that?'

'The Bureau's deputy, Mort Bering, is coming in on tonight's plane with Irena. And staying until at least after her access meeting. Everything will be the same, apart from the sleepovers.'

'Is that all it is, Bering being here?'

Elliott frowned. 'What's that mean?'

Idiot! screamed through Jane's head: why'd she said it, shown her insecurity to be so close to the surface! She had to go on, smooth it down. 'Everything's so good, with us I mean.'

'You're being silly.'

I know! 'I don't mean to be.'

'You have no cause to doubt me in any way. That's what *I* mean.'

'So you don't want me to pack my things when I go back tonight?'

'No, I don't want you to pack your things. And I won't want you to go on being unsure anymore, either.'

Why was it difficult to believe anything any longer? wondered Jane, relieved.

21

THE EMERGENCY COMMITTEE WASN'T TOTALLY DISBANDED BUT greatly reduced. The remaining inner core was made up of the two government mandarins, Sir Peter Pickering with a scaled-down support staff of two and the MI5 three. The secretariat remained the same but the venue was switched to the annexe previously utilized for refreshments no longer judged necessary. An amplified sound system wasn't required, either. The opening session was chaired by Geoffrey Palmer, at whose invitation the attorney-general disclosed that no legal action was to be taken against Harry Jacobson. He was being dismissed under a provision of the Official Secrets Act that amounted to what in open criminal court would be a suspended sentence. As in such sentencing, the relevant Secrets Act section enabled Jacobson's immediate arrest and in camera prosecution if he made any media approach or took any action whatsoever to attract public awareness. There was to be a period of surveillance to guard against that eventuality.

'This would seem to be the appropriate moment to raise another MI6 situation,' came in Jane Ambersom. 'As her liaison to this committee, I've told Rebecca Street the result of yesterday's hearing. She made the point that as MI6's official deputy director, she should be present at these reduced sessions, as well as returning to Vauxhall Cross, which is now without effective headquarters leadership.'

'She called me this morning, making the same point,' said Sir Archibald Bland.

'She's established a rapport with Radtsic,' Pickering pointed out.

'Which was my first thought during our conversation,' said Bland. 'It's a situation that has to be resolved.'

'I don't think we should risk the relationship she appears to have established with Radtsic by assigning another interrogator,' argued Palmer, unnecessarily confirming Aubrey Smith's belief of a prior discussion between the co-chairmen, glad he had forbidden in advance any contribution other than that already made by Jane. He responded blankly to the expectant looks from both civil servants.

'Surely MI6 can't remain rudderless, after all that's happened,' Pickering finally said. 'There should at least be some temporary arrangement.'

'Which you are more than adequately qualified to fulfil, having once been MI6 deputy,' Palmer was forced to say, directly addressing Jane. 'A great deal has already been made of your previous experience in that position.'

'Which is a perfect illustration of how invaluable Jane is to me in a number of other matters,' said Smith, choosing his moment. 'She's the established liaison here with the FBI, who last night flew in Irena Novikov. She was—and still remains, I presume—our conduit with Rebecca Street's dealings with Radtsic and she's also monitoring Natalia Fedova's analysis of what the Novikov woman has so far told the Americans.'

'We're not suggesting more than a token presence, until a proper situation can be re-established at Vauxhall Cross,' assured Bland.

'A guaranteed, strictly limited, *temporary* assignment?' pressed Smith, heavily, determined not to be out of step with two expert exponents of the diplomatic soft-shoe shuffle.

There was a pause, each mandarin waiting for the other to make the commitment.

'Absolutely,' Palmer eventually promised.

Smith turned at last to Jane. 'Yours is the final choice.'

'Guaranteed to be a strictly limited, temporary position?' echoed Jane, as distrustful as the Director-General.

'That's the undertaking,' agreed Bland.

'I also think it important that the appointment, with all its qualifications, is made clear to Rebecca Street when you return her call,' said Jane.

'Is that what this back-and-forth nonsense is all about, assuaging someone's delicate feelings!' demanded a too obviously offended Palmer.

'We're still in the middle of a monumental crisis we don't know how to get out of, instigated by a man—admittedly mentally unwell from every indication—harbouring a promotional grudge,' reminded Aubrey Smith. 'It's reasonable for Rebecca Street, who's not mentally unwell, to believe she's Monsford's logical successor but whose current function is too important for that promotion to be considered. With how much dedication and determination do you imagine she'll perform that function if she thinks she's been passed over for something she believes to be rightfully hers?'

'Aren't you overlooking professionalism?' demanded Palmer, stiffly.

'Not for a moment,' rejected Smith. 'Nor am I overlooking human nature.'

'I will make the situation quite clear to her,' undertook Bland. 'It's by no means automatic, of course, that the directorship will be offered to her.'

'It might be better *not* to include that in what you make quite clear to her,' said Smith.

'You could probably get the permanent appointment if you wanted it,' said Aubrey Smith, when they returned to Thames House.

'I told you before this morning's charade that I don't want it. I'm happy where I am. If I could I wouldn't even move offices.'

'But that would defeat the point,' said Smith. 'You think you can handle everything else, as well?'

'Maybe we could share Irena? I'll stay with Natalia's analysis but you could help with the questioning.'

'That's a good idea,' agreed Smith at once. 'I've assigned Joe Goody.'

'I'm sorry now that I agreed to share,' joked Jane.

'There'll still be the films.'

'The comparison with America will be interesting.'

'Apart from the physical separation of different buildings, we'll be working together as closely as we have been doing up until now.'

Jane laughed, unexpectedly. 'Do you realize you're in the position that Monsford tried to get for himself, spanning both services?'

'Let's hope I make a better job of it than he did.' Which so far, after a late start, he believed himself to be doing.

'I'm too jetlagged for anything: I just want to rest,' immediately announced Irena Novikov, making an instant assessment of the man's timid entry into the library of the house to which she'd been brought the preceding night. 'And I'm not here to be interrogated. I'm here to meet diplomats from my embassy.'

'I always suffer badly from jetlag myself, ma'am,' sympathized Joe Goody. He was a plump, balding, overwhelmingly polite man whose interrogation technique had been perfected during fifteen year's service as a psychologist in Britain's SAS Special Forces.

Irena sniggered at being addressed as ma'am, which in Russian is a term of particular deference. 'Where am I?'

'Quite safe. You're not in any danger, ma'am.'

'I meant what part of England. I came here in the dark, in a closed van.'

'In the south: the whereabouts wouldn't mean anything to you. It's very nice at this time of the year. A lot of flowers are in season. Do you like flowers, ma'am?'

She sniggered again, bemused. Curious at what his reaction might be, she said, 'I couldn't give a shit about flowers.'

'Such a pity, ma'am,' responded Goody, without the disapproving shock she'd expected. 'We could have walked together in the grounds. A former owner was a horticulturalist of some renown. Why don't you sit in the window recess from where the beds can be seen to particular advantage?'

Irena shrugged, content for the man to amuse her, taking the seat he indicated and looking out at the patchwork displays, which really were spectacular if a little too regimented by their different-colour arrangement.

'Would you mind if I sat with you, ma'am?' asked Goody, already lowering himself into a matching chair at the other side of the window bay. 'I particularly like the hyacinths, don't you? That blue merging into purple is quite magnificent, isn't it?'

Irena looked back into the room, smiling. 'Who or what *are* you?'

'Did you get on well with Edwin Birkitt? Such an amenable man, I've always thought.'

'Ah!' acknowledged Irena. 'Don't waste your time. I told you I'm tired and I'm not talking about anything until I've met my embassy people.'

'Probably best, ma'am,' agreed the man, solicitously. 'What you'd have always been trained to do, not knowing what else we have to challenge you. I don't believe there's been a proper response to the access request to you yet. The plastic surgery is very good, isn't it, ma'am? You must be very pleased how it turned out.'

Irena's hand went instinctively towards her repaired face before she became aware of the gesture and she felt stupid, stopping halfway before dropping it back into her lap. 'It's okay.'

'Our surgeons think it's very good, from the pictures they've seen and the talks they've had with the Americans. But they're curious about the original scarring being caused from brandy flambé blown into your face when you were with Stepan Lvov. That's how you told Charlie you got the injury, wasn't it, ma'am?'

Irena began to concentrate, which she hadn't been bothering to do until now. 'That's how it happened.'

'Our surgeons thought a flambé burn wouldn't have caused such original damage. In their opinion it looked more like a petrol burn.'

Irena shrugged, to cover her unease. 'It was caused by too much brandy being added to a flambé pan. I'm very glad it's been removed so well.'

'Oh you would be, ma'am,' again agreed Goody, as if worried at having caused offence. 'And we're arranging for it to be checked, along with the other medical examination.'

'What medical examination?' demanded Irena, irritably. 'I don't need a medical examination: won't have one!'

'It's part of the asylum, the defection, process. Maxim Mikhailovich is undergoing his tomorrow. So's his wife. He's asked after you, incidentally.'

Irena was confused by the man's disjointed, jumbled way of talking. 'I'm not part of any defection process! What did Maxim Mikhailovich say? Is he unwell? Has something happened to him?'

'You went through our defection-protection procedure when you got here with Charlie. We've an obligation to look after you now, ma'am.'

'I didn't know then that I was going to be offered to America, like a sacrifice!'

'Oh dear, ma'am, that must have been most distressing. I can so easily understand you're upset. But now you're back here, safe as I told you earlier.'

'It makes no difference that I'm back here: things might have changed.' Why was this fucking man, with his mixed-up sentences, annoying her so much! He couldn't know: none of them could know.

'Oh but it does, ma'am. We didn't know the full extent to which you'd insinuated Stepan Lvov into the CIA's confidence until you told us. There's some discrepancies there, incidentally: easily explained, I'm sure. But there are things we should talk about, when you're not so jetlagged.'

'What discrepancies! Let's talk about them now!'

'That would be unthinkable, ma'am. You must rest. Maxim Mikhailovich's embassy encounter is coming first.'

'You told me he asked about me. What did he say?'

'I shouldn't really have told you that and now it's on record.' Goody gestured generally around the room to unseen cameras and microphones. 'I'll probably be reprimanded. Are you quite comfortable here? Is there anything you want?'

I want some idea of what you're talking about, thought Irena. 'When's my meeting with the embassy?'

'I'm really not sure at what stage the negotiations are, your being in America. Maybe I could make an enquiry from someone about how it works.'

'There's no maybe about it: it's established practice. What I want is you to find out and let me know, today!'

'Oh I don't think I'll be able to get around to that today, ma'am.'

'Stop fucking me about! I want to know when I'm meeting diplomats from the Russian embassy!'

'You've been very helpful, ma'am.' Goody smiled.

Irena's mouth was a tight line, refusing to say or do anything, her hands gripped together in her lap.

Still smiling, Goody said, 'Thank you very much, ma'am. I'm going to enjoy our conversations.'

Jane Ambersom didn't think of which office she'd occupy until she got to Vauxhall Cross, realizing as she entered to a welcome-back greeting from the front-hall security officers that with her old office now officially that of Rebecca Street, she would have to use Gerald Monsford's suite. Knowing that Monsford had been detained at the conclusion of the Official Secrets hearing, she'd expected it to be in the haphazard disarray in which the man customarily worked. Instead it was immaculate to the point of clinical sterility, the neatness at once drawing her attention to the personally addressed envelope on the pristine desk.

The memo from Matthew Timpson guaranteed that the office and all its ancillary rooms, including the directly adjoining apartment, was completely free from illicit listening devices. The manually operated recording facility James Straughan had installed had been removed, along with the illegal secondary system Straughan had attached. All Monsford's personal affects, including clothes from the apartment, had been removed. Timpson did not foresee any further need for contact between them but assumed Jane knew the procedure if she had any outstanding queries. Beside the envelope were labelled keys to every drawer, cabinet, and cupboard in the suite.

Monsford's personally designed wingback chair had been comfortably big for him, making it physically impossible for Jane to occupy: she couldn't reach either arm if she sat in its centre, and if she leaned against the back the seat was too big for her to bend her legs, which protruded uncomfortably straight out in front of her. Despite Timpson's assurances, Jane filled the time waiting for its replacement by a standard office chair by carefully working her way through every key on the itemized list, seeking one overlooked snippet left by its former occupant. There was nothing: no drawers or closets had so much as lining paper, and the blotter and jotting pads and pens and even toilet rolls were still sealed in their wrappers. The refrigerator was empty, its freezer ice trays unfilled.

There was no trace of Gerald Monsford ever having existed.

Jane's search was broken by the electronic entry request from the chief of staff, who came echoing the earlier welcome-back greeting of the vestibule security.

'Temporary,' contradicted Jane. 'Only very temporary.'

Aubrey Smith intentionally let his concentration switch between the relayed confrontation with Irena Novikov and the two FBI men with him in the purpose-built control barracks set apart from the main house, which was on the edge of the Sussex Downs, close to Petworth. Mort Bering was the most visibly perplexed, constantly frowning sideways for guidance from Barry Elliott, who answered the bewilderment with matching disbelief. It was Elliott who asked the expected question before the end of Joe Goody's initial session.

'Is this guy for real!'

'Very real.' Smith smiled back. 'He's the best I've got.'

'He's like a . . .' groped the deputy FBI director, 'like an English butler. No! An under-servant from a bad movie.'

'Would you believe he was once seconded, at *their* request, to your Green Berets from our SAS?'

'No,' refused Mort Bering. 'I don't believe it. And I won't believe it.'

'He didn't learn diddly-squat: got nothing,' judged Elliott.

'Wouldn't that be a little too much to expect from a first debriefing?'

rhetorically asked Smith. He'd never before met Elliott and was more intently studying the younger American than his older superior, curious at the relationship with Jane Ambersom, hoping that it was genuine, not professionally motivated.

The entry demand took them to the TV monitor showing Joe Goody waiting tentatively outside, not looking directly at the camera he knew to be upon him. He entered hesitantly and addressed both Americans as sir when he was introduced.

'Well?' demanded Smith.

'Something's not right,' declared the psychologist, at once. 'I don't know what it is yet. She's frightened, but not in the way she should be. For someone who did what she did—created the Lvov infiltration but then destroyed it when Charlie confronted her—she's too anxious to see people from her embassy.' He smiled, shyly, towards Bering and Elliott. 'And she thinks I'm stupid but she's not sure. It won't take long to convince her she's right: that she can take advantage of me.'

Just over a hundred miles to the north, Natalia Fedova finished watching all the American filmed recordings of Irena Novikov's questioning in one single, uninterrupted session, just in time to read a bedtime story to Sasha, whom she'd left for the first time for an entire day in Ethel Jackson's care. Ethel had wine poured by the time Natalia returned from the child's bedroom.

'Was it a good idea to do it all in one go?' asked Ethel.

'It was exactly what I needed to do,' said Natalia.

'And?'

'It confirmed what I thought from the flat transcripts. It's wrong.'

'How?'

'That's what I can't work out.'

22

JANE AMBERSOM DID NOT FULLY APPRECIATE THAT ALTHOUGH IT was only a temporary secondment she was now officially responsible for Maxim Radtsic. And that without Straughan, whose function it would have been, that responsibility extended beyond the already organized medical examination to the half-prepared Russian-embassy encounter in Belmarsh Prison. She summoned the formal Foreign Office contingent and while she waited for their arrival went through the travel arrangements with the logistics director, whose authority she formally extended to cover what would have been Straughan's function. She repeated the rehearsal when the diplomats arrived, omitting the complete details of the television and audio monitoring that would operate throughout and the total surveillance to be placed upon the Russian group. Finally she introduced, under their covert operational names, the two MI6 officers who were to make up the British presence.

It was only then that Jane Ambersom called Rebecca Street in Hertfordshire.

'How'd the medical go?' asked Jane.

'Routine,' replied the other woman, dismissively. 'His blood pressure was about five above what they'd like for a man of Radtsic's age but the feeling is that's most likely caused by the understandable stress he's under. All the other immediate checks are fine. We'll get the cholesterol and all the other blood-test results in two or three days. The Russian reference to poor health was obviously a lie.'

'So he's ready for this afternoon?'

'Has been for the last hour, refusing lunch and demanding to know when the transport's arriving.'

'The helicopter is leaving Northolt at noon, ETA with you 1320, arrival at the helipad at 1420. The Foreign Office group, with our two officers, will already be there. They'll get to the prison, with Radtsic and Elena, using the underground access. You're not involved, obviously: we're guessing the FSB with the Russian group will have miniaturized cameras. Radtsic will be brought out the same way. The helicopter will wait, to take you back to Hertfordshire. I'll copy all—'

'How do you know the safe house is in Hertfordshire?' broke in Rebecca.

'You know I'm operating out of Vauxhall Cross,' said Jane.

'No, I don't know,' said Rebecca, flatly.

Shit! thought Jane, awareness settling. 'You're totally committed with Radtsic. Monsford's gone. There needed to be someone at the top here. My being that person is temporary. I refused to accept the secondment without that being completely understood and accepted by Bland and Palmer. You should have been told yesterday by one or the other of them.'

There was no response from the other end.

'Rebecca?'

'I wasn't told.'

'They gave Aubrey Smith and myself separate undertakings that they'd explain everything to you: Bland told us you'd already spoken to him.'

'It must have been quite an extensive conversation in my absence.'

Jane ground her teeth in exasperation. 'Harry Jacobson is being dismissed, under restrictions, so you'll need a supervisor replacement up there.'

'Immediately.'

'I'll organize it today.'

'Try not to forget, like Bland and Palmer.'

'Rebecca, I'm genuinely sorry you weren't told, as it was arranged that you should have been. But I don't want your job, which you obviously consider automatically to be yours. It *will* automatically be if you drain Radtsic of everything he's got to tell us. So let's get professional, shall we?'

'You'll copy me on everything that comes out of the Belmarsh meeting, of course?'

'Of course.' She was right not to like this woman, Jane decided. 'We'll speak when you get back from Belmarsh.'

'Perhaps by then you'll be able to tell me who Jacobson's replacement will be.'

Jane put down the telephone without responding.

The military helicopter took a circuitous route, touching down at Mildenhall air base to justify the filed flight plan before going farther east out over the North Sea to approach London from that direction, finally to land precisely at 1420. Throughout, Radtsic and Elena were linked to the communal voice channel but neither spoke. Nor did Rebecca, churning with impotent, wordless fury at how amateurishly easy she had been outmanoeuvred. It was now so blatantly obvious that the bitch had all along worked not just to get back to Vauxhall Cross but into the Director's chair. Rebecca had only just regained her composure when they landed, thinking rationally, objectively, and totally without any self-confusing anger. So resolved was she, in fact, that Rebecca was actually smiling when she followed the two Russians from the droop-rotored machine.

The British party were already waiting, as Jane had promised. There were no named introductions. At the indication to move off through the underground labyrinth designed to protect the anonymity and safety of those entering and leaving Britain's s highest-security prison, Radtsic turned to the unmoving Rebecca and said, 'You are not coming?'

'I'll be waiting here when you come out.'

'Of course. Stupid of me.'

The corridor was sufficiently wide for four people easily to move abreast, although Radtsic and his wife were an isolated two within the group, walking hand in hand. The bright lighting reflected harshly off the white-tiled floor and walls, forcing them to squint. Telephones were spaced at six-metre intervals. Monitoring cameras tracked their entire journey, warning the waiting uniformed security officers of their approach to a barred control room to which they were admitted only after the head of the Foreign Office delegation produced photographic identification of everyone as well as signed authority for their entry. Two of the security officers led them through more unexpectedly quiet, white-tiled corridors to a lift large enough for them all. It rose two floors to ground level and a distantly noisy area of undesignated, metal-door rooms and barred external windows. There were bars on all the windows in the comparatively small room into which they were finally taken. It was bisected, wall to wall, by a wide, light-coloured wooden-leg table, which in turn was divided up to the ceiling by a thickened glass screen into which, at intervals, microphones were inset. CCTV was installed on all four walls, at the same intervals as along the corridor. A precise number of chairs were set out for the British group. Showing their familiarity with such encounters, the Foreign Office officials put Radtsic and his wife in the very centre, arranging themselves and the two MI6 men at either side. Beneath the bench, the two Russians remained hand in hand.

An abruptly lit red light above the large central door on the opposite side of the glass shield signalled the arrival of the Russian contingent, which included one greying, matronly woman, and for all of whom an exact number of chairs were arranged. The delegation deferred to a squat, obese man tightly corseted in a waistcoated suit, no-one else attempting to sit until he'd settled himself with some chair-shifting difficulty. The woman at once followed, sitting directly alongside and assembling a complicated digital recorder in front of the nearest microphone outlet, towards which she closely erected an aerial. As soon as she settled, the rest of the group arranged themselves at either side and from briefcases unpacked more recorders, notebooks, and folders. One opened a small computer. Two Russians least attentive to the seating process betrayed the likelihood of their being FSB by the intensity with which they studied the wall-mounted CCTV.

'I register an immediate protest,' announced the Russian head. 'According to the understood arrangements, there should be no British presence.' He had the hoarse voice of a persistently heavy smoker. There was a sheen of perspiration on his upper lip and he shifted constantly in his unease.

'The insistence of Maxim Mikhailovich Radtsic upon a British presence, as well as the location of this meeting, was made quite clear and agreed to in the diplomatic exchanges between our two countries,' responded the Foreign Office head, who'd put himself to Radtsic's right. In contrast to the Russian, the diplomat was a tall, thin, impeccably dressed man who remained calm and unmoving.

'I demanded that they be here, as witnesses,' declared Radtsic, authoritatively loud-voiced. He and Elena were no longer hand in hand. She was matching her husband's defiance in the way she sat, arms folded. He had both irritably twitching hands outstretched upon the wide ledge in front of him.

'And I demand that my protest be officially noted,' said the fat man.

'It is noted,' dutifully accepted the British diplomat.

Directly addressing Radtsic, the corpulent Russian said, 'I have come specially from Moscow for this meeting and will remain here in London until this matter is satisfactorily resolved by your being freed. You have the full consular and diplomatic support of the Russian Federation.' The declaration concluded with a gesture of finality, not at Radtsic but at those on either side of the man.

'I do not want the support of the Russian Federation,' rejected Radtsic, his voice clearly controlled. 'I want my son.'

'You were forced, pressured, to come to Britain against your will, weren't you?' insisted the Russian.

'The pressure under which we are being put is by our being deprived of our son,' replied Radtsic. 'I want access to him: a reply to my letter. I want to know that he is being treated properly: that he's not in jail.'

'Your son was rescued before he could be blackmailed by your being held here in England.'

'He was intercepted and prevented from joining me here.'

'How badly have you been treated?'

'I have not been treated badly: subjected to torture.'

'What about your health?' The Russian spokesman twitched, looking inexplicably in both directions to his companions.

'Today I underwent the strictest of medical examinations. As far as I know I do not need any medical treatment. Neither does my wife.'

'This encounter is to make it clear to you that we are making every effort to secure your freedom and your return to Russia, where you will be welcomed as a hero. Once back in Moscow you will undergo medical treatment to recover from whatever drugs are being administered to confuse you.'

'This is all nonsense! I want to speak to my son.'

'You will see your son when you get back to Moscow.'

'This is improper and totally unacceptable,' finally interrupted the head of the British delegation, visibly flushed. 'I shall recommend an official complaint be lodged at your embassy. Maxim Mikhailovich Radtsic was not kidnapped. He is not being ill treated in any way. No drugs are being administered to enforce his presence here. He is in this country at his own request and volition, having strongly expressed the wish to remain here permanently.'

'Let us see our son, talk to him!' Elena's wailed intervention was so unexpected that the Russian negotiator visibly jumped. She'd come forward over the bench, hands out imploringly over it. Radtsic reached out, gripping her arm, but Elena shook him off. 'Don't torture us like this!'

'We will do everything to help you return to Moscow,' said the obese man.

'Let him talk to us on television, a linkup. Or let him reply to my letter. I meant what I said, in my letter. I will tell the British everything I know unless I am allowed to speak to my son. Elena is right. This is torture.'

'We are trying to help your colleagues: see them as we are seeing you. Are you allowed to see them?'

'I'm not interested in seeing anyone but Andrei.'

Elena was back in her chair now, a clenched hand to her face, her other hand still on the table.

The Russian head of mission said, 'Write again. I guarantee a letter will get to him.'

'I can't stand any more of this,' protested Elena.

'Nor can I,' said Radtsic. 'You are the torturers, not the British.'

The warning of the impending return from the prison, where Elena and Radtsic were briefly recovering from the confrontation, came far sooner than Rebecca Street had expected and would have created a problem if Sir Archibald Bland had taken her call. But he hadn't, strengthening Rebecca's conviction that she was being sidelined by those who could have halted Jane Ambersom's manoeuvring. Bland's unnamed executive aide had rejected her request for an immediate meeting with the Cabinet Secretary without bothering to consult the man. With the same peremptory refusal he'd told her that Geoffrey Palmer was also unavailable, both involved in a prior commitment that could not be interrupted. Rebecca didn't completely believe the aide's promise to advise both men of her approach.

And there was no-one else to whom she could directly appeal, Rebecca realized, the returning frustrating impotence tight, like a physically contracting band, around her chest. She'd gain her meeting, eventually, but with a much different approach than she'd intended in the heat of her anger. As her approach to Jane Ambersom would be totally different: her immediate reaction at learning the lesbian cow had taken over Vauxhall Cross had been quite wrong, a mistake from which she had to recover. She'd let Jane Ambersom imagine she'd won, show no irritation or animosity and concentrate upon her one advantage, Maxim Radtsic. And dutifully obey—or appear to obey—exactly what the other woman had ordered, drain everything possible from the Russian and in doing so establish a reputation that would make her indispensable, someone whom those in authority couldn't ignore but automatically thought of instead of Jane Ambersom. And from the very moment she got back to

Vauxhall Cross after achieving that, become the cuckoo in Jane Amber-som's nest. All the mistakes and miscalculations—and there were always mistakes and miscalculations in what they attempted to do—would be those of Jane Ambersom, never Rebecca Street, the acknowledged legend who set Russian intelligence back an entire generation.

There was a stir at the arrival of the Russians and their British diplomatic delegation and Rebecca moved quickly to separate the elder of the two MI6 officers.

'How'd it go?'

'Total waste of time,' said the man. 'I've been with two previous access delegations but never seen anything like this. The Russian negotiator was a total nut. Radtsic held his temper but practically collapsed afterwards.'

'I want a complete CCTV printout at the safe house by the time I get back.'

The man nodded towards his partner. 'We're sure we isolated two FSB. Didn't recognize either from our known embassy list, so at least that's a result.'

Rebecca caught the gesture from the delegation head, moving at once across to the two Russians. 'I'm sorry it wasn't better.'

Radtsic shook his head, visibly bowed. 'Let's get back to the house. There's a lot we've got to talk about.'

'Why didn't Bland or Palmer tell Rebecca, as they promised!' demanded Jane Ambersom, swivelling her new chair to look out over the river towards Thames House and Aubrey Smith's unseen but familiar suite. She'd initiated the first of their end-of-day updating contacts, wishing she could have been there in person instead of talking by telephone.

'We confronted them into making a positive decision: senior civil servants like Bland and Palmer don't like exposing themselves to a responsibility that can be directly attributed to them,' said Smith. 'I should have thought more about it.'

'Are you seriously telling me it was intentional, not an oversight?'

'That's what I'm seriously suggesting, which of course they'd strenuously deny,' said Smith. 'Do you think you mollified Rebecca?'

'I tried, without prostrating myself. We've had enough competing nonsense, haven't we?' On balance the office she was now occupying was far superior to Smith's, she decided, swinging her chair back into the room. But she couldn't imagine sleeping in the king-size apartment bed, despite Matthew Timpson's sterile eradication of any trace of Gerald Monsford. 'I haven't heard anything from her yet about Radtsic's meeting with the Russian delegation but one of our escorts described it as a complete disaster.'

'It was predictable, I suppose, remembering what happened during the French linkup,' remarked Smith. 'I heard from Bland about France just before you called. Everyone's been repatriated, which leaves us just with those still held in Russia.'

'I'm copying you Natalia's full analysis. She's unhappy with what she's seen as well as heard of Irena Novikov's American interrogation. But can't say why. And she's picked up on something else. She says it's wrong that Moscow agreed with Radtsic's meeting being in a prison. She can't understand their agreeing.'

'The uncertainty about Irena chimes with Joe Goody. He says there's something wrong, too: that she's not uncertain or frightened in the way she should be but he can't put his finger on it.' He laughed, in advance. 'And your boyfriend and his boss think Joe's something from another planet who should be preserved in formaldehyde.'

Jane laughed in return. 'I can't wait to hear Barry's version.'

'I can't wait to see the Belmarsh CCTV footage,' said Smith, serious again. 'I'd like to know why Natalia's uncertain about Radtsic's prison meeting.'

He didn't have long to wait.

23

RUSSIA BRILLIANTLY UTILIZED THE BRITISH TIME OF 7:00 A.M. TO maximize the worldwide media pickup that was to follow throughout the next two days. The claimed television exposé was preceded an hour earlier, Moscow time, by an alerting trailer proclaiming the kidnapping of a Russian hero, which was the emblazoned title across a wide-angle, professionally filmed shot of Belmarsh Prison. That was correctly described as Britain's highest security institution and superimposed over it was a clip-by-clip display of the most infamous international terrorists—with the concentration upon Al Qaeda, child-murdering paedophiles, and killers who had been held there. The photographs were pulled together into a composite montage but with one square empty, apart from a question mark against the changed background of prison vans arriving and leaving, for the actual programme's opening sequence. That began with a voice-over repetition of Moscow's accusation that Maxim Radtsic had been kidnapped and his wife tricked into joining him by British intelligence.

The professionally filmed outside footage abruptly changed to an unsteady, grainy film immediately explained to have been shot on a concealed camera by one of a Russian humanitarian group finally allowed access to Radtsic after Moscow threats to raise the seizure before the United Nations. The concentration was upon unsmiling prison officers brusquely checking credentials and constantly locked and unlocked doors in unremittingly barred surroundings, the beehive prisoner hum amplified into a raucous babble. The break was jerky, the film resuming as the unseen Russian group entered the Belmarsh interview room in which the first shot of the waiting British delegation was indistinguishably blurred. It was only slightly clearer when it resumed after the break, the reflected daylight glare from the intervening glass making it difficult to identify individual features. Radtsic and Elena were identified by the commentary to be the two circled in the middle. The commentary described the figures on either side of the couple to be their "inquisitors, drug-inducing psychiatrists, and torturers."

'The incontrovertible proof of which the British never intended to be known,' declared the commentator.

The recorded Belmarsh dialogue did not start until the obese Russian's insistence of being sent from Moscow to secure Radtsic's release, promising the man full consular and diplomatic support.

Radtsic's response was edited to: *'I want the support of the Russian Federation.'*

The Russian negotiator's question—*'How badly have you been treated?'*—again remained untouched, but Radtsic's reply was now: *'I have been subjected to torture,'* and Elena's wailed intervention had been heavily rearranged as well as edited to be: *'Don't let us be tortured like this.'*

That was followed by Radtsic saying, *'Elena is right. This is torture,'* and immediately after by Elena's final remark, *'I can't stand any more of this,'* with Radtsic's rearranged and edited, *'The British are torturers'* directly followed by *'I need treatment.'*

The film broke, to resume with further grained footage of the Russians leaving through the barred jungle, again with an amplified prisoner cacophony. That switched at once to the concluding commentary against a professionally filmed background of a disappearing Belmarsh through the rear window of a departing vehicle and the voice-over insistence that a protest note was that day being presented to the British government.

Attorney-General Sir Peter Pickering, who was the only one not to have seen the original morning broadcast, looked around the others assembled in the Foreign Office annexe and said, 'How in the name of God was that allowed to happen?'

'People didn't plan sufficiently ahead,' said Geoffrey Palmer, leading the co-chairmen's immediate search for a scapegoat.

'We can refute it: show the Russians to be manipulating liars!' declared Pickering, smiling in anticipation. 'We've surely got the originals, CCTV and full digital voice recordings. We simply release the true version to show how it's been twisted.'

'We can't,' at once deflated Aubrey Smith, halting the stir that had begun to move among the reduced committee. Nodding to Passmore, positioned in readiness next to the secretariat, Smith went on, 'I've waited until we're all together to show this. Please pay particular attention to what the Russians do the moment they arrange themselves at the table to confront our people with Radtsic.'

The film was better than the usual CCTV recording, although still short of professional-photographic clarity, but the accompanying soundtrack was corrupted predominantly into whined, screeching sounds. No verbal segment ran longer than four consecutive words: mostly the rest was a hotchpotch of single utterances, none of it possible to translate into anything comprehensible.

'How the hell——?' the permanently bewildered attorney-general began another protest.

'I asked you to watch the Russians settling themselves opposite our people at the beginning,' interrupted Smith, gesturing to Passmore for a replay to impose his own commentary over the Russian compilation. 'Note that each of them unload things from briefcases onto the table in front of the separating screen . . . and there, there and there,' he itemized, 'you can see what appear to be disk recorders or electronic equipment. I went through it, frame by frame, with our electronic technicians last night. Their judgement is that it was quite easy for the Russians to do what they did: those supposed recorders are something like the white-noise listening protection you can buy over the counter in electronic security shops all over London but in this instance reversed to distort or interrupt microphone reception or transmission—'

'No!' broke in Pickering, in turn. 'That won't work! If that's how they did it, they couldn't have got a complete transcript to edit into the lying film we've just seen.'

'Watch again,' urged Smith, nodding for a third repeat, almost at once stopping the transmission to get a freeze-frame of the matronly woman arranging her recording equipment. 'It's quite a conjuring trick, occupying everyone's attention while the others are setting out their stalls. But see how she raises what looks like an aerial next to the microphone directly in front of the fat negotiator next to her, who led the delegation: according to our technicians, she was isolating that particular microphone outlet specifically for their use.'

'Wait! wait!' pleaded Sir Archibald Bland. 'Why weren't they searched: prevented from taking these things in!'

'They couldn't be,' answered the Foreign Office observer, ready for the demand. 'They all produced diplomatic accreditation at the prison security station. Accredited foreign diplomats can't be subjected to physical search of any sort.'

Speaking very slowly, spacing his words, Palmer said, 'Are we being told—and asked to believe—that Russians, some if not all of them spies, entered what is supposedly the most secure penal institution in this country with electronic gadgetry that sabotaged the internal security facilities to enable them to manufacture that anti-British propaganda to which we've just been subjected and which is now circulating around the world!'

'That's exactly what I'm telling you. And what happened,' said Smith. 'And their being accredited Russian diplomats, with diplomatic immunity, really does mean there was nothing whatsoever we could have done to prevent it.'

'As incredible as it appears, I believe you're absolutely and legally right,' conceded Pickering. 'I certainly can't see any way of refuting the propaganda without making ourselves appear even more ridiculous than we've already been made to look.'

'We haven't yet agreed access to the Novikov woman and I'm damned if we're going to now!' said Palmer.

'They're holding two MI6 officers and one MI5 operative, in addition to Charlie Muffin, to none of whom they've agreed access,' reminded the Foreign Office spokesman. 'I wouldn't advise that course of action.'

'Neither would I,' agreed Pickering. 'It would be entirely counter-productive.'

'We've got three of their diplomats on a criminal charge,' persisted Palmer.

'Putting them on trial, entering into the usual tit-for-tat trade-off, isn't going to better what they're achieving practically every day,' dismissed Pickering.

'So all we're left with is a total denial, with the insistence that it's a fabrication that we can't prove?' said Palmer.

'That's all,' agreed the Attorney General.

'Do something!' implored Bland, directly addressing Aubrey Smith and Jane Ambersom. 'Somehow, someway, this nonsense has got to be stopped!'

The interrogation break this time had stretched to almost thirty-six hours, which Charlie used to test himself and was reassured by the self-assessment by the time Mikhail Guzov finally arrived at the dacha that afternoon. There'd been no anxiety, no mentally-undermining speculation about the man's absence, and most satisfying of all, no feeling of dependence upon Guzov at his reappearance. He'd begun slipping into the psychological reliance of a man in helpless solitary confinement but realized it sufficiently early to stop himself sinking further, Charlie congratulated himself. And now it was reversed: *he'd* reversed into the resistant professional he'd always prided himself upon being. It was a good feeling, the best—most encouraging—he'd had for several days.

Most important of all, he was sure now that was how he would continue to feel.

Guzov's briefcase bulged more obviously than on previous interrogations and the man seemed relieved to dump it beside him, smiling his ugly smile as he arranged himself in his customary chair. 'You really are doing very well,' the Russian greeted, enigmatically.

'I think so,' said Charlie, a remark for his own satisfaction.

'We've analyzed everything you've told us, from the moment you and I started talking, and haven't found a single lie.'

If that were true he was doing far better at another level than he'd imagined, Charlie acknowledged. They hadn't found a direct lie because he hadn't been stupid enough to tell one outright. What he had done, according to his meticulous count, was to sow ten misdirecting leads into information the Russians already knew to be accurate and in which he was therefore not disclosing sensitive, unknown information but hopefully causing them wasted months of fruitless follow-up. 'I thought we'd decided from the beginning I'd achieve very little by outright lying. Just as I hoped you'd understand that I wouldn't volunteer anything more than the absolute minimum.' Which again they'd analyze as truthfulness, he knew.

'That's very sensible. That's the decision that's been reached, that you're behaving very sensibly.'

He was, Charlie further congratulated himself, clearly a much better deceiver than the Russian. But then that was the expertise of which he was the proudest. 'London might not agree with you.'

'London's something and somewhere that doesn't need to concern you ever again, although we have told them about you.'

'Told them what?' asked Charlie, keeping everything to a conversational tone but instantly alert for what there might be to learn.

'That you're not badly hurt: fully recovered, in fact. But that you are going to face prosecution.'

'On what charge?' challenged Charlie, at once.

'Operating against the Russian Federation as a member of a foreign intelligence organization, illegal entry into the country under a false identity, activities endangering state security . . .' Guzov shrugged. 'It's a long list: I can't remember the rest.'

Was there anything to be gained by arguing the lack of evidence and the danger of his disclosing the Lvov affair in open court? wondered Charlie. The warning came at once: that's what they'd expect him to do if their eroding psychology was succeeding. 'I suppose you've got to go through the motions of legality.'

'The embassy's response to our contact about you was an official request for their doctor to examine you. Now I can tell them there's no medical need, can't I?'

A smokescreen too easy to see through, thought Charlie, who didn't believe there'd been a medical request. 'You tell them that.'

There was another slight hesitation before Guzov abruptly reached down for his briefcase. 'So let's continue the good work,' urged the man, taking out a thick wad of stiff photographic paper, needing both hands to offer it across the narrow space between them.

Ironically, the weight hurt Charlie's wounded shoulder when he took the bundle, needing both hands, realizing as he did so that each sheet held an average of twelve facial images of men and woman, none of them showing any awareness of their pictures being taken. 'What are these?' asked Charlie, going along with the charade.

'That's what we want you to tell us,' smiled Guzov, the condescension restored. 'They're from British embassies all over the world: itemizing which isn't important. What we want you to do is work your way through them, isolating which are your espionage officers among the genuine diplomats.'

'You know I won't be able to do that!' said Charlie, forcing the indication. 'Officers are kept apart, aren't exposed to each other, precisely to *prevent* their being identifiable to each other and risk exposure.'

'I know that's how the system is *supposed* to work.' Guzov grimaced. 'Just as I know there's a lot of mingling camaraderie between people doing the same job and that if you look very hard there's a lot you'll be able to pick out.'

'They might mingle in the FSB but not in the British system,' persisted Charlie, knowing it was expected of him.

'There appears to be a lot but really there's not that many: it won't take you longer than five or ten minutes to go through each sheet, properly studying the faces.'

'I'll be wasting my time. And yours.'

'That's what we've both got, Charlie, as much time as anything is going to take. But none of it to waste.'

'It seemed obvious to come on over here after Sir Archibald's summons: I could hardly have been closer,' smiled Rebecca Street. It was going to be difficult disguising her total elation after the finally agreed meeting with Sir Archibald Bland.

'Of course it was,' agreed Jane Ambersom, cautiously. 'What's happening with Radtsic and Elena while you're away?'

'Your new security supervisor is in place but they're getting the rest the doctors are insisting upon,' disclosed Rebecca. 'I really thought Radtsic was going to collapse after what happened at the prison yesterday. He was incandescent with rage, demanding we go into debrief the moment we got back to Hertfordshire and simply wouldn't stop. It was past ten last night before he finally called a halt, close to total exhaustion. He got up fine this morning, demanding to start again, but then they saw what's come out of Moscow. They've both been given sedatives.'

Rebecca should have relayed all this earlier and certainly not left them, even if Jacobson's replacement was there, thought Jane. 'How serious is it?' She'd had only an hour's warning of Rebecca's arrival—not knowing until then that the woman was even in London—and had very consciously organized the encounter in the other woman's normal office instead of using the one she was temporarily occupying.

'Physically, not too bad: they should be fine by tomorrow. The more serious danger, according to the medical team, is going to be their final realization that they're never going to see their son again.'

'It was a sensible decision to keep the medical team there,' praised Jane, curious at the total change in the other woman from their last conversation.

'It hardly needed a psychiatric degree to anticipate the strain they were going to be under confronting the Russian delegation. What I didn't anticipate was how it was going to be manipulated.'

'None of us did.'

'I could have gone through all this with you on the telephone,' Rebecca suddenly declared, timing the moment. 'But I'm glad Radtsic's collapse has given me the chance to apologize in person.'

The abruptness disconcerted Jane, who was unsure how to respond without appearing condescending. 'Today's a new day.'

'It's yesterday I want to clear up. I was completely out of order, reacting as I did, and I'm sorry.'

'I'm glad Bland made everything clear to you.'

It was difficult not to collapse into hysterical laugher! 'He didn't, not properly. All he wanted to hear was what Radtsic told me last night and whether it provided anything to get us all out of the immediate problem. The best he managed was to say as I was getting this much out of Radtsic it might be a long time before I got back here. Yours is the assurance I'm talking about.'

'I'm glad it's out of the way,' said Jane. Her relief was entirely professional, glad something she dismissed as trivial didn't become a minimal intrusion into what they were trying to achieve.

Dream on, thought Rebecca. 'So am I.'

'How much *did* Radtsic give us last night?' asked Jane, anxious to move on.

Rebecca shrugged. 'It'll take the analysts a while to sift it down to the gold nuggets but it wasn't confined to Britain. He named assets and sources in Germany—he claims there's still a virtual substrata surviving from the Stasi days even now—and France. But the concentration remains America. I stopped at about thirty keeping a mental count of penetrations he claims the CIA don't know to exist. There's at least a dozen names within the CIA itself. And for the first time that I can remember, he's fingered two FBI officers.'

'What about here?'

'Two MPs, a source within the Treasury, and a senior civil servant in the secretariat of the Chiefs of Staff.'

Jane was literally dumbfounded for several moments. 'This is incredible!'

'That's what Bland said.' Rebecca smiled. As well as guaranteeing her the MI6 directorship along with a damehood to go with the promotion, with an eventual retirement elevation to the House of Lords with the injunction not to disclose the undertakings to anyone, which suited Rebecca perfectly.

'I would have thought this justified the recall of our group,' said Jane, keeping the criticism to its absolute minimum.

'So did I,' easily lied Rebecca, everything scripted. 'That's why I called Sir Archibald first thing this morning, expecting him to convene it. Instead he told me he wanted to hear it personally from me.'

'Congratulations,' allowed Jane. 'You're the only one who's pulling any positive success out of this mess.'

I know and so do the people who matter, thought Rebecca. Aloud she said, 'It's not what I've done, it's what the Russians did.'

'Do you believe her?' demanded Aubrey Smith, when Jane finished recounting the meeting.

'I didn't have anything to challenge her with.' Again Jane was gazing across the river, the telephone cupped into her shoulder.

'Why the hell didn't Bland mention it when we met earlier? Rebecca must have spoken to him by then?'

'She said he wanted to hear it all from her firsthand.'

'It's the sort of trick he'd play, I suppose: wanting to assess the personal protectiveness before any other consideration. Joe Goody's met the same blank wall today. All Irena talked about was how stupid Moscow has made us look: wasn't even fazed when he reminded her it didn't do anything to help her access being agreed.'

'Barry told me last night that Bering isn't impressed by Joe. Thinks he's a joke.'

'I wonder how hard he'll laugh when he hears what Radtsic's said about the FBI penetration?'

'I'll tell you when I hear.'

Jane was on the point of leaving the office when the light on her secure external telephone blinked; recognizing Ethel Jackson's voice immediately, she picked up the receiver.

'I think you'd better come down right away,' said the woman.

'What is it?'

'Natalia thinks she knows what's wrong.'

24

IT WAS A FURTHER SIX HOURS OF CONCENTRATED ACTIVITY
before the government's GCHQ code breakers at Cheltenham gave qualified support to Natalia's conviction, which Jane decided was sufficient to
bring in Aubrey Smith and Joe Goody. Having been with Natalia throughout that time, Jane accepted that before involving others she had to settle
the Russian woman's obvious uncertainty.

'Aubrey Smith is our Director-General. Joe Goody is our senior debriefer, the best we have. And he's formed the same impression as you,
that there's something wrong with Irena Novikov. But like you—until
now, that is—he couldn't decide what it was.'

'I'm basing it on the Russian transmission, which wasn't good. Let's
wait until we get your better original CCTV.'

'Our technical experts think you're right. Their hesitation is about
the deciphering, that's all.'

'Maxim Mikhailovich and Elena were indistinct in the Russian film.
We might be able to see more, be surer, when we see the prison versions.'

'By the time my Director-General gets here, we'll have the better-
quality material,' said Jane, conscious of Ethel Jackson's unease at Natalia
being pressured.

'Your headquarters are under constant surveillance. Your Director-
General will be known to those watching.'

Natalia's real fear, identified Jane. 'He won't be coming from London and he'll be travelling by helicopter, as I did earlier. Joe will come direct from Irena's safe house. There's no way either can guide anyone here.'

'Sasha will be unsettled by a lot of strangers,' persisted Natalia, who'd sat saying little after hesitantly illustrating her belief after Jane's arrival.

'Sasha will be at her lessons. And it will only be two extra people.'

'It would be better if we waited until your specialists give a positive confirmation.'

'Natalia!' pleaded Jane. 'You and Sasha are completely safe: no-one can get to you to cause you any harm. No-one ever will be able to get to you. We're totally trusting you, as Charlie Muffin's wife. Now you've got to trust us.'

'I do trust you,' said Natalia, unconvincingly. 'Everything's happened very quickly.'

'It could be very important in helping Charlie. You mustn't forget that.'

'I'm never likely to.'

'Then you know why I must bring in these people.'

'Yes.' The uncertainty remained.

Aubrey Smith was obviously woken by Jane's call but the alertness was immediate. There was no theatrical reaction. 'GCHQ confirm it?'

'Their reservation is that they can't read it.'

'That's good enough for now,' Smith agreed. 'What about including Rebecca? She's going to be key.'

'Let's wait until we do get the better CCTV prints from the prison as well as our own copies. Natalia's very nervous about bringing in you and Joe. I don't want to crowd her any further.'

'You want me to tell Joe?'

'It would help if you could actually bring him in with you. One of Natalia's several terrors is that the FSB will be led here.'

'We'll be there by nine.'

'So will all the other film I'm having brought in.'

Ethel Jackson had generously filled snifters while Jane spoke. They didn't speak until they'd touched glasses. Sipping her brandy, Ethel said, 'Here's to it being right.'

'GCHQ wouldn't have gone as far as they have if they weren't more than fifty percent sure.'

'It could turn everything totally upside down.'

'I haven't yet worked out just how totally.'

'It's going to take a hell of a lot of analysis.'

'Not so much if GCHQ come good.'

'Their expertise is predominantly in signals intelligence,' cautioned Ethel. 'For this we need the equivalent of Bletchley Park in 1943.'

'It's been a long night. I'm too tired even to contemplate who or what we need,' said Jane, finishing her brandy.

'You were right in what you told Natalia.'

Jane stirred at the tone of the other woman's voice. 'Told her what?'

'That we're unquestionably trusting her,' said Ethel.

'How can you still have doubts about Natalia, after this?'

'I don't have doubts. What I can't completely reconcile myself to is the amount of reliance we're putting in someone who until a month ago was a member of the FSB.'

'And Charlie's wife,' heavily qualified Jane.

'Which is another dichotomy I can't reconcile,' admitted Ethel.

Professional or personal problems? wondered Jane, remembering Ethel's admission about herself and Charlie. 'Let's hope it's not another mistake to add to all the others we've made so far.'

'Yes,' agreed the other woman, pointedly. 'Let's hope.'

By the time Aubrey Smith's helicopter put down, the earlier-arriving technicians had cleared the communal dining room of the security building for the CCTV transmission. Jane was the last into the breakfast room at the nearby safe house. Neither Ethel nor Natalia was eating and Natalia looked as if she'd slept badly. Sasha didn't show the nervousness at the prospect of strangers Natalia had predicted, trying several groping English sentences in anticipation with surprisingly little need to fall back upon Russian. Jane's praise sent the child smiling to her morning's lessons. Jane bothered only with coffee, like the two other women, and got to the security wing with Ethel and Natalia just as the technicians completed their test runs of all the CCTV from Belmarsh Prison. The elder of the two told Jane the facial-recognition difficulty caused by the natural light reflection remained from the frontally positioned camera, although not as badly as the same-position shots the Russians had filmed from their concealed apparatus, but the clarity was greatly improved on the side and rear CCTV. He'd set up to show the frontal recording first. The copied Russian film, enhanced as much as was technically possible, could be shown in parallel if required. They were, of course, separately recording everything that transpired that morning in the communal dining room. Smiling apologetically, the man concluded that whoever was to commentate would need to operate separately the freeze-frame remote control and the laser-beam marker light.

'You all right with that?' Jane asked Natalia.

'I am to be filmed, conducting the session?' questioned Natalia, at once.

'A record has to be made to help GCHQ. Only you can individually point out what you suspect on the Russian film, as you did last night.'

'You know what they are. You can point them up.'

'You know I couldn't: that it's got to be you.'

The hesitation lasted several moments before Natalia eventually nodded, tight lipped. 'I can operate both.'

Only Jane went out to meet Aubrey Smith and Joe Goody. At once Smith said, 'How is she?'

'Shaky,' said Jane. 'Shakier than she was when she first arrived, which I can't understand.'

'Do you doubt what she's saying?' asked Joe Goody.

'I might have started to if it hadn't been for GCHQ's reaction.'

'Which hasn't been positively confirmed,' reminded Smith. 'You think Natalia's having second thoughts herself?'

'Come and decide for yourself,' invited Jane, uncomfortably, leading the way back to the security block.

Natalia was being guided through the two separate remote controls when they entered, her nervousness seeming slightly less during the introductions, even frowning curiously at Goody when the man addressed her as ma'am. During Jane's absence the technicians had finished rearranging the room with seats in front of a wide-screen television. With Natalia beside him, the technician leader repeated the problem of the light reflection on the frontal CCTV and explained that all the digital film had been enhanced to the same degree as the Russian version. All the films were mute, the gibberish left by the Russian sabotage eradicated.

'When you're ready,' prompted the man, leaving Natalia to the left of the screen.

'I believe . . .' started Natalia, faint voiced. She stopped, coughed, and more confidently started again. 'I believe that throughout the encounter in the prison Maxim Mikhailovich and the man who headed the Russian delegation—and Elena, although less so—were communicating in a code, irrespective of the conversation they appeared to be having. . . .' She paused, expecting a reaction. None came from the two forewarned men. She nodded to the waiting technician to start the film.

The enhanced film started with the back-view appearance of the Russian group entering the Belmarsh interview room from beneath the CCTV lens and the hesitation of the rest while the obese man settled in his chosen seat.

'There!' declared Natalia, stopping the transmission and fixing the marker beam upon Radtsic. 'Look at Radtsic's hands—he's just placed them on the table in front of him. The forefinger of his right hand cupped over the back of his left, the other four folded away.' She resumed the film but almost at once stopped it again. 'Now look at the negotiator, who's sat down now. His left forefinger is briefly across the back of his right hand, in response. That's what I believe the code consists of, mostly hand and finger signals, but sometimes there are repeated arm movements. It's a variation of deaf-and-dumb sign language. I'll replay this film more than once, showing those repetitions which I think are too regular to be natural, unmeaning movements. I'll also point out signals from the woman beside the negotiator, which Elena appears to acknowledge.'

It took almost forty-five minutes to go through the entire film from the first CCTV. A positive count maintained on the replay isolated fifty-two possible hand gestures and eighteen specific arm movements, Elena's repeated arm-crossing the most obvious. The hand-shifting count increased to sixty-five and arm gestures to twenty-one on the film shot from the rear CCTV cameras. The separate count from the Russian side was one hundred twenty hand signals and thirty-five different but repeated arm positionings from the assembled Russians.

Aubrey Smith decreed the coffee break after the front and back replays, and as Natalia came to the table where it was laid out he said, 'It's circumstantial but it's very convincing.'

'And you've picked out a lot more than you spotted from the Russian film,' said Jane, recalling the other woman's earlier reluctance to conduct the presentation.

'I'm not sure I would have identified it,' admitted Joe Goody.

'It's an FSB tradecraft technique for hostile situations like hostage-taking,' finally disclosed Natalia. 'It is literally based on sign language and was devised from actual hostage episodes: people crossing their fingers or making some other covert indication that they're being forced to say or write something praising their captors' ideology or political statements. I've never been trained in it, don't know what ciphers or keys they use, but it's common knowledge in Lubyanka. I didn't set out looking for it. It only registered after I'd seen the Russian version three or four times.'

'Radtsic would know about it, of course, although I don't understand how Elena would have the knowledge,' said Jane.

'But why would Radtsic use it?' demanded Smith.

'The man who led the Russian delegation was obviously FSB,' said Ethel. 'Could Radtsic have been threatening what he was going to disclose to use if they didn't let Andrei go?'

Jane shook her head, doubtfully. 'How more impassioned could he have been than in what he actually said during the prison confrontation?'

'We must let the Russians have access to Irena as soon as possible to see if it happens with her,' said Joe Goody.

'We won't have cameras there,' deflated Jane.

'The only function of this signalling is covert, in hostile situations?' questioned Smith.

'Yes,' confirmed Natalia.

'But the hostile situation Radtsic's in is with his own people, not with us,' Smith pointed out, reflectively.

'Unless he really had been kidnapped and is being held hostage,' picked up Jane.

'Which he isn't,' continued Ethel.

'Not according to our understanding,' completed Smith.

'I'm not a cryptologist but I don't imagine this finger-and-thumb code will be easy to decipher without its Rosetta key,' said Goody.

'Do you want to see the remainder of the CCTV?' queried the head technician.

'We're totally reliant upon GCHQ, so we need to give them everything we can: there might be something more,' accepted Smith.

The benefit of side camera CCTV was that it showed both Belmarsh contingents in profile, making it possible simultaneously to co-ordinate hand and arm movements between the sides, which Natalia immediately started to do as she stop-started her way through the first, from the right. She'd itemized three matched exchanges before holding a freeze-frame without indicating any significant movement. For several moments she remained unmoving, finally going within inches of the screen before asking the technician to enlarge the frozen frame. She put herself even closer to the screen for several more minutes before turning back into the room but not immediately speaking.

'What the hell is it now?' demanded Jane.

'It's not Maxim Mikhailovich Radtsic,' Natalia declared.

There was none of Radtsic's usual strutting bombast, Elena actually with her husband's arm cupped supportively as they came in through the french windows from their morning walk. That had been shorter than usual and Rebecca, watching unseen from inside the house beside the duty lip-reading cameraman, had been aware of the Russian's unsteadiness.

Radtsic slumped gratefully into his chair, smiling wanly at Rebecca, 'I hope I haven't kept you waiting.'

The politeness surprised Rebecca almost more than the frailty. 'Of course not. How are you?'

'Tired. And angry, still very angry. I want to teach them a lesson.'

'How?' Rebecca frowned.

'They will be laughing at me: at how they tricked me.'

'Yes?' encouraged Rebecca, doubtfully.

'During the genuine conversation the fat one said he was remaining at the embassy here. I want to meet them again, as we did before.'

Rebecca needed the hesitation. 'Of course I will suggest it, if it's your wish, but I can't imagine we'll agree after what happened the last time. Neither can I imagine your people would agree, either.'

'They won't.' Radtsic smiled more strongly. 'Which is the trick! I want you to film me making the verbal as well as the written approach to the embassy. And when they refuse you will have your rebuttal to what they broadcast. And then, in a continuation of the film, I can refute what was broadcast from Moscow: label it for what it was, a concocted lie.'

Rebecca allowed the second pause. 'There is a lot to consider in what you've said: in what you've suggested. I'll propose it, of course, but I think there will be a lot of practical difficulties.'

'I don't intend just to refute the lies they broadcast to the world. They tricked me—tricked you, too, at the same time. Now I want totally to humiliate them in return. On the same broadcast I want to set out how deeply the FSB manipulated the 2008 global economic collapse that's going financially to undermine the West for years to come.'

'You're surely not suggesting that Russia masterminded that!' challenged Rebecca.

'Of course I'm not! We didn't have to. The financial greed of Wall Street and your City and Frankfurt and the Bourse and every other stock exchange was sufficient to do that for us. What we did, very early on, was to recognize what was happening. And you know what! We actually made a profit buying and selling and all the time stoking up the heat in the world markets. And then pulled out to watch the bubble burst. The Lvov plot didn't begin as part of our financial coup, of course. But we were going to link it at the end. Can you imagine the destruction we would have caused, with Lvov orchestrating the American White House! Ten years from now the world would have been speaking Russian!'

There was no longer any barrier between Rebecca's telephone calls to Sir Archibald Bland, who said when she'd finished talking, 'I am so very glad you're going to be the new MI6 Director.'

25

NO-ONE SPOKE, LOOKING BLANK FACED AT NATALIA IN EXPECTA-
tion of more. When it didn't come, Aubrey Smith said, 'Explain that.'

'He's an impostor: a look-alike, but not Radtsic,' insisted Natalia, her
voice strengthening from her own initial disbelief.

'How can you know that?' demanded Jane.

'There's no mark on his face.' To emphasize the statement, she directed the laser at the freeze-frame to show a clean-shaven, clear-skinned
profile.

'It would help a lot if you told us in more detail what you're talking
about, ma'am,' said Goody.

Natalia straightened, finally composing herself. 'The joke—although
it's not a joke, not to him—in the Lubyanka is that Radtsic looks like
Stalin but has Gorbachev's father. Like Gorbachev, Radtsic's got a facial
birthmark. Everyone's seen Gorbachev's, extending back from his fore-
head although it used to be airbrushed out of all his official photographs
before he came to power. Radtsic's a very vain man and sensitive about
his disfigurement, which stretches down the right side of his face and covers part of his right ear. He wears his hair long, to cover as much of the
mark as he can, and the official portrait in the Lubyanka is taken half
profile, from his left, so that even the airbrushing is completely hidden.
That's the only photograph I've ever seen of the man and that's not publicly issued.' She turned back to the frozen TV screen, again directing the

light beam, and unnecessarily said, 'You can see there's no birthmark: no blemish of any kind.'

The absence of any mark was quite obvious but Jane got up and went closer to the screen as Natalia had, earlier. Turning back to the others but including Natalia, she said, 'That's what all the speculation was about in the artists' drawings when Radtsic's defection was first announced.'

'I've twice been in the presence of the real Maxim Radtsic, although at a considerable distance: seen the disfigurement,' disclosed Natalia. 'It's more purple than the red of a strawberry mark. It's impossible to miss.'

'Are you suggesting it's a huge disinformation trick!' demanded Smith.

'I'm *telling* you that the defector claiming to be Maxim Mikhailovich Radtsic, and whom I understand to be disclosing a lot of KGB and FSB secrets, definitely isn't the executive director of the Sluzhba, which he's supposed to be. The rest is for you to analyze.'

'Disinformation fits with the hand signals: explains them, even though we don't understand what they mean,' offered Goody.

'If Radtsic's a fake, what about Irena Novikov?' questioned Ethel Jackson. 'If it weren't for her and what she told Charlie, we would never have known what the Lvov business was all about. She can't be part of a disinformation scheme.'

'You're right but only up to a point,' qualified Jane, returning from her closer TV examination, but not bothering to sit again. 'What we know—or think we know—of the Lvov operation came *only* from Irena. There's not a shred of independent corroboration.'

'We surely can't have been wrong about everything, not from the very beginning,' protested Goody.

'Why not?' asked Smith. 'Everything we've been working on has come from single, uncorroborated sources: until a few days ago we spent the majority of our time distracted by a mentally disturbed Gerald Monsford, whose supposed coup was netting Radtsic, a man whom we accepted, upon Monsford's say-so, to *be* Radtsic. But whom we now know isn't.'

The attention suddenly concentrated upon Natalia was inadvertent but Natalia showed no uncertainty now. 'And my telling you that you haven't got the genuine Maxim Mikhailovich Radtsic is uncorroborated too, isn't it?'

'If you'd been part of whatever we're looking at here, you wouldn't have identified the hand signals or denounced the Radtsic look-alike,' said Smith.

'I want to study those hand signals before I talk to Irena again,' said Goody, reflectively. 'And I want that talk to be today.'

'And we need to alert London: Rebecca, too,' said Smith, talking to Jane. 'It's essential they all know immediately.'

As they left, Goody went to Natalia, huddling close to the third CCTV replay as she itemized the hand and finger movements of both Russians. Ethel Jackson went to where the coffee was still laid out, pouring for the two MI5 technicians. Smith and Jane returned before she could pour for herself.

Smith said, 'Our Radtsic look-alike has come up with what Bland's calling a major development. Rebecca's already on her way to London for an assessment meeting to which Jane and I have been summoned.'

'We've ordered the security to be doubled at their safe houses,' added Jane. 'We can't imagine that our Radtsic could have found out where he's living and it's even more unlikely he could have discovered where Irena is, but we don't want to lose either to a Russian move until we know what they're really supposed to be doing.'

'What about this safe house?' asked Natalia, her alarm immediate.

'It'll be doubled within an hour,' promised Smith, checking his watch and including Ethel in the reply. 'Mostly men. You remain security supervisor.'

Charlie was surprised the entrapment ritual hadn't been staged earlier. Entering into the performance, he made no attempt to disguise or hide his selection from Mikhail Guzov's photographic montage supposedly from British embassies throughout the world. The betrayal was, though,

still instinctively difficult and he kept his choice to an absolute minimum, mentally apologizing to the innocents whose pictures he identified
as MI5 intelligence agents hopefully to save six of the eight he did recognize, isolating only the remaining two because the Russians probably
knew the identities anyway and he wanted Guzov to imagine he was still
mentally giving way and to a degree co-operating. The objective, after
all, was not to discover undiscovered British intelligence officers but set
him up as a collaborator.

There was no artificial lateness today. Guzov strode purposefully in
promptly at eleven, the time he'd initially established for their interrogation sessions in the psychiatric institute, grimaced his smile, and settled
into the opposite rough-wood chair 'You've completed your assignment?'

Assignment was for the benefit of the film and audio recording, Charlie knew, an exaggerated choice even for an entrapment. 'I warned you I
wouldn't be able to do it: that in our service we're all kept separate from
one another, which I'd always assumed to be your protective system, too.'

'But there were some you recognized, weren't there?'

The question confirmed Charlie's belief that some if not all of those
he'd known were already identified by the Russians. 'I've done the best I
can.'

'I'm glad you're still being sensible, helping us like this.'

'You've told me that before.'

'And want to tell you again. It all contributes to how you'll be treated
in the future.'

'That's the uncertainty, the future,' said Charlie, stirring himself for
the uncertainty they'd expect.

'Yours is fairly predictable, if you continue as you're doing so far.'

A better response than he'd expected, acknowledged Charlie. 'They
won't believe it, you know.'

This time Guzov hesitated. 'You'd be surprised what people believe.'

'I mean the people who know. No matter how well you edit all this and
however or wherever you show it, my people will know I haven't come
across to you.'

'But it's the people in the "however and wherever" that's important to consider, isn't it, Charlie? That's what you'll never know.'

A few days earlier that remark would have tilted him further into a depression, accepted Charlie. Now it didn't, but it would be a mistake to let Guzov know he'd climbed out of the hole into which the man hopefully believed he was slipping.

'You're late!' accused Irena Novikov, before Joe Goody had taken his seat opposite her.

'I'm sorry, ma'am. I was delayed.' Goody very carefully placed his hands on the intervening table, the forefinger of his right hand over the back of his left, the other fingers cupped out of sight.

'Were you on the helicopter?'

Goody had requested the landing place, wanting the woman to see the arrival. 'I won't lie that I enjoyed it but it's such a convenient way of travelling over such long distances in no time at all. You must have moved around a lot that way, though, in Egypt with Stepan Lvov. That's right, isn't it, ma'am: you were in Egypt with Stepan Lvov when your big idea began?'

'When's my embassy meeting?' the woman demanded, ignoring everything Goody had said.

He was sure she'd isolated his hand positioning, which he changed, locking his left thumb between his clenched fist. 'I already warned you that's not going to be straightforward, not after what happened with Maxim Ivanovich. Now it's going to be even more uncertain.'

Irena's lower lip was trapped between her teeth. Appearing to realize it, she tried to cover the instinctive nervousness by openly laughing. 'It's Maxim *Mikhailovich*.'

'Of course it is, ma'am,' apologized Goody, intertwining his forefingers, conscious of her eyes flickering down to the table upon which they rested. 'You learned your lines and acted out your part very well for your great production, didn't you? Irena Yakulova Novikov isn't your real name, either, is it? It's obviously your operational identity.' He cupped his hands together again, leaving the thumbs protruding, and brought her attention up to him by raising the clenched fists to support his chin. 'Don't answer verbally. Hand sign it.'

She laughed again but just failed to stop the quaver at the end. 'You're not making sense . . . talking like an idiot . . . more like an idiot than usual!'

'Ah!' exclaimed Goody, at the first burst of approaching noise. 'Here come the cavalry,' and walked over to the window as another helicopter fluttered into view, located the same landing spot as the first, and roared into touchdown. Over his shoulder Goody said, 'They're called Jolly Green Giants because of all the material and men they can carry. Which is important getting reinforcements in place here.' Goody remained at the window, watching the helicopter disembark the increased protection squad.

'You didn't tell me when I'm meeting the embassy delegation,' tried Irena, a drowning person clinging to the last supporting straw.

Still looking out the window, his back to her, Goody said, 'They'll be in place very shortly, ma'am. There's no way your people could have located your whereabouts but we're not going to risk a rescue attempt, although I personally don't believe they'd risk something as blatant as that, do you, ma'am?'

Irena didn't reply, her lips familiarly clamped shut.

'And we don't want you slipping away, ma'am. You'll be accompanied upon any outside exercise period within the grounds from now on,' continued Goody, coming back to where the woman sat. 'And you'll be fitted with a tracking device: it's like an ankle chain although much more substantial. They're quite comfortable. You'll hardly notice you're wearing it after a while.'

Only someone as professional as Goody would have noticed the physical indication, the slight shoulder sag, the even slighter coming forward of her body. 'We won't bother with any more of these meaningless debriefings, ma'am. There's really no purpose, is there? I'm intellectually intrigued by the sign language, though: look forward to learning it. So simple yet so clever. You know what? I wouldn't be surprised if we didn't copy it: introduce it into our tradecraft. Not actually copy it, I don't mean. Use it as a template to devise a similar communication system of our own. There's lots of potential variations if you think about it, don't you agree, ma'am?'

'Shut up!' suddenly flared Irena. 'And stop addressing me as ma'am!'

Goody finally sat down again. 'I'm sorry. I don't mean to upset you, offend you, in any way. I don't think of us as enemies: we're professionals on opposing sides and I actually admire you for what you've done: what you do. I couldn't do that, not go across to the other side and maintain a pretence as you've done.'

'I'm a Russian national, with the right to consular access. Which I demand.'

'I'll pass that on to those making the decisions but there's a lot for them to take into account now, after what Radtsic—or whatever his real name is—has indicated.'

'What's he said?' It was a blurted demand, her voice fading at the very end in regret at the outburst.

'You know I can't tell you that. But you mustn't condemn him. His strain has been enormous and—'

'No more enormous than mine! I almost saved the operation!'

'I wasn't making a comparison between you and . . . and Radtsic,' said Goody, as if the false name was difficult for him now. 'And I *wouldn't* make the comparison. As I've already told you, I admired you. I'd never be brave enough to go out into the field.'

The woman regarded him steadily for several moments. 'What's he said about me?'

Goody shook his head in refusal again. 'What I can tell you is that Maxim Mikhailovich Radtsic . . . is not a colleague upon whom you can rely for loyalty. But as I don't believe I'm brave enough to do what you and Radtsic—'

'Demin,' burst in Irena. 'The bastard's name is Yuri Georgevich Demin and I argued against his inclusion from the very beginning!'

'I give you my word that I'll do all I can to prevent everything being laid at your door,' promised Goody.

He managed to reach Aubrey Smith on a secure line from the West Sussex safe house just before the Director-General went into the Foreign Office meeting.

On a day of surprises the further unexpected was the inclusion of Mort Bering and Barry Elliott in the hurriedly assembled group. Both Americans were already in the room when Aubrey Smith and Jane entered. Elliott was prepared but Jane wasn't and Smith admired her totally unruffled composure, easily reciprocating Elliott's smiled nod, suspecting as he watched the exchange that Rebecca Street, also already there, was the more disconcerted of the two women. Rebecca sat apart from the two newcomers, her blotter already assembled with jotter and pens as it always had been when she accompanied Monsford. There was a large-screen television positioned conveniently for everyone to see, to the woman's left a security-cleared technician in readiness.

Sir Archibald Bland opened the session without any explanation of the FBI presence, called the preceding twelve hours bewildering, and with a nod to Rebecca said the established chronological presentation would be maintained.

Rebecca began hesitantly, unsettled not just by the Americans but by Bland's apparent urgency. She'd requested the meeting because of the international implications of disclosures promised earlier that morning by Maxim Radtsic. There was a filmed record but in summary Radtsic was promising to detail the exacerbating FSB intrusion into 2008's near-total global financial collapse, an operation from which Moscow had profited by billions and which had established Russia's future intended intelligence target to be the destabilization of world economies.

'I'd like now . . .' she tried to continue, turning to the waiting technician, but Aubrey Smith said, 'I think I should intervene here. There's no point in watching any more film or listening to anything more of what Maxim Radtsic wants to tell us. He's a planted impostor, a phoney, like his name and everything he's ever told us.'

It took almost three hours for Jane to play and replay the Belmarsh CCTV ahead of that morning's film of Natalia Fedova identifying the hand-signal cryptograph. Jane studiously avoided directing her attention towards Elliott, although she savoured the thought of his upon her, but early in the presentation became aware of Rebecca's stone-faced concentration at being so cursorily dismissed by Aubrey Smith.

'So what's it say, this code!' demanded Rebecca, the moment the transmission finished.

'We don't know, not yet,' admitted Aubrey Smith, taking over from Jane. 'But GCHQ are confident enough that it *is* a code. They've had less than twenty-four hours to decipher it.'

'So it's not positively confirmed to *be* one, not yet?' persisted Rebecca.

'Not by GCHQ,' conceded Smith, recognizing the woman's irritation. Allowing the condescension, he went on, 'But we definitely know it is a code. Irena Novikov's interrogator, Joe Goody, copied some of the movements and bluffed her after watching what you've just seen: conned her into thinking Radtsic had somehow been caught out or made a mistake and broken down. Radtsic's real name, according to Irena, is Yuri Georgevich Demin.'

Rebecca eased back into her seat, totally rebuffed. Jane was surprised at Smith's ruthlessness, another newly emerged trait she wished he hadn't chosen that moment to demonstrate.

Mort Bering said, 'You guys have done damned well in the time you've had. I'd like to bring some of our cryptologists in on the decoding.'

'You're welcome,' accepted Smith, without consulting either co-chairman.

'Yes, of course. There's no objection at this late stage to it becoming a joint operation,' hurriedly agreed Palmer. 'But what's your interpretation of it all?'

Smith only just held back the sigh. 'I don't have an interpretation. I know the people we knew as Maxim Radtsic and Irena Novikov are not the genuine defectors we took them to be and I know that Radtsic communicated with other Russians. That's as far as I've got.'

'What about the other gal, Natalia?' insisted Bering. 'What's her part in all this?'

'She hasn't got one, not in the deception,' came in Jane, defensively. 'It was Natalia who told us it wasn't the real Radtsic, not Irena. And it was Natalia who spotted the hand code: it's FSB tradecraft, apparently.'

'I think, at last, that we might be ahead in this mess,' said Bland, briskly. 'How do you propose we take it forward?'

'By letting Joe Goody loose on Radtsic—I suggest we stay with the name we're familiar with, for the sake of easy understanding—knowing now that the man's a phoney,' said Smith.

'I'm debriefing Radtsic,' broke in Rebecca, too quickly.

'No you're not,' rejected Smith, at once. 'You're being conned—until now we've all been conned—by the man. Joe's a professional interrogator, the best my service has got. You're not: he'd go on trying to use you and we haven't got time for that. I want to play one off against the other. Their treating us like fools has ended. Now it's our turn and that's what's going to happen to them: they're going to be turned like pigs on a spit when we decipher the tictac sleight of hand. It also means, Ms Street, that you can return to MI6 and my deputy can come back to her position in my service.'

'Obviously sensible, all the way round,' decreed Bland, bustling on. 'What else?'

'I can't see any way Radtsic could have learned the location of his safe house, nor that of the Novikov woman, but I've already drafted in additional personnel to guard against their disclosure in that code we still can't read—'

'Do you seriously believe the Russians might physically attempt to get to both of them ... take them back to Russia?' stopped Palmer.

'I seriously believe if they knew where either were—and believed their covers blown—that the Russians would attempt their assassination to prevent the deception being understood or becoming public,' said Smith. 'Consider for a moment how well their deaths would fit the propaganda they've managed so far.'

'Why don't you move them?' asked Bering.

'I intend to if the code isn't broken quickly,' said Smith.

'I believe Radtsic is officially MI6's responsibility,' reminded Rebecca, tightly.

'You are part of this group,' reminded Smith. 'No decisions are taken without your being involved in the consultation. I moved extra protection in as a matter of urgency when I failed to make contact with you. I was told you'd already left for this meeting.'

'For the forethought and quickness of which I think we're all grateful,' said Bland, as Rebecca subsided again in her seat, a flush of anger for the first time visible.

'And in view of today's involvement of our FBI partners, I think they should be included in our subsequent sessions until this is concluded,' continued Smith. 'Which will be on our terms: for the first time ours is the strongest position.'

26

'WHO ARE YOU!'

'The person you and your wife are going to be talking to from now on, sir.'

'I decide who we talk to,' insisted Radtsic, the arrogance perfectly pitched. 'Get the woman back. You can go.'

Goody smiled, shaking his head. 'I want you to believe that I admire very much how you've handled your assignment, sir: you too, ma'am. I genuinely respect professionalism, which is what you've both shown. I'm looking forward to our association.'

The Russian turned the flush of uncertainty into feigned anger, eyes bulging as he came forward in his chair. 'Get out and do what I told you, get the woman back! I want to talk to someone in authority: someone I can trust and understand. You're a madman and I don't talk to madmen.'

Beside Radtsic, Elena remained totally unmoving, arms outstretched along the sides of her chair, hands cupped tightly over each edge, looking fixedly at Goody.

'Trust! That's the touchstone, isn't it, sir? When you're working with a partner, no matter how long you prepare—and to be fair to Irena Yaku-lova, neither of you could have had long to prepare for an assignment like this—there has to be trust, a reliance, upon your partner not to collapse as Irena Yakulova has collapsed. It's all over once that happens, isn't it, sir?'

'I won't talk to you, deal with anyone except the woman. Get out!'

'I didn't expect you to, not as quickly as this, Yuri Georgevich: didn't even come prepared for you to do so. I suppose you'd call this a courtesy visit, to let you both know how things are going to be from now on. You'll both remain here for the time being, but you're technically under arrest now: the helicopter you obviously saw arrive this morning has doubled the security here, so don't think of escape or anything silly like that. It really would be stupid and I don't believe either of you are stupid. . . .' Goody snapped his fingers, making Elena visibly jump. 'I've forgotten the code, haven't I! Now that's something I really do admire, Yuri Georgevich. I think that's all for the moment. I'm not sure when I'll be back: Irena Yakulova is going to take up a lot of our time for the moment but if—'

'I want contact with my embassy,' stopped Elena.

Radtsic turned sharply to look at her but didn't speak.

'They'll be informed of your detention, of course, but it's far too early for talk of consular access.' Goody smiled again. 'And when—if—it comes, you'll be able to talk openly, not bother with those juggling gestures, won't you?'

'I demand to know what charges we are being held upon!' declared Radtsic.

'Your not being in a position to demand anything is probably the most difficult adjustment you'll have to make now that it's all over, Yuri Georgevich. That's who you are now, Yuri Georgevich Demin, no longer play-acting the part of one of the most important men in the Russian Federation. From now on, for as long as we choose for you to remain here, you'll be told what to do.'

'What does that mean, for as long as we remain here?' asked Elena.

'You surely don't imagine you're going to stay here, in surroundings like this! As soon as we're ready you'll be moved to another secure establishment which I'm afraid will be much inferior to this. Split up, I'd expect, between different secure establishments.'

'A prison, you mean!' demanded the woman, her voice flickering apprehensively.

'That's what I would expect,' agreed Goody, affably. 'After all, one of the most likely reactions from Moscow learning their scheme has gone wrong will be to try to eliminate the embarrassment of your being here, which would make prison the safest place for you to be.'

'You cannot hold us without charge, nor prevent our having consular access,' insisted the man, dropping the arrogant Radtsic persona.

'Yuri Georgevich! As far as Moscow is concerned, you and Elena have buried yourselves deeply into our confidence, telling us all your carefully rehearsed stories. You even told them so, at the prison meeting. They believe the same about Irena and will go on believing it until we choose to tell them otherwise. Which we've no intention of doing for a long time yet. And do, please, drop the nonsense about there needing to be specific charges and the rights of consular access. We don't operate within the law, giving ourselves those rights. We accord them if it suits us and if it doesn't, we don't bother. . . .' Goody gestured broadly around the conservatory. 'Enjoy all this for a couple of days, until I get back. Although I'm not—'

'I want to discuss things,' declared Elena.

'I really don't have time, not today.'

'When . . . ? Tomorrow . . . ?'

'Look, why don't you talk things through, the two of you, and when you decide what—and how much—you want to tell me, you let the guards know. And that's what they are, from now on. Your guards. Get used to it because whatever happens, guards are going to become a very positive feature of your lives for some time to come yet.'

It required positive willpower for Rebecca to suppress the easily aroused frustration, despite realistically acknowledging that Thames House was the obvious venue for her to be summoned under the revised circumstances, in which she was now very much the junior participant. Aubrey Smith and Jane Ambersom were already in the conference room when Rebecca arrived. The only other person she recognized was Joe Goody, intent upon a selection of illustrated wall charts still in the process of being hung by three strangers. A lectern separated the charts from two wide-screen television sets placed side by side in readiness. The Director-General nodded in greeting to Rebecca but didn't speak, also more occupied with the charts. Jane smiled and said it had to be good to at last be back at Vauxhall Cross, resettling herself, and Rebecca smiled back and agreed that it was, concealing her impression of the other woman's gloating satisfaction at her relegation to the periphery of what they were now confronting. The two newly seconded Americans were the last to arrive, with apologies for their lateness. Mort Bering extended that apology with the admission that neither the FBI, the CIA, nor the National Security Agency code breakers had so far penetrated the finger-and-arm exchanges beyond agreeing with Britain's GCHQ that it unquestionably had been a coded exchange between Radtsic and the Russian delegation.

'Which is scarcely surprising, considering how little time your experts have had to work on it,' took up Aubrey Smith, introducing a plump, pink-faced man he beckoned towards the lectern as head of GCHQ's linguistic division. 'What have we learned from having had more time?'

'Not as much as we would have liked,' conceded the unidentified man, putting himself between the wall charts and the inactive televisions and accepting a marker light from one of his waiting companions. 'It's very clever encryption that's going to be very difficult satisfactorily to break. We've made some preliminary progress but not enough. We think we've got close, in places, but so far we're beaten by what we believe to be the deciphering being open to different, even contradictory, interpretations....'

'I'm having difficulty following this,' complained Rebecca. It was a professionally objective remark.

'As we are,' smiled the man. 'The code is composed of what I can only describe as several different linguistic or communicative elements. There's deaf-and-dumb sign woven into what we've identified as apparently randomly introduced Middle Eastern picture and some identifiable Asian picture languages: the code depends predominantly on straight-line imagery, with adjustments for slightly bent digits using the human hand. There are differences, in phonetically based sign, between word languages: we've isolated some, but not all. There are, obviously, complete differences between Middle East and Asian picture scripts. Again, we think we've identified some. What we don't have—nor any way of discovering—is whether in addition to the various picture-and-sign languages there's been introduced a mathematical manipulation, remembering that mathematics is the core base of most codes: whether to subtract, add, or multiply by a specific number sequence or amount the letter or symbol represented in the recognizable exchange.'

'How the hell can we work that out?' demanded Barry Elliott.

'We can't, just as Bletchley Park couldn't have broken the Enigma code without actually having a captured machine to reverse engineer,' said the linguistic scientist. 'With the cipher, children of ten could communicate as easily as they're doing now on the Internet. Without it, we'll never be sure that our translation, which we'll eventually get in full and which will probably read quite coherently, is actually what was communicated between the two Russians in that prison interview room.'

'Would it be a static cipher, relevant to every exchange?' asked Rebecca, another objective query.

The man smiled. 'A clever question. That's the value of ambiguous meanings. The positive definitions, if they are mathematically governed, are probably fixed by the particular day of the exchange: let's say Monday is numbered one, Tuesday is two, Wednesday is three, and so on. Each number would dictate the definition for its appropriate day. Radtsic's prison meeting was on a Wednesday. That day's definitions could—and probably would—be different from those of Thursday.'

'What you're telling us is that without the day-by-day cipher—if one even exists—we're beaten,' said Aubrey Smith.

'Not completely,' qualified the expert. 'Eventually we'll get a virtually complete translation of what passed between Radtsic and those who confronted him in Belmarsh for that Wednesday, but every word—and more importantly every picture symbol, all of which have a number of variations—will have to be considered: we'll eventually be able to provide you with possibly four different versions of the same code.'

'Which is a roundabout way of saying that we're beaten,' repeated Smith.

'Not necessarily,' contradicted Goody. 'Can you take us through what you are so far able to read?'

It took a long time, the marker beam almost permanently alight, stop-starting the television recordings between the actual Belmarsh encounter and the separated, itemized code examples, switching at every break to the wall-chart illustrations of each individual symbol, word, gesture, and sign. A reliance emerged upon single-, two-, or three-finger improvisations, sometimes topped by single or double finger positioning to create Mandarin Chinese or Japanese symbols ('Chinese is the root of the Japanese language'), and some Hebrew straight-line characters recreated with finger representation—even one ancient Sumerian triangular symbol—to support an arm-brushing sign gesture designating a road, a route, or a distance. There was easily decipherable disability sign for water, river, sea, or lake, and a combination of Cantonese and Japanese to designate a person, people, or a number of people, conceivably sufficient to constitute a crowd. None of the hybrid mishmash had grammatical prefix, preposition, or suffix to identify plural or singular.

There was a protracted silence at the end of the dissertation, broken only when Goody looked up, smiling, from his note scribbling. 'I'm surprised and impressed, sir. You got a lot, accepting all the caveats: far more than I expected from your earlier presentation. I wouldn't normally ask such a favour, but I wonder, sir, if you couldn't save me valuable time by suggesting what minimal interpretation you've so far reached?'

The linguist's smile of appreciation remained throughout Goody's remarks. 'Accepting all the caveats?' he qualified.

'Absolutely.'

The marker beam came on again, now with only one television operating. 'Two, maybe connected, possibilities: and I want you to understand that we're not working from the obvious supposition of what a defector—or supposed defector—would want to convey,' embarked the man, pink face flushed from the interrogator's praise. 'One of the simplest translations of that mixture of Mandarin script and lower-class Japanese that the leader of the Russian delegation is using is *success* or *progress*. There's the immediate deaf-and-dumb response,' identified the man, switching the beam upon Radtsic's hands. 'It's *yes* or *agreement*: certainly an affirmative.' The beam jumped. 'I have a question here but I'll delay it, to avoid a pre-judgement. Here's the Chinese—Japanese combination I pointed out earlier that could indicate people or a single person. We've only been asked to assess the encounter of a single person, Maxim Radtsic.' The beam danced through several freeze-frames. 'The repetition makes us believe the reference is to more than one person: maybe two or three. There's no grammar or tense, as I've explained, but we're surmising from Radtsic's responses here. . . .' The beam jabbed to a series of deaf-and-dumb sign. 'Here's the marking for *water* or *river* or *lake* and here's Radtsic's reply, *no*. Here's *forest* or *trees* or *woods* and here's Radtsic replying in the affirmative. And look here, at the repeated sign for *distance* or *road* or *route*. Our initial assessment is that the Russian delegation was trying to establish location: where Radtsic was being held. Now you help us, as far as tense is concern. The code for *people* or *a single person*: what is it, plural or singular?'

'Plural,' replied Jane. 'It could be as many as four but more like three—Radtsic, his supposed wife, and Irena.'

'That'll help us,' thanked the GCHQ expert.

'I still don't understand the significance of it all,' said Jane.

'Radtsic was telling the delegation that he—maybe even the others—were succeeding in their mission or assignment but wasn't able to identify where he or the others were being housed,' elaborated the man.

'That's more than enough for me,' said Goody.

'It would have been more than enough for Natalia, too,' Jane remarked sideways to Aubrey Smith.

'You lied: tried to trick me,' accused Mikhail Guzov. 'You pretended not to recognize five of the photographs I showed you of people we'd definitely identified to be MI5 operatives: your colleagues.' The man was hunched aggressively forward in his rustic chair, the door behind him still swinging back and forth from the force with which he'd burst into the dacha.

'I didn't lie or trick you,' refused Charlie, unmoved by the performance. 'I told you from the beginning that MI5 field officers don't mix or fraternize, *precisely* to prevent one being able to identify another in a hostile situation. I picked out those I thought I could recognize. If you'd already identified others the trickery was yours, trying to trap me.' Acting out the feigned anger—anger becoming genuine at the rejection—Guzov wasn't bothering with his grotesque impression of a smile: Charlie was grateful. He decided against mocking the man further by getting up to close the unsecured door.

'You're good at lying, aren't you?' persisted the Russian.

'Isn't it essential to our trade, until it's pointless, as it now is?' said Charlie, cautiously.

'I mean particularly good.'

This was prepared, maybe even rehearsed from someone else's script. 'I don't know what you expect me to say to that: I don't understand it.'

'Tell me about Edwin Sampson.'

The immediate chill, an actual sensation, rose like nausea throughout Charlie's body, physically numbing him, but his mind remained clear but racing. Edwin Sampson was the British traitor with whom he'd faked defection to Moscow and succeeded in discrediting during those initial, first-day debriefings with Natalia. 'It was a professional assignment.'

'Sampson wasn't the phoney you convinced us he was. It was you who were the phoney, cheating us so well we didn't believe anything Sampson told us.'

They had Natalia: Sasha, too! Why had they waited this long: there wasn't any logic. *Don't panic*, Charlie warned himself. He had to stick to the story they'd rehearsed over and over again: the story to which she'd be clinging to save herself and their daughter. And she was clinging to it: if she weren't, they wouldn't be bothering with this charade, waiting for him to make a slip. 'It was a professional assignment. I beat your man who interrogated me. He was old, past it.'

'Man?' seized Guzov, accusingly.

Guzov wouldn't outwit him, determined Charlie. He was better, quicker, than the Russian, whom he was sure was following someone else's psychology. He wouldn't—couldn't—fail Natalia. Or Sasha. 'A colonel, according to the uniform epaulettes. I never knew his name, of course, although the debriefing went on for a long time, daily for what must have been more than a month in the very beginning.'

'That wasn't how it was at the beginning, was it, Charlie?' challenged Guzov. 'Your initial debriefer was a woman, not a man.'

Charlie shook his head, frowning. 'It's vague now, so long ago. There was a woman, though. Very briefly, no more than one or two sessions. My impression was that she was very new, probably only just qualified. I assumed that's why someone more senior took over.'

'Was that really how it was, Charlie?'

This was goading, not how a professional interrogator would have asked the question. 'You hold all the records.' Records that Natalia had assured him she'd so very carefully manufactured to prove that after her opening session his questioning had been transferred to a senior colonel who'd died within a year of their affair beginning.

'I've read all the records,' said Guzov, his tone thick with doubt. 'I've read everything we could find.'

It had to be the official Hall of Weddings documentation of his marriage to Natalia, when he'd hoped to persuade her to come back with him to England. Charlie was tensed, although not showing it, waiting for the triumphant coup de grace. *Admit nothing, offer nothing,* he reminded himself. 'Then you have the advantage over me, after such a long time.'

'That's exactly what I've got, Charlie—the total advantage over you. That's what I told you that first day in the hospital, remember?'

'Your special hospital,' snatched Charlie, trying to deflect the man from his script.

'Where there's still a place permanently available for you.'

This wasn't right, decided Charlie. Where was the denouement to which Guzov had so carefully, so obediently to his instructions, built up; to the declaration of Natalia and Sasha's seizure, at which they expected him to collapse! They couldn't have detained them after all! They'd tried a bluff, which Guzov had enacted quite well, in the hope that he *would* collapse: her escape to London would have automatically led to her entire KGB and FSB career being scrutinized, and the coincidence of his edited early encounter and his seizure at the same time as her disappearance would be more than sufficient to justify this confrontation. And perhaps, interpreting that last remark, his pulling himself back from his near psychological decline had been detected by the permanently recording cameras and there was a determination to reduce him back into a mentally malleable state of career confession that he'd refused with the photographic recognition. Choosing that for a response, Charlie said, 'That's a pointless threat. I've told you why I couldn't identify more of those pictures.'

'The hospital specialists there tell me they have treatments that can help memory and recollection but I don't really want to descend to that sort of help,' said Guzov, grimacing his smile at last.

'It would be pointless as I'm trying to co-operate as much as I can,' said Charlie. He walked back to one of the inner door supports he'd established not to be covered by any camera lens to scratch his back, more irritated than concerned by the episode, hoping yet again that the nonsense didn't go on for much longer.

Mort Bering's presence in London disrupted their established routine and it was past ten that night before Elliott got back to his apartment and Jane Ambersom waiting expectantly in bed. 'Didn't mean to be so late,' apologized the American. 'But the Bureau and Langley are in a mutual state of chaos at the thought of being tricked a second time by Russian intelligence. Everyone, that is, except Mort, who's switched everything around to make it appear he's the guy who's caught out Irena and Radtsic.'

'Excluding you?' asked Jane, protectively, briefly pulling her head away from his naked shoulder.

'Oh no,' reassured Elliott. 'I'm very much Robin to his Batman. I know who's really sorting fact from fiction, don't I?'

'The last we heard from Joe Goody was that he's going to let Irena and Radtsic sweat until tomorrow,' said Jane, knowing Elliott was anxious to hear what had transpired at meetings to which he and Bering had not been included.

'Goody suddenly doesn't seem to be in any great hurry,' complained the American.

'He insists this'll be the quickest way,' contradicted Jane. 'Our attorney-general was at this afternoon's assessment meeting. He wants to confront Moscow right away to get a people exchange under way. After all the shit the Russians have shovelled onto us over the past weeks, it's turning into a personal advantage contest between him, Bland, or Palmer to establish who can come up with the best total recovery counter-attack.'

'And all I thought important was upholding the honest reputation of our two countries,' remarked Elliott.

'The inscription on that FBI badge of yours?' prompted Jane, matching the cynicism. 'Which out of Fidelity, Bravery, and Integrity don't you understand?'

27

GUIDED BY THE INITIAL LANGUAGE IDENTIFICATION OF BRITAIN'S GCHQ, America's combined intelligence organizations, led by the Maryland—headquartered National Security Agency, massively concentrated their overnight code search between specialized Asian and Middle Eastern lexicologists and cryptologists, enabling Mort Bering to convene a breakfast meeting in the FBI section of the U.S. embassy in Grosvenor Square with three virtually complete but alternative-choice transcriptions waiting on each table setting. Apart from coffee, the offerings were eggs hardening on a warmer, bagels, blueberry muffins, and sweet rolls. Most satisfied themselves with coffee.

'Our conclusions are substantially the same as your guys', yesterday,' opened Bering, generous in the knowledge that the American decryptions were far more comprehensive. 'In addition to how it's going and where are you, there's repeated insistence, mostly in sign, for Radtsic to insist on further meetings. . . .' Bering nodded to Rebecca. 'Which fits with what he said to you the day after the prison encounter. There's alternative-version inferences to time gaps and interruptions, which we think is for some estimate of how long Radtsic imagines the supposed debriefing will continue. And there's confirmation that Radtsic's being asked about others. . . .' Bering gestured with his transcription copy. 'You see it's the same on all three versions and it's repeated from more than one member of the Russian delegation. Our interpretation is that it's important to them, close to being the focus of the meeting.'

'They surely can't imagine we'd have Irena, Radtsic, and Elena at the same location?' said Rebecca. There wasn't any resentment today. The embassy was neutral territory and she'd decided she couldn't give a damn about Aubrey Smith virtually ignoring her, particularly after being singled out by Bering.

'We're fairly satisfied that Irena and Radtsic are working the same scheme, right?' suggested Jane. 'Natalia isn't. How about the location demand being to find her?'

'That's feasible,' agreed Smith. 'She's completely rejected any consular approach. Getting to her another way would continue the success Moscow's so far achieved everywhere else.'

'And still imagine they're achieving,' reminded Jane. 'But why should they believe for a moment we'd allow contact between any of them? That would never happen: it's ridiculous and they'd know it.'

'We're overlooking another possibility,' declared Rebecca, seizing an opening that no-one else appeared to have considered. 'Why should it be Natalia? Let's think like the intelligence professionals we're supposed to be. Moscow came inches close to pulling off their coup of the century with Stepan Lvov. This, somehow we still don't understand, is a continuation: certainly there's a connection. Wouldn't they have established a Control, a conduit between Radtsic, Elena, and Irena, to ensure each was telling the same coherent story so that we'd never suspect any of them? Which we wouldn't have ever done if the uninvolved Natalia hadn't picked up on the code.'

'That's a reasonable speculation that's been too long in coming from any of us,' complimented Jane. 'But it obviously can't work. Radtsic and Elena don't know where Irena is, nor does Irena know their location. There's no way of their communicating through an unknown outside Control. How could they link up?

'Through the second *known*, outside conduit, the Russian delegation who announced in Belmarsh that they were remaining in England,' identified Rebecca, triumphantly. 'Look at the number of references to other meetings! Radtsic finds out where he is, to tell them, they press for consular access to Irena to learn where she is and give both to their patiently waiting, already emplaced and unknown link between Radtsic, Elena, and Irena.'

'To perform or provide what function?' demanded Barry Elliott.

'I don't know,' openly admitted Rebecca, confident of leading the meeting. 'I'm speculating upon what we believe we've got. What's your alternative suggestion?'

Joe Goody put aside a half-eaten muffin to cover the impasse. 'I can't promise all the answers but from what we've now got I'll be disappointed if I can't provide most of them. Yesterday all I had was bluff. Now I've got sufficient to make each of them think the other's made full confessions.'

'And you've still got a full day ahead of you,' encouraged Smith.

'Do you know what occurred to me back there?' Aubrey Smith asked Jane, on their way back to Thames House.

'What?'

'How much the idea of an intermediate conduit between Radtsic and Irena fits Gerald Monsford's insistence that there's a hostile penetration, a mole, in MI6.'

'I thought we'd proven that to be a deranged invention?' said Jane.

'So did I,' said Smith.

Irena broke.

She'd been left the longest by Goody, but, upon his instructions, never for a moment been free from the doubled-up security guards. A female officer even accompanied her to the bathroom, the separating lavatory doors kept open, and the moveable, light-identifying cameras were constantly visible to her, tracking her every movement throughout the West Sussex house. She was escorted by three guards, always one female, during outside exercise. Again following Goody's orders, none of the guards, inside or outside the house, verbally responded to Irena's increasingly angry demands. Distinguishably different-coloured and insignia-marked helicopters regularly passed overhead: every day since her uncovering at least one landed a security-staff changeover. Floodlights kept the immediately encircling grounds—and therefore, inevitably, the complete exterior and reflected interior of the house—in perpetual daylight illumination. There was persistent noise from ground-patrolling guard dogs.

Goody was intentionally visible as he disembarked from an arriving helicopter and remained in apparently deep, arm-gesturing discussion with assembled guards, in the middle of whom he eventually disappeared inside the house. It was a further thirty minutes before he entered the drawing room in which Irena sat, forcing a relaxed calmness.

'According to the interrogation manuals, I'm supposed to be gibbering by now, begging to confess to whatever you want, aren't I?'

Goody ignored that and said, 'We've officially informed the embassy of your detention, ma'am: of the others', too.'

'At last, someone with a speaking part!'

'There's to be no diplomatic access, not until the investigation's complete. Which will probably take some time, despite everything that Demin's telling us,' said Goody, continuing his monologue.

'I'm sure your mummers will tire of their silent performance before I do.' There was the slightest catch in Irena's voice at the reference to Yuri Demin.

Goody gave no indication of instantly detecting it. 'It's required, according to the international conventions, that you're told of an impending prosecution, ma'am.'

'They're really not very good mummers, none of them.'

Goody gestured to the identifiably lighted camera. 'The fact that I've complied with that requirement will have been recorded, audibly and on film.' Goody fumbled papers and a pen from a document valise. 'I'd be grateful, ma'am, if you'd sign the official acknowledgement.'

'Go to hell!' exploded the woman, abandoning the artless mockery.

'Of course, ma'am,' said Goody, as if accepting the instruction. 'It's not immediately essential and it's on camera, as I've indicated. Your legal advisor will guide you later upon the formalities. I know you would have been given some idea of the procedure in the event of your capture during your briefing for this assignment. Yuri Georgevich certainly hasn't adhered to it. You're going to be moved from here, of course. A London women's prison will be more convenient, not that we think there's any need for protracted interviews. Your lawyer will doubtless need a lot of time with you to go through what Yuri Georgevich has alleged against you.'

'What is he saying?' asked Irena, thin voiced, appearing oddly to become physically smaller as the resistance seeped from her.

'I don't think it would be right, legally acceptable even, for me to tell you in detail. Suffice to say he's given us a very full account of everything, particularly confirming the importance of your role . . . not in the actual Lvov concept, I don't mean . . . what you've done, or rather tried to do, afterwards—'

'He's done a deal, hasn't he!' broke in Irena. 'He and the bitch Marina Raina, whose most acclaimed performance is opening her legs, have done a deal. . . .'

'We have agreed some concessions, particularly about accommodation, prior to any court hearings,' conceded Goody. 'In the women's prison we're considering, it would probably be sensible to elect for solitary confinement.'

Irena settled herself positively in her chair, glancing up at the audio-equipped camera that Goody had earlier indicated. 'Now listen to the proper story.'

Goody settled back, too. 'Tell me about the finger code.'

'I appreciate your coming personally,' thanked Natalia. 'And for showing me the relevant footage.' She'd become increasingly subdued during the transmission.

'You're owed our complete honesty, for what you've done,' thanked Jane, in return. 'As well as all the reassurance we can offer neither you nor Sasha is in any personal danger. There's absolutely no possibility of your whereabouts being discovered.'

'I'm the third person—Sasha as well as me, because of me—referred to in the coded exchanges,' declared Natalia, looking out the window to where Ethel and Sasha were solemnly enacting a tea party for Luda the doll. 'So thank you, too, for increasing the security.'

'Increasing the security isn't a contradiction of the assurance I've just given you,' insisted Jane, urgently. 'It would be unthinkable in these new circumstances for us not to have done so.'

'I'm a definite target now, for refusing to meet anyone from the embassy.'

'They can't ever, won't ever, be able to get to you or Sasha,' persisted Jane.

'Is what's happened enough to get Charlie out?' abruptly demanded Natalia.

'We're going to make it enough.'

'I hope you're right.'

'Being right about getting Charlie out is another absolute guarantee I'm giving you.'

'There won't be any more footage for me to assess or analyze, now that we've caught them out, will there?'

'I wouldn't have thought so, but there still might be something.'

'It'll be good not to be so involved. I've been neglecting Sasha: not giving her enough of my time.'

'I'll keep you up-to-date about Charlie.'

'I've just told her we're going to bargain Charlie's freedom,' disclosed Jane, after Natalia swapped places with Ethel at the doll's tea party. 'I'd expected a very different response from what I got.'

'I warned against the television interpretation of a search for a third person,' reminded Ethel.

'I also told her that she's not in any danger of being found.'

'She's in the business!' protested Ethel. 'She knows you can't positively guarantee that, just as you and I know it. And if they find her, they find Sasha, who's the total focus of Natalia's life. She was starting to relax, occupied by what we were asking her to do. Now that's over and she's just been told there's a search for her, she's terrified.'

'There's no absolute certainty about Natalia being the third person!' insisted Jane. 'It could be someone—a group, even—with no connection whatsoever to Natalia. The deciphering could be wrong: there might not even *be* a third involvement.'

'I'll accept each and all of that,' said Ethel. 'Natalia won't acknowledge a single word of it.'

'You're telling me I shouldn't have shown her the deciphering?'

'You're my deputy director-general.'

'As which I'm asking you to answer the question.'

'No,' said Ethel. 'You shouldn't have shown her.'

One hundred twenty miles away, Joe Goody's helicopter put down on the far lawn of the Hertfordshire safe house.

It was difficult for Charlie not to sink back. If they had Natalia and Sasha, there was only one conceivable psychological move: to goad him, as Guzov had goaded, but to have ended with the destroying disclosure, maybe even with a forlorn, weeping photograph or even a pleading film of Natalia begging him truthfully to co-operate. But maybe . . . ? Maybe what? He didn't believe Guzov had the psychological awareness to realize how low he'd sunk, nor how he'd pulled back, but the films would have been analyzed by professionals who would have recognized his recovery and wanted to push him down again until his resistance was completely crushed. Known, too, that Natalia and Sasha were his weakness with which to do it. Would a weeping, pleading film or photograph do it during the next confrontation with the grimacing man? It was a question Charlie couldn't answer: didn't want to answer because he feared what that answer would be, despite and against all the training and all the self-belief.

From the security control room in Hertfordshire, Joe Goody told Aubrey Smith, 'I've got it all, from both of them. All on film, of course; every word recorded.'

'You too tired for a meeting tonight?' asked Smith.

'Absolutely not. I like travelling by helicopter,' said the interrogator.

For once the man hadn't called him sir, Smith realized.

28

AS THERE HAD BEEN SO MANY TIMES BEFORE, THERE WAS SI-
lence at the conclusion of Joe Goody's presentation, but for the first time
the atmosphere in the small Foreign Office conference room was of pal-
pable, gradually smiling satisfaction. The only immediate movement
was Goody heavily drinking two glasses of water in quick succession after guiding everyone through his filmed confessions of the three known
as Maxim and Elena Radtsic and Irena Novikov.

'The Lvov concept was brilliant but this, as a total disinformation follow-up to create the maximum chaos in America and here with invented
accounts of penetrations and deeply embedded agents, was almost in the
same league,' declared Sir Archibald Bland, in begrudging admiration.

'And devised in less than six weeks, from the time the Lvov emplacement began to go wrong,' supported Geoffrey Palmer. 'That's a theatrical
tour de force.'

'That's what those serving in the KGB and FSB's disinformation bureau are and always have been, consummate actors,' reminded Aubrey
Smith, less effusive. 'That's the very reason for their induction into the
Russian service, to play whatever role they're called upon to perform.' He
gesture to the now-black screens. 'And don't forget what the phoney
Radtsic said—he's been the real Radtsic's stand-in at a lot of official
events in Russia: he not only looks like the man, apart from the facial
disfigurement, he knows how to behave like him: he's had a long rehearsal time.'

'Learning all they had to learn in such a short period is still a remarkable feat of memory,' insisted Bland.

'I'm surprised all three collapsed so quickly, even faced with Joe's threats of indefinite imprisonment while cases were prepared against them,' said John Passmore, who'd been included in that night's assessment, along with Attorney-General Sir Peter Pickering.

'I'm not,' said Rebecca, anticipating the approaching conclusion to the entire affair that would clear the way for her promised promotion. 'They're *actors*, pure and simple. They didn't go through field training, weren't taught how to resist interrogation. Their schooling was in deceit and pretence and, in the case of both the women, in seduction. On the film you've just seen both Irena and Elena admitted working as swallows, sexually entrapping selected foreigners for blackmail. But all three would always, until now, have worked within Russia, never outside. They don't know how to withstand the tricks of interrogation. . . .' She smiled towards Goody, on his third glass of water.

'What about their accommodation from now on?' asked Jane, as always wanting to look forward. 'At the moment they're in minor stately homes taking up a hell of a lot of manpower. I'm not suggesting we actually do put them in jail, but shouldn't we scale the luxury down a little?'

'Doesn't that depend on how satisfied we are that we've got everything, which is, I suppose, a question for you, Joe,' questioned Passmore. 'It certainly looks as if we've got enough to face the Russians down and get our guys back, but do you think you've got it all?'

'I probably haven't,' conceded Goody, at once. 'As you've seen and heard, for a majority of the interviews I let their admissions run without intruding too many qualifying questions. My concentration *was* upon getting what you needed to bargain our people's release. To go deeper I'd need to analyze each previous interrogation to isolate specific disclosures—which means all the American film and audio recordings of Irena's questioning—and go through each individual claim and revelation item by item.'

'Irena talked for a total of maybe sixteen hours,' said Mort Bering, looking at Rebecca. 'How long did Radtsic take?'

'Twenty, at least.'

'To tooth-comb that lot would take weeks,' gauged Barry Elliott, anxious to make a contribution in front of his deputy director.

'More like months, maybe as many as three to four, to do it thoroughly,' corrected Goody. 'That's the least amount of time I'd like to set aside.'

'We know it's all disinformation to misdirect and confuse us that can now be ignored,' said Bland, impatient for a successful conclusion that would end the implied doubt about his cabinet-office role. 'There are two absolute essentials here: publicly exposing the whole Russian business for what it was to restore our credibility completely, and getting our people back.'

'I wouldn't agree with that order of things,' immediately challenged Smith. 'I believe the threat of exposure is the weapon to repatriate Charlie and the others.'

'Pedantic,' dismissed Palmer, as anxious as his co-chairman for a quick conclusion.

'I'm inclined to agree on a time limit,' said Bering. 'I think the bastards have made us run around in circles for far too long. I think it's payback time.'

'And I want to get the repatriation moving right away,' said Sir Peter Pickering. 'Nothing's going to happen immediately. There must be particular claims that appear more important than others. Why don't we concentrate the re-examination upon those while the bargaining runs its course?'

'That sounds an excellent compromise,' declared Bland, to Palmer's nodded agreement.

'Which brings us back to my question,' reminded Jane. 'Do we let them go on living where they are or move them to somewhere more realistic . . . prison, even, if it would create the pressure to help Joe with his restricted schedule?'

'I'm still opposed to actual imprisonment,' cautioned Pickering. 'It's different with the three Russians who burgled Charlie's flat, even though they are diplomats. Burglary is a criminal offence. I can—and will—set out charges against Radtsic and the two women. We can move them somewhere less salubrious, but don't put them behind bars.'

'We might as well leave them where they are,' bustled Bland. 'Politically we need this to be over as soon as possible: moving them from a five- to one-star safe house won't achieve anything apart from unnecessary upheaval.'

'I'll be glad when I can get my man back at a proper time at night,' said Jane, in mock complaint as Barry Elliott came into the bedroom.

'Tonight was Mort's celebration time,' announced the American, a slur in his voice.

'Celebrating what?' asked Jane, pushing herself farther up in the bed.

The man began to undress, which needed concentration. 'I was speaking to guys in D.C. earlier today. The word is there's going to be a big reshuffle back there: Mort gets the top job for what he's done here.'

'Which was sitting and listening to other people's successes,' judged Jane, cynically.

Elliott gave a lopsided grin, needing very positively to sit down to remove his trousers. 'We spent the early part of tonight talking about disinformation, remember? What you know to have happened here and how it's been relayed back to Pennsylvania Avenue are two very different stories. I told you already, Mort is Batman under deep cover.'

'What you told me was that you were Robin to his Batman,' reminded Jane, seriously.

'Reword that,' suggested Elliott, matching the seriousness. 'While he's been here, I've been the gofer for the big man upon whose goodwill my future career depends. And I thought I detected quite a bit of career jockeying going on around that Foreign Office conference table earlier tonight. You want a nightcap?'

'Haven't you had enough?'

'You're not going to turn into a shrew, reminding me of that play we saw at Stratford, are you?'

'Small ones.' Jane sat even more fully up against the bed head while he fetched the drinks, curious at his reference to the very beginning of their affair. Accepting the brandy from him, she said, 'Is that how you define all that eagerness to wrap everything up, as career protection?'

'As far as Mort was concerned it was job promotion but I thought your two civil-service guys were in a hell of a hurry.' He touched his glass to Jane's.

'I thought there was too much hurry, too,' admitted Jane. 'So does Aubrey. Against which, we're in a hurry ourselves to get our people out, particularly Charlie Muffin. We still don't have a proper idea of how badly he's hurt.'

'What about Rebecca, who was being conned so rotten by Radtsic?'

'That's not strictly fair: we were all being conned rotten until Natalia identified the coded exchanges,' defended Jane.

'You want to be careful about that Christian fairness crap. Where we exist, it's regarded as a failing.'

'But let's go on with it between ourselves,' urged Jane, putting her unwanted brandy aside. 'Are you going to be staying here in London? Or are you likely to get a career change too?'

The man put his drink aside as well, turning more fully to Jane. 'I don't know. Nothing's been said.'

'But?' she pressed, detecting the uncertainty in his voice.

'It's a possibility.'

'Oh.'

'Would you consider leaving your service to be with me?'

'Is that a clumsy proposal of marriage?'

'I suppose it is. So what's your answer?'

'I don't know.'

'That isn't an answer and doesn't help.'

'I wish it did; that I had an answer,' said Jane.

When it finally came, the too-long-overdue British rebuttal of Moscow's propaganda blitz was all-encompassing. The close-to-dawn, intentionally ambiguous government release of an important forthcoming statement on arrested Russian spies, calculated against the time difference between London and Moscow, gained its intended coverage on every early-morning radio and television news channel as well as in daytime print publications. The announcement also alerted global news media, additionally guaranteeing coverage and publication in countries with similar time zones.

There was a further announcement, an hour later, to ensure its unstated connection to the first, that the British government was calling in the Russian ambassador to be given the strongest possible protest note concerning his country's totally unacceptable intelligence activities. That was quickly supplemented by strictly unattributable briefings to British and foreign London-based journalists that a particularly specialized and newly arrived group of spies, whose identities were known to the counter-intelligence agencies, were inside the Kensington embassy. The tightest, twenty-four-hour surveillance had been imposed and arrests were intended if any of them emerged from what was technically Russian territory.

In the afternoon, Prime Minister's Questions were delayed for ten minutes for the British foreign secretary to make a personal statement to the House of Commons, adding his public protest to that already officially notified to Moscow through its London ambassador. Few details could at that stage be disclosed beyond making it as clear as possible that the Russian activities were totally unacceptable. Whether it would be possible to go further into the complained details depended upon Moscow's response to each and every accusation directly levelled against it.

The sensation of the eventual statement was not its content but the simultaneous issue of photographs of Maxim and Elena Radtsic and Irena Novikov. All were captioned under their assumed names, with what they claimed to be their genuine identities listed in the accompanying text. The kidnap allegation was a total fantasy, along with every other claim and allegation made by the Russian Federation in recent weeks. Those allegations had been an attempt to conceal a potentially devastating international intelligence operation that had been defeated by British counter-intelligence. The full details of that operation would possibly emerge during the intended trials of every Russian involved in the conspiracy, including those now hiding inside the Russian embassy.

'Well?' demanded Ethel Jackson, turning away from the BBC broadcast that had taken almost twenty minutes to complete.

'They'll consider it aggressive. And the real Radtsic will see himself to be humiliated.'

'Natalia!' exclaimed the security supervisor, bewildered at the other woman's muted response. 'The genuine Radtsic would have known what was happening: initiated it, even. What's he expect when he's caught out? He brought about his own humiliation.'

'It might have been better to have begun with a softer approach.'

'What are you frightened of, Natalia?' Ethel asked, directly.

'Not getting Charlie out. What he might be like if we do get him out.'

'This is the beginning, not the end of what we can do,' said Ethel, encouragingly.

'Moscow has kept ahead all the time. They might still have something we haven't anticipated.'

'On the other hand they might not,' balanced Ethel, reluctant to concede that the Russian might be right.

Charlie Muffin became conscious of vehicle noise before he was properly awake and was already out of bed when that week's guard, the originally assigned Georgian who'd saved him from the *spetsnaz* dogs, hurried into the room.

'You're going,' announced the man.

'Where?'

'Get dressed. You've no time to wash, shave.'

'What's the hurry? Where am I being taken?'

'They're waiting.'

The most likely destination was the psychiatric hospital, Charlie supposed, struggling into the only clothes he had. But why? The only purpose for his being taken there would be to reduce him medically to a malleable puppet, and there was no benefit for them in doing that because they wouldn't be able to trust his deranged ramblings any more than they had been able to accept what he'd already told Guzov. A different but still harsher regime, their having lost patience at learning nothing from the Guzov charade? That was a possibility. Which still left the question: where? The Lubyanka topped the list. But there was also Moscow's Lefortovo jail, legendary for crushing defiance from political prisoners.

'Let's go!' demanded the house guard, from the door.

Charlie was relieved that the three waiting soldiers were not wearing *spetsnaz* insignia. There were two men in civilian clothes and another in a blue unidentified type of uniform similar to what Charlie remembered from the psychiatric institute. The woman housekeeper was at the kitchen door, looking apprehensively at the soldiers. Charlie didn't catch the full exchange between the waiting group and the house guard but thought he detected "specific orders."

The man turned to him and said, 'You're to go with them. Goodbye.'

'Where?' asked Charlie again.

'Just go.' shrugged the man.

A long, small-windowed prison-type van was pulled up directly outside the dacha, its rear doors already open. One of the soldiers pushed Charlie in first, leaving him to choose his own seat on one of the side-mounted benches. The Russian escort filed in behind him. A soldier heavily settled on either side of him.

'Where am I being taken?' demanded Charlie.

'Back to the city,' said the blue-suited man.

'What for? Where to?'

'Moscow,' repeated the man, dully.

Charlie was tensed for the uneven track but there was still sharp, jabbing pain in his shoulder as the van jarred and bumped over the ruts. Conscious of the concentration of the two civilians, Charlie didn't give any indication of discomfort.

As the van reached the smoother blacktop, the one in blue said, 'Are you all right?'

'No,' said Charlie, turning the question. 'I don't know where we're going. Or what for.'

'It won't be long,' avoided the man.

It wasn't. Charlie guessed it took only twenty minutes before the van
was slowed by Moscow traffic, the sounds of which became increasingly
loud. From the briefness with which they obviously travelled upon the
ring road, Charlie guessed the destination was neither the Lubyanka nor
the Lefortovo, which was confirmed when the rear doors opened in the
yard of the psychiatric institute. Charlie hesitated at the point of getting
out of the vehicle, gazing up at the window-barred building. Would he
leave it sane, he wondered: if he left at all.

The blue-uniform man led Charlie into the institute, the two unspeaking civilians escorting from behind. The soldiers remained by the
van. They went past the reception desk without stopping for the waiting
elevator but went up only two floors. The bearded surgeon was waiting,
smiling, in an office large enough to accommodate at least six of his
usual entourage.

'This time you come to me,' announced the man, whom Charlie had
last seen with Guzov at the dacha in the hills.

Again all Charlie's questions were ignored. He was escorted, by medical
staff now, to a radiology department where his shoulder was X-rayed from
both front and back and then to an adjoining operating theatre where he
remained stripped to the waist but was allowed to sit, not lie, on the table
for the surgeon to examine the healed wound. An assistant took his blood
pressure and a blood test, the result of which the surgeon brought with
him when he entered the office in which Charlie, dressed now, had been
told to wait.

'You're surprisingly fit for a man who's obviously neglected himself so
much in the past,' announced the surgeon. 'And your injury is completely
healed.'

'You've already told me that,' said Charlie, who'd been surprised at the smallness of the entry and exit wounds they'd held mirrors for him to see for the first time.

'It'll never cause you any trouble in the future.'

'That's reassuring,' said Charlie. 'So what happens now?'

The man shrugged. 'You're completely out of my hands now.'

A saloon car was where the van had earlier been when Charlie left the building. The two civilian escorts positioned themselves on either side of him in the rear. There was a third man in the passenger seat, beside the driver.

'Are any of you going to tell me where I'm going?' tried Charlie.

'No,' refused the man in the front seat. 'Be quiet.'

It was a short journey, the ring road ignored to get into the old part of the city, where there were still pre-revolutionary buildings. But it was into a modern high-rise that they abruptly turned, anonymous until they got through an arched entrance into an inner courtyard in which some of the parked vehicles were official government ZiLs.

Not the time for any questions, Charlie realized, bewildered but hopeful. He got out as instructed, walked unresisting between his backseat escorts into a foyer, and obediently stood aside while the third man went through document signing and exchanges at a reception desk, from behind which a man immediately came to gesture Charlie farther along a corridor. Almost at the end the man opened a door and said, 'Wait in there.'

Almost at once the door opened again, as if the newcomer had been waiting conveniently close, in the next room, even. The man was tall, as impeccably dressed as Mikhail Guzov had always been, but unusually for a Russian wore a crested ring on the little finger of his left hand.

The man frowned disbelievingly, examining Charlie's kulak-smocked figure from top to bottom and in cut-crystal English said, 'Are you *really* Charlie Muffin?'

'Yes,' said Charlie. 'Who are you?'

'Chambers, second secretary at the embassy. I've come to get you home.'

29

IT WAS DIFFICULT FOR CHARLIE TO ADJUST QUICKLY ENOUGH TO take control but he did, just. He refused any small talk and determinedly avoided the most personally vital question, for which he doubted the diplomat would have the answer. Unable to accept what was happening and unwilling to risk another, different entrapment, Charlie went as far as warning the embassy driver against speeding or ignoring any other traffic regulation and actually held back from taking off the demeaning kulak smock until they'd passed unimpeded through the embassy gates to an unsuspected reception.

Peter Warren was the only person Charlie recognized. The ambassador was much younger than the predecessor who'd so disastrously failed to supervise the embassy six months earlier, at once assuring Charlie that every assistance was available and suggesting a personal meeting when Charlie had settled. By similar contrast, the new, grey-haired, Mancunian-accented third secretary was an older man than the preceding, incompetent incumbent who'd done nothing to correct his superior's failings. The frustration burning through him at the enforced delay, Charlie assured the instantly attentive embassy doctor that he was fit enough to travel and that he'd undergo the medical examination when he reached London, which it was important he do as quickly as possible. His only request was for clothes to replace those in which the FSB had humiliated him as part of their mentally disorientating captivity.

As they entered the MI5 *rezidentura*, Warren got as far as, 'So you don't—?' before Charlie cut him off.

'Natalia! What happened to Natalia and Sasha!'

'Both safe, in England. There wasn't a hitch. Your shooting ensured that.'

There was no single emotion. It was a colliding combination of relief, continuing confusion, uncertainty, and satisfaction that finally merged into impatience. 'I've been totally isolated, don't know anything of what's happened from the moment I was shot. Tell me from that moment.'

'The Director-General wants to talk to you at once.'

'He can wait until I've got some idea what he'll be talking about.'

'I got a bottle of Islay single malt from your commissary records when you were here.'

'That's thoughtful,' accepted Charlie, who managed two whiskies in the time it took Warren to set out everything that had followed the Vnukovo ambush.

'And I don't know it all, just the basic outlines,' concluded Warren. 'There's a lot that's gone on in London that I obviously haven't been told about.'

'I'm the only one released: the others from the original back-up team, apart from you, are still being held?'

'Wilkinson got out under another identity through Poland after Preston was picked up at the airport on a test run. We've no idea where MI6's Denning and Beckindale are.'

'Any access granted?'

'No.'

'How much notice was there of my release?'

Warren poured himself an Islay malt, head curiously to one side. 'An hour. And for someone who's been totally isolated, you're talking as if you know something that no-one else does?'

Charlie shook his head, refusing the question. 'What about embassy surveillance?'

'Substantially increased,' confirmed Warren. 'And after what happened to Preston I'm a prisoner here as much as the Russians who saw Radtsic in Belmarsh are trapped in their London embassy. Aubrey Smith's thought is that I'll be okay coming out as your escort: that they'll expect someone to travel with you.'

'Which is precisely why you're not coming with me.'

'Charlie! What the hell's going on!'

'I won't know, not until I get back to London. Which I want to do today.'

'There's two tickets booked on the six o'clock plane, Moscow time: one of them was for me,' said Warren, miserably.

'Here you're safe. Outside you won't be,' said Charlie. 'It's time I talked to the Director.'

'How much do you know?' was Aubrey Smith's opening demand when the connection was established from the suspended, totally secure communications pod in the embassy's communications room.

'I don't at the moment need to know any more of what happened after I was shot. There's something more immediately important. My release isn't right. I think I know what it is but I can't get proof until I get back tonight. And I'm doing that alone. I don't want to give the FSB any excuse—'

'We've already arranged your arrival at Heathrow,' broke in Smith.

'Scrap it,' insisted Charlie. 'What's the nearest hospital to London airport?'

There was a pause. 'I don't know. Hammersmith, maybe.'

'Make it Hammersmith,' said Charlie. 'Warn the hospital director—but no-one else—that I'll be arriving. No preparations in advance. I'll make my own way there from the airport.'

'What's the problem?'

Charlie took a deep breath, knowing yet again that he was nakedly splaying himself out for self-offered sacrifice if he were wrong and that if he were he would never again be accorded trust or loyalty from a man who'd already shown him an abundance of both. 'I'm not sure there is one. Trust me until tonight.'

There was a pause from London. 'I'll have people at the hospital.'

'I'll be followed from the airport: keep everything at a distance.'

'Are you in physical danger?'

'Not yet. The defectors are, totally.'

'Including Natalia?'

'Very much including Natalia. We shouldn't take risks with any of them.'

'We're not,' guaranteed Smith. 'They're all under complete shut-down.'

'They need to be: absolute, total shutdown.'

'Trust, as always,' isolated Aubrey Smith, allowing the criticism at last.

'Trust is all I've got to offer at the moment.'

'Your cover name at the hospital will be Simpkins,' supplied Smith.

'That's one I've never had before,' accepted Charlie.

'It's the name of my cat,' said Smith.

None of the jackets offered to Charlie after his brief, noncommittal courtesy encounter with the ambassador fitted him any better than the enveloping smock. Charlie accepted Warren's raincoat—along with an already prepared replacement passport—to cover the Russian-supplied work shirt and trousers. Thinking not as himself but as those who would be watching the embassy, Charlie abandoned his original intention to get to Sheremetyevo by airport bus because it was unthinkable he would have travelled that way, but once more cautioned the embassy driver against motoring risks. He arrived an hour ahead of the required schedule, was among the first through the check-in line, and, for the benefit of the surveillance he wasn't bothering to identify, allowed himself one vodka before embarking, curious at how many FSB were inevitably following him onto the flight. He believed he identified two, one actually sitting in the opposite aisle seat, but was sure there would be more. He considered the in-flight meal, having refused anything at the embassy, but decided against it and made the one unwanted whisky last until the co-pilot's announcement of the London landing.

Charlie had expected to feel relief—a minimal sensation at least—but there was nothing. His troublesome feet, more extensively exercised in less than one day than they had been over the previous fortnight, prevented his hurrying to the passport check-in queue for which he waited patiently, conscious of the two suspected FSB watchers on the plane unprofessionally anxious to keep level in the non-EU-passenger queue. Charlie switched his search for MI5 protectors he knew would be in the passenger hall and was encouraged at failing to isolate any. He had to walk in front of the foreign-passport checks as he made his way down to the baggage hall, aware as he passed of his aisle-seat companion in a gesticulating dispute with an immigration officer.

Without luggage to claim, Charlie passed straight through to the arrivals concourse and was relieved at the shortness of the taxi queue, although there were at least six intervening customers and only three available vehicles between him and his followers when he got his cab. As it picked up the M4 into London, Charlie had the first sensation he supposed to be relief but it was too fleeting for him to be sure. He wished he were surer of a lot of other beliefs and emotions.

Charlie didn't bother to check for pursuit as he went into the hospital, glad there was an unoccupied receptionist at the desk. 'I have an appointment with the director. My name is Simpkins.'

The bespectacled woman frowned, shuffling through paper from a cubby hole in front of her. 'There's no note here.'

'Please check his office.'

'There's always a note.'

'Please check,' repeated Charlie.

The woman hesitated but then with obvious reluctance dialed on an internal line, the frown deepening as she replaced the receiver. 'You're to go to level F, administration. There should have been a note.'

'I'll tell them when I get there,' promised Charlie.

'He's landed safely,' announced Jane, as she returned from the control room.

'Definitely free?' pressed Natalia.

'Definitely,' confirmed Jane, smiling between the two other women in the sitting room of the safe house.

'How badly was he hurt?'

'He'll have an immediate medical check. He was well enough to travel alone.'

'Do you think champagne's in order?' suggested Ethel.

'Absolutely,' agreed Jane.

'Where's he being taken?' asked Natalia.

'Into London,' generalized Jane.

'Has anyone spoken properly to him yet?'

'Not yet. Not like you mean.'

Ethel handed glasses around and said, 'Congratulations. You've got him back, Natalia. And it's largely as a result of all that you did.'

'Yes,' said the woman, the last to sip her wine. 'Will he be brought here?'

'Not immediately. He has to be debriefed. We've no idea what's been happening to him since Vnukovo.'

'Of course.'

'His first question was about you and Sasha,' said Jane, who'd read Warren's account from Moscow before flying down to Hampshire.

Natalia smiled, faintly. 'That's good to hear.'

'You haven't drunk your champagne,' complained Ethel, hovering over the Russian after topping up the two other glasses and waiting while Natalia made room for more wine.

'You don't seem very excited,' finally accused Jane.

'I'm frightened,' Natalia admitted, openly. 'I never really thought it would work, that they'd let him go. I still can't properly understand it and I'm frightened.'

'I think anyone would be frightened, after what you've both been through,' encouraged Ethel. 'And that's up to now. There's still the adjustments you've got to make.'

'Yes,' agreed Natalia. 'There'll need to be a lot of adjustments.'

'Why aren't I being allowed television anymore? Or radio or newspapers?' demanded Irena.

'You should be grateful you're being allowed to stay here, ma'am,' said Joe Goody, registering the similarity of the protest with that of Radtsic and Elena, earlier.

'I want to know what's going on!'

'I've told you what's going on,' said Goody, patiently. 'You've been exposed as a Russian intelligence agent working against the interests of this country, for which you're going to face trial on charges still being formulated. They will automatically carry a custodial sentence the length of which could be mitigated by the degree of assistance you continue to give us.'

'I'm not telling you any more, don't want to see you again, until I'm allowed access to diplomats from my embassy.'

'I've also told you that arrest warrants have been issued against the Russian intelligence agents who saw Radtsic in prison and who have taken refuge in your London embassy,' politely continued Goody. 'There is no question of consular access to you, Radtsic, or Elena while that situation exists. There's also the matter of your safety that has to be considered.'

'What safety?' demanded the woman, the belligerence slightly lessening.

'We have reason to believe that if your service discovered your whereabouts you'd be in considerable physical danger.'

'Elimination!' exclaimed the woman derisively. 'Don't be ridiculous. We'll go home heroes.'

'We don't believe we are being ridiculous, ma'am,' said Goody, forever mild, also noting the similarity with Radtsic's earlier rejection. 'We believe your service consider all three of you a severe political embarrassment that they're anxious to eradicate to prevent your publicly appearing in a British court of law.'

'You're bluffing,' accused Irena, unable to keep the uncertainty from her voice.

'What I want you very carefully to consider is properly, genuinely, defecting to us and telling us precisely what the disinformation was in everything you told the Americans.'

'Go fuck yourself!'

'I'll see you tomorrow, ma'am. And don't worry. As long as you're here, protected as completely are you are, you'll remain quite safe.'

'You're right!' declared the security-cleared surgeon, squinting at the X-ray pictures on the viewing screen. 'I've never seen anything like this before. And as minuscule as that is, I'm not sure a radiologist would have spotted it if the precise location hadn't been pointed out in advance.'

'Another Russian miracle of miniaturization technology,' dismissed Charlie. 'Is it going to be difficult to get out?'

'Piece of cake,' assured the man, turning away from the screen to where Charlie sat on the edge of the operating table, naked to the waist, which he wished didn't bulge so much over the ill-fitting trousers. 'They didn't actually put it in the wound socket. That would have risked an infection. They created a skin pocket, next to it, using scar tissue as concealment. I can get it out with a local anaesthetic but I'd want you to stay in overnight.'

'I already reserved a private room before knowing what you thought had been planted in your body,' said John Passmore. 'You sure it's limited to being a tracker?'

'I tested it where they kept me,' said Charlie. 'Worked every time I disappeared into the woods: there was someone—once a troop—with me in minutes. But every one of those times and on ordinary exercise in view of their cameras I kept repeating, aloud, that I knew I had a bug embedded in my shoulder. It was never picked up.'

'How did you know?' asked the surgeon. 'I wouldn't have imagined there'd be much pain.'

'There wasn't,' agreed Charlie. 'But it itched like hell.'

It took less than fifteen minutes from the time the local anaesthetic was administered for the tracker device to be taken from Charlie's shoulder and soundlessly laid, at Charlie's urging, on a waiting gauze pad.

'Why so much care?' asked Passmore.

'I don't want any indication that it's been taken out. How many people have you got with you?'

'Enough to make sure you're totally protected.' Passmore frowned.

'Where do buses go from here?' Charlie asked the surgeon.

The man shrugged. 'All over.'

'What's the longest route?'

The man shrugged again. 'The 211 to Waterloo, right over to the other side of London.'

'Get someone to take the tracker, catch the 211, and stash it down the back of a seat,' Charlie told Passmore. 'Maybe have him get off after a couple of stops. You'll have enough time to get an arrest squad in place at Waterloo station to pick up everyone in the car that will be following, as well as whoever's still on the bus.'

'To charge them with what?' demanded Passmore.

'Nothing,' said Charlie, simply. 'I want them delivered back to the embassy to go with the others who are trapped inside. I want Moscow to know that in the end I beat them, the bastards.'

30

EXTRA AMBULANCES WERE THE FOLLOWING MORNING DRAFTED to Hammersmith hospital to create the diversion and as they departed en masse, some sounding their alarm bells, Charlie walked quietly and unaccompanied to the unwashed Ford waiting in the car park. The driver took a surveillance-checking route down Fulham Palace Road and crossed Putney Bridge before the surrounding escort vehicles declared them to be undetected. They recrossed the river at Wandsworth but stayed parallel with it into Chelsea to the safe house originally allocated to Charlie after his initial Moscow investigation into the death of the one-armed man. The MI5 triumvirate was already inside, waiting.

'How's the shoulder?' greeted Aubrey Smith.

'Stiff, which is a lot better than the constant irritation.'

'Have you seen any television or newspapers?' asked Jane.

'No.'

She pressed the Start button on the already set up recorder and at once the TV screen was filled by a melee of television and still cameramen and journalists jostling around a closed van from which six men, all trying to cover their faces with their coats or hands, were abruptly released outside the Russian embassy. Its outer gates were closed, trapping the scrambling men against the railings: their intercom pleas to be admitted, in Russian and clearly identifying themselves by name, were distinctly audible and obviously enabled the still photographs from routine intelligence surveillance to have been provided for the collage strip across the top of the screen. The live footage below continued with the gates finally swinging back for the frantic men to scramble towards the tentatively opened embassy door; halfway there, two of the Russians stumbled into each other and fell, one punching the other in the face in frustrated fury. The voice-over commentary described the six as spies seized during part of the already exposed Russian espionage debacle who were to be declared persona non grata by the British government, who were summoning the Russian ambassador to receive yet another official protest note against Moscow's unacceptable spying activities.

'We tweaked your idea.' Smith smiled. 'And we kept that pinhead bug they put in your shoulder. It's much more advanced than anything our technical division has got. We're going to reverse engineer it to produce our own version.'

'Any movement on the rest of our people held in Moscow?' asked Charlie, anxious to reach his own conclusions about possible FSB reactions.

'It's too soon,' judged the Director-General. 'But as well as today's new protest the ambassador's going to be given new demands for access and their immediate release. We're also giving Moscow a court-appearance date for the three who burgled your flat.'

'Prichard and Blackwater,' abruptly announced Charlie, realizing the tit-for-tat potential from his naming the two MI5 officers from the photographs Mikhail Guzov had produced at the dacha. 'I had to identify them from eight photographs of our people to convince them I was cooperating and for them to believe all the misinformation I was sowing.'

'Prichard got back from Rome last week: his rotation was up,' said Passmore, already moving towards the telephone. 'Blackwater's in Canberra.' From where he stood, telephone in hand, he called to Charlie, 'You got the names of the other six?'

Charlie crossed to the operations director to avoid shouting the identifications. As Charlie returned to where he'd been sitting, Aubrey Smith said, 'We should have been told that last night.'

'Last night I didn't know about the Russian-embassy siege,' apologized

Charlie. 'Or what you were going to do with those who followed me from the airport.'

'That's got nothing to do with it,' refused the Director-General.

'I know,' Charlie conceded. 'I made a mistake.' He didn't make professional mistakes like that, thought Charlie, anguished.

'Is there any more identification—anything at all sensitive—to which we've got to react?' demanded Jane.

'No,' assured Charlie, tightly.

Passmore had remained by the telephone and answered it on its first ring. 'We're lucky that it's eleven at night in Australia,' he announced, replacing the receiver. 'Blackwater's in bed, in the compound. Nothing's so far happened to the others, all of whom are being recalled to their embassies.'

'Definitely lucky all around,' agreed Smith, the continued criticism of Charlie unmistakable. 'I think we should begin your debriefing right away.'

'So do I,' agreed Charlie. There was surely nothing else about which he could be caught out!

'Ahead of which, why do you believe they implanted that tracker in your back?' questioned Passmore, finally returning to his seat.

'Improvisation,' said Charlie. 'And opportunity, utilized by some brilliant FSB forward thinking. I couldn't have been more completely trapped, bandaged up like a mummy in a psychiatric hospital, for my brain and everything it held about British intelligence to be taken apart. But here in England they had three active agents who could be uncovered at any minute. Which they were, far more quickly than Moscow expected, because of the help you got from the genuine defector, Natalia. The tracker was their insurance against that discovery, if they'd had more time to spread the intended confusion. Losing whatever I would have been drugged into disclosing was a more acceptable sacrifice than losing what they hoped to achieve through Irena and Radtsic's doppelganger: let's not forget the damage they've already inflicted on the CIA for believing Lvov was genuine. They calculated I would inevitably be reunited with Natalia: the tracker, which we know they were following from my arrival at Heathrow, would have led them to her. As it would have led them to Irena: it was more than an even possibility that I'd see Irena, whom we all thought I'd trapped when I exposed Lvov, an operation they'd already abandoned for the lesser success of planting Irena and Radtsic on us. Both Irena and Natalia—perhaps even Sasha—would have been taken out by an assassination squad. So would I. And when he learned they'd been killed, there would have been very little chance of Radtsic disclosing any real intelligence, would there?'

'But you found the tracker?' said Passmore, admiringly.

'*Suspected* the tracker,' qualified Charlie. It was a relief to have rid himself of its irritation but there was still the pulsating foot discomfort Charlie always felt when he was treading, figuratively, on dangerous ground.

'His identifying Prichard and Blackwater should have been the first thing Charlie Muffin told you at the hospital,' declared Aubrey Smith, who'd insisted upon an instant analysis of the safe-house encounter when they got back to Thames House.

'I checked with Warren,' said Passmore, who'd detoured to the control room before joining the other two in the Director-General's suite. 'He didn't tell Charlie about our blockading the Russian embassy and Charlie certainly didn't know what we were going to do with those who followed the bus: when I left him we hadn't decided to do it ourselves!'

'And when he wasn't in a Moscow mental institute having bugs planted in his back he was being held in virtual isolation,' supported Jane.

'He identified two fellow agents whom he should have done everything to protect at the first opportunity,' persisted the Director-General. 'Charlie's the total professional: it should have been an automatic reaction.'

'He's insisting on being completely debriefed *and* seeing the recordings of the Radtsic and Irena interviews ahead of seeing his wife!' Jane pointed out. 'That's pretty damned professional.'

'And no harm's been done,' reminded Passmore. 'He's acknowledged his mistake. And we don't yet have a complete picture of what he went through in Moscow. I think we should make allowances.'

'Two field agents have got to be withdrawn for their own safety and protection. It'll be a long time, if ever, before we can reassign them,' argued Smith.

'It was always accepted when I was across the river that it was inevitable an officer would break under duress,' remembered Jane. 'I thought there would be the same acceptance here.'

'Under duress,' qualified Smith, heavily. 'Did he appear to you to have been someone subjected to extreme duress?'

Jane broke the brief silence that followed. 'I wouldn't go as far as "extreme duress." He's certainly more subdued than I expected.'

'That's my impression, too,' agreed Passmore. 'And I ascribe that to his not knowing until a few hours before I met him last night what had happened to his wife and child: whether, even, he'd make it to the hospital knowing there was a Russian assassination squad right behind him. Charlie *is* a complete professional. Okay, he made a mistake about the two he named, for which I believe there's a mitigating excuse. What he won't have made any mistake about is knowing, having screwed the Russians for a second time, exactly how big the target is that he's pinned on himself, Natalia, and even their daughter. I think Charlie's got more than enough to be subdued about.'

'Points taken,' said Aubrey Smith.

But not accepted, guessed Jane.

Charlie's debriefing was conducted by two anonymous interrogators and a psychologist, also unnamed, each of whose specific function was the verbal and mental examination of agents subjected to hostile interrogation. It took an unbroken six hours, which included an as-accurate-as-possible identification from a greatly enlarged aerial photograph of the dacha area in which he'd been held as well as estimates of *spetsnaz* barracks and possible weekend-dacha locations of government hierarchy. An additional hour was taken up by a point-by-point review of everything he'd volunteered and every answer he'd given to every detailed question.

Charlie remained absolutely truthful throughout, openly admitting his professional failure in not instantly warning of his naming fellow agents, but held back from telling the psychologist of his mental deterioration in his bizarre forest isolation. The three left anticipating a further session after more-detailed analysis.

It was approaching nine o'clock when Charlie, his second Islay malt already poured, dialed the Hampshire number. He used the identification code supplied by Jane Ambersom to authorize the transfer from the control building to the safe house on a secure line and had a further five minutes to prepare himself with a brief reunion conversation with Ethel Jackson. Natalia didn't immediately speak when the connection was finally made, although he knew she'd picked up the receiver.

'Natalia?'

'Yes.'

'Are you all right?'

'Yes. You were hurt?'

'Not seriously. I'm all right now.'

'I was worried.' Her voice caught, at the end.

'So was I. I didn't know if you'd got out or not.'

'This is being recorded, isn't it?' she asked, professionally.

'Of course. It's automatic.'

'Was it bad for you?'

'No.'

'That's a lie!'

For the first time there was emotion in her voice. 'It's over now. I'll be seeing you and Sasha very soon. But not immediately. A day or two.'

'I know.'

'How is she?'

'Fine. Getting the language well. Ethel's been very good to us. You know her.'

'We worked together a long time ago.'

'Don't take any risks, getting here.'

'Don't you want to see me?' He tried to make it light but it didn't work.

'Why did you say that!'

'It was a joke.'

'A bad one.'

'Answer it as a serious question then.'

'You know how much I want to see you.'

'I want very much to see you, too. Just a day or two.'

'Promise you'll be careful.'

'I promise. And don't forget we've got people being careful for us.' It had ended better than it had begun, Charlie decided. But only minimally. There was a long way to go.

Charlie missed his self-imposed deadline to view the filmed interrogations of the three Russians, despite working an eighteen-hour day, eating what little food he bothered with as he watched, and limiting the Islay malt intake. He was slowed, though, by itemized reruns, which he logged for separate, independent assessment, and the care with which he watched the several-times-replayed Belmarsh prison encounter. Forcing objectivity, Charlie challenged himself to isolate the finger code and awarded himself a 60 percent success score at the same time as conceding it was far behind Natalia. He was relieved his three debriefers dismissed the need for a follow-up session but uncomfortable at having three protection officers assigned to get him to the Foreign Office on the fourth day.

That discomfort remained at Charlie's discovery that he was appearing before what was left of the original emergency committee, with the addition of FBI officers. It grew at the stage-strutting-by-association of Sir Archibald Bland's reference to the implanting of the tracker as if it had been life-threatening and Geoffrey Palmer's account, from his debriefing report, of the *spetsnaz* ambush as another reflected-glory waste of time. There was no proper direction of the encounter until Sir Peter Pickering disclosed that the international humiliation of dumping the FSB assassination squad on the doorstep of the Russian embassy had finally forced a reaction from Moscow and asked for further pressuring ideas, the need for which heightened with Joe Goody's admission that Radtsic, Elena, and Irena were refusing any further disclosures. Rebecca proposed separating Radtsic from the woman pretending to be his wife, and Mort Bering suggested taking Irena back to America ('in a transporter, not telling her where the hell she's going, which wouldn't be a comfortable safe house when she got there'). Pickering dismissed another of Bering's proposals by insisted that putting Radtsic on a genuine CIA rendition flight wasn't acceptable after the Guantanamo outcry and Bland finally, impatiently, intervened with a waving-down, calming hand gesture.

'I'm going to propose we go with what we've got, the three diplomats on the burglary charge,' said the Cabinet Secretary, reverting to the government eagerness to conclude the episode. 'We've given Moscow a court date. Let's appoint prosecuting counsel: offer the embassy a list of British counsel to represent their diplomats and let it be known we'll proceed with a hearing in open court. We know they'll cave in and that we'll get our people back. Which will be the end of the whole business. There's no need to bother with any more re-interrogation of the Radtsic fellow and his supposed wife. Or the other woman. We *know* everything they've told us is lies, disinformation. We just ignore it all.'

Charlie looked around the table, waiting, conscious of the nodded agreement of the co-chairman and the shrug of acceptance from Mort Bering.

'So it's agreed then?' invited Palmer.

'No!' Charlie at last protested, although too loudly.

'What!' demanded Bland, in affronted surprise.

'You can't ignore anything—not as much as one word—of what Radtsic and Elena and Irena have said!' pleaded Charlie. 'Every single claim, every single episode, has to be gone through word-for-word and then gone through all over again. Every single person they've named has got to be investigated and re-investigated, along with everyone close to them, because it might not be the person they've identified but a wife or a lover—'

'Who!' demanded Bland, the outrage positive now.

'The spy or source or minister being blackmailed, whom we don't know about,' listed Charlie. 'And there'll be an episode or a case we've misinterpreted or misunderstood and which we've got to know about to correct. There will be people genuinely and knowingly sacrificed—as they've sacrificed Andrei, who was clearly intended to be an embedded sleeper until a more necessary need arose for him—to ensure we check everything as we've got to scrutinize everything.'

'But that will take—' Bland began to protest.

'Years and years,' agreed Charlie. 'And we can't afford not to do it and America can't afford not to do it. The FSB's already caused incalculable damage to the CIA with Lvov, even though they didn't install him as President of the Russian Federation. And now they've done it all over again, with Irena, Radtsic, and Elena. They've won not once, but twice. . . .' Charlie paused, looking directly at Rebecca. 'And it doesn't matter that Monsford's been identified: he's not important, not involved, anymore. But Radtsic, who'll eventually be repatriated, will take to Moscow a very full and detailed description of you, whom I understand to be the new MI6 Director.'

'How long would you have given Charlie before intervening yourself?' questioned Jane, glad Passmore had accompanied Charlie back to Chelsea to go through the annotated DVDs, leaving her to walk back to Thames House alone with Aubrey Smith.

'Not long,' admitted the Director-General. 'It was a simple test. Charlie either spoke up to stop the nonsense or he didn't.'

'And he did, spoiling Rebecca's chances of promotion in the process. Are you satisfied now that all Charlie's suffering from is the effects of solitary Russian confinement? How about remorse at changing sides?'

'We're going to have to watch him carefully, make sure it's a complete recovery,' avoided the man. 'I never imagined Charlie the sort of agent to be as badly affected so quickly as he clearly has been.'

31

AWARE OF THE RENEWED APPREHENSION IT WOULD CAUSE NATA-
lia, whose fear he'd been assured by Ethel Jackson had begun to diminish,
Charlie argued against a protective escort, disappointed at Aubrey Smith's
final insistence, but he persuaded them to let him disembark alone from
the helicopter and keep several yards behind to approach the Hampshire
safe house. It would have helped if Natalia's ground security hadn't so
obviously emerged from the surrounding woodland to make their additional presence so obvious.

Charlie was still some way from the house when Natalia hesitantly
emerged from the veranda doors, paused, and then more determinedly
pressed on to meet him. Charlie stopped, wanting to distance their initial
encounter as far away as possible from the perpetually watching cameras. Keeping to their agreed arrangements, Charlie's personal escorts
stopped, too, to keep their distance. It took at least five minutes for Natalia to reach him, so far from the house had the helicopter considerably
landed to avoid the disruption of its downdraft. Natalia was serious-faced,
looking beyond Charlie to his bodyguards.

'So you are at maximum protection level?' she recognized, stopping
more than an arm's length away.

'It's an over-reaction,' dismissed Charlie. 'You know how everything's
been escalated. You look wonderful.' She didn't. Her hair was perfectly
prepared—although shorter than he remembered from their last Moscow

meeting—and the off-white dress was uncreased but she was visibly thinner, her face lined with strain.

She said, 'For someone who lies a lot for a living, you're not very good at it personally. But you've certainly dressed for the occasion. Blue suits you.'

'Jane Ambersom's choice. The shoes are new, too. They hurt.' But weren't entirely responsible for his discomfort, he thought.

'Do you want to come inside? Sasha will be at her lessons for another hour.'

'No,' refused Charlie, positively. 'Let's walk around here for a while.'

Natalia looked away to the escorts and then back to Charlie. 'They'll have the house cameras on us, lip reading what they can of our conversation, won't they?'

'It's all part of the routine,' reminded Charlie.

'I know. But I hate it.'

'I'm not enjoying it, either.'

She fell in step beside him, walking parallel to the house, but still not putting herself close to him. 'And you've got a permanent bodyguard?'

'It won't be forever.'

'It'll have to be, for a very long time,' refused Natalia. 'Moscow will work out the full extent of the damage we caused.'

'They've caused a lot of damage to us—and to America—in return,' argued Charlie. 'It comes out about even.'

Natalia shook her head in continued refusal. 'It won't be even for them until they find us: punish us in the only way they know.' Her voice clogged at the end.

'They'll never do that.'

Natalia didn't reply but followed as he turned away from the tree line to put their backs to the house.

Natalia said, 'I didn't know you were shot, not when I was at the airport.'

'It wouldn't have made any difference if you had, would it? I told you to go on, whatever happened. That's what you would have done, isn't it?'

Natalia didn't reply at once. 'I don't know,' she said, doubtfully.

'That was the arrangement.'

'I still don't know.'

'You had Sasha with you!'

'Yes.'

They walked on in silence for several moments, still apart, their heads lowered against the cameras.

Natalia said suddenly, 'I'm very frightened.'

'Yes,' said Charlie, unhelpfully.

'You know, don't you? You've worked it out.'

'Yes.'

'Does anyone else know?'

'No.'

'Sasha will be safe, with you.'

Charlie ignored the remark. 'How did they find out about us?'

'I hadn't sanitized the records as well as I thought I had.'

'And that led them to the marriage records?'

Natalia nodded. 'I did what I could to warn you: give you signs. Told you the FSB didn't suspect me anymore and that I'd seen false documentation about Radtsic's background on an investigation committee to which I would never have been appointed.'

'You got me there with telephone calls that you were suspected by the FSB. Why didn't you include an earlier indication?'

Instead of replying, Natalia said, 'We always had a pact, didn't we, Charlie? That Sasha was the most important thing to both of us—more important than either of us to the other.'

'What was the FSB deal?' demanded Charlie, avoiding the question.

'If I got you back to Moscow, to be punished for destroying their Lvov scheme, I'd be allowed out with Sasha. If I didn't, it would be what we'd always agreed could never happen—Sasha would be put into a state orphanage after I'd been put into a camp.'

'It wasn't a choice,' accepted Charlie.

'It was and I made it,' contradicted Natalia. 'I was told to agree to consular access: that was to be my signal that if I were asked I'd do everything to confirm what Irena Novikov and Radtsic were telling their debriefers: as your wife with every reason to defect I would have been believed without question. I refused the access request, once I got here: they would have known I'd reneged. Instead I agreed to do everything I could to get you out. I didn't expect to be so totally included in the verification of Irena and the Radtsics. Or to be able to identify the code.'

'If you hadn't done that, I'd never have been released,' acknowledged Charlie.

'It was the best, the only, thing I could do. And I knew you'd withstand whatever the interrogation was. Which you did, didn't you?'

'Yes,' lied Charlie.

'Will you forgive me?'

'You know I will.' *I hope,* thought Charlie.

'Sasha will be waiting,' said Natalia, finally extending her hand.

Charlie's hesitation at reaching out to take it was only mental so he knew Natalia wouldn't have detected it.